Wants a Wife

REBECCA WINTERS
EMILY FORBES
MARGARET BARKER

Published in Great Britain 2015
by Mills & Boon, an imprint of Harlequin (UK) Limited,
Eton House, 18-24 Paradise Road, Richmond, Surrey, TW9 1SR

THE GREEK WANTS A WIFE © 2015 Harlequin Books S.A.

A Bride for the Island Prince, Georgie's Big Greek Wedding? and *Greek Doctor Claims His Bride* were first published in Great Britain by Harlequin (UK) Limited.

A Bride for the Island Prince © 2012 Rebecca Winters
Georgie's Big Greek Wedding? © 2012 Emily Forbes
Greek Doctor Claims His Bride © 2009 Margaret Barker

ISBN: 978-0-263-25227-9
eBook ISBN: 978-1-474-00406-0

05-0815

A BRIDE FOR THE ISLAND PRINCE

BY
REBECCA WINTERS

Rebecca Winters, whose family of four children has now swelled to include five beautiful grandchildren, lives in Salt Lake City, Utah, in the land of the Rocky Mountains. With canyons and high alpine meadows full of wild flowers, she never runs out of places to explore. They, plus her favourite vacation spots in Europe, often end up as backgrounds for her romance novels, because writing is her passion, along with her family and church. Rebecca loves to hear from readers. If you wish to e-mail her, please visit her website at www.cleanromances.com.

I'd like to dedicate this book to JULIE, the speech therapist at the elementary school. With her sunny smile and dedication, she helped my children work through a difficult period for them and I'll always be grateful.

CHAPTER ONE

PRINCE Alexius Kristof Rudolph Stefano Valleder Constantinides, Duke of Aurum and second in line to the throne of Hellenica, had been working in his office all morning when he heard a rap on the door. "Yes?" he called out.

"Your Highness? If I might have a word with you?"

"What is it, Hector?" The devoted assistant to the crown poked his head in the door. Hector, who'd been the right hand to Alex's father and grandfather, had been part of the palace administrative staff for over fifty years. He knew better than to disturb Alex unless it was urgent. "I'm reading through some important contracts. Can't this wait until after lunch?"

"The national head of the hospital association is here and most eager to thank you for the unprecedented help you've given them to build four new hospitals our country has needed so badly. Would it be possible for you to give him a little of your time?"

Alex didn't have to think about it. Those facilities should have been built long before now. Better health care for everyone was something he felt strongly about. "Yes. Of course. Show him to the dining room and I'll be there shortly."

"He'll be very pleased. And now, one other matter, Your Highness."

"Then come all the way in, Hector."

The substantial-looking man whose salt-and-pepper hair was thinning on top did Alex's bidding. "The queen instructed me to tell you that Princess Zoe has had another of her moments this morning." In other words, a temper tantrum.

He lifted his dark head. His four-year-old daughter meant more to him than life itself. For this reason he was alarmed by the change in her behavior that was making her more and more difficult to deal with.

Unfortunately the queen wasn't well, and Alex had to shoulder his elder brother Stasio's royal responsibilities while he was out of the country. He knew none of this was helping his daughter.

For the past four months her meltdowns had been growing worse. He'd been through three nannies in that period. At the moment Alex was without one for her. In desperation he'd turned to Queen Desma, his autocratic grandmother, who, since the death of his grandfather, King Kristof, was the titular head of Hellenica, a country made up of a cluster of islands in the Aegean and Thracian seas.

She had a soft spot for her great-granddaughter and had asked one of her personal maids, Sofia, to look after her until a new nanny could be found. What his grandmother really wanted was for Alex to take a new wife. Since by royal decree he could only marry another princess, rather than being able to choose a bride from any background, Alex had made the decision never to marry again. One arranged marriage had been enough.

Lately Zoe had been spending most of her time in the

quarters of her great-grandmother, who'd been trying in her unsubtle way to prepare Zoe for a new mother. The queen had been behind the match between Alex and his deceased wife, Teresa. Both women were from the House of Valleder.

Now, with Teresa gone, his grandmother had been negotiating with the House of Helvetia for a marriage between her grandson and the princess Genevieve, but her machinations were wasted on Alex.

"I had breakfast with her earlier this morning and she seemed all right. What happened to set her off with Sofia?"

"Not Sofia," he clarified. "But two new situations *have* arisen. If I may speak frankly."

Only two? Alex ground his teeth in worry and frustration. He'd had hopes this was a phase that would pass, but the situation was growing worse. "You always do."

"Her new American tutor, Dr. Wyman, just handed in his notice, and her Greek tutor, Kyrie Costas, is threatening to resign. As you know, the two have been at odds with each other over the proper curriculum for the princess. Dr. Wyman is out in the hall. Before he leaves the palace, he requests a brief audience with you."

Alex got to his feet. Two weeks ago he'd been forced to withdraw her from the preschool classes she went to three times a week because her teacher couldn't get her to participate. Fearing something was physically wrong with Zoe, he'd asked his personal physician to give her a thorough examination. But the doctor had found nothing wrong.

Now her English tutor had resigned? Alex's wife, who'd spent a portion of her teenage years in America, had died of a serious heart condition. Before passing away she'd made him promise Zoe would grow up to be fluent in English. He'd done everything in his power to honor her wishes, even hiring an American tutor. Alex himself made an effort to speak English with her every day.

He took a fortifying breath. "Show him in."

The forty-year-old American teacher had come highly recommended after leaving the employ of Alex's second cousin, King Alexandre Philippe of Valleder, a principality bordering the Romanche-speaking canton of Switzerland. No longer needing a tutor for his son, the king, who was best friends with Alex's brother, had recommended Dr. Wyman to come to Hellenica and teach Zoe.

"Your Highness." He bowed.

"Dr. Wyman? Hector tells me you've resigned. Is my daughter truly too difficult for you to handle any longer?"

"Lately it's a case of her running away when she sees me," he answered honestly. "It's my opinion she's frightened about something and hardly speaks at all. What comes out I don't understand. Mr. Costas says it's my method, but I disagree. Something's wrong, but I'm only a teacher."

Since Zoe's medical exam, Alex had considered calling in a child psychiatrist for a consultation. Dr. Wyman said she was frightened. Alex agreed. This behavior wasn't normal. So far he'd thought it was a case of arrested development because Zoe had been born premature. But maybe not having a mother had brought on psychological problems that hadn't been recognizable until now.

"If she were your child, what would you do?"

"Well, I think before I took her to a child psychologist, I'd find out if there's a physiological problem that is preventing her from talking as much as she should. If so, maybe that's what is frightening her."

"Where could I go for that kind of expertise?"

"The Stillman Institute in New York City. Their clinic has some of the best speech therapists in the United States. I'd take my child there for an evaluation."

"I'll look into it. Thank you for your suggestion and your help with Princess Zoe, Dr. Wyman. I appreciate your honesty. You leave the palace with my highest recommendation."

"Thank you, Your Highness. I hope you get answers soon. I'm very fond of her."

So am I.

After Dr. Wyman left, Alex checked his watch. By the time he'd had lunch with the head of the hospital association, the clinic in New York would be open. Alex would call and speak to the director.

Dottie Richards had never ridden in a helicopter before. After her jet had touched down in Athens, Greece, she was told it was just a short journey to Hellenica.

The head of the Stillman Speech Institute had picked her to handle an emergency that had arisen. Apparently there was an important little four-year-old girl who needed diagnostic testing done ASAP. A temporary visa had been issued for Dottie to leave the country without having to wait the normal time for a passport.

For security reasons, she hadn't learned the identity of the little girl until she was met at the helicopter pad in Athens by a palace spokesman named Hector. Apparently the child was Princess Zoe, the only daughter of Prince Alexius Constantinides, a widower who was acting ruler of Hellenica.

"Acting ruler, you say?"

"Yes, madame. The heir apparent to the throne, Crown Prince Stasio, is out of the country on business. When he returns, he will be marrying Princess Beatriz. Their wedding is scheduled for July the fifth. At that time the dowager queen Desma, Princess Zoe's great-grandmother, will relinquish the crown and Prince Stasio will become king of Hellenica.

"In the meantime Prince Alexius is handling the daily affairs of state. He has provided his private helicopter so you can be given a sightseeing trip to the palace, located on the biggest island, also called Hellenica."

Dottie realized this was a privilege not many people were granted. "That's very kind of him." She climbed aboard and the helicopter took off, but the second it left the ground she grew dizzy and tried to fight it off. "Could you tell me what exactly is wrong with Princess Zoe?"

"That's a subject for you to discuss with the prince himself."

Uh-oh. "Of course."

Dottie was entering a royal world where silence was the better part of discretion. No doubt that was why Hector had been chosen for this duty. She wouldn't guess the older man was the type to leave the royal household and write a book revealing the dark secrets of the centuries-old Constantinides family. Dottie admired his loyalty and would have told him so, but by then she was starting to experience motion sickness from the helicopter and was too nauseated to talk any more.

Several years earlier, Dottie had seen pictures of

the Constantinides brothers on various television news broadcasts. Both had playboy reputations, like so many royal sons. They'd been dark and attractive enough, but seen in the inside of a limo or aboard a royal yacht, it was difficult to get a real sense of their looks.

Dottie had never been anywhere near a royal and knew nothing about their world except for their exposure in the media, which didn't always reflect positively. But for an accident of birth, she could have been born a princess. Anyone could be. Royals were human beings after all. They entered the world, ate, slept, married and died like the rest of humanity. It was what they did, where they did it and how they did it that separated them from the masses.

Raised by a single aunt, now deceased, who'd never married and had been a practical thinker, Dottie's world hadn't included many fairy tales. Though there'd been moments growing up when Dottie had been curious about being a queen or a princess. Now an unprecedented opportunity had arisen for her to find out what that was like.

Dottie had seen and heard enough about royals involved in escapades and scandals to feel sorry for them. The trials of being an open target to the world had to be worse than those of a celebrity, whose popularity waxed strong for a time in the eyes of public adulation and curiosity, then waned out of sight.

A royal stayed a royal forever and was scrutinized ad nauseum. A prince or princess couldn't even be born or die without a crowd in attendance. But as Dottie had learned during an early period in her life, the trials of an ordinary human were sometimes so bad they drew unwanted attention from the public, too. Like with King

George VI of England, her own severe stuttering problem had been an agony to endure. However, to be human and a royal at the same time placed one in double jeopardy.

At the age of twenty-nine and long since free of her former speech problem, Dottie loved her anonymity. In that sense she felt compassion for the little princess she hadn't even met yet. The poor thing was already under a microscope and would remain there for all the days of life she was granted. Whether she had a speech problem or something that went deeper, word would get out.

One day when the motherless princess was old enough to understand, she'd learn the world was talking about her and would never leave her alone. If she had a physical or a noticeable psychological problem, the press would be merciless. Dottie vowed in her heart she'd do whatever possible to help the little girl, *if* it were in her power.

But at the moment the helicopter trip was playing havoc with her stomach and the lovely sightseeing trip had been wasted on her. The second they landed and she was shown to her quarters in the glistening white royal palace, she lost any food she'd eaten and went straight to bed.

It was embarrassing, but when she was green around the gills and unable to rally, nothing except a good night's sleep would help her to recover. When her business was finished here and she left the country to go back to the States, she would take a flight from Hellenica's airport to Athens before boarding a flight to New York. No more helicopter rides.

* * *

Alex eyed his ailing, widowed grandmother, whose silvery hair was still thick at eighty-five. She tired more easily these days and kept to her apartment. Alex knew she was more than ready for Stasio to come home and officially take the worries of the monarchy from her shoulders.

No one awaited Stasio's return with more eagerness than Alex. When his brother had left on the first of April, he'd promised to be home by mid-May, yet it was already the thirtieth with his wedding only five weeks away. Alex needed out of his temporary responsibilities to spend more time with Zoe. He'd built up his hopes that this speech therapist could give him definitive answers. It would be a step in the right direction; his daughter was growing unhappier with each passing day.

"Thank you for breakfast," he said in Greek. "If you two will excuse me, I have some business, but I'll be back." He kissed his petite daughter, who was playing with her roll instead of eating it. "Be good for *Yiayia*."

Zoe nodded.

After bowing to his grandmother, he left her suite and hurried downstairs to his office in the other part of the palace. He'd wanted to meet this Mrs. Richards last evening, but Hector had told him she'd never ridden in a helicopter before and had become ill during the flight. There'd been nothing he could do but wait until this morning and wonder if her getting sick was already a bad omen.

He knew better than to ask Hector what she was like. His assistant would simply answer, "That's not for me to say, Your Highness." His tendency not to gossip was a sterling quality Alex admired, but at times it drove Stasio insane.

For years his elder brother had barked at Hector that he wasn't quite human. Alex had a theory that the reason why Hector irked Stasio was because Stasio had grown up knowing that one day he'd have to be king. Hector was a permanent reminder that Stasio's greatest duty was to his country, to marry Princess Beatriz and produce heirs to the throne.

Like the queen, who wanted more great-grandchildren for the glory of Hellenica, Alex looked forward to his brother producing some cousins for Zoe. His little girl would love a baby around. She'd asked Alex for a sister, but all he could say was that her uncle Stasi would produce a new heir to the throne before long.

After reaching his office, he scowled when he read the fax sent from Stasio, who was still in Valleder. *Sorry, little brother, but banking business will keep me here another week. Tell Yiayia I'll be home soon. Give Zoe a hug from her uncle. Hang in there. You do great work. Stasi.*

"Your Highness? May I present Mrs. Richards."

He threw his head back. Hector had come in the office without him being aware of it and was now clearing his throat. A very American-looking woman—down to the way she carried herself—had entered with him, taller than average, with her light brown hair swept up in a loose knot. Alex was so disappointed, even angered by his brother's news, he'd forgotten for a moment that Hector was on his way down. Stasio had taken advantage of their bargain.

"One month, little brother," he'd said when he'd left.

"That's all I need to carry out some lucrative banking negotiations. Philippe is helping me." But Stasio had been gone much longer and Alex wasn't happy about it. Neither was the queen, the prime minister or the arch-bishop, who were getting anxious to confer with him about the coronation and royal nuptials coming up soon.

Pushing his feelings aside, Alex got to his feet. "Welcome to Hellenica, Mrs. Richards."

"Thank you, Your Highness."

She gave an awkward curtsey, no doubt coached by Hector. He hated to admit she looked fresh, appeal-ing even, as she stood there in a pale blue blouse and skirt that tied at her slender waist, drawing his atten-tion to the feminine curves revealed above and below. He hadn't meant to stare, but his eyes seemed to have a will of their own as they took in her long, shapely legs.

Alex quickly shifted his gaze to her face and was caught off guard again by the wide, sculpted mouth and the cornflower-blue of her eyes. They reminded him of the cornflowers growing wild alongside larkspurs on Aurum Island where he normally lived.

He missed his private palace there where he con-ducted the mining interests for the monarchy, away from Hellenica. The big island drew the tourists in hordes, Aurum not quite so much. He shouldn't mind tourists since they were one of his country's greatest financial resources, but with his daughter in such dis-tress, everything bothered him these days. Especially the woman standing in front of him.

A speech therapist could come in any size and shape. He just hadn't expected *this* woman, period. For one thing, she looked too young for the task ahead of her. No wonder Hector hadn't dropped a clue about her.

"I've been told you suffered on your helicopter ride. I hope you're feeling better."

"Much better, thank you. The view was spectacular."

One dark brow dipped. "What little you saw of it in your condition."

"Little is right," she acknowledged in a forthright manner. "I'm sorry your generous attempt to show me the sights in your helicopter didn't have the desired outcome." Her blunt way of speaking came as a surprise. "Will I be meeting your daughter this morning?"

"Yes." He flicked his glance to Hector. "Would you ask Sofia to bring Zoe to us?"

The older man gave a brief bow and slipped out of the office, leaving the two of them alone. Alex moved closer and invited her to sit down on the love seat. "Would you care for tea or coffee?"

"Nothing for me. I just had some tea. It's settling my stomach, but please have some yourself if you want it."

If *he* wanted it? She was more of a surprise than ever and seemed at ease, which wasn't always the case with strangers meeting him.

"My boss, Dr. Rice, told me your daughter is having trouble communicating, but he didn't give me any details. How long since your wife passed away?"

"Two years ago."

"And now Zoe is four. That means she wouldn't have any memory of her mother except what you've told her, and of course pictures. Did your wife carry Zoe full term?"

"No. She came six weeks early and was in the hospital almost a month. I feared we might lose her, but she finally rallied. I thought that could be the reason why she's been a little slower to make herself understood."

"Was her speech behind from infancy?"

"I don't really know what's normal. Not having been around children before, I had no way to compare her progress. All I know is her speech is difficult to understand. The queen and I are used to her, but over the past few months her behaviour's become so challenging, we've lost her art, English and dance teachers and three nannies. Her Greek tutor has all but given up and she's too much for the teacher to handle at her preschool."

"It's usually the caregiver who first notices if there's a problem. Would that have been your wife?"

"Yes, but a lot of the time she was ill with a bad heart and the nanny had to take over. I took charge in the evenings after my work, but I hadn't been truly alarmed about Zoe until two weeks ago when I had to withdraw her from preschool. As I told you earlier, I'd assumed that being a premature baby, she simply hadn't caught up yet."

"Has she had her normal checkup with the pediatrician?"

"Yes."

"No heart problem with her."

He shook his dark head. "I even took her to my own internist for a second opinion. Neither doctor found anything physically wrong with her, but they gave me the name of a child psychiatrist to find out if something else is going on to make her behind in her speech. Before I did that, I decided to take Dr. Wyman's advice. He recommended I take her to the Stillman Institute for a diagnosis before doing anything else."

"I see. What kind of behavior does she manifest?"

"When it comes time for her lessons lately, Zoe has tantrums and cries hysterically. All she wants to do is hide in her bed or run to her great-grandmother's suite for comfort."

"What about her appetite?"

This morning Zoe had taken only a few nibbles of her breakfast, another thing that had alarmed him. "Not what it should be."

She studied his features as if she were trying to see inside him. "You must be frantic."

Frantic? "Yes," he murmured. That was the perfect word to describe his state of mind. Mrs. Richards was very astute, but unlike everyone else in his presence except the queen and Stasio, she spoke her mind.

"Imagine your daughter feeling that same kind of emotion and then times it by a hundred."

Alex blinked. This woman's observation brought it home that she might just know what she was talking about. While he was deep in contemplation, his daughter appeared, clinging to Sofia's hand. Hector slipped in behind them.

"Zoe?" Alex said in English. "Come forward." She took a tentative step. "This is Mrs. Richards. She's come all the way from New York to see you. Can you say hello to her?"

His daughter took one look at their guest and her face crumpled in pain. He knew that look. She was ready for flight. With his stomach muscles clenched, he switched to Greek and asked her the same question. This time Zoe's response was to say she wanted her *yiayia*, then she burst into tears and ran out of the room. Sofia darted after her.

Alex called her back and started for the door, but Mrs. Richards unexpectedly said, "Let her go."

Her countermand surprised him. Except for his own

deceased father, no one had ever challenged him like that, let alone about his own daughter. It was as if their positions had been reversed and she was giving the orders. The strange irony set his teeth on edge.

"She probably assumes I'm her new nanny," she added in a gentler tone. "I don't blame her for running away. I can see she's at her wit's end. The first thing I'd like you to do is get her in to an ear, nose and throat specialist followed up by an audiologist."

He frowned, having to tamp down his temper. "As I told you a minute ago, Zoe has already been given two checkups."

"Not that kind of exam," she came back, always keeping her voice controlled. "A child or an adult with speech problems could have extra wax buildup not noticeable with a normal check-up because it's deep inside. It's not either doctor's fault. They're not specialists in this area. If there's nothing wrong with her ears and I can't help her, then your daughter needs to see a child psychiatrist to find out why she's regressing.

"For now let's find out if more wax than normal has accumulated recently. If so, it must be cleaned out to help improve her hearing. Otherwise sounds could be blocked or distorted, preventing her from mimicking them."

"Why would there be an abnormal amount of wax?"

"Does she get earaches very often?"

"A few every year."

"It's possible her ear canals are no longer draining as they should."

That made sense. His hands formed fists. Why hadn't he thought of it?

Her well-shaped brows lifted. "Not even a prince

can know everything." She'd read his mind and her comment sent his blood pressure soaring. "Will you arrange it? Sooner would be better than later because I can't get started on my testing until the procedure has been done. That child needs help in a hurry."

As if Alex didn't know... Why else had he sent for *her*?

He didn't like feeling guilty because he'd let the problem go on too long without exploring every avenue. Alex also didn't like being second-guessed or told what to do. But since it was Zoe they were talking about, he decided to let it go for now. "I'll see that a specialist fits her in today."

"Good. Let me know the results and we'll go from there." She turned to leave.

"I haven't excused you yet, Mrs. Richards."

She wheeled back around. "Forgive me, and please call me Dottie." Through the fringe of her dark, silky lashes, her innocent blue gaze eyed him frankly. "I've never worked with a parent who's a monarch. This is a new experience."

Indeed, it was. It appeared Alex was an acquired taste, something he hadn't known could happen. He wasn't a conceited man, but it begged the question whether she had an instant dislike of him.

"Monarch or not, do you always walk away from a conversation before it's over?"

"I thought it was." She stood firm. "I deal with preschoolers all the time and your little girl is so adorable, I'm hoping to get to the bottom of her problem right away. I'm afraid I'm too focused on my job. Your Highness," she tacked on, as if she weren't sure whether to say it or not.

She was different from anyone he'd ever met. Not rude exactly, yet definitely the opposite of obsequious. He didn't know what to think of her. But just now she'd sounded sincere enough where his daughter was concerned. Alex needed to take the advice his mother had given him as a boy. Never react on a first impression or you could live to regret it.

"I'm glad you're focused," he said and meant it. "She's the light of my life."

The briefest glint of pain entered her eyes. "You're a lucky man to have her, even if you *are* a prince."

His brows furrowed. "Even if I'm a prince?"

She shook her head. "I'm sorry. I meant— Well, I meant that one assumes a prince has been given everything in life and is very lucky. But to be the father of a darling daughter, too, makes you that much luckier."

Though she smiled, he heard a sadness in her words. Long after he'd excused her and had arranged for the doctor's appointment, the shadow he'd seen in those deep blue eyes stayed with him.

CHAPTER TWO

DOTTIE stayed in her room for part of the day, fussing and fuming over a situation she could do little about. *I haven't excused you yet, Mrs. Richards.*

The mild rebuke had fallen from the lips of a prince who was outrageously handsome. Tall and built like the statue of a Greek god, he possessed the inky-black hair and eyes of his Hellenican ancestry. Everything—his chiseled jaw, his strong male features—set him apart from other men.

Even if he weren't royal, he looked like any woman's idea of a prince. He'd stood there in front of his country's flag, effortlessly masculine and regal in a silky blue shirt and white trousers that molded to his powerful thighs.

He'd smelled good, too. Dottie noticed things like that and wished she hadn't because it reminded her that beneath the royal mantle, he was human.

Already she feared she might not be the right person for this job. Dr. Rice, the head of her department at the Stillman clinic, had said he'd handpicked her for this assignment because of her own personal experiences that gave her more understanding. Fine, but in order to give herself time to get used to the idea, she should have been told she was coming to a royal household before she boarded the jet in New York.

The atmosphere here was different from anything Dottie had known and she needed time to adjust. There was so much to deal with—the stiffness, the protocol, the maids and nannies, the teachers, the tutors, a prince for a father who'd been forced to obey a rigid schedule his whole life, a princess without a mother....

A normal child would have run into the room and hugged her daddy without thinking about it, but royal etiquette had held Zoe back from doing what came naturally. She'd appeared in the doorway and stood at attention like a good soldier.

The whole thing had to be too much for a little girl who just wanted to be a little girl. In the end she'd broken those rules and had taken off down the hall, her dark brown curls bouncing. Despite his calling her name, she'd kept going. The precious child couldn't handle any more.

Dottie's heart ached for Zoe who'd ignored her father's wishes and had run out of his office with tears flowing from those golden-brown eyes. She must have gotten her coloring from her mother, who'd probably been petite. His daughter had inherited her beauty and olive skin from her father, no doubt from her mother, too.

The vague images Dottie had retained of him and his brother through the media had been taken when they were much younger, playboy princes setting hearts afire throughout Europe. In the intervening years, Zoe's father had become a married man who'd lost his wife too soon in life. Tragic for him, and more tragic for a child to lose a parent. Unfortunately it had happened.

Dottie was the enemy of the moment where Zoe was concerned, and she'd would have to be careful how she approached her to do the testing. Soon enough she would discover how much of Zoe's problem was emotional or physical. Probably both.

With a deep sigh she ate the lunch a maid had brought her on a tray. Later another maid offered to unpack for her, but Dottie thanked her before dismissing her. She could do it herself. In fact she didn't want to get completely unpacked in case she'd be leaving the palace right away. If the little princess had a problem outside of Dottie's expertise, then Dottie would soon be flown back to New York from the island.

At five o'clock the phone rang at the side of her queen-size bed. It was Hector. The prince wished to speak to her in his office. He was sending a maid to escort her. It was on the tip of Dottie's tongue to tell him she didn't need help finding the prince's inner sanctum, but she had to remember that when in Rome... Already she'd made a bad impression. It wouldn't do to alienate him further, not when he was so anxious about his daughter.

She thanked Hector and freshened up. In a minute, one of the maids arrived and accompanied her down a different staircase outside her private guest suite to the main floor. The prince was waiting for her.

Out of deference to him, she waited until he spoke first. He stood there with his hands on his hips. By the aura of energy he was giving out with those jet-black eyes playing over her, she sensed he had something of significance to tell her.

"Sit down, please."

She did his bidding, anxious to hear about the result of the examination.

"Once we could get Zoe to cooperate, the doctor found an inordinate amount of wax adhering to her eardrums from residual fluid. She hated every second of it, but after they were cleaned out, she actually smiled when he asked her if she could hear better. The audiologist did tests afterwards and said her hearing is fine."

"Oh, that's wonderful news!" Dottie cried out happily.

"Yes. On the way back to the palace, I could tell she did understand more words being spoken to her. There was understanding in her eyes."

Beneath that formal reserve of his, she knew he was relieved for that much good news. A prince could move mountains and that's what he'd done today by getting her into an ear specialist so fast. In fact, he'd made it possible for Dottie to come to Hellenica instead of the other way around. What greater proof that the man loved his daughter?

"This is an excellent start, Your Highness."

"When do you want to begin testing her?"

"Tomorrow morning. She needs to have a good night's sleep first. After what she's been through today, she doesn't need any more trauma."

"Agreed." She heard a wealth of emotion in that one word. Dottie could imagine the struggle his daughter had put up. "Where would you like to test her?"

Since the prince was still standing, Dottie got to her feet to be on par with him, but she still needed to look up. "If you asked her where her favorite place is to play, what would she tell you?"

After a moment he said, "The patio off my bedroom."

That didn't surprise Dottie. His little girl wanted to be near him without anyone else around. "Does she play there often?"

She heard his sharp intake of breath. "No. It's not allowed unless I'm there, too." Of course not. "My work normally goes past her bedtime."

"And mornings?"

"While we've been at the palace, I've always had breakfast with her in the queen's suite. Zoe's the most comfortable there."

"I'm talking before breakfast."

"That's when I work out and she takes a swimming lesson."

Dottie fought to remain quiet, but her impulse was to cry out in dismay over the strict regimen. "So what times does she get to play with you on your patio?"

He pursed his lips. "Sunday afternoons after chapel and lunch. Why all these questions?"

She needed to be careful she didn't offend him again. "I'm trying to get a sense of her day and her relationship with you. When is her Greek lesson?"

"Before her dinner."

"You don't eat dinner with her, then?"

"No."

Oh. Poor Zoe. "You say she was attending a preschool until two weeks ago?"

"Yes. The sessions went in two-hour segments, three times a week. Monday, Wednesday and Friday. But lately I haven't insisted for the obvious reasons."

"When does she play with friends?"

"You mean outside her school?"

"Yes. Does she have friends here at the palace?"

"No, but we normally live on Aurum where she has several."

"I see. Thank you for giving me that information. Would it be all right with you if I test her out on your patio? I believe she'll be more responsive in a place where she's truly happy and at ease. If you're there, too, it will make her more comfortable. But with your full schedule I don't suppose that's poss—"

"I'll make time for it," he declared, cutting her off.

No matter how she said things, she seemed to be in the wrong. It wasn't her intention to push his buttons, but she was doing a good job of it anyway. "That would be ideal. It's important I watch her interaction with you. Before you come, I'd like to set up out there with a few things I've brought."

His brows lifted. "How much time do you need?"

"A few minutes."

He nodded. "I'll send a maid to escort you at eight. Zoe and I will join you at eight-twenty. Does that meet with your approval?"

Eight-twenty? Not eight-twenty-one? *Stop it, Dottie. You're in a different world now.* "Only if it meets with yours, Your Highness."

This close to him, she could see a tiny nerve throbbing at the corner of his compelling mouth. His lips had grown taut. "If I haven't made it clear before, let me say this again. My daughter is my life. That makes her my top priority." She believed him.

"I know," Dottie murmured. "While I'm here, she's mine, too."

A long silence ensued before he stepped away. "I've instructed Hector to make certain you're comfortable while you're here. Your dinner can be served in the small guest dining room on the second floor, or he'll have it brought to your room. Whatever you prefer. Anything you want or need, you have only to pick up the phone and ask him and he'll see to it."

"Thank you. He's been so perfect, I can hardly believe he's real."

"My brother and I have been saying the same thing about him for years." The first glimmer of an unexpected smile reached his black eyes. He did have his human moments. The proof of it set off waves of sensation through her body she hadn't expected or wanted to feel.

"If you'll eat your eggs, I have a surprise for you." Zoe jerked her head around and eyed Alex in excitement. "I'm going to spend time with you this morning and thought we'd play out on my patio. That's why I told Sofia to let you wear pants."

She made a sound of delight and promptly took several bites. The queen sent him a private glance that said she hoped this testing session with the new speech therapist wasn't going to be a waste of time. Alex hoped not, too. No one wanted constructive feedback more than he did.

After Zoe finished off her juice, she wiggled down from the chair and started to dart away. Alex called her back. "You must ask to be excused."

She turned to her grandmother. "Can I go with daddy, *Yiayia*?"

The queen nodded. "Have a good time."

Alex groaned in silence, remembering the way his daughter had flown out of his office yesterday after one look at Dottie.

Zoe slipped her hand into his and they left for his suite. She skipped along part of the way. When he saw how thrilled she was to be with him, he found himself even more put out with Stasio.

As soon as his brother got back from Vallader, Alex planned to take more time off to be with his daughter. While he'd had to be here at the palace doing his brother's work plus his own, he'd hardly had a minute to spend time with her. Maybe they'd go on a mini vacation together.

The curtains to the patio had been opened. Zoe ran through the bedroom ahead of him, then suddenly stopped at the sight of the woman sitting on the patio tiles in jeans and a pale orange, short-sleeved cotton top.

"Hi, Zoe," she spoke in English with a smile. Dottie had put on sneakers and her hair was loose in a kind of disheveled bob that revealed the light honey tones among the darker swaths. "Do you think your daddy can catch this?" She threw a Ping-Pong ball at him.

When he caught it with his right hand, Zoe cried out in surprise. He threw it back to Dottie who caught it in her left. Their first volley of the day. For no particular reason his pulse rate picked up at the thought of what else awaited him in her presence.

"Good catch. Come on, Daddy." Her dancing blue gaze shot to his. "You and Zoe sit down and spread your legs apart like this and we'll roll some balls to each other." She pulled a larger multicolored plastic ball from a big bag and opened those long, fabulous legs of hers.

Alex could tell his daughter was so shocked by what was going on, she forgot to be scared and sat down to imitate Dottie once he'd complied. Dottie rolled the ball to Zoe, who rolled it back to her. Then it was his turn. They went in a round, drawing Zoe in. Pretty soon their guest pulled out a rubber ball and rolled it to his daughter right after she'd sent her the plastic ball.

Zoe laughed as she hurried to keep both balls going. His clever little girl used her right and left hand at the same time and sent one ball to Dottie and one to him. "Good thinking!" she praised her. "Shall we try three balls?"

"Yes," his daughter said excitedly. Their guest produced the Ping-Pong ball and fired all three balls at both of them, one after the other, until Zoe was giggling hysterically.

"You're so good at this, I think we'll try something else. Shall we see who's better at jumping?" She whipped out a jump rope with red handles and got to her feet. "Come on, Zoe. You take this end and I'll hold on to the other. Your daddy's going to jump first. You'll have to make big circles like I'm doing or the rope will hit him in the head."

"Oh, no—" Zoe cried.

"Don't worry," Dottie inserted. "Your daddy is a big boy. It won't hurt him."

So their visitor *had* noticed. Was that a negative in her eyes, too?

Zoe scrutinized him. "You're a boy?"

"Yes. He's a very big one," Dottie answered for him and his daughter laughed. Soon Zoe was using all her powers of concentration to turn the rope correctly and was doing an amazing job of it. After four times to get it right he heard, "You can jump in anytime now, Daddy."

Alex crouched down and managed to do two jumps

before getting caught around the shoulders. He was actually disappointed when their leader said, "Okay, now it's Zoe's turn. How many can you do?"

She cocked her dark brown head. "Five—"

"Well, that's something I want to see. Watch while we turn the rope. Whenever you think you're ready, jump in. It's okay if it takes you a whole bunch of times to do it, Zoe. Your daddy isn't going anywhere, right?"

She didn't look at him as she said it. He had a feeling it was on purpose.

"We're both in your hands for as long as it takes, Dorothy." He'd read the background information on her and knew it was her legal name.

"I never go by my given name," she said to Zoe without missing a beat while she continued to rotate the rope. "You can call me Dottie."

"That means crazy, doesn't it?" he threw out, curious to see how she'd respond.

"Your English vocabulary is remarkable, Your Highness."

"Is she crazy?" Zoe asked while she stood there, hesitant to try jumping.

"Be careful how you answer that," Dottie warned him. "Little royal pitchers have big ears and hers seem to be working just fine."

Alex couldn't help chuckling. He smiled at his daughter. "She's funny-crazy. Don't you think?"

"Yes." Zoe giggled again.

"Come on and jump." After eight attempts accompanied by a few tears, she finally managed a perfect jump. Dottie clapped her hands. "Good job, Zoe. Next time you'll do more."

She put the rope aside and reached into her bag of

tricks. His daughter wasn't the only one interested to see what she would pull out next. "For this game we have to get on our tummies."

The speech therapist might as well have been a magician. At this point his daughter was entranced and did what was suggested without waiting for Alex. In another minute Dottie had laid twenty-four cards facedown on the floor in four rows. She turned one card over. "Do you know what this is, Zoe?"

His daughter nodded. "Pig."

"Yes, and there's another card just like it. You have to remember where this card is, and then find the other one. When you do, then you make a book of them and put the pile to the side. You get one turn. Go ahead."

Zoe turned over another card.

"What is it?"

"Whale."

"Yes, but it's not a pig. So you have to put the card back. Okay, Daddy. It's your turn."

Alex turned over a card in the corner.

"Tiger, Daddy."

Before he could say anything, he saw their eyes look to the doorway. Alex turned around in frustration to see who had interrupted them.

"Hector?"

"Forgive me, Your Highness. There's a call for you from Argentum on an urgent matter that needs your attention."

Much as Alex hated to admit it, this had to be an emergency, otherwise Bari would have sent him an email. Barisou Jouflas was the head mining engineer on the island of Argentum and Alex's closest friend since college. He always enjoyed talking to him and got to his feet, expecting an outburst from Zoe. To his astonishment, Dottie had her completely engrossed in the matching game.

"I'll be back as soon as I can."

Dottie nodded without looking at him.

"Bye, Daddy," his daughter said, too busy looking for a matching card to turn her head.

Bye, Daddy— Since when? No tantrum because he was leaving?

Out of the corner of her eye Dottie watched the prince disappear and felt a twinge of disappointment for his daughter. They'd all been having fun and it was one time when he hadn't wanted to leave, she felt sure of it. But there were times when the affairs of the kingdom did have to take priority. Dottie understood that and forgave him.

He might be gone some time. Dottie still had other tests to do that she preferred to take place outside the palace. Now would be a good time to carry them out while Zoe was still amenable. Her speech was close to unintelligible, but she was bright as a button and Dottie understood most of what she was trying to say because of her years of training and personal experience.

Once they'd concluded the matching game she said, "Zoe? Do you want to come down to the beach with me?" The little girl clapped her hands in excitement.

"All right, then. Let's do it." Dottie got up and pulled a bag of items out of the bigger bag. "Shall we go down from here?"

"Yes!" Zoe stood up and started down the stairs at the far end of the patio. Dottie followed. The long stairway covering two stories led to the dazzling blue water below.

It was a warm, beautiful day. When they reached the beach, she pulled out a tube of sunscreen and covered both of them. Next she drew floppy sun hats from the bag for them to put on.

"Here's a shovel. Will you show me how you build a castle?"

Zoe got to work and made a large mound.

"That's wonderful. Now where do you think this flag should go?" She handed her a little one.

"Here!" She placed it on the very top.

"Perfect. Make a hole where the front door of the castle is located."

She made a big dent with her finger at the bottom. Dottie rummaged in the bag for a tiny sailboat and gave it to her. "This is your daddy's boat. Where do you think it goes?"

"Here." Zoe placed it at the bottom around the side.

"Good." Again Dottie reached in the bag and pulled out a plastic figure about one inch high. "Let's pretend this is your daddy. Where does he live in the castle?"

Zoe thought about it for a minute, then stuck him in the upper portion of the mound.

"And where do you sleep?" Dottie gave her a little female figure.

"Here." Zoe crawled around and pushed the figure into the mound at approximately the same level as the other.

"Do you sleep by your *Yiayia*?"

"No."

"Can you show me where she sleeps?" Dottie handed her another figure. Zoe moved around a little more and put it in at the same height. Everyone slept on the second floor.

"I like your castle. Let's take off our shoes and walk over to the water. Maybe we can find some pretty stones to decorate the walls. Here's a bucket to carry everything."

They spent the next ten minutes picking up tiny, multicolored stones. When they returned to the mound Dottie said, "Can you pour them on the sand and pick out the different colors? We'll put them in piles."

Zoe nodded, eager to sort everything. She was meticulous.

"Okay. Why don't you start with the pink stones and put them around the middle of the castle." Her little charge got the point in a hurry and did a masterful job. "Now place the orange stones near the top and the brown stones at the bottom."

While Zoe was finishing her masterpiece, Dottie took several pictures at different angles with her phone. "You'll have to show these pictures to your daddy. Now I think it's time to put our shoes on and go back to the palace. I'm hungry and thirsty and I bet you are, too. Here—let me brush the sand off your little piggies."

Zoe looked at her. "What?"

"These." She tugged on Zoe's toes. "These are your little pigs. Piggies. They go *wee wee wee*." She made a squealing sound.

When recognition dawned, laughter poured out of Zoe like tinkling bells. For just a moment it sounded like her little boy's laughter. Emotion caught Dottie by the throat.

"Mrs. Richards?" a male voice spoke out of the blue, startling her.

She jumped to her feet, fighting the tears pricking her eyelids, and looked around. A patrol boat had pulled up on the shore and she hadn't even heard it. Two men had converged on them, obviously guards protecting the palace grounds. "Yes?" She put her arm around Zoe's shoulders. "Is something wrong?"

"Prince Alexius has been looking for you. Stay here. He'll be joining you in a moment."

She'd done something wrong. Again.

No sooner had he said the words than she glimpsed the prince racing down the steps to the beach with the speed of a black panther in pursuit of its prey. The image sent a chill up her spine that raised the hairs on the back of her neck.

When he caught up to them, he gave a grim nod of dismissal to the guards, who got back in the patrol boat and took off.

"Look what I made, Daddy—" His daughter was totally unaware of the byplay.

Dottie could hear his labored breathing and knew it came from fright, not because he was out of shape. Anything but. While Zoe gave him a running commentary of their beach adventure in her inimitable way, Dottie put the bucket and shovel in the bag. When she turned around, she discovered him hunkered down, examining his daughter's work of art.

After listening to her intently, he lifted his dark head and shot Dottie a piercing black glance. Sotto voce, he said, "There are pirates in these waters who wait for an opportunity like this to—"

"I understand," she cut him off, feeling sick to her stomach. She'd figured it out before he'd said anything. "Forgive me. I swear it won't happen again."

"You're right about that."

His words froze the air in her lungs before he gripped his daughter's hand and started for the stairs.

"Come on," Zoe called to her.

Dottie followed, keeping her eyes on his hard-muscled physique clothed in a white polo shirt and dark blue trousers. Halfway up the stairs on those long, powerful legs, he gathered Zoe in his arms and carried her the rest of the way to the patio.

"The queen is waiting for Zoe to have lunch with her," he said when she caught up to him. "A maid is waiting outside my suite to conduct you back to your room. I've asked for a tray to be sent to you. We'll talk later."

Dottie heard Zoe's protests as he walked away. She gathered up the other bag and met the maid who accompanied her back to her own quarters. Once alone, she fled into the en suite bathroom and took a shower to wash off the sand and try to get her emotions under control.

No matter how unwittingly, she'd endangered the life of the princess. What if his little daughter had been kidnapped? It would have been Dottie's fault. All of it. The thought was so horrific, she couldn't bear it. The prince had every right to tell her she was leaving on the next flight to Athens.

This was one problem she didn't know how to fix. Being sorry wasn't enough. She'd wanted to make a difference in Zoe's life. The princess had passed every test with flying colors. Dottie was the one who'd never made the grade.

After drying off, she put on a white linen dress and sandals, prepared to be driven to the airport once the prince had told her he no longer required her services.

As she walked back into the bedroom, there was a knock on the door.

Dottie opened it to a maid who brought her a lunch tray and set it on the table in the alcove. She had no appetite but quenched her thirst with the flask of iced tea provided while she answered some emails from home. As she drained her second glass, there was another knock on the door.

"Hector?" she said after opening it. Somehow she wasn't surprised. He'd met her at the airport in Athens for her helicopter ride, and would deposit her at Hellenica's airport.

"Mrs. Richards. If you've finished your lunch, His Highness has asked me to take you to his office."

She deserved this. "I'm ready now."

By the time they reached it, she'd decided to leave today and would make it easy for the prince. But the room was empty. "Please be seated. His Highness will be with you shortly."

"Thank you." After he left, she sat on the love seat and waited. When the prince walked in, she jumped right back up again. "I'm so sorry for what happened today."

He seemed to have calmed down. "It's my fault for not having warned you earlier. There was a kidnapping attempt on Zoe at her preschool last fall."

"Oh, no—" Dottie cried out, aghast.

"Fortunately it failed. Since then I've tripled the security. It never occurred to me you would take Zoe down that long flight of stairs, even if it is our private beach. We can be grateful the patrol boats were watching you the entire time. You're as much a target as Zoe and you're my responsibility while you're here in Hellenica."

"I understand."

"Please be seated, Mrs. Richards."

"I—I can't," she stammered. Dottie bemoaned the fact that earlier during the testing, he'd called her Dorothy and had shown a teasing side to his nature. It had been unexpected and welcome. Right now those human moments out on the patio might never have been.

He eyed her up and down. "Have you injured yourself in some way?"

"You know I haven't," she murmured. "I wanted to tell you that you don't need to dismiss me because I'm leaving as soon as someone can drive me to the airport."

His black brows knit together in a fierce frown. "Whatever gave you the idea that your services are no longer required?"

She blinked in confusion. "*You* did, on the beach."

"Explain that to me," he demanded.

"When I swore to you that nothing like this would ever happen again, you said I was right about that."

His inky-black eyes had a laserlike quality. "So you jumped to the conclusion that I no longer trusted you with my daughter? Are you always this insecure?"

Dottie swallowed hard. "Only around monarchs who have to worry about pirates and kidnappers. I didn't know about those incidents and can't imagine how terrifying it must have been for you. When you couldn't find us today, it had to have been like déjà vu. I can't bear to think I caused you even a second's worry."

He took a deep breath. "From now on, whether with Zoe or alone, don't do anything without informing me of your intentions first. Then there won't be a problem."

"I agree." He was being much more decent about this than she had any right to expect. A feeling of admiration for his willingness to give her a second chance welled up inside her. When their eyes met again, she felt something almost tangible pass between them she couldn't explain, but it sent a sudden rush of warmth through her body, and she found herself unable to look away.

CHAPTER THREE

THE prince cleared his throat, breaking the spell. "After spending the day with my daughter, tell me what you've learned about her."

Dottie pulled herself together. The fear that she'd alienated the prince beyond salvaging almost made her forget why she'd come to Hellenica in the first place.

"I'll give you the bad news first. She has trouble articulating. Research tells us there are several reasons for it, but none of it matters. The fact is, she struggles with this problem.

"Now for the good news. Zoe is exceptionally intelligent with above-average motor and cognitive skills. Her vocabulary is remarkable. She understands prepositions and uses the right process to solve problems, such as in matching. Playing with her demonstrates her amazing dexterity. You saw her handling the balls and jumping rope. She has excellent coordination and balance.

"She follows directions the first time without problem. If you took a good look at that castle, it proves she sees things spatially. Her little mound had a first floor and a second floor, just like the palace. She understands her physical world and understands what she hears. Zoe only has one problem, as I said, but it's a big one since for the most part she can't make herself understood to anyone but you and the queen and, I presume to some extent, Sofia."

Alex nodded. "So that's why she's withdrawing from other people."

"Yes. You've told me she's been more difficult over the past few months. She's getting older and is losing her confidence around those who don't have her problem. She's smart enough to know she's different and not like everyone else. She wants to avoid situations that illuminate the difference, so she runs away and hides. It's the most natural instinct in the world.

"Zoe wants to make herself understood. The more she can't do it, the angrier she becomes, thus the tantrums. There's nothing wrong with her psychologically that wouldn't clear up immediately once she's free to express herself like everyone else does. She pushes people away and clings to you because you love her without qualification. But she knows the rest of the world doesn't love her, and she's feeling like a misfit."

The prince's sober expression masked a deep fear. She saw it in his eyes. "Can she overcome this?"

"Of course. She needs help saying all her sounds, but particularly the consonants. *H*'s and *T*'s are impossible for her. Few of her words come out right. Her frustration level has to be off the charts. But with constant work, she'll talk as well as I do."

He rubbed the back of his neck absently. "Are you saying you used to have the same problem?"

"I had a worse one. I stuttered so severely, I was the laughingstock of my classes in elementary school.

Children are cruel to other children. I used to pretend to be sick so I wouldn't have to go to school."

"How did you get through it?" He sounded pained for her.

"My aunt raised me. She was a stickler for discipline and sent me to a speech therapist every weekday, who taught me how to breathe, how to pace myself when I talked. After a few years I stuttered less and less. By high school it only showed up once in a while.

"Zoe has a different problem and needs to work on her sounds every day. If you could be the one encouraging her like a coach, she would articulate correct sounds faster. The more creativity, the better. I've brought toys and games you can play with her. While she's interacting with you, she'll learn to model her speech after you. Slowly but surely it will come."

"But you'll be here, too."

"Of course. You and I will work with her one on one, and sometimes the three of us will play together. I can't emphasize enough how much progress she'll make if you're available on a regular basis."

He shifted his weight. "How long do you think this will take?"

"Months to possibly several years. It's a gradual process and requires patience on everyone's part. When you feel confident, then another therapist can come in my place and—"

"I hired *you*," he interrupted her, underlining as never before that she was speaking to a prince.

"Yes, for the initial phase, but I'm a diagnostician and am needed other places."

His eyes narrowed on her face. "Is there a man in New York waiting for you to get back to him?"

No. That was a long time ago, she thought sorrowfully. Since then she'd devoted her time to her career. "Why does my personal life have to enter into this discussion?"

"I thought the point was obvious. You're young and attractive."

"Thank you. For that matter so are you, Your Highness, but you have more serious matters on your mind. So do I."

There she went again, speaking her thoughts out loud, offending him right and left. He studied her for a long time. "If it's money…"

"It's not. The Institute pays me well."

"Then?" He left the word hanging in the air.

"There is no *then*. You have your country to rule over. I have a career. The people with speech problems are *my* country. But for the time I'm here, I'll do everything in my power to get this program going for Zoe."

An odd tension had sprung between them. "Zoe only agreed to stop crying and eat lunch with the queen as long as she could return to the patio to play with you this afternoon," he said. "She had a better time with you this morning than I think she's ever had with anyone else."

Dottie smiled. "You mean besides you. That's because she was given the nonstop attention every child craves without being negatively judged. Would it be all right with you if she comes to my room for her lessons?"

"After the grilling you gave me, will I be welcome, too?" he countered in a silky voice that sent darts of awareness through her body. The prince was asking *her* permission after the outspoken way she'd just addressed him?

"I doubt Zoe will stay if you don't join us. Hopefully in a few days she'll come to my room, even when you can't be there. The alcove with the table makes it especially convenient for the games I've brought. If you'll make out a schedule and rules for me to follow, then there won't have to be so many misunderstandings on my part."

"Anything else?" She had a feeling he was teasing her now. This side of him revealed his charm and added to the depth of the man.

"Where does her Greek tutor teach her?"

"In the library, but she's developed an aversion to it and stays in her bedroom."

"That's what I used to do. It's where you can sleep and have no worries. In that room you can pretend you're normal like everyone else." Maybe it was a trick of light, but she thought she saw a glimmer of compassion radiate from those black depths. "As for your patio, I think it ought to remain your special treat for her."

"So do I. Why don't you go on up to your room. I'll bring Zoe in a few minutes. Later this evening you'll join me in the guest dining room near your suite and we'll discuss how you want to spend your time while you're in Hellenica when you're not with my daughter."

"That's very kind of you," Dottie murmured, but she didn't move because she didn't know if she'd been dismissed or not. When he didn't speak, she said, "Do I need to wait for a maid to escort me back to my room?"

His lips twitched, causing her breath to catch at the sight of such a beautiful man whose human side was doing things to her equilibrium without her consent. "Only if you're afraid you can't find it."

She stared into his eyes. "Thank you for trusting me. With work, Zoe's speech *will* improve."

On that note she left his office, feeling his all-seeing gaze on her retreating back. She hurried along the corridor on trembling legs and found the staircase back to the guest suite. Now that she'd discovered she was still employed by him, she was ravenous and ate the lunch she'd left on the tray.

Before he came with Zoe, she set things up to resemble a mini schoolroom; crayons, scissors, paper, building blocks, beads to string, hide-and-seek games, puzzles, sorting games. Flash cards. She'd brought several sets so he could keep a pack on him. All of it served as a device while she helped his daughter with her sounds.

That's why you're here, Dottie. It's the only reason. Don't ever forget it.

Alex found Dottie already seated in the guest dining room when he joined her that evening. She looked summery in a soft blue crochet top and white skirt that followed the lines and curves of her alluring figure.

He smiled. "May I join you?"

"Of course."

"You're sure?"

"I came from New York to try to be of help."

It wasn't the answer he'd wanted. In truth, he wasn't exactly sure what he wanted, but he felt her reserve around him when she wasn't with Zoe and was determined to get to the bottom of it. He sat down opposite her and within a minute their dinner was served.

Once they were alone again he said, "Whenever you wish to leave the palace, a car and driver will be at your disposal. Hector will arrange it. A bodyguard will always be with you. Hopefully you won't find my security people obtrusive."

"I'm sure I won't. Thank you." She began eating, but the silence stretched between them. Finally she said, "Could I ask you something without you thinking I'm criticizing you or stepping over the line?"

"Because I'm a prince?"

"Because you're a prince, a man and a father." She lifted her fabulous blue eyes to him. "I don't know which of those three people will be irked and maybe even angered."

Alex tried to keep a straight face. "I guess we won't know until I hear your question."

A sigh came out of her. "When did you stop eating dinner with Zoe as part of your natural routine?"

He hadn't seen that question coming. "After my wife died, I had to make up for a lot of missed work in my capacity as overseer of the mining industry of our country. Hellenica couldn't have the high quality of life it enjoys without the revenue paid by other countries needing our resources. It requires constant work and surveillance.

"I spent my weekends with Zoe, but weekdays my hours were long, so she ate dinner with her nannies and my grandmother, who could get around then and spent a lot of her time on Aurum with us. However, I never missed kissing my daughter good-night and putting her to bed. That routine has gradually become the norm.

"With Stasio gone the past six weeks, I've had to be here and have been stretched to the max with monarchy business plus my own work."

"Do you mind if I ask what it is you do for your

brother? I've often wondered what a crown prince's daily routine is really like."

"Let me put it this way. On top of working with the ministers while he runs the complex affairs of our country on a daily basis, Stasio has at least four hundred events to attend or oversee during a year's time. That's more than one a day where he either gives a speech, entertains international dignitaries, attends openings or christens institutions, all while promoting the general welfare of Hellenica."

"It's very clear his life isn't his own. Neither is yours, obviously. Where did you go today after our session with Zoe?"

Alex was surprised and pleased she'd given him that much thought. "I had to fly to one of the islands in the north to witness the installation of the new president of the Thracian college and say a few words in Stasio's place. I should have stayed for the dinner, but I told them I had another engagement I couldn't miss." Alex had wanted to eat dinner with her. He enjoyed her company.

"Do you like your work? I know that probably sounds like an absurd question, but I'm curious."

"Like all work, it has its good and bad moments, but if I were honest I'd have to say that for the most part I enjoy it—very much, in fact, when something good happens that benefits the citizenry. After a lot of work and negotiations, four new hospitals will be under construction shortly. One of them will be a children's hospital. Nothing could please me more."

"Does Zoe know about this hospital? Do you share some of the wonderful things you do when you're with her?"

Her question surprised him. "Probably not as much as I should," he answered honestly.

"The reason I asked is because if she understood what kinds of things take up your time when you're away from her, she'd be so proud of you and might not feel as much separation anxiety when you're apart."

He looked at her through shuttered eyes. "If I didn't know better, I'd think you were a psychiatrist."

She let out a gentle laugh. "Hardly. You appear to have an incredible capacity to carry your brother's load as well as your own and still see to your daughter's needs. I'm so impressed."

"But?"

"I didn't say anything."

"You didn't have to. It's there in your expression. If I ate dinner with my daughter every evening, her speech would come faster."

"Maybe a little, but I can see you're already burning the candle at both ends out of concern for your country and necessity. It would be asking too much of you when you're already making time for her teaching sessions." She sat back. "I'm so sorry you lost your wife, who must have been such a help to you. It must have been a terrible time for you."

"It was, but I had Zoe. Her smiling face made me want to get up in the morning when I didn't think I could."

Moisture filmed her eyes. "I admire you for the wonderful life you're giving her."

"She's worth everything to me. You do what you have to do. Don't forget I've had a lot of help from family and the staff."

"Even so, your little Zoe adores you. It means what-

ever you're doing is working." She pushed herself away
from the table and got to her feet. "Good night, Your
Highness. No, no. Don't get up. Enjoy that second cup
of coffee in peace.

"What with worrying about your grandmother, too,
you deserve a little pampering. From my vantage point,
no one seems to be taking care of you. In all the fairy
tales I read as a child, they went to the castle and lived
happily ever after. Until now I never thought about the
prince's welfare."

Her comment stunned him before she walked out of
the dining room.

Two nights later, while Alex was going over a new
schedule he'd been working out with his internal affairs
minister, a maid came into his office with a message.
He wasn't surprised when he heard what was wrong.
In fact he'd half been expecting it.

"If you'll excuse me."

"Of course, Your Highness."

Pleased that he'd been able to arrange his affairs so
he could eat dinner with Zoe and Dottie from now on,
he got up from the desk and headed for Zoe's bedroom.
He heard crying before he opened the door. Poor Sofia
was trying to calm his blotchy-faced daughter, who took
one look at him and flung herself against his body.

Alex gathered her in his arms. "What's the matter?"
he asked, knowing full well what was wrong. She'd
been having the time of her life since Dottie had come
to the palace and she didn't want the fun to stop.

Sofia shook her head. "She was asleep, and then suddenly she woke up with a nightmare. I haven't been able

to quiet her down, Your Highness. She doesn't want me to help her anymore."

"I understand. It's all right. You can retire now. Thank you."

After she went into the next room, where she'd been sleeping lately, Zoe cried, "I want my mommy."

She'd never asked for her mother before. From time to time they'd talked about Teresa. He'd put pictures around so she would always know what her mother looked like, but this was different. He pulled one of them off the dresser and put it in her hand. To his shock, she pushed the photo away. "I want Dot. She's my mommy."

Alex was aghast. His daughter had shortened Dottie's name, but the sound that came out would make no sense to anyone except Alex, who understood it perfectly. "No, Zoe. Dottie's your teacher."

She had that hysterical look in her eyes. "No—she's my mommy. Where did she go?"

"Your mommy's in heaven."

"No—" She flung her arms around his neck. "Get my mommy!"

"I can't, Zoe."

"Has she gone?" The fright in her voice stunned him.

Alex grabbed the photograph. "This is your mommy. She went to heaven, remember?"

"Is Dot in heaven?"

Obviously his daughter's dreaming had caused her to awaken confused. "Dottie is your teacher and she went to her room, but she's not your mommy."

"Yes, she is." She nodded. "She's my new mommy!" she insisted before breaking down in sobs.

New?

"I want her! Get her, Daddy! Get her!" she begged him hysterically.

Feeling his panic growing, he pulled out his cell phone to call Hector.

"Your Highness?"

"Finds Mrs. Richards and tell her to come to Zoe's suite immediately."

"I'll take care of it now."

Alex could be thankful there was no one more efficient than Hector in an emergency.

When Dottie walked into the room a few minutes later with a book in her hand, his daughter had calmed down somewhat, but was still shuddering in his arms.

"Dot—" Zoe blurted with such joy, Alex was speechless.

"Hi, Zoe. Did you want to say good-night?"

"Yes."

"She thought you were gone," Alex whispered in an aside.

Dottie nodded. "Why don't you get in bed and I'll read you a story. Then *I* have to go to bed, too, because you and I have a big day planned for tomorrow, don't we?"

Zoe's lips turned up in a smile. "Yes."

Like magic, his daughter crawled under the covers. Dottie pulled up a chair next to the bed. "This is the good-night book. See the moon on the cover? When he's up there, everyone goes to sleep. Freddie the frog stops going *ribbbbbit* and says good-night." Zoe laughed.

Dottie turned the page. "Benny the bee stops *buzzzz-ing* and says good-night." She showed each page to his daughter who was enchanted. "Charlie the cricket stops *chirrrping* and says good-night. Guess who's on the last page?" Zoe didn't know. Dottie showed it to her. There was a mirror. "It's *you!* Now *you* have to say goodnight."

Zoe said it.

"Let's say the *g* again. Mr. G is a grumpy letter." Zoe thought that was hilarious. "He gets mad." She made a face. "Let's see if we can get as mad as he does. We have to grit our teeth like this. Watch my mouth and say *grrr.*"

Alex was watching it. To his chagrin he'd been watching it on and off for several days. After half a dozen tries Zoe actually made the *grrr* sound. He couldn't believe it. In his astonishment his gaze darted to Dottie, but she was focused on his daughter.

"You sounded exactly like Mr. G, Zoe. That was perfect. Tomorrow night your father will read it to you again. Now Dot has to go to sleep. I'll leave the book with you." She slipped out of the room, leaving the two of them alone.

Zoe clasped it to her chest as if it were her greatest treasure. Alex's eyes smarted because lying before him was *his* greatest treasure. She fell asleep within minutes. As soon as she was out, he left the room knowing Sofia was sleeping in the adjacent room and would hear her if she woke up.

He strode through the palace, intending to talk to Dottie before she went to bed. Hector met him as he was passing his grandmother's suite on his way to the other wing.

"The queen wants to see you before she retires."

His brows lifted. "You wouldn't by any chance be spying on me for her, would you, Hector?"

"I have never spied on you, Your Highness."

"You've been spying for her since the day Stasi and I were born, but I forgive you. However, Stasi might not be so forgiving once he's crowned, so remember you've been warned. Tell the queen I'll be with her in ten minutes."

He continued on his way to Dottie's apartment. After he knocked, she called out, "Yes?"

"It's Alex."

The silence that followed was understandable. He'd never used his given name with her before, or given his permission for her to use it. But considering the amount of time they'd been spending together since her arrival at the palace, it seemed absurd to say anything else now that they were alone. "Would you be more willing to answer me if I'd said it's Zoe's father, or it's your Royal Highness?"

He thought he heard her chuckle before she opened the door a couple of inches. "I was on the verge of crawling into bed."

Alex could see that. She'd thrown on a pink toweling robe and was clutching the lapels beneath her chin. "I need to talk frankly with you. Zoe has decided you're her new mommy. She got hysterical tonight when I tried to tell her otherwise."

"I know. She's told me on several occasions she wishes I were her mother. This happens with some of my youngest students who don't have one. It's very normal. I just keep telling them I'm their teacher. You need to go on telling her in a matter-of-fact way that Princess Teresa was her mommy."

"I did that."

"I know. I saw the photograph and see a lot of the princess's beauty in Zoe. What's important here is that if you don't fight her on it, she'll finally get the point and the phase will pass after a while."

"That's very wise counsel." He exhaled the breath he'd been holding. "You made a breakthrough with her tonight."

"Yes. I've wanted her to feel confident about one sound and now it has happened."

"How did you know she would do it?"

"I didn't, but I hoped. Every success creates more success."

Talking through the crack in the door added a certain intimacy to their conversation, exciting him. "Her success is going to help me sleep tonight."

"I'm glad. Just remember a total change isn't going to happen overnight. Her vowels are coming, but *G* is only one consonant out of twenty-one. Putting that sound with the rest of a word is the tricky part."

"Tricky or not, she mimicked you perfectly and the way you read that book had her spellbound."

"There was only one thing wrong with it."

"What's that?" He found himself hanging on her every word, just like his daughter.

"It didn't have a page that said the prince stopped *rrrruling* and said good-night."

Alex broke into full-bodied laughter.

Her eyes smiled. "If you'll forgive me, you should do that more often in front of Zoe, Your Highness."

"What happened to Alex? That is my name."

"I realize that."

"Before I leave, I wanted you to know that I've worked things out with my internal affairs minister so I can eat dinner with my daughter every night. From now on he'll take care of the less important matters for me during that time period."

"Zoe's going to be ecstatic!" she blurted, displaying the bubbly side of her nature that didn't emerge as often as he would have liked to see.

"I hope that means you're happy about it, too, since you'll be joining us for our meals. Good night, Dottie."

"Good night, Alex."

She shut the door on him before he was ready to leave. After being with her, he wasn't in the mood to face his grandmother. As he made his way back to her suite, he thought about his choice of words. The only time he'd ever *faced* the queen was when he'd been a boy and had a reason to feel guilty about something.

Tonight he had a strong hunch what she wanted to discuss with him. After Zoe's nightmare, now he knew why. If she'd told *Yiayia* that Dottie was her new mommy, nothing would have enraged his grandmother more. She would have told Zoe never to speak of it again, but that wouldn't prevent his daughter from thinking it in her heart.

Until the phase passed, Dottie had said.

What if it didn't? That's what disturbed Alex.

Zoe's insistence that Dottie was her new mommy only exacerbated his inner conflict where the speech therapist was concerned. Since he'd peered into a pair of eyes as blue as the flowers fluttering in the breeze around the palace in Aurum, he couldn't get her out of his mind.

In truth he had no business getting physically involved with someone he'd hired. He certainly didn't need the queen reminding him of what he'd already been telling himself—keep the relationship with Mrs.

Richards professional and enjoy the other women he met when he left the country for business or pleasure.

Too bad for his grandmother that he saw through her machinations and had done so from an early age. She always had another agenda going. Since Teresa's funeral, she'd been busy preparing the ground with the House of Helvetia. But until Stasi married, she was biding her time before she insisted Alex take Princess Genevieve of Helvetia to wife for the growth and prosperity of the kingdom.

Lines darkened his face. The queen would have to hide away forever because Stasi would be the only one doing the growing for the Constantinides dynasty. He was the firstborn, Heaven had picked him to rule Hellenica. Ring out the bells.

Alex had a different destiny and a new priority that superseded all else. He wanted to help his daughter feel normal, and that meant coaching her. With Dottie's help, it was already happening. She understood what was going on inside Zoe. Her story about her own stuttering problem had touched him. He admired her strength in overcoming a huge challenge.

His first order of business was to talk to Stasio tonight. His brother needed to come home now! With Alex's work schedule altered, he could spend the maximum amount of time with Zoe and Dottie throughout the day. It was going to work, even though it meant dealing with his ministers in the early morning hours and late at night when necessary.

Once Stasio was home, Alex would move back to the island of Aurum, where he could divide his attention between helping Zoe and doing the work he'd been overseeing for the country since university. With Dottie installed and a palace staff and security waiting on them, Zoe couldn't help but make great strides with her speech and he'd convince Dottie she couldn't leave yet.

CHAPTER FOUR

LIKE pizza dough being tossed in the air, Dottie's heart did its own version of a flip when the prince entered her schoolroom a few days later with Zoe. They must have just come from breakfast with the queen. Zoe was dressed in pink play clothes and sneakers.

Dottie hardly recognized Alex. Rather than hand-tooled leather shoes, he'd worn sneakers, too. She was dazzled by his casual attire of jeans and a yellow, open-necked sport shirt. In the vernacular, he was a hunk. When she looked up and saw the smattering of dark hair on his well-defined chest, her mouth went dry and she averted her eyes. Zoe's daddy was much more man than prince this morning, bringing out longings in her she hadn't experienced in years.

He'd been coming to their teaching sessions and had cleared his calendar to eat dinner with Zoe. Dottie was moved by his love and concern for his daughter, but she feared for him, too. The prince had the greatest expectations for his child, but he might want too much too soon. That worry had kept her tossing and turning during the night because she wanted to be up to the challenge and help Zoe triumph.

But it wasn't just that worry. When she'd told Alex

she'd had other patients who'd called her mommy, it was a lie. Only one other child had expressed the same wish. It was a little boy who had a difficult, unhappy mother. In truth, Zoe was unique. So was the whole situation.

Normally Dottie's students came by bus or private car to the institute throughout the day. Living under the palace roof was an entirely different proposition and invited more intimacy. Zoe was a very intelligent child and should have corrected her own behavior by now, but she chose to keep calling Dottie Mommy. Every time Zoe did that, it blurred the lines for Dottie, who in a short time had allowed the little girl to creep into her heart.

To make matters worse, Dottie was also plagued by guilt because she realized she wanted Alex's approval. That sort of desire bordered on pride. Her aunt had often quoted Gibran. "Generosity is giving more than you can, and pride is taking less than you need." If she wanted his approval, then it was a gift she had to earn.

Did she seek it because he was a prince? She hoped not. Otherwise that put her in the category of those people swayed by a person's station in life. She refused to be a sycophant, the kind of person her aunt had despised. Dottie despised sycophants, too.

"GGGRRRRRR," she said to Zoe, surprising the little girl, who was a quick study and *gggrrrred* back perfectly. Alex gave his daughter a hug before they sat down at the table.

"Wonderful, Zoe." Her gaze flicked to him. "Good morning, Your Highness." Dottie detected the scent of the soap he'd used in the shower. It was the most marvelous smell, reminding her of mornings when her husband—

But the eyes staring at her across the table were a fiery black, not blue. "Aren't you going to *gggrrr* me? I feel left out."

Her pulse raced. "Well, we don't want you to feel like that, do we, Zoe?" The little girl shook her head, causing her shiny brown curls to flounce.

Dottie had a small chalkboard and wrote the word *Bee*. "Go ahead and pronounce this word for us, Your Highness." When he did, she said, "Zoe? Did you hear *bee*?"

"Yes."

"Good. Let's all say *bee* together. One, two three. *Bee*." Zoe couldn't do it, of course. Dottie leaned toward her. "Pretend you're a tiny goldfish looking for food." Pressing her lips together she made the beginning of the *B* sound. "Touch my lips with your index finger." Her daddy helped her. In the process his fingers brushed against Dottie's mouth. She could hardly breathe from the sensation of skin against skin.

"Now feel how it sounds when I say it." Dottie said it a dozen times against Zoe's finger. She giggled. "That tickled, didn't it? Now say the same sound against my finger." She put her finger to Zoe's lips. After five tries she was making the sound.

"Terrific! Now put your lips to your daddy's finger and make the same *B* sound over and over."

As Zoe complied with every ounce of energy in that cute little body, Alex caught Dottie's gaze. The softness, the gratitude she saw in his eyes caused her heart to hammer so hard, she feared he could hear it.

"You're an outstanding pupil, Zoe. Today we're going to work on the *B* sound."

"It's interesting you've brought up the *bee*," Alex interjected.

"They make honey," said Zoe.

"That's right, Zoe. Did you know that just yesterday I met with one of the ministers and we're going to establish beekeeping centers on every island in Hellenica."

"How come?"

"With more bees gathered in hives, we'll have more honey to sell to people here as well as around the world. It's an industry I'd like to see flourish. With all the blossoms and thyme that grow here, it will give jobs to people who don't have one. You know the honey you eat when we're on Aurum?" She nodded. "It comes from two hives Inez and Ari tend on our property."

Zoe's eyes widened. "They do? I've never seen them."

"When we go home, we'll take a look."

Zoe smiled and gave her father a long hug. As he reciprocated, his gaze met Dottie's. He'd taken her suggestion to share more with his daughter and it was paying dividends, thrilling her to pieces.

"I'm going to give your daddy a packet of flash cards, Zoe. Everything on it starts with a *B*. He'll hold up the card and say the word. Then you say it. If you can make three perfect *B* sounds, I have a present for you."

Zoe let out a joyous sound and looked at her daddy with those shiny brown eyes. Dottie sat back in the chair and watched father and daughter at work. Zoe had great incentive to do her best for the man she idolized. The prince took his part seriously and proceeded with care. She marveled to watch them drawing closer together through these teaching moments, forging closer bonds now that he was starting to ease up on his work for the monarchy.

"Bravo!" she said when he'd gone through the pack of thirty. "You said five *B*'s clearly. Do you want your present now or after your lesson?"

Zoe concentrated for a minute. "Now."

Alex laughed that deep male laugh. It resonated through Dottie to parts she'd forgotten were there. Reaching in the bag in the corner, she pulled out one of several gifts she'd brought for rewards. But this one was especially vital because Zoe had been working hard so far and needed a lot of reinforcement.

Dottie handed her the soft, foot-long baby. "This is Baby Betty. She has a *bottle*, a *blanket* and a *bear*."

"Oh—" Zoe cried. Her eyes lit up. She cradled it in her arms, just like a mother. "Thank you, Mommy."

The word slipped out again. Dottie couldn't look at Alex. His daughter had said it again. These days it was coming with more frequency. The moment had become an emotional one for Dottie, who had to fight her own pain over past memories that had been resurrected by being around her new student.

"I'm not your mommy, Zoe. She's in heaven. You know that, don't you."

She finally nodded. "I wish you were my mommy."

"But since I'm not, will you please call me Dot?"

"Yes."

"Good girl. Guess what? Now that you've fed Betty, you have to burp her." Puzzled, Zoe looked up at her. "When a baby drinks milk from a bottle, it drinks in air, too. So you have to pat her back. Then the air will come out and she won't have a tummyache. Your mommy used to pat your back like that when you were a baby, didn't she, Your Highness?"

Dottie had thrown the ball in his court, not knowing what had gone on in their marriage. He'd never discussed his private personal life or asked Dottie about hers.

"Indeed, she did. We took turns walking the floor with you. Sometimes very important people would come in the nursery to see you and you'd just yawn and go to sleep as if you were horribly bored."

At that comment the three of them laughed hard. Dottie realized it provided a release from the tension built up over the last week.

From the corner of her eye she happened to spot Hector, who stood several feet away. He was clearing his throat to get their attention. How long had he been in the room listening?

"Your Highness? The queen has sent for you."

"Is it a medical emergency?"

"No."

"Then I'm afraid she'll have to wait until tonight. After this lesson I'm taking Zoe and Mrs. Richards out on the *boat*," he said emphasizing the B. "We'll work on her *B* sounds while we enjoy a light *buffet* on *board*, won't we, Zoe?" He smiled at his daughter who nodded, still gripping her baby tightly. "But don't worry. I'll be back in time to say good-night to her."

"Very well, Your Highness."

Dottie had to swallow the gasp that almost escaped her throat. Lines bracketed Hector's mouth. She looked at the floor. It really was funny. Alex had a quick, brilliant mind and a surprising imp inside him that made it hard for her to hold back her laughter, but she didn't dare laugh in front of Hector.

After Hector left, Dottie brought out a box containing tubes of blue beads, so Zoe and Alex could make a bracelet together. They counted the beads as they did so, and Dottie was pleased to note that Zoe's *B* sounds were really coming along.

Satisfied with that much progress, Dottie cleaned everything up. "That's the end of our lesson for today." She got up from the chair, suddenly wishing she weren't wearing a T-shirt with a picture of a cartoon bunny on the front. She'd hoped Zoe would ask her about it and they could practice saying the famous rabbit's name. But it was Alex who'd stared at it several times this morning, causing sensual waves to ripple through her.

He swept Zoe in his arms. "I'm very proud of you. Now let's show Dot around the island on the sailboat." His daughter hugged him around the neck. Over her shoulder he stared at Dottie. "Are you ready?"

No. Sailing with him wasn't part of her job. In fact it was out of the question. She didn't want to feel these feelings she had around him. Yearnings...

"That's very kind of you, Your Highness, but I have other things to do this afternoon, including a lot of paperwork to send in to the Institute. In case you don't get back from sailing by dinnertime, I'll see you and Zoe in the morning for her lesson."

He lowered his daughter to the floor. "I insist."

She took a steadying breath. "Did you just give me a command?"

"If I did, would you obey it?"

There was nothing playful about this conversation. The last thing she wanted to do was offend him, but she refused to be anything but Zoe's speech therapist. With his looks and charismatic personality, he could ensnare any woman he wanted. That's what royal playboys did.

Alex might be a widower with a daughter, but as far as she was concerned, he was at the peak of his manhood now and a hundred times more dangerous. She was reminded of that fact when he'd eyed her T-shirt. A little shiver went through her because he was still eyeing her that way and she was too aware of him.

Dottie needed to turn this around and make it right so he wouldn't misunderstand why she was refusing the invitation. Using a different tactic she said, "I gave you that pack of flash cards. You should take your daughter on your sailboat this afternoon and work with her while the lesson is fresh in her mind."

In a lowered voice she added, "I might be her speech therapist, but outside this classroom I can only be a distraction and cause her more confusion over the mommy issue. She wants your undivided attention and will cooperate when you do the cards with her because she'd do anything for you. There's a saying in English. I'm sure you've heard of it. 'Strike while the iron's hot.'"

"There's another saying by the great teacher Plato," he fired back. "'We can easily forgive a child who is afraid of the dark; the real tragedy of life is when men are afraid of the light.'" He turned to his daughter. "Come with me, Zoe."

Dottie trembled as she watched them leave. Alex had her figured out without knowing anything about her. She *was* afraid. Once upon a time her world had been filled with blinding, glorious light. After it had been taken away, she never wanted to feel it or be in it again. One tragedy in life had been too much.

* * *

Alex put his daughter to bed, but he had to face facts. After the outing on the sailboat and all the swimming and fun coaching moments with the flash cards, it still wasn't enough for his little girl. She didn't want Sofia tending to her.

He'd read the good-night book to her six times, but the tears gushed anyway. She was waiting for her favorite person. "Have you forgotten that Dottie had a lot of work to do tonight? You'll see her in the morning. Here's Betty. She's ready to go to sleep with you." He tucked the baby in her arm, but she pushed it away and sat up.

"Tell Dot to come."

Alex groaned because these tears were different. His daughter had found an outlet for her frustration in Dottie who understood her and had become her ally. What child wouldn't want her to be her mommy and stay with her all the time? Alex got it. She made every moment so memorable, no one else could possibly measure up. Dottie was like a force of nature. Her vivacious personality had brought life into the palace.

Earlier, when he'd asked Hector about Dottie's activities, he'd learned she'd refused a car and had left the grounds on foot. Security said that after she'd jogged ten miles in the heat, she'd hiked to the top of Mount Pelos and sat for an hour. After visiting the church, she'd returned to town and jogged back to the palace.

"Zoe? If you'll stay in your bed, I'll go get her."

The tears slowed down. She reached for her baby. "Hurry, Daddy."

Outside the bedroom he called Dottie on his cell phone, something he'd sworn he wouldn't do in order to keep his distance, but this was an emergency. When she picked up, he asked her to come to Zoe's bedroom.

He sensed the hesitation before she said, "I'll be right there."

It pleased him when a minute later he heard footsteps and watched Dottie hurrying towards the suite with another book in her hand.

"Alex—" she cried in surprise as he stepped away from the paneled wall.

He liked it that she'd said his name of her own volition. "I wondered when you would finally break down."

Dottie smoothed the hair away from her flushed cheek. Her eyes searched his. Ignoring his comment she said, "Did Zoe have another nightmare?"

He moved closer. "No. But she's growing more and more upset when you're not with us. Why didn't you come today? I want the truth."

"I told you I had work."

"Then how come it was reported that you went jogging and climbed Mount Pelos, instead of staying in your room? Were you able to see the sail of my boat from the top?"

A hint of pink crept into her cheeks. She *had* been watching for him. "I saw a lot of sailboats."

"The security staff is agog about the way you spent your day. Not one visit to a designer shop. No shopping frenzy. You undoubtedly wore them to a frazzle with your jogging, but it was good for them."

A small laugh escaped her throat. He liked it that she didn't take herself seriously.

"I'll ask the question again. Why didn't you come with us this afternoon?"

"Surely you know why. Because I'm worried over her growing attachment to me."

"So am I, but that's not the only reason you kept your distance from me today. Are you afraid of being on a boat? Don't you know how to swim?"

"Don't be silly," she whispered.

"How else am I to get some honesty out of you? It's apparent you have a problem with me, pure and simple. My earlier reputation in life as Prince Alexius may have prejudiced you against me, but that was a long time ago. I'm a man now and a father the world knows nothing about. Which of those roles alarms you most?"

She folded her arms. "Neither of them," she said in a quiet voice.

His brows met in a frown. "Then what terrible thing do you imagine would have happened to you today if you'd come with us?"

"I'd rather not talk about it, even if you are a prince." She'd said that "even if you are a prince" thing before. After retaining his gaze for a moment, she looked away. "How did your afternoon go with Zoe?"

"Good, but it would have been better if you'd been along. She won't go to sleep until you say good-night. Tonight she fired Sofia."

"What?"

"It's true. She doesn't want a nanny unless it's you. To save poor Hector the trouble of having to summon you every night, why don't you plan to pop in on her at bedtime. In the end it will save my sanity, too."

She slowly nodded. "Since I won't be here much longer, I can do that."

"Let's not talk about your leaving, not when you barely got here."

"I— I'll go in now." Her voice faltered.

"Thank you." For several reasons, he wasn't through with her yet, but it could wait until she'd said goodnight to his daughter. Alex followed her into the bedroom. Zoe was sitting up in her bed holding her baby. She glowed after she saw Dottie.

"Hi, Zoe. If I read you a story, will you go to sleep?"

"Yes. Will you sit on the bed?"

"I can read better on this chair." Dottie drew it close to the bed and sat down. Once again Alex was hooked by Dottie's charm as she read the tale about a butterfly that had lost a wing and needed to find it.

She was a master teacher, but it dawned on him she always kept her distance with Zoe. No hugs or kisses. No endearments. Being the total professional, she knew her place. Ironically his daughter didn't want hugs or kisses from her nannies who tried to mother her, but he knew she was waiting for both from Dottie.

Zoe wasn't the only one.

The second she'd gone to sleep, Dottie tiptoed out of the room. Alex caught up to her in the hall. She couldn't seem to get back to her suite fast enough. They walked through the corridors in silence. As she reached out to open the door to her apartment, he grasped her upper arms and turned her around.

They were close enough he could smell her peach fragrance. She was out of breath, but she was in too good a shape for the small exertion of walking to produce that reaction. "Invite me in," he whispered, sensing how withdrawn she'd become with him. "I want an answer from you and prefer that we don't talk out here in the hall where we can be observed."

"I'm sorry, but we have nothing to talk about. I'm very tired."

"Too tired to tell me what has you so frightened, you're trembling?"

A pained expression crossed over her face. "I wish I hadn't come to Hellenica. If I'd known what was awaiting me, I would have refused."

"For the love of heaven, why? If I've done something unforgivable in your eyes, it's only fair you tell me."

"Of course you haven't." She shook her head, but wouldn't look at him. "This has to do with Zoe."

"Because she keeps calling you Mommy?"

"That and much more."

At a total loss, he let go of her with reluctance. "I don't understand."

She eased away from him. "Five years ago my husband and son were killed by a drunk driver in a horrific crash." Tears glistened on her cheeks. "I lost the great loves of my life. Cory was Zoe's age when he died."

Alex was aghast.

"He had an articulation problem like hers, only he couldn't do his vowel sounds. I'd been working with him for a year with the help of a therapist, and he'd just gotten to the point where he could say *Daddy* plainly when—"

Obviously she was too choked up to say the rest. His eyes closed tightly for a moment. He remembered the pain in hers the other day.

"I've worked with all kinds of children, but Zoe is the only one who has ever reminded me of him. The other day when she laughed, it sounded like Cory."

"You didn't let on." His voice grated.

"I'm thankful for that." He thought he heard a little

sob get trapped in her throat. "It's getting harder to be around her without breaking down. That's why I didn't go with you today. I—I thought I'd gotten past my grief," she stammered, "but coming here has proven otherwise."

He sucked in his breath. "You may wish you hadn't come to Hellenica, but keep in mind you're doing something for my daughter only you can do. Watching Zoe respond to your techniques has already caused me to stop grieving over her pain.

"No matter how much you're still mourning your loss, doesn't it make you feel good to be helping her the way you once helped your son? Wouldn't your husband have done anything for your son if your positions were reversed?"

She looked away, moved by his logic. "Yes," came the faint whisper, "but—"

"But what? Tell me everything."

"It's just that I've felt…guilty for not being with them that terrible day."

"You're suffering survivor's guilt."

"Yes."

"In my own way I had the same reaction after Teresa passed away. It took me a long time to convince myself everything possible had been done for her and I had to move on for Zoe's sake."

She nodded.

"Then it's settled. From now on after her morning lessons, we'll have another one during the afternoons in the swimming pool. We'll practice what you've taught her while we play. After finding your strength and solace in furthering your career, don't you see you can make a difference with Zoe and maybe lay those ghosts to rest? It's time to take a risk. With my schedule changed, I can spend as much time as possible with both of you now."

"I've noticed." After a pause, she added, "You're a remarkable man."

"It's because of you, Dottie. You're helping me get close to my daughter in a whole new way. I'll never be able to thank you enough for that."

"You don't need to thank me. I'm just so glad for the two of you." Dottie wiped the moisture from the corners of her eyes. "Tomorrow we'll work on her *W* sounds. Good night, Alex."

CHAPTER FIVE

WHAT luxury! Dottie had never known anything like it until she'd come to the palace ten days ago. After a delicious lunch, it was sheer bliss to lie in the sun on the lounger around the palace pool enjoying an icy fruit drink.

Zoe's morning lesson with her daddy had gone well. Her *B* and G sounds were coming along, but she struggled with the *W*. It might be one of the last sounds she mastered on her long journey to intelligible speech.

Dottie was glad to have the pool to herself. While they were changing into their swimsuits, she was trying to get a grip on her emotions. She'd been doing a lot of thinking, and Alex had been right about one thing. If she'd been the one killed and Cory had been left with his speech problem, then she would have wanted Neil to stop at nothing to find the right person to help their son. At the moment, Dottie was the right person for Zoe.

Deep in her own thoughts, she heard a tremendous splash followed by Zoe's shriek of laughter. Dottie turned her head in time to see Zoe running around the rim of the pool in her red bathing suit, shouting with glee. She was following a giant black whale maybe five feet long skimming the top of the water with a human torpedo propelling it.

Suddenly Alex's dark head emerged, splashing more water everywhere. Zoe got soaked and came flying toward Dottie, who grabbed her own towel and wiped off her shoulders. "You need some sunscreen. Stand still and I'll put it on you." Zoe did her bidding. "I didn't know a whale lived in your pool."

The child giggled. "Come with me." She tugged on Dottie's arm.

"I think I'd rather stay here and watch."

Alex stared at Dottie with a look she couldn't decipher, but didn't say anything. By now Zoe had joined him and was riding on top of the whale while he helped her hold on. The darling little girl was so happy, she seemed to burst with it.

Dottie threw her beach wrap around her to cover her emerald-colored bikini and got up from the lounger. She walked over to the side of the pool and sat down to dangle her legs in the water while she watched their antics.

All of a sudden it occurred to her she was having real fun for the first time in years. This was different than watching from the sidelines of other people's lives. Because of Alex she was an actual participant and was feeling a part of life again. The overpowering sense of oneness with him shook her to the core. So did the desire she felt being near him. That's why she didn't dare get in the water. Her need to touch him was overcoming her good sense.

"I think we need to name Zoe's whale," he called to her.

Dottie nodded. "Preferably a two syllable word starting with *W*."

Both she and Alex suggested a lot of names, laughing into each other's eyes at some of their absurd suggestions. Zoe clapped her hands the minute she heard her daddy say *Wally*. Though it wasn't a name that started with *Wh* like whale, it was the name his daughter wanted. When Zoe pronounced it, the sound came out like *Oye-ee*.

Dottie was secretly impressed when he came up with the idea of Zoe pretending she was a grouper fish. Evidently his daughter knew what one looked like and she formed her mouth in an *O* shape, opening and closing it. After a half hour of playing and practice, the *wa* was starting to make an appearance.

"Well done, Your Highness." Dottie smiled at him. "She wouldn't have made that sound this fast without your help."

He reciprocated with a slow, lazy smile, making jelly of her insides. The afternoon was exhilarating for Dottie, a divine moment out of time. Anyone watching would think they were a happy family. Before she knew it, dinner was served beneath the umbrella of the table on the sun deck. Zoe displayed a healthy appetite, pleasing her father and Dottie.

Toward the end of their meal he said, "Attention, everyone. I have an announcement to make." He looked at Zoe. "Guess who came home today?"

She stopped drinking her juice. "Uncle Stasi?"

"Yes. Your one and only favorite uncle."

"Goody!" she blurted. "He's funny."

"I've missed him, too. Tonight there's going to be a

party to welcome him back. I'm going to take you two ladies with me."

Zoe squealed in delight.

"After we finish dinner, I want you to go upstairs and get ready. Put on your prettiest dresses, because there's going to be dancing. When it's time, I'll come by for you."

Dancing?

Adrenalin surged through Dottie's body at the thought of getting that close to him. Heat poured off her, but she couldn't attribute all of it to the sun. She suspected his announcement had caused a spike in her temperature.

Her mind went through a mental search of her wardrobe. The only thing possibly presentable for such an affair was her simple black dress with her black high heels.

"Will it be a large party, Your Highness?"

He darted her a curious glance. "Thirty or so guests, mostly family friends. If you're both finished with dinner, let's go upstairs."

After gathering their things, Dottie said she'd see them later and she hurried back to her bedroom for a long shower and shampoo. She blowdried her hair and left it loose with a side part, then put on her black dress with the cap sleeves and round neck.

While she was applying her coral-frost lipstick, she thought she heard a noise in the other room. When she went to investigate, she saw Zoe looking like a vision in a long white dress with ruffles and a big yellow sash. But her face was awash in tears. She came running to her.

Without conscious thought, Dottie knelt down and

drew her into her arms. It was the first hug she'd given her, but she could no longer hold back. Zoe clung to her while she wept, exactly the way Cory had done so many hundreds of times when he'd needed comfort.

"What's wrong, darling?"

"Daddy's going to get married."

Dottie was trying to understand. "Don't you mean your uncle?"

"No—I heard *Yiayia* tell Sofia. My daddy's going to marry Princess Genevieve. But I want *you* to be my new mommy. When I kissed *Yiayia* good-night, she told me Princess Genevieve will be at the party and I had to be good."

A stabbing pain attacked Dottie until she could hardly breathe. "I see. Zoe, this is something you need to talk to your daddy about, but not until you go to bed. Does he know you're here with me?"

"No."

Dottie stood up. "I need to phone Hector so he can tell your daddy you ran to my room."

When that was done, she took Zoe in the bathroom. After wetting a washcloth, she wiped the tears off her face. "There. Now we're ready. When we get to the party, I want you to smile and keep smiling. Can you do that for me?"

After a slight hesitation, Zoe nodded.

Dottie clasped her hand and walked her back in the other room. "Have I told you how pretty you look in your new dress?"

"Both of you look absolutely beautiful," came the sound of a deep, familiar voice.

Alex.

Dottie gasped softly when she saw that he'd entered

the room. Since Zoe had left the door open, he must not have felt the need to knock. The prince, tall and dark, had dressed in a formal, midnight-blue suit and tie, taking her breath. His penetrating black eyes swept over her, missing nothing. The look in them sent a river of heat through her body.

"Zoe wanted to show me how she looked, Your Highness. In her haste, she forgot to tell Sofia."

He looked so handsome when he smiled, Dottie felt light-headed. "That's understandable. This is my daughter's first real party. Are you ready?"

When Zoe nodded, he grasped her other hand and the three of them left the room. He led them down the grand staircase where they could hear music and voices. Though Zoe lacked her usual sparkle, she kept smiling like the princess she was. Her training had served her well. Even at her young age, she moved with the grace and dignity of a royal.

Some of the elegantly dressed guests were dancing, others were eating. The three of them passed through a receiving line of titled people and close friends of the Constantinides family.

"Zoe?" her father said. "I'd like you to meet Princess Genevieve."

For a minute, Dottie reeled. She'd seen the lovely young princess in the news. Zoe was a trooper and handled their first meeting beautifully. One royal princess to another. Dottie loved Zoe for her great show of poise in front of the woman she didn't want for her new mother.

Dottie was trying to see the good. It was natural that Alex would marry again, and Zoe desperately needed a mother's love. Plus their match would give Alex more children and Zoe wouldn't have to be the only child. In that respect it was more necessary than ever that her speech improve enough that when Alex married Princess Genevieve, his daughter could make herself understood. Zoe also needed to be strong in her English speech because she would be tested when French was introduced into their household. Princess Genevieve would expect it. The House of Helvetia was located on the south side of Lake Geneva in the French-speaking region.

Now that she knew of Alex's future plans, Dottie had to focus on the additional goal to pursue for his daughter. She needed to help prepare Zoe for the next phase in her life and—

"My, my. What have we here?"

A male voice Dottie didn't recognize broke in on her thoughts. She turned her head to discover another extremely attractive man with black hair standing at the end of the line. Almost the same height as Alex, he bore a superficial resemblance to him, but his features were less rugged. The brothers could be the same age, which she estimated to be early to mid-thirties.

When she realized it was Crown Prince Stasio, she curtsied. "Welcome home, Your Highness."

He flashed her an infectious smile. "You don't need to do that around me. My little brother told me you're working with Zoe. That makes us all family. Did anyone ever tell you you're very easy on the eyes?" His were black, too. "Alex held back on that pertinent fact."

What a tease he was! "Zoe told me you were funny. I think she's right."

The crown prince laughed. She noticed he had a fabulous tan. "Tell me about yourself. Where have you been hiding all my life?" He was incorrigible and so different from Alex, who was more serious minded. Of the two, Dottie privately thought that Zoe's father seemed much more the natural ruler of their country.

"I'm from New York."

His eyes narrowed. "Coming to Hellenica must feel like you dropped off the edge of the planet, right?"

"It's paradise here."

"It is now that I've got my little Zoe to dance with." He reached over and picked up his niece. After they hugged, he set her down again. "Come on. I'm going to spin you around the ballroom."

Zoe's smile lit up for real as he whirled her away. Dancing lessons hadn't been wasted on her either. She moved like a royal princess who was years older, capturing everyone's attention. People started clapping. Dottie couldn't have been prouder of her if she'd been Zoe's real mother.

While she watched, she felt a strong hand slip around her waist. The next thing she knew Alex had drawn her into his arms. His wonderful, clean male scent and the brush of his legs against hers sent sparks of electricity through her system. In her heels, she was a little taller and felt like their bodies had been made for each other.

"Why won't you look at me?" he whispered. "Everyone's going to think you don't like me."

"I'm trying to concentrate on our dancing. It's been a long time." The soft rock had a hypnotizing effect on her. She could stay like this for hours, almost but not quite embracing him.

"For me, too. I've been waiting ages to get you in my arms like this. If it's in plain sight of our guests, so be it. You feel good to me, Dottie. So damn good you're in danger of being carried off. Only my princely duty keeps me from doing what I feel like doing."

Ah… Before Zoe's revelations in the bedroom tonight, Dottie might have allowed herself to be carried away. The clamorings of her body had come to painful life and only he could assuage them.

"I understand. That's why I'm going to say goodnight after this dance. There are other female guests in the ballroom no doubt waiting for their turn around the floor with you. You're a terrific dancer, by the way."

"There's only one woman I want to be with tonight and she's right here within kissing distance. You could have no idea the willpower it's taking not to taste that tempting mouth of yours." He spoke with an intensity that made her legs go weak. "While we were out at the pool, I would have pulled you in if Zoe hadn't been with us."

"It's a good thing you didn't. Otherwise your daughter will be more confused than ever when she sees you ask Princess Genevieve to dance."

His body stiffened. She'd hit a nerve, but he had no clue it had pierced her to the depths. "I know you well enough to realize you had a deliberate reason for bringing up her name. Why did you do it?"

Dottie's heart died a little because the music had stopped, bringing those thrilling moments in his arms to an end. She lifted her head and looked at him for the first time since they'd entered the ballroom. "When you put Zoe to bed tonight, she'll tell you. Thank you for an enchanting evening, Your Highness. I won't forget. See you in the morning."

She eased out of his arms and walked out of the

ballroom. But the second she reached the staircase, she raced up the steps and ran the rest of the way to her room.

"Dot," Zoe called to her the next morning as she and her father came into the classroom. "Look at this?" She held up a CD.

"What's on it?"

"It's a surprise. Put it in your laptop," said Alex.

After giving him a curious glance, Dottie walked around to the end of the table and put it in. After a moment they could all see last night's events at the party on the screen, complete with the music. There she was enclosed in Alex's arms. Princess Genevieve would not have been happy.

Whoever had taken the video had caught everything, including what went on after Dottie had left the ballroom. Her throat swelled with emotion as she watched Alex dance with his daughter. If he'd asked Princess Genevieve to dance, that portion hadn't been put on the CD.

She smiled at Zoe. "You're so lucky to have a video of your first party. Did you love it?"

"Yes!" There weren't any shadows in the little girl's eyes. Whatever conversation had taken place between father and daughter at bedtime, she looked happy. "Uncle Stasi told me I could stand on his feet while he danced with me. He made me laugh."

"The crown prince is a real character." Her gaze swerved to Alex. "He made me laugh, as well. I've decided you and your brother must have given certain people some nervous moments when you were younger."

Alex's grin turned her heart right over. "Our parents

particularly. My brother was upset you left the party before he could dance with you."

"Maybe that was for the best. My high heels might have hurt the tops of his feet."

At that remark both he and Zoe laughed. Dottie was enjoying this too much and suggested they get started on the morning lesson.

They worked in harmony until Alex said it was time for lunch by the pool. After they'd finished eating, Zoe ran into the cabana to get into her swimsuit. Dottie took advantage of the time they were alone to talk to him.

"I'm glad we're by ourselves for a minute. I want to discuss Zoe's preschool situation and wondered how you'd feel if I went with her to class in the morning. You know, just to prop up her confidence. We'll come back here for lunch and enjoy our afternoon session with her out here. What do you think?"

He sipped his coffee. "That's an excellent suggestion. Otherwise she'll keep putting off wanting to go back."

"Exactly."

Alex released a sigh. "Since our talk about her friends, I've worried about her being away from the other children this long."

Dottie was glad they were on her same wavelength. "Is there any particular child she's close to at school?"

Their gazes held. "Not that she has mentioned. As you know, school hasn't been her best experience."

"Then tell me this. Who goes to the school?"

"Besides those who live in Hellenica, there are a few children of some younger diplomats who attend at the various elementary grade levels."

"From where?"

"The U.K., France, Italy, Bosnia, Germany, the States."

The States? "That's interesting." Dottie started to get excited, but she kept her ideas to herself and finished her coffee.

Alex didn't say anything more, yet she felt a strange new tension growing between them. Her awareness of him was so powerful, she couldn't sit there any longer. "If you'll excuse me, I'll go change into my bathing suit."

"Not yet," he countered. "There's something I need to tell you before Zoe comes out."

Her pulse picked up speed. "If it's about her running to my room last eve—"

"It is," he cut in on her. "After what Zoe told me while I was putting her to bed, I realize this matter needs to be cleared up."

"Your marriage to Princess Genevieve is none of my business. As long as—"

"Dottie," he interrupted her again, this time with an underlying trace of impatience. "There will be no marriage. Believe me when I tell you there was never any question of my marrying her. I impressed that on Zoe before she went to sleep."

Dottie had to fight to prevent Alex from seeing her great relief and joy.

"Since Teresa's death, it has been my grandmother's ambition to join the House of Helvetia to our own. Zoe had the great misfortune of overhearing her tell Sofia about her plans. In her innocence, Zoe has expressed her love for you and has told *Yiayia* she wants *you* to be her new mommy."

"I was afraid of that," she whispered.

"Last night I spoke to my grandmother. She admitted that she arranged last night's party for me, not Stasi. She hoped that by inviting Princess Genevieve, it would put an end to Zoe's foolishness."

"Oh, dear."

"The queen has taken great pains to remind me once again what a wonderful mother Teresa was and that it is time I took another wife. Naturally she's grateful you've identified Zoe's problem, but now she wants you to go back to New York. I learned she's already found another speech therapist to replace you."

Dottie's head reared. "Who?"

"I have no idea, but it's not important. My grandmother is running true to form," he said before Dottie could comment further. "She tried to use all her logic with me by reminding me Zoe will have to be taken care of by a nanny until maturity; therefore it won't be good to allow her to get any more attached to you."

"In that regard, she's right."

Anger rose inside him. "Nevertheless, the queen stepped way out of bounds last night. I told her that I had no plans to marry again. She would have to find another way to strengthen the ties with Helvetia because Zoe's welfare was my only concern and you were staying put."

His dark eyes pierced hers. "I'm sure my words have shocked you, but it's necessary you know the truth so there won't be any more misunderstandings."

"Daddy?" They both turned to see Zoe trying to drag out her five-foot inflated whale from the cabana, but it was stuck. "I need help!"

Before he moved in her direction he said, "My grandmother may still be the ruler of Hellenica, but I rule over my own life and Zoe's. My daughter knows she doesn't have to worry about Princess Genevieve ever again, no matter what her *yiayia* might say."

With that declaration, he took a few steps, then paused. "Just so you know, after I've put Zoe to bed tonight, I'm taking you to the old part of the city, so don't plan on an early night."

Alex stayed with Zoe and read stories to her until she fell asleep. Since she realized he wasn't going to marry Princess Genevieve, his daughter actually seemed at peace for a change. With a nod to Sofia in the next room to keep an eye on her, he left for his own suite.

He showered and shaved before dressing in a sport shirt and trousers. On his way out of the room, he called for an unmarked car with smoked glass to be brought around to his private entrance. With Stasio in the palace, Alex didn't need to worry about anything else tonight. He called security and asked them to escort Dottie to the entrance.

After she climbed in the back with him, he explained that they were driving to the city's ancient amphitheater to see the famous sound and light show. "We're going to visit the site of many archaeological ruins. As we walk around, you'll see evidence of the Cycladic civilization and the Byzantium empire."

Alex had seen the show many times before with visiting dignitaries, but tonight he was with Dottie and he'd never felt so alive. The balmy air caused him to forget everything but the exciting woman who sat next to him.

Throughout the program he could tell by her questions and remarks that she loved it. After it was over he lounged against a temple column while she explored.

The tourists had started leaving, yet all he could see was her beautiful silhouette against the night sky. She'd put her hair back so her distinctive profile was revealed. She was dressed in another skirt and blouse, and he was reminded of the first time he'd seen her in his office.

"Dottie?" he called softly in the fragrant night air as he moved behind her. She let out a slight gasp and swung around.

He caught her to him swiftly and kissed her mouth to stop any other sound from escaping. Her lips were warm and tempting, but he didn't deepen the kiss. "Forgive me for doing that," he whispered against them, "but I didn't want you to say *Your Highness* and draw attention. Come and get in the car. It's late."

He helped her into the backseat with him and shut the door. "I'm not going to apologize for what I did," he murmured against her hot cheek. "If you want to slap me, you have my permission. But if I'm going to be punished for it, I'll take my chances now and give you a proper reason."

Alex's compelling mouth closed over Dottie's with a hunger that set her knees knocking. She'd sensed this moment was inevitable. Since her arrival in Hellenica, they'd been together early in the morning, late at night and most of the hours in between. He possessed a lethal sensuality for which she had no immunity.

Knowing he had no plans to marry Princess Genevieve, Dottie settled deeper into his arms and found herself giving him kiss for kiss. It was time she faced an ironic truth about herself. She wasn't any different than the rest of the female population who found the prince so attractive, they'd give anything to be in her position.

Royal scandal might abound, but she'd just discovered there was a reason for it. Forbidden fruit with this gorgeous male made these moments of physical intimacy exquisite. When a man was as incredibly potent and exciting as Alex, you could blot out everything else, even the fact that the driver ferrying them back to the palace was aware of every sound of ecstasy pouring out of her.

She finally put her hands against his chest and tore her mouth from his so she could ease back enough to look at him. Still trying to catch her breath, she asked, "Do you know what we are, Your Highness?" Her voice sounded less than steady to her own ears. She hated her inability to control that part of her.

"Suppose you tell me," he said in a husky voice.

"We're both a cliché. The prince and the hired help, nipping out for a little pleasure. I've just confirmed everything I've ever read in books and have seen on the news about palace intrigue."

"Who are you more angry at?" he murmured, kissing the tips of her fingers. "Me, for having taken unfair advantage? Or you, for having the right of refusal at any time which you didn't exercise? I'm asking myself if I'm fighting your righteous indignation that served you too late, or the ghost of your dead husband."

She squirmed because he'd hit the mark dead center. "Both," she answered honestly.

"Tell me about your husband. Was it love at first sight with him?"

"I don't know. It just seemed right from the beginning."

"Give me a few details. I really want to know what it would be like to have that kind of freedom."

Dottie stirred restlessly, sensing he meant what he said. "We met in Albany, New York, where I was raised. I went to the local pharmacy to pick up a prescription for my aunt. Neil had just been hired as a new pharmacist. It was late and there weren't any other customers.

"He told me it would take a while to get it ready, so we began talking. The next day he phoned and asked me out with the excuse that he'd just moved there from New York City and didn't know anyone. He was fun and kind and very smart.

"On our first date we went to a movie. After it was over, he told me he was going to marry me and there was nothing I could do about it. Four months later we got married and before we knew it, Cory was on the way. I was incredibly happy."

Alex's arm tightened around her. "I envy you for having those kinds of memories."

"Surely you have some wonderful ones, too."

A troubled sigh escaped his lips. "To quote you on several occasions, even if I am a prince, the one thing I've never had power over was my own personal happiness. Duty to my country came first. My marriage to Teresa was planned years before we got together, so any relationships I had before the wedding couldn't be taken seriously.

"She was beautiful in her own way, very accomplished. Sweet. But it was never an affair of the heart or anything close to it. On his deathbed, my father commanded me to marry her. I couldn't tell him I wouldn't."

Dottie shuddered. "Did you love him?"

"Yes."

"I can't comprehend being in your shoes, but I

admire you for being so devoted to your father and your country. Did Teresa love you?"

He took a steadying breath. "Before she died, she told me she'd fallen in love with me. I told her the same thing, not wanting to hurt her. She told me I was a liar, but she said she loved me for it."

"Oh, Alex… How hard for both of you."

"I wanted to fall in love with her, but we both know you can't force something that's not there. Zoe was my one gift from the gods who brood over Mount Pelos."

Her gaze lifted to his. "Not to be in love and have to marry—that's anathema to me. No wonder you seek relief in the shadows with someone handy like me. I get it, Alex. I really do. And you *didn't* take unfair advantage of me. It's been so long since I've been around an attractive man, my hormones are out of kilter right now."

"Is that what this tension is between us? Hormones?" he said with a twinge of bitterness she felt pierce her where it hurt most.

"I don't have a better word for it." She buried her face in her hands. "I loved Neil more than you can imagine. Thank heaven neither of us had a royal bone in our bodies to prevent us from knowing joy."

He stroked the back of her neck in a way that sent fingers of delight down her spine. "How did you manage after they were killed?"

"My aunt. She reminded me not everyone had been as lucky as I'd been. Her boyfriend got killed when he was deployed overseas in the military, so she never married. In her inimitable way she told me to stop pitying myself and get on with something useful.

"Her advice prompted me to go to graduate school

in New York City and become a speech therapist. After graduation I was hired on by the Stillman Institute. Little did I know that all the time I'd been helping Cory with his speech that last year, I was preparing for a lifetime career."

"Is your aunt still alive?"

"No. She died fourteen months ago."

"I'm sorry. I wish she were still living so I could thank her for her inspired advice. My Zoe is thriving because of you." He pulled her closer. "What about your parents?"

"They died in a car crash when I was just a little girl."

"It saddens me you've had to deal with so much grief."

"It comes to us all. In my aunt's case, it was good she passed away. With her chronic pneumonia, she could never recover and every illness made her worse."

"My mother was like that. She had been so ill that Stasi and I were thankful once she took her last breath."

"What about your father?"

"He developed an aggressive cancer of the thyroid. After he was gone, my grandmother took over to make sure we were raised according to her exacting Valleder standards. She was the power behind my grandfather's throne."

"She's done a wonderful job. I'll tell her that when I leave Hellenica." Dottie took a deep breath and sat back in the seat. "And now, despite her disapproval that I haven't left yet, here I am making out in an unmarked car with Prince Alexius Constantinides. How *could* you have given Zoe such an impossible last name? Nine consonants. *Nine!* And two of them are *T*'s," she half sobbed as the dam broke and she felt tears on her cheeks.

Alex reached over and smoothed the moisture from her face. He put his lips where his hand had been. "I'm glad there are nine. I won't let you go until she can pronounce our last name perfectly. That's going to take a long time."

"You'll have gone through at least half a dozen speech therapists by then."

"Possibly, but you'll be there in the background until she no longer needs your services."

"We've been over this ground before."

"We haven't even started," he declared as if announcing an edict. "Shall we get out of the car? We've been back at the palace for the past ten minutes. My driver probably wants to go to bed, which is where we should be."

She didn't think he meant that the way it came out, but with Alex you couldn't be absolutely sure when his teasing side would suddenly show up. All she knew was that her face was suffused with heat. She flung the car door open and ran into the palace, leaving him in the proverbial royal dust.

The death of her husband had put an end to all fairy tales, and that was the only place a prince could stay. She refused to be in the background of his life. It was time to close the storybook for good.

CHAPTER SIX

AT ELEVEN-FORTY-FIVE the next morning, Alex did something unprecedented and drove to the preschool to pick up Zoe and Dottie himself. He'd decided he'd better wear something more formal for this public visit and chose his dove-grey suit with a white shirt and grey vest. He toned it with a darker grey tie that bore the royal crest of the monarchy in silver, wanting to look his best for the woman who'd already turned his world inside out.

The directress of the school accompanied him to the classroom, where he spotted his daughter sitting in front and Dottie seated in the back. As the woman announced the arrival of Prince Alexius Constantinides, Dottie's blue eyes widened in shock. Her gaze clung to his for a moment.

He heard a collective sound of awe from the children, something he was used to in his capacity as prince. Children were always a delight. He was enjoying this immensely, but it was clear Dottie was stunned that he'd decided to come and get them. He knew in his gut her eyes wouldn't have ignited like that if she hadn't been happy to see him.

The teacher, Mrs. Pappas, urged the roomful of

twelve children to stand and bow. Zoe stood up, but she turned and smiled at Dottie before saying good morning to His Royal Highness along with the others. Alex got a kick out of the whole thing as the children kept looking at Zoe, knowing he was her daddy.

He'd never seen his daughter this happy in his life, and he should have done this before now. It lit up her whole being. Dottie was transforming his life in whole new ways. Because of her influence, Alex wanted to give his struggling preschooler a needed boost this morning. But she wasn't so struggling now that she had Dottie in her court.

He shook hands with everyone, then they returned to the palace. After changing into his swimming trunks, he joined them at the pool for lunch. With Zoe running around, he could finally talk to Dottie in private.

"How did my daughter do in class?"

"She participated without hanging back."

"That's because you've given her the confidence."

"You know it's been a team effort. While I've got you alone for a minute, let me tell you something else that happened this morning."

Alex could tell she was excited. "Go ahead."

"I arranged to talk with the directress about Zoe and was given permission to visit the other preschool class. One of the boys enrolled is an American from Pennsylvania named Mark Varney. He's supposed to be in first grade, but his parents put him back in preschool because he has no knowledge of Greek and needs to start with the basics. The situation has made him unhappy and he's turning into a loner."

"And you've decided that two negatives could make a positive?"

"Maybe." She half laughed. "It's scary how well you read my mind. Here's the thing—if you sanctioned it and Mark's parents allowed him to come back to the palace after school next time, he and Zoe could have some one-on-one time here in the pool, or down on the beach. I'd help them with their lessons, but the rest of the time they could have fun together. A play date is what she needs."

"I couldn't agree more."

"Oh, good! The directress says he's feeling inadequate. If his parents understood the circumstances and explained to him about Zoe's speech problem, he might be willing to help her and they could become friends in the process. That would help his confidence level, too."

Alex heard the appeal in Dottie's voice. "I'll ask Hector to handle it and we'll see how the first play date goes."

Light filled her blue eyes, dazzling him. "Thank you for being willing."

"That's rather ironic for you to be thanking me. I'm the one who should be down on my knees to you for thinking of it. She's a different child already because of you."

"You keep saying that, but you don't give yourself enough credit, Alex. When she saw you walk into the schoolroom earlier today, her heart was in her eyes. I wish I'd had a camera on me so I could have taken a picture. Every father should have a daughter who loves him that much. The extra time you've spent with her lately is paying huge dividends. I know it's taking time away from your duties, but if you can keep it up, you'll never regret it."

He rubbed his lower lip with the pad of his thumb,

staring at her through shuttered eyes. "That's why I sent for Stasi to come home. With you showing me the way, I'm well aware Zoe needs me and am doing everything in my power to free myself up."

"I know." She suddenly broke away from his gaze to look at Zoe. "She's waiting for us. Today we'll work on the letter *C*. Her preschool teacher brought her own cat to class. The children learned how to take care of one. Zoe got to pet it and couldn't have been more thrilled."

Dottie had inexplicably changed the subject and was talking faster than usual, a sign that something was going on inside her, making her uncomfortable. When she got up from the chair, he followed her over to the edge of the pool and listened as she engaged his daughter in a conversation that was really a teaching moment. She had a remarkable, unique way of communicating. Zoe ate it up. Why wouldn't she? There was no one else like Dottie.

Dottie was more than a speech therapist for his daughter. She was her advocate. Her selfless efforts to help Zoe lead a normal life couldn't be repaid with gifts or perks or money she'd already refused to accept. The woman wanted his daughter to succeed for the purest of reasons. She wanted it for a stranger's child, too. That made Dottie Richards a person of interest to him in ways that went deep beneath the surface.

Alex took off his sandals and dove into the deep end. After doing some underwater laps, he emerged next to his daughter, causing her to shriek with laughter. The day had been idyllic and it wasn't over.

As he did more laps, his thoughts drifted to his conversation with Dottie last night. When he'd turned eighteen, his family had arranged the betrothal to Princess

Teresa. However, until he'd been ready to commit to marriage, he'd known pleasure and desire with various women over the years. Those women had understood nothing long lasting could come of the relationship. No one woman's memory had lingered long in his mind. Forget his heart.

When Zoe came along, their daughter gave them both something new and wonderful to focus on. With Teresa's passing, Zoe had become the joy of his life. There'd been other women in the past two years, but the part of his psyche that had never been touched was still a void.

Enter Dottie Richards, a woman who'd buried a son and husband. He could still hear her saying she'd lost the great loves of her life. She'd experienced the kind of overwhelming love denied him because of his royal roots. He really envied her the freedom to choose the man who'd satisfied her passion at its deepest level and had given her a child.

Though it was an unworthy sentiment, Alex found himself resenting her husband for that same freedom. If Alex had been a commoner and had met her in his early twenties—before she'd met her husband—would she have been as attracted to him as he was to her? Would they have married?

She wasn't indifferent to Alex. The way she'd kissed him back last night convinced him of her strong attraction to him. He'd also sensed her interest at odd times when he noticed her eyes on him. The way she sometimes breathed faster around him for no apparent reason. But he had no way to gauge the true depth of her emotions until he could get her alone again.

As for his feelings, all he knew was that she'd lit a

fire inside him. In two weeks, even without physical intimacy, Dottie affected him more than Teresa had ever done during the three years of their marriage.

For the first time in his life he was suddenly waking up every morning hardly able to breathe until he saw her. For the only time in his existence he was questioning everything about the royal legacy that made him who he was and dictated his destiny.

His jealousy terrified him. He'd seen his brother's interest in her. Stasi's arranged marriage would be happening on his thirty-fifth birthday, in less than three weeks now. Until then it didn't stop him from enjoying and looking at other women. But it had angered Alex, who felt territorial when it came to Dottie. That's why he hadn't let Stasi dance with her. Alex had no right to feel this way, but the situation had gone way beyond rights.

Alex *wanted* his daughter's speech therapist. But as he'd already learned, a command from him meant nothing to her. A way had to be found so she wouldn't leave, but he had to be careful that he didn't frighten her off.

He swam back to Zoe, who hung on to the edge of the pool, practicing the hard *C* sound with Dottie. Without looking him in the eye, Dottie said, "Here's your daddy. Now that your lesson is over, I have to go inside. Zoe, I need to tell you now that I won't be able come to your bedroom to say good-night later. I have plans I can't break, but I'll see you in the morning." She finally glanced at him. "Your Highness."

Alex had no doubts that if she'd dared and if it wouldn't have alarmed Zoe, Dottie would have run away from him as fast as she could. Fortunately one of the positive benefits of being the prince meant he could keep twenty-four-hour surveillance on her.

After she'd left the sun deck, he spent another half hour in the pool with his daughter before they went inside. But once in her room, Zoe told Sofia to go away. When Alex tried to reason with her and get her to apologize, she broke down in tears, begging him to eat dinner with her in her room. She didn't want to be with *Yiayia*.

Dottie's announcement that she wouldn't be coming in to say good-night had sent the sun behind a black cloud. Naturally Dottie had every right to spend her evenings the way she wished. That's what he told Zoe. He had to help his daughter see that, but the idyllic day had suddenly vanished like a curl of smoke in the air.

"Make her come, Daddy."

A harsh laugh escaped his lips. You didn't make Dottie do anything. He didn't have that kind of power. She had to do it herself because she wanted to.

What if she *didn't* want to? What if the memory of life with her husband trapped her in the past and she couldn't, or didn't want to, reach out? On the heels of those questions came an even more important one.

Why would she reach out? What did a prince have to offer a commoner? An affair? A secret life? The answers to that question not only stared him in the face, they kicked him in the gut with enough violence to knock the wind out of him.

Once Zoe was asleep, Alex left for his suite, taking the palace stairs three steps at a time to the next floor. The last person he expected to find in his living room was Stasio with a glass of scotch in his hand.

He tossed back a drink. "It's about time you made an appearance, little brother." For a while now a cross-grain tone of discontent had lain behind Stasi's speech and it had grown stronger over the last few months. No crystal ball was needed here. The bitter subject of arranged marriages still burned like acid on his tongue as it did on Stasi's.

"Did you and *Yiayia* have another row tonight?" Alex started unbuttoning his shirt and took off his shoes.

"What do you mean, another one?" Stasio slammed his half-empty glass on the coffee table, spilling some of it. "It's been the same argument for seventeen years, but tonight I put an end to it."

"Translate for me," Alex rapped out tersely.

Stasio's mouth thinned to a white line. "I told her I broke it off with Beatriz while I was in Valleder. I can't go through with the wedding."

Alex felt the hairs on the back of his neck stand on end. He stared hard at his brother. All the time Stasi had put off coming home, something in the back of Alex's mind had divined the truth, but he hadn't been able to make his brother open up about it.

Since Stasio had been old enough to comprehend life, he'd been forced to bear the burden of knowing he would be king one day. That was hard enough. But to be married for the rest of his life to a woman he didn't love would have kept him in a living hell. No one knew it better than Alex.

"How is Beatriz dealing with it?"

"Not well," he whispered in agony.

"But she's always known how you truly felt. No matter how much this has hurt her, deep down it couldn't have come as a complete surprise. I thought she would have broken it off a long time ago."

"That miracle never happened. She wanted the marriage, just the way Teresa wanted yours." Alex couldn't deny it. "What always astounded me was that you were able to handle going through with your marriage to her."

Alex wheeled around. "The truth?"

"Always."

"It was the last thing I wanted. I wouldn't have married her, but with Father on his deathbed making me promise to follow through with it, I couldn't take the fight with him any longer and caved. The only thing that kept me sane was the fact that I wouldn't be king one day, so I wouldn't have to be in the public eye every second. And then, Zoe came along. Now I can't imagine my life without her."

Stasio paled. "Neither can I. She's the one ray of sunshine around this tomb." He took a deep breath. "Under the circumstances I should be grateful *Yiayia* isn't taking her last breath because there will be no forced wedding with Beatriz. Philippe has backed me in this and he holds a certain sway with our grandmother."

Alex was afraid that was wishful thinking on Stasio's part. Not only was Philippe his best friend, he'd been one of the lucky royals who'd ended up marrying the American girl he'd loved years earlier. They'd had a son together and the strict rules had been waived in his particular case.

But the queen hadn't approved of Philippe's marriage, so it didn't follow she would give an inch when it came to Stasio's decision. In her eyes he'd created a monumental catastrophe that could never be forgiven.

"So what's going to happen now?"

"Beatriz's parents have given a statement to the press. It's probably all over the news as we speak or will be in a matter of hours. Once the story grows legs, I'll be torn apart. I had to tell *Yiayia* tonight to prepare her for what's coming."

"What was our grandmother's reaction?"

"You know her as well as I do. Putting on her stone face, she said the coronation would go ahead as scheduled to save the integrity of the crown. A suitable marriage with another princess will take place within six months maximum. She gave me her short list of five candidates."

Alex felt a chill go through him. "Putting the cart before the horse has never been done."

"The queen is going to have her way no matter what. Let's face it. She's not well and wants me to take over."

"Stasi—"

Sick for his brother, he walked over and hugged him. "I'm here for you always. You know that."

"I *do*. A fine pair we've turned out to be. She told me you're still resisting marriage to Princess Genevieve."

"Like you, I told her no once and for all," he said through clenched teeth. "I sacrificed myself once. Never again."

"She's not going to give up on Genevieve. I heard it in her voice."

"That's too bad because my only duty now is to raise Zoe to be happy."

With the help of Dottie, he intended that to become a reality. Walking over to the table, he poured himself a drink. He lifted his glass to his brother.

"To you, Stasi," he said in a thick-toned voice. "May God help you find a way to cope." *May God help both of us*.

* * *

After a sleep troubled with thoughts of Alex, Dottie felt out of sorts and anxious and only poked at her breakfast. Since he hadn't brought Zoe for her morning session yet, she checked her emails. Among some posts from her friends at the Institute in New York she'd received a response to the email she'd sent Dr. Rice. With a pounding heart, she opened it first.

Dear Dottie:

Thank you for giving me an update on Princess Zoe. I'm very pleased to hear that she's beginning to make progress. If anyone can work miracles, it's you. In reference to your request, I've interviewed several therapists who I believe would work well with her, but the one I think could be the best fit might not be available as soon as you wanted. She's still working with the parent of another child to teach them coaching skills. I'll let you know when she'll be free to come. Give it a few more days.

By the way, it's all over the news about Crown Prince Stasio calling off his wedding to Princess Beatriz. She's here in Manhattan. I saw her on the news walking into the St. Regis Hotel. What a coincidence that you're working for Prince Alexius. Have you ever met his brother? Well, take care. I'll be in touch before long. Dr. Rice.

She rested her elbow on the table, covering her eyes with her hand. Prince Stasio's teasing facade hid a courageous man who'd just done himself and Princess Beatriz a huge favor, even if talk of it and the judgments that would follow saturated the news.

The world had no idea what went on behind the closed doors of a desperately unhappy couple, royal or otherwise. What woman or man would want to be married to someone who'd been chosen for them years earlier? Alex's first marriage had been forced. It boggled the mind, yet it had happened to the royals of the Constantinides family for hundreds of years in order to keep the monarchy alive.

Poor Zoe. To think that dear little girl would have to grow up knowing an arranged marriage was her fate. Dottie cringed at the prospect. Surely Alex wouldn't do that to his own daughter after what he and his brother had been through, would he?

"Dot?" Zoe came running into the alcove and hugged her so hard, she almost fell off the chair.

Without conscious thought Dottie closed her eyes and hugged her back, aching for this family and its archaic rules that had hung like a pall over their lives. When she opened them again, there was Alex standing there in a navy crew neck and jeans looking bigger than life as he watched the two of them interact.

She saw lines and shadows on his striking face that hadn't been there yesterday. But when their eyes met, the black fire in his took her to the backseat of the car where the other night they'd kissed each other with mindless abandon.

"We're here to invite you out for a day on the water," he explained. "The galley's loaded with food and drink. We'll do lessons and have fun at the same time."

As he spoke, Zoe sat down to do one of the puzzles on the table out of hearing distance. It was a good thing, because Alex's invitation had frightened Dottie. Though her mind was warning her this would be a mistake, that vital organ pumping her life's blood enlarged at the prospect.

The other night she'd almost lost control with him and the experience was still too fresh. To go with him would be like watching a moth enticed to a flame fly straight to its death.

"Perhaps it's time you enjoyed one day without me along. It won't hurt Zoe to miss a lesson." She'd said the first thing to come into her mind, frantically searching for an excuse not to be with him.

Lines marred his arresting features. "I'm afraid this is one time I need your cooperation. There's something critically urgent I must discuss with you."

Dottie looked away from the intensity of his gaze. This had to be about his brother. The distinct possibility that Prince Stasio needed Alex to do double duty for him right now, or to spend more time with him, crossed her mind. Of necessity it would cut short the time he'd been spending with Zoe. If that was the case, she could hardly turn him down while he worked out an alternative plan with her.

"All right. Give me a minute to put some things in the bag for our lesson."

"Take all the time you need." His voice seemed to have a deeper timbre this morning, playing havoc with the butterflies fluttering madly in her chest.

After Zoe helped pack some things they'd need, Dottie changed into a sleeveless top and shorts. When she emerged from the bathroom with her hair freshly brushed, the prince took swift inventory of her face and figure, whipping up a storm of heat that stained her cheeks with color. Once she'd stowed her swimsuit in the bag, she put on her sunglasses and declared she was ready to go.

Dottie had assumed they'd be taking his sailboat. But once they left the palace grounds, Alex informed her he had business on one of the other islands so they were going out on the yacht. The news caused a secret thrill to permeate her body.

That first morning when she and Zoe had gone down to the private beach, she'd seen the gleaming white royal yacht moored in the distance. Like any normal tourist, she'd dreamed of touring the Aegean on a boat while she was in Hellenica. Today the dream had become reality as she boarded the fabulous luxury craft containing every amenity known to man.

With the sparkling blue water so calm, Zoe was in heaven. Wearing another swimsuit, this one in lime-and-blue stripes, she ran up and down the length of it with her father's binoculars, looking for groupers and parrot fish with one of the crew.

Alex settled them in side-by-side loungers while the deck steward placed drinks and treats close enough to reach. With Zoe occupied for a few minutes, Dottie felt this would be the best time to approach him about his brother and turned in his direction. But he'd removed his shirt. One look at his chest with its dusting of black hair, in fact his entire masculine physique, and she had to stifle a moan.

The other night she'd been crushed against him and, heaven help her, she longed to repeat the experience. Fortunately the presence of Zoe and the crew prevented anything like that from happening today.

Admit you want it to happen, Dottie.

After losing Neil, she couldn't believe all these feelings to know a man's possession had come back this strongly. For so long she'd been dead inside. She was frightened by this explosion of need Alex had ignited. She had to hope Dr. Rice would email her the good news that her replacement could be here by next week because she could feel herself being sucked into a situation that could only rebound on her.

Not for a moment did she believe Alex was a womanizer. He was a man, and like any single male was free to find temporary satisfaction with a willing woman when the time and opportunity presented itself. With her full cooperation he'd acted on one of those opportunities and she'd lost her head.

It wasn't his fault. It was *hers*. She'd been an idiot.

Unless she wanted a new form of heartache to plague her for the rest of her life, she couldn't afford another foolish moment because of overwhelming desire for Alex. There was no future in it. She'd be gone from this assignment before long. Nothing but pain could come from indulging in a passionate interlude with a prince. *Nothing*.

"Alex. The head of my department at Stillman's responded to one of my emails this morning."

He removed his sunglasses and shifted his hard-muscled body on the lounger so he faced her. "Was that the one asking him to find another therapist for Zoe?" he inquired in a dangerously silky voice. An underlying tone of ice sent a tremor through her body.

"Yes. He says he'll probably have someone to replace me within another week. By then Zoe ought to have more confidence in herself and will work well with the new speech teacher."

Paralyzing tension stretched between them before

eyes of jet impaled her. "You don't believe that piece
of fiction any more than I do. In any event, there can't
be a question about you leaving, not with the coronation almost upon us."

She sat up in surprise. "You mean there's still going
to be one?"

Like lightning he levered himself from the lounger.
"Why would you ask that question?"

"At the end of Dr. Rice's email, he told me there were
headlines about Prince Stasio calling off his wedding
to Princess Beatriz."

"So it's already today's news in New York." He
sounded far away. She watched him rub the back of
his neck, something he did when he was pondering a
grave problem.

Growing more uneasy, Dottie stood up. "Forgive me
if I've upset you."

He eyed her frankly. "Forgiveness doesn't come into
it. They were never suited, but I didn't know he'd made
the break official until he told me last night."

She rubbed her arms in reaction. "What a traumatic
night it must have been for all of you and your grandmother."

"I won't lie to you about that." His pain was palpable.

Dottie bit her lip. "For both their sakes I'm glad he
couldn't go through with it, but you'll probably think
I'm horrible for saying it."

"On the contrary," Alex ground out. "I'd think something serious was wrong with you if you hadn't. His
life has been a living hell. He should have ended the
betrothal years ago."

Alex... She heard the love for his brother.

"Does it mean the queen will go on ruling?" she

asked quietly. "I'm probably overstepping my bounds to talk to you like this, but after meeting your brother, I can't help but feel terrible for what he must be suffering right now, even if he didn't want the marriage."

"Between us, he's in bad shape," he confided, "but the coronation is still on. Our grandmother is failing in small ways and can't keep up her former pace as sovereign, but she's still in charge. She has given him six months to marry one of the eligible royals on her list."

"But—"

"There are no buts," he cut her off, but she knew his anger wasn't directed at her. "I just have to pray he'll find some common ground with one of the women." His voice throbbed. Again Dottie was horrified by Prince Stasio's untenable situation. "Since there's nothing I can do except stand by him, I'd rather concentrate on Zoe's lesson. What do you have planned for today?"

Heartsick as Dottie felt, she'd been sent to Hellenica to do a job and she wanted desperately to lift his spirits if she could. "Since we're on the yacht, I thought we'd work on the *Y* sound. She can already say *Yiayia* pretty well."

"That's where her Greek ought to help."

"Why don't you say hello to her in Greek and we'll see what happens."

Together they walked toward the railing at the far end. Zoe saw them coming and trained the binoculars on them.

"Yasoo," her father called to her. The cute little girl answered back in a sad facsimile of the greeting.

Dottie smiled. "Do you like being on this boat?"

"Yes."

Today they'd work on *ya*. Another day they'd work

on *yes*. "Do you know what kind of a boat this is?" Zoe shook her head. "It's called a yacht. Say *yasoo* again." Zoe responded. "Now say *ya*." She tried, but the sound was off with both words.

"I can't."

Dottie felt her frustration.

Alex handed Dottie the binoculars and picked up his daughter. "Try it once more." He wanted her to make a good sound for him. Dottie wanted it, too, more than anything. But this was a game of infinite patience. "Be a parrot for daddy, like one of those parrot fish you were watching with its birdlike beak. Parrots can talk. Talk to me. Say *ya*."

"Ya."

"Open your mouth wider like your daddy is doing," Dottie urged her. "Pretend he's the doctor looking down your throat with a stick. He wants to hear you. Can you say *ya* for him?"

She giggled. "Daddy's not a doctor."

The prince sent Dottie a look of defeat. "You're right." He kissed Zoe's cheek. "Come on. Let's have a lemonade." As soon as he put her down, she ran back to the table by the loungers to drink hers.

Clearly Zoe wasn't in the mood for a lesson. Who would be on a beautiful day like this? The translucent blue water was dotted with islands that made Dottie itch to get out and explore everything. She put the binoculars to her eyes to see what was coming next. "What's the name of that island in the distance?"

"Argentum."

"You mine silver there?"

"How did you figure that out?"

"You told me you lived on Aurum. Both islands have Latin names for gold and silver."

His eyes met hers. "You're not only intelligent, but knowledgeable. We'll anchor out in the bay. The head mining engineer is coming aboard for a business lunch. He's also my closest friend."

"Where did you meet?"

"We were getting our mining engineering degrees at the same time, both here and in Colorado at the school of mines."

"That's why your English is amazing. Is your friend married?"

"Yes. He has a new baby."

"That's nice for him."

"Very nice. He's in love with his wife and she with him."

Dottie couldn't bear to talk about that subject. "Tell me about the tall island beyond Argentum with the green patches?"

"That's Aurum, where Zoe and I normally live." He hadn't put on his shirt yet. She could feel his body radiating heat. "As you guessed correctly, rich gold deposits on the other side of the mountain were discovered there centuries ago. Bari and I are both passionate about our work. There are many more mining projects to be explored. I'm anxious to get back to them."

By now she was trembling from their close proximity. Needing a reason to move away from him, she put the binoculars on the table and picked up her lemonade. "Do you miss Aurum?"

"Yes." His dark gaze wandered over her, sending her pulse rate off the charts. "Zoe and I prefer it to Hellenica. The palace there is much smaller with more trees and vegetation that keep it cooler. We'll take you next week so Zoe can show you the garden off her room."

Dottie let the comment pass because if she were still here by then, she had no intention of going there with him. It wouldn't be a good idea. Not a good idea at all. "Do you get her to preschool by helicopter, then?"

He nodded. "Once she's in kindergarten, she'll go to a school on Aurum, but nothing is going to happen until after the coronation." After swallowing the contents of his drink without taking a breath, he reached for his shirt. "Shall we go below and freshen up before Bari comes on board?"

She followed the two of them down the steps of the elegant yacht to the luxurious cabins. "Come with us." Zoe pulled on her hand.

Dottie bent over. "I have my own cabin down the hallway."

"How come?"

"Because I'm a guest."

She looked at her daddy. "Make her come."

"Zoe? We have our room, and she has hers," he said in his princely parental voice as Dottie thought of it.

To the surprise of both of them, Zoe kept hold of Dottie's hand. "I want to be with you."

"It's all right, Your Highness," Dottie said before he could protest. "Zoe and I will freshen up together and meet you on deck in a little while." Their family was going through deep turmoil. The burden of what his brother had done had set off enormous ramifications and Alex was feeling them.

For that matter, so was Zoe, who'd behaved differently today. With the advent of Prince Stasio's stun-

ning news, she couldn't have helped but pick up on the
tension radiating from the queen and her father during
breakfast. She might not understand all that was going
on, but she sensed upheaval. That's why she'd given up
on her lesson so easily.

His eyes narrowed in what she assumed was speculation. "You're sure?"

"Do you even have to ask?" Dottie had meant what
she'd told him last week about his needing some pampering. He had work to do with Mr. Jouflas, but no one
else was there to help him with Zoe the way he needed
it. Dottie found she wanted to ease his burden. He'd
made sacrifices for the love of his country. Now it was
her turn, no matter how small.

"You're operating under an abnormal amount of
strain right now. You could use a little help. I don't
know how you've been doing this balancing act for such
a long time." She smiled at Zoe. "Come on."

Dottie saw the relief on his face and knew she'd said
the right thing. "In that case I'll send the steward to your
cabin with a fresh change of clothes for her."

"That would be perfect."

CHAPTER SEVEN

DOTTIE felt Alex staring at her before they disappeared inside. Since she'd been trying so hard to keep a professional distance with his daughter, he knew this was an about-face for her. But no one could have foreseen this monarchial disaster.

Alex was being torn apart by his love for his brother, his grandmother and the future of the crown itself. He was Atlas holding up the world with no help in sight. This was a day like no other. If Dottie could ease a little of his burden where Zoe was concerned, then she wanted to.

"I've got an idea, Zoe. After you shower, we'll take a little nap on the beds. The heat has made me sleepy."

"Me, too."

There were two queen beds. Before long she'd tucked Zoe under the covers.

"Dot? Will you please stay with Daddy and me forever? I know you're not my mommy, but Daddy said you were once a mommy."

She struggled for breath. "Yes. I had a little boy named Cory who had to work on his speech, just like you."

"What happened to him?"

"He died in a car accident with my husband."

"So you're all alone."

"Yes," she murmured, but for the first time it wasn't hard to talk about. The conversation with Alex last night had been cathartic.

"My mommy died and now Daddy and I are all alone."

"Except that you have your great-grandmother and your uncle."

"But I want you."

Dottie wanted to be with Zoe all the time, too. Somehow she'd gotten beyond her deep sadness and would love to care permanently for this child. But it was impossible in too many ways to even consider.

"Let's be happy we're together right now, shall we?" she said in a shaky voice.

"Yes." Zoe finally closed her eyes and fell asleep.

Dotti took her own shower and dressed in a clean pair of jeans and a blouse. When she came out of the bathroom, the other bed looked inviting. She thought she'd lie down on top while she waited for Zoe to wake up.

The next thing she knew, she heard a familiar male voice whispering her name. Slightly disoriented, she rolled over and discovered Alex sitting on the side of the bed. She'd been dreaming about him, but to see his gorgeous self in the flesh this close to her gave her heart a serious workout. His eyes were like black fires. They trapped hers, making it impossible for her to look away.

"Thank you for stepping in."

She studied his features. "I wanted to."

"With your help I was able to conclude our business lunch in record time and came in to bring Zoe a change of clothes. Do you have any idea how beautiful you are lying there?"

Dottie couldn't swallow. She tried to move away, but he put an arm across her body so she was tethered to him. "Please let me go," she begged. "Zoe will be awake any minute now."

He leaned over her, running a hand up her arm. The feel of skin against hot skin brought every nerve ending alive. "I'll take any minute I can steal. Being alone with you is all I've been able to think about."

"Alex—" she cried as his dark head descended.

"I love it when you say my name in that husky voice." He covered her mouth with his own in an exploratory kiss as if this were their first time and they were in no hurry whatsoever. He took things slow in the beginning, tantalizing her until it wasn't enough. Then their kiss grew deeper and more sensuous. His restless lips traveled over every centimeter of her face and throat before capturing her mouth again and again.

The other night he'd kindled a fire in her that had never died down. Now his mastery conjured the flames licking through her body with the speed of a forest fire in full conflagration.

Out of breath, he buried his face in the side of her neck. "I want you, Dottie. I've never wanted any woman so much, and I know you want me."

"I think that's been established," she admitted against his jaw that hadn't seen a razor since early morning. She delighted in every masculine line and angle of his well-honed body. With legs and arms entwined, their mouths clung as their passion grew more frenzied. They tried to appease their hunger, but no kiss was long enough or deep enough to satisfy the desire building.

He'd taken them to a new level. She felt cherished. Like the wedding vow repeated by the groom, it seemed as if Alex was worshipping her with his body. But in the midst of this rapture only he could have created, she heard the blare of a ship's horn. With it came the realization that this was no wedding night and a groan escaped her throat.

She'd actually been making out with Prince Alexius of Hellenica on his royal yacht! Never mind that it was the middle of the day and his daughter was asleep in the next bed. What if Zoe had awakened and had been watching them?

Horrified to have gotten this carried away, Dottie wrenched her mouth from his and slipped out of his arms. So deep was his entrancement, she'd caught him off guard. Thankfully she was able to get to her feet before he could prevent it, but in her weakened state she almost fell over.

"Dottie?" he called her name in longing, but she didn't dare stay in here and be seduced by the spell he'd cast over her. On the way out of the cabin she grabbed her purse and hurried down the corridor to the stairs.

At the top of the gangway the deck steward smiled at her. "Mrs. Richards? We've docked on Hellenica. You're welcome to go ashore whenever you please."

Could he tell she'd been kissed breathless by the prince? The sun she'd picked up couldn't account for mussed hair and swollen lips, too.

The queen didn't deserve to hear this bit of gossip on top of Prince Stasio's shocking news. Every second Dottie stayed on board, she was contributing to more court intrigue. She couldn't bear it. In fact she couldn't believe they were back at the main island already. She'd been in such a completely different world with Alex, she'd lost track of everything including her wits.

"Th-thank you," her voice faltered. Without hesitation, she left the yacht and got in the waiting limousine. While she was still alone, she brushed her hair and applied some lipstick, trying to make herself presentable.

A few minutes later Alex approached the car with Zoe. "Dot!" she cried and climbed in next to her.

"Did you just wake up?" Dottie concentrated on Zoe, studiously avoiding his eyes. "You were a sleepyhead."

Zoe thought that was funny. She chatted happily with her daddy until they reached the palace where Hector stood outside the entry.

"Welcome back, Your Highness. The queen is waiting for you and the princess to join her and Prince Stasio in her suite."

A royal summons. It didn't surprise Dottie. She'd had visions of the queen herself waiting for them as they drove up to the entrance. For an instant she caught Alex's enigmatic glance before he alighted from the car. All their lives he and Stasio had been forced to obey that summons. A lesser person would have broken long before now.

She might be an outsider, yet she couldn't help but want to rebel against this antiquated system she'd only read about in history books. Unbelievable that it was still going on in the twenty-first century!

Alex helped them out of the backseat. "Come on, Dot." Zoe's hand had slipped into hers. She had to harden herself against Zoe's plea. The child's emotional hold on her was growing stronger with every passing day.

"I'm sorry. The queen has asked for you and your

daddy to come, and I have to speak to my director in New York." Aware Alex's eyes were on her she said, "You have to go with him. I'll see you tomorrow when we leave for your preschool."

Gripping the bag tighter, Dottie hurried inside the palace doors and raced up the stairs. She fled to her suite pursued by demons she'd been fighting from the beginning. Since this afternoon when she'd fallen into Alex's arms like a ripe plum, those demons had gained a foothold, making her situation precarious.

Her instincts told her to pack her bags and fly back to New York tonight. But if she were to just up and leave Hellenica, it would only exacerbate an already volatile situation with Zoe, who'd poured her heart out to her earlier.

Without hesitation she marched over to the bed and reached for the house phone. "This is Mrs. Richards. Could you bring a car around for me? I'm going into the city." She'd eat dinner somewhere and do some more sightseeing. After the nap she'd had, it might take hours before she was ready for bed again.

Alex waited for Hector to alert him on the phone. When the call came, he learned Dottie had just returned to the palace. He checked his watch. Ten to ten.

He left Zoe's bedroom and waited for Dottie at the top of the stairs leading to her suite. This time he didn't step out of the shadows. He stood there in full view. Halfway up she caught sight of him and slowed her steps. Alarm was written all over her beautiful face. She'd picked up some sun earlier in the day, adding appealing color.

"Alex? What's wrong?"

Anyone watching them would never know what had gone on between them on the yacht. He'd nearly made love to her and her passion had equalled his. Her breathtaking response had changed his life today.

"Let's just say there's a lot wrong around here. Since your arrival in Hellenica, you've got me skulking in every conceivable place in order to find time alone with you. At this point you'd have reason to think I'm your personal phantom of the opera." He drew in a harsh breath. "We have to talk, but not here." When he saw her stiffen he said, "I know you can't be commanded, but I'm asking you to come with me as a personal favor." He'd constructed his words carefully.

Tension sizzled between them as he started down the stairs toward her. To his relief she didn't fight him. Slowly she followed him to the main floor. They went down the hallway and out a side door where he'd asked that his sports car be brought around.

Alex saw the question in her eyes. "I bought this ten years ago. It's my getaway car when I need to be alone to think." He intentionally let her get in by herself because he didn't trust himself not to touch her. After leaving the grounds, he headed for the road leading to an isolated portion of the coast with rocky terrain.

"But you're *not* alone," she said in a haunted whisper.

"If you mean the bodyguards, you're right." He felt her nervousness. "Relax. If I had seduction in mind, we wouldn't be in this. I purposely chose it in order to keep my hands off you tonight."

"Alex—"

"Let me finish," he interrupted. "Whatever you may think about me, I'm not in the habit of luring available women to my bed when the mood strikes me. You came to Hellenica at my request in order to test Zoe. Neither of us could have predicted what would happen after you arrived.

"I can't speak for you, but I know for a fact that even if your husband's memory will always be in your heart, the chemistry between us is more powerful than anything I've ever felt in my life. We both know it's not going to go away."

She lowered her head.

"One night with you could never be enough for me." He gripped the steering wheel tighter. "I know you would never consent to be my mistress, and I would never ask you. But until the coronation is over, I'm requesting your help with Zoe."

She shifted in the seat. "In what way?"

"Stasio and my daughter both need me desperately, but I can't be in two places at the same time and still manage the daily affairs of the crown. My brother is going through the blackest period of his life. He's clinging to me and shutting out our grandmother. She's beside herself."

"I can only imagine."

"I'm worried about both of them and asked the doctor to come. He's with them now, seeing what can be done to get them through this nightmare. He says I need to be there for Stasio 24/7. I've asked our cousin Philippe to fly here and stay for a few days so my brother has someone to talk to he trusts."

"I'm so sorry, Alex."

"So am I," he muttered morosely. "This situation is something that's been coming on for years. Unfortunately it's had a negative impact on Zoe. When we got back to the palace today, it took me an hour to settle her down. She wanted to go to your room with you. Tonight she begged me to let you become her official nanny."

Alex heard a half-smothered moan come out of Dottie. The sound tore him up because any kind of connection to keep her with him was fading fast. "It wouldn't work."

"You think I don't know that?" he bit out. "But as a temporary solution, would you be willing to stay at the palace on Aurum with her until the coronation? She loves it there, especially the garden. One of the staff has grandchildren she plays with. I'd fly over each evening in the helicopter to say good-night.

"When the coronation is over, I'll be moving back to Aurum with Zoe, and you can return to New York. Hector will see to your flight arrangements. I assume your replacement will arrive soon after that, if not before. But until then, can I rely on your help?"

She nodded without looking at him. "Of course."

The bands constricting his breathing loosened a little. "Thank you. On Saturday I'll run you and Zoe over in the cruiser. We'll skip her preschool next week."

"Are you still going to go ahead with the arrangements for the Varney boy to come home with Zoe after class tomorrow?"

"Yes," he murmured. "Any distraction would be better than her being around my grandmother, who's not in a good way right now. She's always been a rock, but she never saw this coming with Stasio."

"You sound exhausted, Alex. Tomorrow will be here before we know it. Let's go back to the palace."

She sounded like Hector. *Go back. Do your duty. Forget you're a man with a man's needs.*

Full of rage, he made a sharp U-turn and sped toward the palace tight-lipped, but by the time they reached the entry, he'd turned into one aching entity of pain. He watched the only person who could take it away for good rush away on her gorgeous legs.

Dottie could tell Zoe felt shy around Mark Varney. She stuck close to her daddy at the shallow end of the pool.

They'd just returned home from the preschool. Mark was a cute, dark blond first grader who sported a marine haircut and was a good little swimmer already. He didn't appear to be nervous as he floated on an inner tube at the deep end, kicking his strong legs. Dottie sat on the edge by him.

"My mom told me she talks funny. How come?" he said quietly.

"Sometimes a child can't make sounds come out the way they want. But I'm working on them with her. One day she'll sound like you, but for now I'm hoping to get your help."

He blinked. "How? She's a princess."

She looked at his boyish face with its smattering of freckles. "Forget about that. She's a girl. Just be friends with her. In a way, you can be her best teacher."

His sunny blue eyes widened. "I can?"

"Yes. You're older and you're an American who speaks English very well. If you'll play with her, she'll listen to you when you talk and she'll try to sound like you. You're a guy, and guys like to dare each other, right?"

He grinned. "Yeah."

"Well, start daring her. You know. Tell her you bet she can't say *bat*."

"Bat?" He laughed.

"She's working on her *B*'s and *T*'s. Make a game out of it. Tell her that if she can say *bat* right, you'll show her your MP3 player. I saw you playing with it in the limo on the drive to the palace."

"Don't tell my dad. I'm not supposed to take it to school."

She studied him for a minute. "If he finds out, I'll tell him you're using it to help Zoe. She's never seen one of those. There's an application on it that makes those animal sounds."

"Oh, yeah—"

"It'll fascinate her."

"Cool."

"See if you can get her to say *cool*, too."

"Okay. This is fun."

Dottie was glad he thought so. After trying to learn Greek at school and home, it had to be a big release for him to speak English. "Let's go have a war with her and her daddy." She took off her beach coat and slipped into the water. "You get on the whale. I'll push you over to them and we'll start splashing."

"Won't the prince get mad?"

"Yes." Dottie smiled. "Real mad."

His face lit up and they took off.

Hopefully Alex would get mad enough to forget his own problems for a little while. She'd suffered for him and his family all night. No matter her misgivings about spending full days with Zoe until the coronation, she couldn't have turned Alex down last night. The look in his expression had been a study in anguish, aging him.

Once they reached their destination, the happy shrieks coming out of Zoe were just the thing to get their war started. For a good ten minutes they battled as if their lives depended on it. The best sound of all was Alex's full-bodied laughter. After knowing how deeply he'd been affected by his family's problems, Dottie hadn't expected to hear it again.

When she came up for air after Alex's last powerful dunk, his eyes were leveled on her features. "You've been holding out on me. All this time I thought maybe you couldn't swim well. I was going to offer to teach you, but I was afraid you'd think I was a lecherous old man wanting to get my hands on you. After I showed up in your cabin on the yacht, now you know it's true."

She was thankful for the water that cooled her instantly hot cheeks. In the periphery she noticed Mark pushing Zoe around on the whale. He was talking a blue streak and had captured her full attention. The ice had been broken and they were oblivious to everyone else. Dottie couldn't have been more pleased.

Alex followed her gaze. "Your experiment is working. She's so excited by his attention, she hasn't once called for either of us."

"I've asked him to help her. He's a darling boy." In the next few minutes she told Alex about their conversation. "If all goes well today, how would you feel about Mark coming home with us from school on Friday?"

"I'm open to anything that will help her speech improve and make her happy."

"Mark seems to be doing both. I've learned he's been unhappy, so I was thinking maybe he could even come to Aurum with us on Saturday. Naturally you'd have to talk to his parents. If they're willing, maybe he could make a visit to the island next week. You know, after his morning class at preschool. Zoe would have something exciting to look forward to and I know it would be good for him, too."

His eyes glinted with an emotion she couldn't read. "I can see where you're going with this. If you think his being there will prevent her attachment to you from growing deeper, you couldn't be more wrong. But as a plan to entertain them and help her, I like the idea."

"Honestly?"

He ran suntanned hands through his wet black hair. Adonis couldn't possibly have been as attractive. "I wouldn't have said so otherwise."

She expelled the breath she'd been holding. "Thank you. I was thinking Zoe and I could ride the ferry to Hellenica and meet him at the dock after he's out of class. He could ride back with us and we could eat lunch on board. Mark can help her pronounce the names of foods, and she can teach him some more Greek words."

Alex nodded. "I'll fly him back with me in the helicopter in the evening."

"You'd be willing to do that?"

He frowned. "By now I thought it was clear to you I'd do anything to help my daughter. In order to ensure that you stay with her until her uncle Stasi has been proclaimed king, I've even gone so far as to promise I won't touch you again."

She knew that and already felt the cost of it.

If he had any comprehension of how hard this was for her, too... They had no future together, but that didn't mean she found it easy to keep her distance. She'd come alive in his arms. Because she was unable to assuage these yearnings, the pleasure had turned on her so she was in continual pain. This was the precise reason she didn't want to have feelings for any man, not ever again, but it was far too late for that.

"Your Highness?"

Hector's voice intruded, producing a grimace from Alex. Dottie hadn't realized he'd come out to the pool. It seemed like every time she found herself in a private conversation with Alex, some force was afoot that kept wedging them further apart, At this point she was a mass of contradictions. Her head told her the interruption was for the best, but her heart—oh, her heart. It hammered mercilessly.

"King Alexandre-Philippe has arrived from Valleder and your presence is requested in the queen's drawing room. The ministers have been assembled."

Hearing that news, Alex's face became an inscrutable mask. "Thank you, Hector. Tell her I'll be there shortly."

His gaze shot to Dottie's. "I'm afraid this will be a long night. I'd better slip away now while Zoe's having fun."

"I think that's a good idea. We'll walk Mark out to his parents' car before dinner. She can eat with me. Later I'll take her to her bedroom and put her down."

"You couldn't have any comprehension of what it means to me to know you're taking care of my daughter. Sofia will be there to help. I'll try to get away long enough to kiss her good-night, but I can't promise."

"I understand."

"If I don't make it, I'll see you at nine in the morning. After I've talked to Mark's parents, we'll see if he wants to join us on Saturday. I thought we'd take the cruiser to Aurum. Sofia will know what to pack for Zoe."

"We'll be ready."

She heard his sharp intake of breath. "Zoe trusts you and loves being with you. Under the circumstances, it's an enormous relief to me."

"I'm glad. As for me, she's a joy to be with, Your Highness." She had to keep calling him by his title to remind herself of the great gulf between them no ordinary human could bridge. If she were a princess...

But she wasn't! And if she'd been born a royal, he would have run in the other direction.

For him, any attraction to her stemmed from forbidden fruit. She was a commoner. It was the nature of a man or woman to desire what they couldn't or shouldn't have. In that regard they were both cursed!

Fathoms deep in turmoil, she noticed his eyes lingering on the curve of her mouth for a moment. She glimpsed banked fires in those incredibly dark recesses. He was remembering those moments on the yacht, too. Dottie could feel it and the look he was giving her ignited her senses to a feverish pitch.

With effortless male agility he suddenly levered himself from the pool and disappeared inside the palace. When he was gone, the loss she felt was staggering.

CHAPTER EIGHT

"Hi, Mark!"

"Hi!"

He got out of his father's limo and hurried along the dock to get in the cruiser. Zoe's brown eyes lit up when she saw him. The two fathers spoke for a minute longer before Alex joined them and made sure everyone put on a life preserver.

The prince piloted the boat himself and they took off. Excitement suffused Dottie, crowding out any misgivings for the moment. She found the day was too wonderful. It seemed the children did, too. Both wore a perpetual smile on their animated faces. Zoe pointed out more fish and birds as they drew closer to their destination. While they were communicating, Alex darted Dottie an amused glance.

She wondered if he was thinking what she'd been thinking. What if his daughter and Mark were to share a friendship that took them through childhood to the teenage years? What if… But she forced her mind to turn off and think only happy thoughts. The island of Aurum was coming up fast. She'd concentrate on it.

Somehow she'd assumed it shared many of the characteristics of Hellenica, but the mountains were higher and woodier. As they pulled up to the royal dock, Dottie had to admit her adrenaline had been surging in anticipation of seeing where they lived. When Alex talked about Aurum, she noticed his voice dropped to a deeper level because he loved it here.

He'd explained that the mountainous part of the island where the palace was located had been walled off from the public. This had been his private residence from the age of eighteen and would continue to be for as long as he retained the title of Duke of Aurum. She'd learned it had its own game preserve, a wildlife sanctuary, a bird refuge and a stable.

Somehow she'd expected this palace to resemble the white Cycladic style of that on Hellenica. Nothing could have been further from the truth. Through the heavy foliage she glimpsed a small gem of Moorish architecture in the form of a square, all on one level.

"Oh!" she cried out in instant delight the second she saw it from the open limo window.

Alex heard her. "This area of the Aegean has known many civilizations. If you'll notice, the other palace leaves the stairs and patios open. Everything tumbles to the sea. You'll see the reverse is true here. The Moors liked their treasures hidden within the walls."

"Whoa!" Mark exclaimed. His eyes widened in amazement. He'd stopped talking to Zoe. *Whoa* was the perfect word, all right.

Dottie marveled over the exterior, a weathered yellow and pale orange combination of seamless blocks delineated by stylized horizontal stripes, exquisite in detail. The limo passed a woman who looked about fifty standing at the arched entry into a courtyard laid out in ancient tiles surrounding a pool and an exquisite garden. At its center stood a latticed gazebo. This was the garden Alex had referred to last week.

As he helped them from the car, a peacock peered from behind some fronds and unexpectedly opened its plumage. The whirring sound startled Dottie and Mark, but Zoe only laughed. It walked slowly, displaying its glorious fan.

"Whoa," their guest said again, incredulous over what he was seeing. It *was* hard to believe.

Dottie eyed Alex. "We're definitely going to have to work on the *P* sound."

One corner of his mouth curved upward. He ran a hand over his chest covered by a cream-colored polo shirt. "Don't look now," he said quietly, "but there's a partridge in the peach tree behind you."

Slowly she turned around, thinking he was teasing her while he made the *P* sounds. But he'd told the truth!

Transfixed, she shook her head, examining everything in sight. A profusion of pink and orange flowers grew against the gazebo. She walked through the scrolling pathway toward it. Inside she discovered a lacy looking set of chairs and a table inlaid with mother-of-pearl. Dottie felt as if she'd just walked inside the pages of a rare first-edition history book of the Ottoman empire. This couldn't possibly be real.

Alex must have understood what she was feeling because he flashed her a white smile. But this one was different because it was carefree. For a brief moment she'd been given a glimpse of what he might have looked like years ago, before he'd had a true understanding that he was Prince Alexius Constantinides with obligations and serious responsibilities he would have to shoulder for the rest of his life.

There was a sweetness in his expression, the same sweetness she saw in Zoe when she was really happy about something, like right now. But the moment was bittersweet for Dottie when she thought of the pain waiting for him back on Hellenica. A myriad of emotions tightened her chest because her pain was mixed up in there, too.

"Do you want to see my room?" Zoe asked Mark.

"I want to follow the peacock first."

"Okay." She tagged along with her new friend, still managing to carry Baby Betty in her hands.

Alex spread his strong arms. "Guys and girls. Human nature doesn't change." Dottie laughed gently, sharing this electric moment with him.

Porticos with bougainvillea and passion flowers joined one section of the palace to the other. The alcoved rooms were hidden behind. Zoe's was a dream of Moorish tiles and unique pieces of furniture with gold leaf carved years ago by a master palace craftsman of that earlier civilization.

A silky, pale pink fabric formed the canopy and covering of her bed. Near a tall hutch filled with her treasures stood an exquisite pink rose tree. When Dottie looked all the way up, she gasped at the sheer beauty of the carved ceiling with hand-painted roses and birds.

Alex had been watching her reaction. "Your room is next door. Would you like to see it?"

Speechless, she nodded and followed him through an alcove to another masterpiece of design similar to Zoe's except for the color scheme. "Whoever painted the cornflowers in this room must have had your eyes in mind, Dottie. They grow wild on the hillsides. You'll see them when you and Zoe go hiking or horseback riding."

She was spellbound. Her eyes fell to the bed canopied with blue silk. "Was this the room you and your wife used? It's breathtaking."

In a flash his facial muscles tensed up. "Teresa never lived here with me. Like my grandmother, she preferred the palace on Hellenica. She thought this place too exotic and isolated, the mountains too savage. This room was used during my mother's time for guests. Since Teresa's death, Zoe's string of nannies have lived in here."

Dottie couldn't help but speculate on how much time he and his wife must have spent apart—that is, when they didn't have to perform certain civic duties together. Separation went on in unhappy marriages all over the planet, but this was different. He'd been born into a family where duty dictated his choice of bride. Even cocooned in this kind of luxury only a few people would ever know, the onlooker could expect such an arrangement to fail.

As Dottie's aunt had often told her, "You're a romantic, Dottie. For that reason you can be hurt the worst. Why set yourself up, honey?" Good question. Dottie's heart ached for Alex and Stasio, for Teresa and Beatriz, for Genevieve, for every royal who had a role and couldn't deviate from it.

"My apartment is through the next alcove. The last section houses two more guest rooms plus the kitchen and dining room. There's a den where I do my work. It has television and a computer. All of it is at your disposal for the time you're here."

"I've never seen anything so unusual and beautiful."

"Those are my sentiments, too. You saw Inez when we drove in. She and her husband, Ari, head the staff here. There's the gamekeeper, of course, and Thomas who runs the stable. All you have to do is pick up the phone and Inez will direct one of the maids to help you."

"Thank you. I didn't expect to find paradise when I came to Hellenica. I don't think your brother believed me when I told him it really does exists here."

"Paradise implies marital bliss. You'll have to forgive him for being cynical over your naïveté."

Alex's comment bordered on mockery, revealing emotions too raw for him to hide. She shuddered and turned away, not wanting to see the bleakness she often saw in his eyes when he didn't know she was looking.

"I'd better go check on Zoe." She hurried through to the other bedroom, but there was still no sign of her.

Alex came up behind Dottie, close enough for her to feel the warmth of his breath on her neck. "I'll give you one guess where she's gone."

"Well, Mark is pretty cute. She doesn't know she's playing with fire yet." The words came out too fast for her to stop them.

"That's true," Alex said in a gravelly voice before she was spun around and crushed against him. "But I do, and right now I don't give a damn. I want you so badly I'm shaking." He put her hand on his chest. "Feel that thundering? It's my heart. That's what you do to me. I know I promised not to touch you, but I'm not strong enough to keep it. You're going to have to give me help."

The moment had caught her unaware. He had a slumberous look in his eyes. His mouth was too close. She couldn't think, couldn't breathe. Dottie tried to remove her hand, but found her limbs had grown weak with longings that had taken over.

"Alex—" She half groaned his name before taking the initiative to kiss him. When she realized she'd been the one to make it happen, it was too late to change her mind. Their mouths met in mutual hunger. She wrapped her arms around his neck, wanting to merge with him.

With one hand cupping the back of her head, his other wandered over her spine and hips, drawing her closer. The kiss she'd started went on and on. She desired him too terribly to do anything that would cut off the divine experience of giving and taking pleasure like this.

In the background she heard the children's muffled laughter. She didn't know if they'd peeked in this room and had seen them or not, but the sound was too close for comfort. Much as she never wanted to leave Alex's arms, she slid her hands back down his chest and tried to ease away from him so he would relinquish her mouth.

"I heard them," he whispered before she could say anything. Alex had the uncanny ability to read her mind.

"I hope Zoe didn't see us."

He sucked in his breath and cupped her face in his hands. "I hate to break this to you, but she woke at the last minute on the yacht."

Guilt swept through her, making her whole body go white-hot.

"Every little four-year-old girl has seen the movie of *Snow White*. My Zoe knows that when Prince Charming kissed the princess awake, it was true love that worked the charm."

What he was telling her now caused Dottie's body to shake with fright. "You don't think she really sees us that way—"

His handsome features hardened. "Who's to say? In her eyes you're her mommy. Zoe has never seen me kiss another woman. I *have* brought you to my castle. The way you and I were devouring each other just now has probably set the seal in her mind."

Aghast, Dottie propelled herself away from him. "Then you have to unset it, Alex."

"I'm afraid it's too late. You might as well know the rest."

She folded her arms to her waist to stay calm. "What more is there?"

"Sofia had a private word with me this morning before I left the palace. Just as Hector spies for my grandmother, Sofia is my eyes and ears where Zoe is concerned. It seems my daughter told her grandmother that you and I were leaving for Aurum today. But she told her not to cry. When we have the baby, we'll bring it to see *Yiayia.*"

Dottie didn't know whether to laugh or cry, but the tears won out. The sound that escaped her lips was probably as unintelligible as Zoe's word for Hector. Four consonants. All difficult. "Your grandmother's world truly has come crashing down on her."

She saw his body tauten before he caught her in his arms once more. He shook her gently. "What has happened between you and me wasn't planned. For two years I've been telling the queen I'll never marry again, so it's absurd for you to be feeling guilt of any kind over Genevieve." He kissed her wet eyelids, then her whole face.

"It's not so much guilt as the *fear* I feel for Zoe. She's attached herself to me because of her speech problem. I won't be here much longer, but every day that I stay, it's going to make the ultimate separation that much harder."

A shudder passed through his body she could feel. "You think I'm not aware of that?"

She broke free of him. "I know you are, but we've got to lay down some ground rules. I don't ever want her to see us together like we are now. We can't be alone again. This has to be the end so she won't fantasize about us, Alex. It's no good. I'm going to my room to unpack and settle in. Go be with her and Mark right now. Please."

Blind with pain, she left him standing there ashen-faced.

On Wednesday evening of the following week, Alex's mood was as foul as Stasio's. Five days ago Dottie had virtually told him goodbye on the island, but he couldn't handle it any longer and needed to see her. Something had to be done or he was going to go out of his mind.

Philippe had just left to fly home to Vallader, but he would be coming back with his family to attend the coronation on Saturday just a week off now. Until then Alex and his brother were alone.

Stasio cast him a probing glance. "I do believe you're as restless as I am."

Alex gritted his teeth. "You're right." He shot to his feet. "Alert security and come with me. I'm leaving for Aurum to say good-night to Zoe."

"*And* Dottie?"

"I don't want to talk about her. After Zoe's asleep we'll do some riding and camp out in the mountains."

At least that was what he was telling himself now. Wild with pain, he spun around.

"When it comes to a woman, I can't have what I really want. Even if I could, she wouldn't want me. She adored her husband. Why do you think she's still single? No man measures up. The day after your coronation, she'll be leaving the country whether the new speech therapist replacing her has arrived or not."

"Zoe won't stand for it."

"She'll *have* to," he said in a hoarse whisper. "We're all going to have to go on doing our duty. You've never been able to have what you really wanted. You think I don't know what's been going on inside of you? It's killing me."

Stasio stopped midstride. His tormented expression said it all. "What do you want to do, little brother?"

Alex's brows had formed a black bar above his eyes. "Let's get out of here. Gather anything you need and I'll meet you at the helipad."

Before long they were winging their way to Aurum. Once they'd landed, Zoe came running with a couple of the other children who lived on the estate. Inez chatted with him for a minute.

Alex picked up his daughter and hugged her hard. "I've missed you."

"I've been waiting for you, Daddy. I missed you, too."

He kissed her curls. "Where's Dottie?"

"In town." Tears crept down her cheeks. "She said I couldn't go with her."

Naturally Zoe hadn't been happy about that. Though Alex couldn't argue with Dottie's decision, the news sent his heart plunging to his feet. She'd warned him that she would never be alone with him again and she'd meant it.

"How about a hug for me!" Stasio drew her into his arms to give Alex a chance to pull himself together.

Inez gathered up the other children, leaving the men alone with Zoe. They talked about Mark. "I'm sorry he had a cold and couldn't come today."

"Do you think he can come tomorrow?"

"I'll find out."

"I know he wants to come. Dot told us that after our lesson she'd take us out to look for ducks. He can't wait!"

Of course he couldn't. Any time spent with Dottie was pure enchantment.

"Will you ask his mommy?"

"You know I will."

Stasio put a hand on his shoulder. "I'll be at the stable getting the horses ready."

He nodded. "Come on, my little princess. It's getting late. Time to go to bed."

As she chatted with him, he realized he was starting to hear true sounds coming out of her and she was doing a lot more talking. In a month's time Dottie had already made a profound difference in her. All the thanks in the world would never be able to express his gratitude adequately to her.

For the next half hour he read stories to Zoe, then it was time for her prayers. At the end she said, "Bless my daddy and my Dot."

He blinked. She'd said *Dot* distinctly! He'd heard the *D* and the *T*, plus the *ah* in the middle.

Tears sprang to his eyes. This was Dottie's doing. She'd been trying to get her to say *Dot* instead of *mommy.* Just now the word had passed Zoe's lips naturally. A miracle had happened. He wanted to shout his elation, but he didn't dare because she was ready to go to sleep.

The sudden realization hit Alex hard. He loved Dottie Richards. He loved her to the depth of his being. He wanted her in his life forever and needed to tell her so she wouldn't leave him or Zoe. There had to be a way to keep her here and he was going to find it.

Once his daughter was dead to the world, he stole out of her room and raced to the stable to tell his brother there'd been a major breakthrough with Zoe. It was providential he and Stasio were going riding. Alex did his best thinking on the back of a horse. Tonight he would need all his powers of reasoning to come up with a solution.

But as he approached his brother, Stasio's phone rang. One look at his face after he'd picked up and Alex knew there was trouble.

"That was Hector," he said after ringing off. "*Yiayia* isn't well. The doctor is with her, but he thinks we should come home." They stared at each other. With the queen ill, their best-laid plans would have to wait.

Alex informed Inez. By tacit agreement they left for the helipad. Tonight's shining moment with Zoe had been swallowed up in this new crisis with their grandmother. When they arrived back on Hellenica, Hector was waiting for them in their grandmother's suite.

"The doctor has already left. He says the queen's ulcer is acting up again. He gave her medicine for it and now she's sleeping comfortably. I'm sorry to have bothered you."

Stasio eyed Alex in relief. "Thanks for letting us

know, Hector. It could have been much more serious. We're glad you told us."

"Thank you for your understanding, Your Highness."

"You've been with our grandmother much longer than we have. No one's been more devoted." Stasio's glance rested on Alex. "Shall we go to my suite?"

He nodded at his brother. Both of them needed a good stiff drink about now. As he turned to leave, Hector cleared his throat. "Prince Alexius? If I may have a private word with you first."

Something strange was going on for Hector to address him so formally. Alex eyed his brother who looked equally baffled. "I'll be with you in a minute, Stasi."

After he walked off, Hector said, "Could we talk in your suite, Your Highness?"

"Of course." But the request was unprecedented. As they headed to his apartment, Alex had an unpleasant foreboding. Their grandmother was probably sicker than Hector had let on, but he didn't want to burden Stasio, who walked around with enough guilt for a defeated army. The decision to call off his wedding to Beatriz had dealt a near-lethal blow to their grandmother, and poor Hector had been caught in the fallout.

Once they'd entered the living room, Alex invited the older man to sit down, but he insisted on remaining standing, so they faced each other.

"You have my complete attention, Hector. What is it?"

"When's my daddy coming?"

Dottie had been swimming in the pool on Aurum with Zoe while they waited for Alex. "Last night he told you he would be here after your lesson, didn't he?"

"Yes. I want him to hurry. I hope Mark's still not sick."

"We'll find out soon enough, because I can hear your daddy's helicopter." They both looked up.

When Dottie saw it, the realization that Alex would be walking out here in a few minutes almost put her into cardiac arrest. No mere hormones or physical attraction to a man could cause these feelings that made her world light up just to hear his name or know he was in the vicinity.

She was in love. She knew that now. She was in love again, for the second time in her life, and she cried out at the injustice. Her first love and son had been struck down so cruelly, she'd wondered how she could ever build another life for herself.

Now here she was carrying on with her career and doomed to love again, only this man was a prince who was off-limits to her. By the time of the coronation, Zoe would be snatched from her, too, and she'd be left a totally empty vessel. Blackness weighed her down. *What am I going to do?*

While Zoe shouted with excitement and hurried across the tiles to meet her father, who'd be striding through the entry any second, Dottie got out of the pool and raced to her own room. To be with him would only succeed in pouring acid on a newly opened wound that would never heal.

Knowing Alex needed time alone with his daughter, Dottie would give it to him. Quickly she showered and changed into denims and a top before checking her emails. Dr. Rice had sent her another message.

Dear Mrs. Richards,
Success at last. Your replacement's name is Mrs.
Miriam Hawes. She'll be arriving in Athens to-
morrow. All the arrangements have been made.
When you return to New York, I have a new three-
year-old girl who needs testing. We'll enjoy hav-
ing you back. Good luck and keep me posted.
Dr. Rice.

Dottie read the words again before burying her face in her hands. While she was sobbing, a little princess came running into her room and caught her in the act.

"Why are you crying?" She put her face right up against Dottie's. "Do you have a boo-boo?"

Zoe could say boo-boo well enough to be understood. Nothing could have pleased Dottie more, but right now pain consumed her. Yes. Dottie had a big boo-boo, one that had crumbled her heart into tiny pieces.

She sniffed and wiped the moisture off her face. "I hurt myself getting out of the pool." It wasn't a lie. In her haste she'd scraped her thigh on the side, but she would live. "Did Mark come?"

"Yes. He's running after the peacock." Dottie laughed through the tears. "Can he pull out one of its big feathers?"

"No, darling. That would hurt it."

"Oh." Obviously she hadn't thought about that aspect. "Daddy wants you to come."

Dottie had wondered when the bell would toll. She had no choice but to walk out and say hello to Alex and Mark, who were already in the pool whooping it up. Zoe ran to join them.

"Good afternoon, Your Highness."

His all-encompassing black gaze swept over her. "Good afternoon," he said in his deep, sensuous voice. Her body quickened at the change in him from last Saturday when there'd been nothing but painful tension between them.

"I'm glad you brought Mark with you. How are you feeling today, Mark?"

"Good. I didn't have a temperature, so my mom said I could come."

Dottie took her usual place on the edge and dangled her bare feet in the water. "Well we're very happy you're here, aren't we, Zoe?" She nodded while she hung on to her daddy's neck. "Zoe tells me you'd like to take a peacock feather home for a souvenir."

"Yeah. Could I?"

The sudden glance Alex flashed Dottie was filled with mirth. He wasn't the same man of a few days ago. She hardly recognized him. "What do you say about that, Prince Alexius?"

By now he'd put Zoe up on his powerful shoulders. He looked like a god come to life. "Tell you what, Mark. That peacock is going to moult in another month. When he does, he'll shed his tail feathers. You and Zoe can follow him around. When he drops them, you can take home as many as he leaves."

"Thanks!"

"Cool, Daddy."

Alex burst into laughter. "What did you just say to me?"

"'Cool,'" Mark answered for her.

"That's what I thought she said."

"I've been teaching her."

Zoe patted her daddy's head. "Can Mark come to Uncle Stasi's coronation?"

Alex's black eyes pinned Dottie's body to the tiles at the edge of the pool. The day after she was leaving Hellenica. "His family has already been invited."

"*My* family?" Mark's eyes had rounded like blue marbles.

"*Yiayia* says we have to be quiet," Zoe warned him.

"I won't talk."

"It's going to be a very great occasion in the cathedral," Dottie explained to him. "Hellenica is going to get a new king. You'll be able to see the crown put on his head."

She nodded. "It gave my *pappou* a headache."

Dottie broke down laughing. Despite the fact that part of her was dying inside, she couldn't hold it back.

"Hey—that's not funny!" Stasio's voice broke in. "Do you know the imperial crown of Hellenica weighs over five pounds? I'll have to wear a five-pound sack of flour on my head the whole day before to get used to it."

"Uncle Stasi!" Zoe called to him in delight and clapped her hands. Dottie hadn't realized he'd come with Alex.

"That's my name." He grinned before doing a belly flop in the pool. The splash got everyone wet. When he came up for air, he looked at the children. "You'd better watch out. I heard there was a shark in here."

"Uh-oh." While the children shrieked, Dottie jumped up. "This is where I opt out."

Without looking back she walked across the tiles to her room. She thought she was alone *until* she saw Alex. He'd followed her dressed in nothing more than his wet black swimming trunks. Dottie's heartbeat switched to hyperspeed. "You're not supposed to be in here. That was our agreement."

He stood there with his hands on his hips. "Last night that agreement was rendered null and void."

"Why?" she whispered in nervous bewilderment.

His eyes narrowed on her features. "You may well ask, but now isn't the time to answer that question. The queen has been sick, but she's starting to feel better and is missing Zoe. I promised to take her back to Hellenica. Stasi has volunteered to babysit the children on the flight while you and I take the cruiser. We'll leave here as soon as you're ready. Pack what you want to take for overnight." On that note, he disappeared.

Dottie gathered up some things, not surprised the queen wanted to see Zoe. It would lift her spirits. Before long they were ready and left with Alex for the dock in the limo. Once on board, he maneuvered the cruiser out of the small bay at a wakeless speed, then opened the throttle and the boat shot ahead.

The helicopter dipped low and circled above them so the children could wave to them. Dottie waved back. She could tell they were having the time of their lives. Alex beeped the horn three times before the helicopter flew on.

"That's precious cargo up there," she told him. "The two little sad sacks of a month ago have undergone a big transformation. I had no idea if the experiment would work, but I honestly think they like each other."

He squinted at her. "You only think?"

"Well, I don't know for sure. Mark might be pretending because he wants to haul off some of those peacock feathers."

Alex's shoulders shook in silent laughter. While his spirits seemed so much improved, she decided to tell him about the email from Dr. Rice.

He nodded. "I was already informed by him."

Naturally he was. She cleared her throat. "Under the circumstances I thought the new therapist could come to Aurum and stay in one of the guest rooms. We'll let Zoe get used to her and I'll involve her in our games."

When Alex didn't respond she got nervous and said, "Mrs. Hawes will have her own techniques to try out on your daughter, of course. By the time of the coronation, they'll be used to each other. I know it will be difficult for Zoe to say goodbye to me, so we need to handle that carefully."

"I agree." He sounded remote. "I'll think on it."

With those few words, Alex remained quiet, but she didn't mind because his mellow mood was so different from the way he'd been, she was able to relax. For a little while she could pretend they were a normal couple out enjoying each other on this glorious blue sea with the same color of sky above them. Despite her aunt's warnings, Dottie still had a tendency to dream forbidden thoughts, if only for the few minutes they had until they reached the shore.

In this halcyon state she noticed him turn his dark head toward her. "After we dock, you're free until this evening. At eight-thirty I'll send for you. In light of Mrs. Hawes's imminent arrival, we'll finalize the termination of your contract tonight. For Zoe's sake it will be best if you don't drop by her suite to say good-night."

The trip between islands hadn't taken long. Dottie

had been given her few minutes of dreaming, but that was all. With one royal pronouncement, even that brief time had been dashed to smithereens.

CHAPTER NINE

TONIGHT was different from all the other nights in Alex's life. As he'd told Dottie last week, he couldn't be in two places at once. In order to help his brother, he'd sent her and Zoe to Aurum. But this night he needed to be alone with the woman who'd turned the lights on for him. Only Dottie had known the location of the secret switch. Through her magic, she'd found it and now no power could turn it off.

After eating dinner with Zoe and putting her to bed, Alex asked his brother to read her some stories until she fell asleep. While he did that, Alex slipped away to shower and dress in a black silk shirt and trousers, just formal enough to let Dottie know what this night meant to him.

He flicked his gaze around the private dining room of his own jet. It was one of the few places where they could have privacy and be secure away from the palace. The steward had set up the preparations for their intimate dinner, complete with flickering candlelight.

Alex had never used his plane for anything but transportation and business meetings. Tonight it would serve as his portal to a future he'd never dared dream about. Now that he could, his body throbbed at every pulse point. When he pulled the phone from his pocket to answer it, his hand trembled.

Hector was outside. He'd brought Dottie to the airport in the limousine. "Tell her to come aboard."

He moved to the entrance of the plane. When she saw him, she paused midway up the steps in a pink-and-white-print dress he hadn't seen before. She looked breathtaking. Her honey blond-hair had been swept into a knot.

Though she'd picked up a golden tan over the past month, she had a noticeable pallor. He hoped to heaven it was because the thought of leaving him was killing her. Maybe it had been cruel to set her up this way, but he'd wanted proof that she couldn't live without him either. If he'd misread the radar...

"Come all the way in, Dottie. I've got dinner waiting for us."

She bit her lower lip. "I couldn't possibly eat, Alex. I'm sorry for any trouble you've gone to. We could have taken care of business in your office."

He lounged against the opening, half surprised at that response. "We could have, but the office is too public a place for the proposal I have in mind."

By the look in her blue eyes, she acted as if she'd just had a dagger plunged into her heart. "There can't be anything but indecent proposals between you and me." Her wintry comment might have frozen him if he didn't know certain things she wasn't aware of yet.

His black brows lifted. "If you'll finish that long walk into the plane, I'll enlighten you about a very decent one you wouldn't have thought of."

She remained where she was. "If you've decided to abandon your family and the monarchy and hide away in some distant place for the rest of your life, then you're not the prince I imagined you to be."

Her answer thrilled him because it meant she'd not only thought of every possibility for finding a way the two of them could be together, she'd actually put voice to it.

"Then you like it that I'm Prince Alexius?"

He could tell she was struggling to pretend her breath hadn't almost left her lungs. "That's an absurd question. You couldn't be anyone else. It's who you are."

"In other words I'm *your* highness, and you're *my* lowness."

She averted her eyes. "Don't joke about serious matters like this."

"Joking is how I've gotten through life this far."

Her head flew back. "That's very tragic. Why did you have me driven here?" she cried. "The truth!"

"Can you stand to hear it?" he fired back in a quiet voice.

"Alex—" She'd dispensed with his title. That was progress.

"I have a plan I want to talk over with you."

He could see her throat working. "What plan? There can be no plan."

"If you'll come aboard, I'll tell you. In case you think I'm going to kidnap you, I swear this jet won't leave the ground. But since I'm a target for the press, who have their Telephoto lenses focused on us as we speak, I'd prefer we talked in private."

He felt her hesitation before she took one step, then another, until she'd entered the plane. His steward closed the door behind them.

"This way." Alex refrained from touching her. The

time wasn't right. As soon as they entered the dining room, he heard her soft cry. She looked at everything as if she was in some sort of daze. He'd been in one since last night.

"Why did you go to all this trouble?"

"Because it occurred to me you've done all the work since you came to Hellenica. I thought you deserved a little fuss to be made over *you* for a change." He held out a chair for her, but she didn't budge.

"Alex—it's *me* you're talking to. Mrs. Richards, the speech therapist. If there are lies between us, then this meeting is pointless. Please stop dancing around the subject. What's the purpose in my coming here?"

"More than you know."

"You're being cryptic. I can't do this." She turned away from him but he caught her arm.

"All I ask is that you hear me out."

The beautiful line of her jaw hardened. "What if I don't want to listen?"

They stood there like adversaries. "I thought that after everything we've been through together, you trusted me. I think you know I trust you with my life, but apparently I've made a mistake about you." Alex took a calculated risk and let go of her hand. "If you don't want anything more to do with me, then you're free to leave now."

Dottie stayed planted to the same spot. Her breathing sounded labored. "Is this about Zoe?"

"About Zoe. About you. About me. If you'll sit down, Hector will explain."

Her eyes widened. "Hector—"

"Yes. I'll phone him now."

The older man had a certain gravitas even Dottie recognized. While she continued to stand where she was, he rang the older man. Within a minute, Hector joined them.

"Your Highness?" He bowed.

"Would you please tell Mrs. Richards what you told me last night?"

"Certainly." Hector cleared his throat and proceeded to explain what Stasio had jokingly said earlier was Alex's get-out-of-jail-free card. "Before Prince Alexius married, his father, King Stefano, knew of Princess Teresa's heart condition and worried about it. Eventually he made a legal proviso that cannot be broken.

"Simply stated, it reads that should she precede him in death and he wishes to marry again, he—who is second in line to the crown—would have the constitutional right to choose his own wife whether she be of royal blood or a commoner. However, any children born of that union would have no claim to the throne."

Alex watched Dottie slowly sink to the chair he'd pulled out for her. When the older man had finished, he thanked him.

"I'm happy to be of service, Your Highness. If you need me, I'll be out in the limo." He exited the plane while Dottie rubbed her arms with her hands, as if she were chilly.

"The gods on Mount Pelos have heard me," Alex began. "Until I met you, Dottie, I never wanted to marry again. And now, thanks to my father, I'm now able to ask you to marry me." He stared at her for a long moment. "I'm making you an honorable, legally binding offer of marriage."

She finally looked at him. The pupils of her eyes had grown so large, she was obviously in shock. "I couldn't be happier that because of your father's intervention, you've suddenly been given your free agency to choose your own wife. For him to think that far ahead for your welfare shows he really did love you. What I don't understand is why didn't Hector come forward ages ago so you could have found someone else by now?"

Alex was thunderstruck by her question. Had his proposal of marriage meant nothing to her?

"Hector didn't tell me why, but I suspect it's because he secretly loves Zoe like his own granddaughter. He never married or had children. I'm convinced that seeing her so happy with you and so unhappy at the prospect of becoming the stepdaughter of Princess Genevieve prompted him to come forward. The queen may have his allegiance, but Zoe has his heart. Hector has seen the three of us together and knows I'll always put my daughter first."

"But you've only known me for a month, Alex! You're *young!* You've got years to find the kind of relationship you've dreamed of having."

He leaned forward. "I've already had years of relationships that filled the loneliness from time to time, but now I have a daughter who's as precious to me as your son was to you. If I'd searched the world over, I couldn't have found the more perfect mother for her than you."

"So that's all you want? A mother?"

"After what we've shared, you know better than to ask me that. I'm in love with you and you know it, but even though you've responded to me physically, I'm aware your heart died when you lost your husband and son. I live in the hope that one day you'll come to love me with the same intensity. As for Zoe, she loves you so much, she was calling you mommy almost from the beginning."

"Yes, but—"

"It would be a second chance for both of us to find happiness," he spoke over her. "We could make a home anywhere you want. If you prefer to stay in New York and further your career, we'll buy a house there. Our home will be our castle."

An incredulous expression broke out on her face. "What are you talking about?"

"What all normal couples talk about when they're discussing marriage. I want you to be happy."

"But your place is here in Hellenica!"

"Listen to me, Dottie. I'll always be Prince Alexius, but I don't have to live here. Not now. Thanks to technology, it won't matter where we settle down because I can do my mining engineering work anywhere."

"Be serious—your family and friends are here!"

"Yes, and we'll come for visits."

"I'm talking about your life!"

"My life will be with my own little family. You have no idea how much I want to take care of you. I love you. You'll be my first priority."

"You think the queen is going to stand for that?" She sounded frightened.

"She has no say in this matter."

"You're really serious, aren't you?"

"Of course."

In the quiet that followed, Dottie stared into the candle flames. "I feel like I'm in some kind of strange dream. What if I didn't exist?" she cried out. "What would you be planning to do with this new freedom?"

It appeared he was wrong about her feelings. The

knowledge that they could be together legitimately hadn't changed anything for her.

"It's a moot point. You *do* exist, and you've won Hector around, otherwise he would never have come forward with that document." At this point Alex couldn't comprehend life without her, but maybe he'd been mistaken in thinking there was a future for them. "After the coronation, I plan to live with Zoe on Aurum as always. Shall I consider this your answer?"

When she didn't say anything, Alex's burgeoning hopes disintegrated into blackness. He pushed himself away from the table and got to his feet. "If you're ready to leave, I'll walk you out to the limo and Hector will see you get back to the palace."

Once she'd said good-night to Hector, Dottie hurried to her room so torn up inside she didn't know how she was going to make it through the night. Alex's marriage proposal had turned her world upside down.

He'd told her he'd fallen in love with her, but that had to be his desire talking. She knew he desired her, but feared it would eventually wear off now that she was no longer forbidden fruit. If they married and then he grew tired of her, she couldn't bear it.

She still couldn't comprehend that one minute he was doomed to the life he'd been born into, and the next minute he was free to take a commoner for his wife. It was too convenient. If she hadn't heard it from his own lips—from Hector's—she wouldn't have believed it, not in a million years.

Didn't he realize he could marry any woman he wanted? The idea that he'd move to New York for her was a pipe dream. You didn't take the prince out of the man no matter how hard you tried. She didn't want to do that to him. She loved Alex for who he was, but she wasn't about to ruin his life by condemning him to another prison.

Dottie was painfully in love with him, but she wasn't his grand passion. Once his gratitude to her wore off, he'd want his freedom. She couldn't handle that. It was better to remain single and just do her job. The time had come for her to watch out for herself and what she wanted.

Full of adrenaline, she went to the closet for her luggage and started packing. Mrs. Hawes would be on the job in the morning. Zoe wouldn't be happy about it, but in time she'd adjust. Her speech was improving every day. She was already getting some self-confidence. Alex would keep working with her.

As Dottie cleaned out the schoolroom, she kept telling herself Zoe was going to be fine. She and her daddy had each other. That was the important thing. After another hour she had everything packed and finally crawled into bed, praying for sleep to come. But her pillow was wet before oblivion took over.

The next time she had cognizance of her surroundings, she heard a child crying. The sound tugged at her deepest emotions.

"Cory?" she murmured. Her eyes opened.

"Dot," a voice called out her name clearly in the early morning light. It was Zoe! "Dot?"

"I'm right here."

"Mommy," she cried her other name for her and climbed onto the bed.

Dottie pulled her close and rocked her in her arms. "Did you have a bad dream?"

"No. *Yiayia* says a new teacher has come to help me. Don't go, Mommy. Don't go." Her little body shook from her tears. She clung to Dottie.

"Shh. It's all right." Dottie kissed her wet eyes and cheeks. Her dear little face was flushed. She sang some songs she used to sing to Cory. After a few minutes Zoe started to quiet down. Just when it appeared she'd fallen asleep and Dottie could alert the staff, the palace phone rang, startling both of them.

Zoe lifted her head. "I want to stay here."

Dottie reached for the receiver and said hello.

"Dottie—" The anxiety in Alex's voice was that of any frantic parent who couldn't find his child.

"Zoe's with me. I was just going to let you know."

"Thank heaven. I'll be right there."

Alex must have broken the speed record. By the time she'd thrown on her robe, he'd entered her bedroom out of breath and looking so pale it worried her. He was still dressed in the stunning black silk shirt and trousers he'd worn on the jet. It meant he'd been up all night, which made her feel so guilty she wanted to die.

Zoe stood up in the bed. "Don't be mad, Daddy."

A sound of anguish escaped his throat as he reached for her and hugged her tight. "I went to your room to kiss you good morning, but you weren't there."

"I know. I came to see Dot."

"How did you get past the guards?"

"I ran when they didn't see me."

Dottie heard his groan. "You gave me a fright."

"*Yiayia* said I have a new teacher and Dot is leaving. I don't want a new teacher. Please don't let Dot leave—" The pain in her voice was too much for Dottie, who couldn't stop her own tears.

"I can't make Dottie stay, Zoe." The sound that came out of him seeped from a new level of sadness and despair, finding a responding chord in her.

"Yes, you can," Zoe fought her father.

He shook his dark head and kissed her curls. "You're going to learn you can't force people to do things they don't want to do. Come on. Let's take a walk on the beach and then we'll have breakfast."

"No—" she screamed as he started to carry her out. Still in his arms, Zoe turned her head to look at Dottie. "Don't leave, Mommy. I don't want to go. Stop, Daddy—"

Dottie had a vision of them walking out that door. What if she never saw them again? The day of the car accident Neil had grabbed Cory to take him on an errand. Both of them were smiling as he carried their son out the front door. Dottie never saw them alive again.

The thought of never seeing Alex or Zoe again was unthinkable.

"Wait, Alex—"

He'd already started out the door. The momentum caused him to take a few more steps before he swung around. His haunted expression tore her heart to shreds.

"You really want to marry me?" she whispered shakily.

He slowly lowered Zoe to the marble floor and started toward her. "Would I have asked, otherwise?"

It was the moment of truth. She had to have faith that their marriage could work. He'd told her he loved her. He was willing to move to New York, willing to give her the opportunity of loving his wonderful daughter. What more could a woman ask?

But she'd been thinking about it all night. Her deepest fear was that this royal prince, who'd been denied the possibility of a happy marriage the first time, was jumping impulsively into another marriage he'd regret down the road. He was a free man. If he chose to, he could go where he wanted and live like a commoner with another woman.

After what had happened to Neil and Cory, Dottie wanted a guarantee of happiness. But as her aunt had told her, there were no guarantees. *You're a romantic, Dottie. For that reason you can be hurt the worst. Why set yourself up, honey?*

Her aunt's advice had come too late. For better or worse, Dottie *had* set herself up.

She closed the distance between them. "I love you, Alex. So much, you have no idea." Emotion was almost choking her. "I want to be your wife more than anything in the world."

"Darling—" He crushed her to him, wrapping his arms all the way around her. "I adore you, Dottie. I was up all night plotting how to get you to love me," he whispered against her lips before kissing her long and hard. "We need to get married right away."

"I agree," she cried, kissing him back hungrily. "I think we'd better tell Zoe."

"You think?" His smile lit up her insides before he said, "Why don't we do it right here in the alcove."

His arms reluctantly let her go before he drew Zoe over to the table where they'd spent so many delightful times together. Still trembling from the look he'd just given her, Dottie took her place across from them, her usual teacher position. She checked her watch. It was ten to seven in the morning.

Zoe eyed both of them curiously. She'd seen them

kissing and knew something was going on. "Are we going to have school *now*?"

Alex's lips twitched that way they sometimes did when he was trying to hold back his laughter. When he did that, Dottie thought there could be no more attractive man on earth.

"No," he answered. "This morning is a very special morning and we have plans to make because Dottie has just said she would marry me."

The sweetest smile broke out on Zoe's face. "Then you're going to be my real mommy, like Mark's?"

"Yes." Dottie reached across the table to squeeze her hands.

"They're going to have a baby. Mark told me."

"I didn't know that," he answered, trying to keep a deadpan face. Dottie wasn't as successful.

"Can we have one, too?"

Dottie laughed through the tears. "For now you have Baby Betty."

Alex's dark eyes swerved to hers. The look of desire in them took her breath. "If the gods on Mount Pelos are kind, maybe a new baby will come."

Zoe beamed. "A big boy like you, Daddy!"

He trapped Dottie's gaze midair. Her soon-to-be daughter was precocious to a fault, just like her father. Both of them were remembering the jump-rope game. It was the day she fell so hard for Prince Alexius, she hadn't been the same since. She didn't know which moment was the most surreal. But one thing was absolutely certain. She'd committed herself and there was no going back now.

"I tell you what," Alex said. "Let's all get dressed

and have breakfast in my suite while we make plans. After that we'll tell the family."

Zoe stared at her father before giving him a huge kiss. Then she got down and ran around the table to hug Dottie. "I love you, Mommy."

"I love you, too." Over her brown curls she looked at the man she'd just told she was going to marry. "I love you both beyond belief."

Dottie had been to Alex's apartment once before, but her thoughts had been so focused on her diagnostic session with Zoe, she hadn't really looked around and appreciated the magnificence of her surroundings.

During their fabulous breakfast out on the patio, a delivery came for Dottie. She opened the long florist box and discovered two dozen long-stemmed red roses with the most heavenly fragrance. The little card said, *For the first time in my life, I feel like a king whose every wish has come true.* Coming from Alex, those words had unique significance.

After kissing Dottie hungrily, he excused himself to go visit his grandmother and make sure she was up. He told Dottie and Zoe he'd be coming by for them in a few minutes, at which point they would go to the queen's drawing room and tell her their news.

After Stasio had refused to marry Princess Beatriz, Alex's announcement was going to be another terrible disappointment. Dottie feared it might be too much for Zoe's *yiayia* and she would suffer from something worse than ulcers. In a way Dottie had it in her heart to feel sorry for the dowager whose world was crumbling before her very eyes.

The older woman had grown up knowing nothing

but her duty. Somehow she had made her own marriage work, and so had Alex's parents. Deep down it had to be very hard on her to see her two wonderful grandsons so terribly unhappy up to now.

Dottie played with Zoe out on the patio, but she kept waiting for Alex to appear. A maid brought them some much-appreciated refreshments. Dottie asked for a vase so she could put the gorgeous roses in water. The gesture from Alex was one of the reasons she loved him so much.

After being in the apartment for two hours with no word from him, she started to get nervous. Perhaps his grandmother had suffered a setback from the news. He and Stasio were probably sequestered with her because Alex's news had shattered another dream. Twice Dottie started to pick up the palace phone and ask to speak to him, then thought the better of it.

Zoe seemed perfectly content to play with her toys, but Dottie was turning into a mass of nerves. Another hour went by, still no word about anything. When 7:00 p.m. rolled around, their dinner was brought in, but no news from Alex. When she didn't think she could stand it a second longer, Hector appeared on the patio where they'd started to eat.

"If I might speak to you in private."

Thank goodness. "I'll be right back, Zoe. I'm just going to the living room."

"Okay."

Dottie followed him into the other room. "Obviously something's wrong. It's been ten hours since Alex told me he'd be back."

"He had to fly to Zurich today and might not return until morning."

She blinked. "As in Switzerland?"

"Yes. He asked me to assure you that he would never have left you and the little princess unless it was an emergency. He would like you to stay in his suite."

No doubt Alex had told him they were getting married. "Then we will."

Hector knew what the emergency was, but he would never tell Dottie. Whatever was going on had to be serious for Alex to go away today. She rubbed her arms nervously. "Is he all right?"

The slight hesitation before he said, "Of course," spoke volumes. "If there's anything else you need, you only have to ask."

"We're fine, Hector. Thank you for telling me. Good night."

"Good night."

Hector was always perfectly correct. He'd served the monarchy all his adult life. Like the queen, he didn't deviate from his role. It would be too much to ask of anyone. She thought of Alex who'd told her he would live in New York if she wanted. She had no doubt he could do it and make the most of it, but he'd been raised a prince. That would never change.

Full of musings, she walked out to the patio. "Zoe?"

"Did Daddy come?"

"Not yet. Something came up."

"I know. It's business."

Dottie smiled. Just then Zoe sounded a hundred years old. "Why don't we get you in the tub for a nice bath, then I'll read you some stories."

"Are we going to sleep in Daddy's bed?"

"Yes. At least until he calls or comes."

A little sound of happiness escaped the little girl's lips.

Dottie rang for a maid to bring them some things from their rooms. Within the hour both of them were ready for bed. Zoe picked out the stories she wanted and they climbed under the covers. Dottie looked around the sumptuous room, hardly able to believe she would be marrying the man who slept in this royal bedchamber when he was on Hellenica.

Though she was filled with anxiety over the reason for Alex's absence, the feel of the warm little body nestled against her brought a comfort to her heart she hadn't known in years. When they read the last book, she kissed her. "I'm so thankful you're going to be my daughter soon. I love you, Zoe."

"I love you. Good night, Mommy."

No one slept more peacefully than a child who wasn't worried about anything. Zoe had her new mommy-to-be, her daddy and her Baby Betty. Her world was complete. Dottie wished she could say the same for herself, but without Alex here to tell her what was going on, she was too anxious to sleep.

Instead of lying there tortured by fears she couldn't even identify, she slid out of bed and threw on her robe. Zoe preferred the patio to any other place in the palace. Dottie was drawn to it, too, and wandered out there where she wouldn't disturb Zoe with her restlessness.

CHAPTER TEN

AT ONE in the morning, Alex stepped off his jet into the limo and headed for the palace. He'd been prepared to stay all night in Valleder with Philippe and Stasio, but both men urged him to go back to Hellenica and be with Dottie and Zoe.

There was nothing Alex wanted so much in this life, but since the last time he'd seen Dottie, his entire world had changed. He couldn't reverse time and put it back to the way it was before he'd gone to his grandmother's apartment to let her know he'd returned from Aurum.

He said good-night to Hector, then entered the palace and went straight to his apartment. But he was so torn up in his soul by the events of the past fifteen hours, the burden of what he had to tell Dottie made his limbs heavy. He felt like an old man as he continued up the steps and down the hall to his suite.

No lights had been left on. The place was quiet as a tomb. He tiptoed to the bedroom and was surprised to see Zoe asleep alone. Instinct told him Dottie was out on the patio and he headed for it.

His thoughts flew back to that first day. He'd walked Zoe out there to be tested. When Dottie had thrown him that Ping-Pong ball, she'd set an energy in motion that had turned him into a different man. Now all the dynamics were different because Mrs. Dottie Richards had agreed to become Mrs. Dottie Constantinides. Or so she'd thought.

This happened to be his favorite time of night, when the moon was on the rise over the Aegean. It was the time when the heat of the day released the perfume from the jasmine, filling the warm air with its heavenly scent. Instead of it being day, this was the night of his engagement. It was a singular irony that his daughter occupied his bed.

He stepped out on the patio and glimpsed his bride-to-be at the other end. His pounding heart almost suffocated him as he moved toward her. She stood at the wall and had put her hands on either side of the ledge, taking in the unparalleled view etched in his mind from childhood. With her standing there, a new softly rounded, feminine sculpture had been added to the landscape.

"Dottie?" he murmured. A cry escaped her lips. She turned toward him in surprise. "Enjoying the view?"

"This kind of beauty goes beyond perfection."

He sucked in his breath. "It does now." She looked gorgeous yet maidenlike standing there in the moonlight in her simple pink robe. Alex found it hard to believe she'd given birth to a child in another time and place.

"Hector said you might not be home before morning."

"I thought I might have to stay in Valleder until tomorrow, but my brother and Philippe sent me back."

Her eyes searched his. "Why did you have to go to Philippe's? What's happened?"

"You deserve a full explanation and you're going to

get one, but it's going to take a while. Maybe you should sit down."

"That sounded ominous." Her voice trembled. "I think I'd prefer to stand."

"The bottom line is, Stasio submitted papers to the ministers and has taken the steps to abdicate from the monarchy."

In the silence that followed, he watched her face pale. "*What* did you say?"

"Apparently he's been planning it for a long time. When you suggested that I might have decided to abdicate in order to marry you, the idea wasn't so far-fetched after all. You just happened to apply it to the wrong prince."

A hand went to her throat. "He's really stepping down?"

"Yes. After Stasi called off his betrothal, I should have guessed this would be the next step, but I've been so caught up in my feelings for you, I'm not the same person anymore."

"Darling…"

"It's true, Dottie. The reason he was out of the country so long was because he had to work things out with Philippe."

"What things?"

"Stasi has persuaded our second cousin to rule as king over Hellenica."

She shook her head. "I don't believe it."

"Philippe will be able to reign over both countries without problem. The Houses of Valleder and Constantinides are intrinsically entwined. He's well loved in Valleder. It will be the same here."

She looked shellshocked. "Aren't *you* the second in line to the throne?"

"Yes. But Stasio knows how I feel and would never put me in that position, especially now that I'm going to marry you and move to New York. Zoe is third in line and, if she wishes, will rule one day when Philippe is no longer king."

"So does that mean the coronation has been called off?"

"Yes. The announcement will go out on the news tomorrow evening. My grandmother will continue to be the head of the monarchy until Philippe is installed."

Dottie stared out at the sea. "I'm surprised the queen isn't in the hospital by now."

"She may end up there, but she hasn't given up the fight yet. This change to install Philippe has to be voted on by the ministers of the parliament. She has powerful friends there. So does Stasi. I believe the votes for Philippe will prevail. She's calling for an emergency assembly."

"What if they vote against installing your cousin?"

"Then she'll continue to reign until her death, issuing her edicts through the head of parliament."

"And after that?"

"The parliament will convene to find an heir from the Constantinides line. We have a fourth cousin living on the island of Cuprum in the Thracian Sea. He's in his sixties and could be brought up for consideration. However, we have no idea how long my grandmother will live. She has a strong constitution and could outlive him."

"This is all so unbelievable. Your poor grandmother.

Poor Stasio," she whispered, wringing her hands. "To be so desperate for his freedom, he'd give up everything…"

"Actually, I never saw anyone happier than he was when I left him. He's been in love with a woman from Norway for the past ten years and had to make a choice. In the end he chose Solveig. He's a different man now."

"I can only imagine. The second you said abdicate, I thought there had to be a woman. Only a powerful love could cause him to make a break with your family."

"I told him he was insane if he ever wasted another moment feeling guilty about what he's done."

"You're a wonderful brother to say that to him."

"Stasi would do the same for me. Fortunately our father provided that escape clause for me in his will. Otherwise there would have been two abdications."

"You don't really mean that." Her voice shook.

He gave an elegant shrug of his shoulders. "After Teresa died, I put the idea of marriage completely out of my mind. Much later I realized I wanted to marry you, and knew I would have to have papers drawn up for my abdication because there was no way I was going to let you get away from me. I loved you from the moment I saw you. When Hector heard you were leaving, he acted on my father's wishes and told me about the codicil to his will. As you said, it takes a powerful love."

Her breathing had changed. "You loved me from the beginning?"

"I realize now that I fell for you the moment you walked into my office and treated me like an ordinary man. You had no idea what that did to me. My world changed and I knew I had to have you, even if it meant turning my back on my heritage."

"Alex—

"I love you desperately. When we reach New York, I plan to show you what you mean to me. I'll do whatever I have to in order to make our marriage work."

"So will I," she declared. "Don't you know I'm so crazy about you, I'd do anything for you, too? At first I feared the only reason you wanted to marry me was because I was forbidden fruit and able to be a mother figure for Zoe. But I took the risk and said yes to you anyway because I'm so in love with you, nothing else matters."

"Do you have any concept of what those words mean to me, Dottie? I raced back here from Valleder fearing maybe all this was a fantastic dream. It's so hard to believe that I've found the only woman for me, and she loves me, too."

"Then believe this—I don't want to go back to New York with you. I don't want to live there."

"Of course you do. It's your home."

"It was once, but then I came to your world and I've grown to love it here. *You're* here. I would never expect you to cast aside your whole way of life for me. Being Zoe's therapist has brought me smack-dab into the heart of your world. I've learned so much and I'm still learning."

The blood was pounding in his ears. "You're just saying this because it's what you think I want to hear."

"Well, isn't it? Besides the fact that what I'm telling you is true, what do you think those wedding vows are going to be about? I plan to love, honor and serve you through the good and the bad. This is a bad time for your family. Without Stasio, you need me to help you keep the monarchy together.

"Your grandmother needs you. Even though I haven't

met her, I like her, Alex. I really do. She has tried to do her duty the way she's seen fit and Zoe adores her. Why should King Philippe or any other royal family member have to be brought in when you're the son meant to take up the reins? I believe your father knew that."

Alex couldn't believe what he was hearing.

"Alex, you've already been carrying a lot of the load your whole life. Stasio tried his best to shield you by turning to Philippe. He did everything in his power to help you, but you don't need his help.

"I've watched and listened. Your marriage to Teresa proves to me you cared more for the kingdom than you know, or like Stasio you would have abdicated a long time ago. To my mind, you were born to be king. Your country means everything to you, otherwise you wouldn't have agreed to serve in Stasio's place while he's been away. I love you, Alex. I revere you for wanting to do the noble thing and I love the idea of helping you."

Her brilliant blue eyes flashed like the sapphire of the ring he hadn't given her yet. It was still in his suite on Aurum. Those eyes let him know the truth. It was pouring from her soul. "All you have to do is turn around and accept the crown, my love."

There was a swelling in his chest that felt as though it might be a heart attack.

"You and I will always have each other and you and Stasio will be able to live without any guilt. He can marry the woman he loves. They can come and visit, have children, give Zoe a cousin or two. Hector will be thrilled. The queen can take a well-earned rest and Zoe will always be our darling girl. It's the best of all worlds."

Her logic moved him to tears, but he shook his head. "You don't understand. I can't rule with a commoner for a wife, and I refuse to give you up."

"Who says you can't?" she shot back. "I didn't hear about that when Hector explained the contents of your father's codicil to me. It only said that if we have a child or children together, they won't have claim to the throne. That will be Zoe's privilege."

Alex rubbed the back of his neck. "Everything you've said makes perfect sense, but it's never been done."

"That still doesn't make it impossible. Let's go to the queen right now. Wake her up if you have to and tell her you're willing to rule Hellenica with me at your side. Since your father broke the rules when he made that extension to his will, it stands to reason his mother could be moved to convince the ministers to vote in our favor for the good of the monarchy.

"There's no one who can do greater good for the country than you, Alex. You've already been running everything singlehandedly and doing a brilliant job. Maybe it was a presentiment on my part, but the night of the party I watched you and thought you should be king, not Stasio."

In the next instant he reached blindly for her. "You don't know what you're saying."

"I think I do." She clutched his arms. "All I need to know is one thing. Look me in the eye and tell me you don't want to salvage the House of Constantinides. If you're not truthful with me now, then the marriage we're about to enter into is a sham and won't last."

He crushed her in his arms, rocking her long and hard. With his face buried in her hair he whispered, "What have I ever done to deserve you?"

"It'll take me a lifetime to tell you everything, but first we have to tell the queen. Phone your grandmother now. She needs help. Who better than the father of her beloved Zoe?"

Alex kissed the side of her neck. "Whether or not I become king—whether or not my grandmother decides she wants us to have a public wedding here on Hellenica at the time of the coronation—it doesn't matter as long as for once in my life I do get to do the thing I thought I'd never be able to do."

"What's that?" Dottie asked breathlessly.

He cupped her face in his hands. "Marry the woman of my dreams in the chapel on Aurum tomorrow."

"Alex—"

"It will be a very private ceremony just for us. The tiny church located on the palace grounds isn't open to the public. It was erected for the family's use. Father Gregorius will marry us. I'll ask him to perform the ceremony in English."

"He doesn't have to go to that trouble."

"Yes, he does. I'm marrying the bride of my heart and want to say my vows in English for your sake. My friend Bari will be our witness along with Inez and Ari. And, of course, Zoe."

Dottie clung to Alex's hand as he escorted her and Zoe inside the dark interior of the church that smelled strongly of beeswax candles and incense. She wore her white dress with the yellow sash. Dottie had dressed in the pink print and had left her hair down because Zoe had told her earlier that her daddy loved her hair like that.

Inez stepped forward. She handed Dottie a bouquet

of cornflowers. Against Dottie's ear Alex whispered, "I asked her to gather these this morning. They match the incredible blue of your eyes."

She felt tears start and soon saw that another, smaller bouquet had been picked for Zoe to hold. Alex was wearing a light blue summer suit. After putting two cornflowers inside his lapel, he led her and Zoe to the front where the priest stood at the altar. Inez beckoned Zoe to stand by her.

Despite the fact that Alex would always be a prince, Dottie realized he'd dispensed with all artifice for their wedding. She knew the last thing he wanted was for her to feel overwhelmed. Her heart quivered with her love for him as the ceremony began.

"Do you, Prince Alexius Kristof Rudolph Stefano Valleder Constantinides, Duke of Aurum, take Dorothy Giles Richards to be thy wedded wife? To love, honor and serve her unto death?"

"I do."

Dottie trembled.

"Do you, Dorothy Giles Richards, take Prince Alexius to be thy wedded husband? To love, honor and serve him unto death?"

"I do," she whispered, scarcely able to believe this was really happening.

"Then by the power invested in me, I proclaim you husband and wife from this day forth. What God has blessed, let no man put asunder. In the name of the Trinity, Amen."

"Amen," Alex declared after Dottie spoke.

"You wish to bestow tokens?"

"I do, Father." He reached for Dottie's left hand and slid the one-carat sapphire onto her ring finger.

"You may kiss your bride."

The significance of this moment shook Dottie to her very roots. Alex was her husband now. Her life! Without caring about anything else, she raised her mouth to his, needing his kiss like she needed the sun on her face and air to breathe.

While they stood locked together, Zoe ran over to them and hugged their legs. She felt her little arms, reminding her she and Alex were probably giving Father Gregorius a coronary for letting their kiss go on so long. No doubt she was blushing, but the others wouldn't be able to tell until they went outside.

"Are you married now, Daddy?"

Alex relinquished Dottie's mouth and picked up his daughter to kiss her. "We're very, very married."

She giggled and turned to reach for Dottie, who hugged her.

Bari stepped forward and gave Alex a bear hug before bestowing a kiss on Dottie's cheek.

"Congratulations, Your Highness." Inez and Ari curtsied to him and Dottie, then handed her the bouquet. "Your Highness."

"Thank you," Dottie answered.

Alex shook their hands. "We appreciate all your help."

"It's been our pleasure."

"Let's go outside for some pictures," Bari suggested.

The priest stayed long enough for a group photo in front of the ancient doors, then he had to be on his way to the city. Alex invited Bari to have a drink with them. At Zoe's suggestion they celebrated in the gazebo. Bari drank to their health and happiness. After one more picture, he left to get back to work.

Inez brought out a tray of salad, sandwiches and a pitcher of iced tea. By now they were all hungry, including Zoe. A month ago her appetite had diminished to the point they'd both worried about it, but no longer.

The peacock happened to walk past the gazebo just then. Zoe scrambled out of her chair and went after it, leaving them alone for a minute. Alex caught her in his arms. "Alone at last. Happy wedding day, Mrs. Constantinides."

"I love you, darling," she blurted. "Thank you for the simple, beautiful ceremony. I loved it. I love my ring. I'll treasure this day forever. I'm only sorry I didn't have a ring for you."

He kissed her passionately on the mouth. "I didn't want one. I don't like rings and would prefer not to wear one. Yet I have seven of them, all with precious gems encrusted. The only one that doesn't have stones is this one." He flexed his right hand where he wore the gold ducal crest. "Since I have to wear it, I'll take it off and let you put it on the ring finger of my left hand."

He removed it and handed it to her.

At first she was all thumbs. Finally she took hold of his hand and slid it home. "Did you wear it on this hand when you were married to Zoe's mother?" she asked without looking at him.

"No. She gave me a ring from the House of Valleder. I took it off after she died and put it with the other rings that Zoe will inherit one day."

As she stared into his eyes, she sensed something else was on his mind. "You have news. I can tell."

"Yes. For one thing, Hector explained the situation to Mrs. Hawes and she's been given a free two-week vacation here if she wants. Now you don't have to worry about her needless trip."

"Oh, thank you, darling. That's so generous of you."

"After meeting you, I realized how hard-working and dedicated you therapists are. She deserves every perk we can offer."

Dottie bit her lip. "What else were you going to tell me?"

His expression grew more solemn. She saw the slightest look of vulnerability in his eyes. "Before we left Hellenica this morning, my grandmother told me the vote from the parliament was unanimous. They want me to be king. So does she."

His news was so wonderful, she threw her arms around his neck. "You're going to be the greatest king this country ever had. I'm the luckiest woman in the world because I'm your wife. I promise to help make your life easier. I swear it."

"Dottie—" He pulled her tightly against him. "You realize what this means. The day after tomorrow will be my coronation. The queen wants us to come to the palace immediately to discuss the arrangements for our wedding. We're going to have to go through another ceremony, and then I will be crowned king. She wants to meet the commoner who stole the hearts of her great-granddaughter and grandson."

This time tears rolled down Dottie's cheeks. She grasped his handsome face in her hands. "I can't wait to meet her. I can't wait to say my vows again. I love you," she cried, covering his face with kisses.

The archbishop of Hellenica closed the coronation ceremony with "God Save the King." Dottie adored this great man she'd just married for the second time. He'd now been crowned king in this magnificent cathedral and was so handsome and splendid in his dark blue ceremonial suit and red sash, it hurt to look at him.

Zoe, dressed in a tiara and frilly white floor-length dress, sat on a velvet chair like a perfect little princess between Dottie and her great-grandmother, who'd come in a wheelchair. Stasio sat opposite them in his ceremonial dress. Solveig, the woman he loved, had come and was seated in the crowd. Dottie liked her already and imagined there'd be a wedding soon.

King Philippe and his pregnant American wife sat next to Stasio. Over the past few days Dottie had gotten to know her and couldn't wait to spend more time with her.

When the archbishop bid Princess Dorothy rise to join Alex for the processional out of the church, Dottie realized it was *she* he meant and blushed like mad. Her husband noticed she'd been caught off guard and his black eyes flashed fire as she walked toward him to grasp his hand. Zoe followed to carry the train.

In an intimate appraisal, his gaze swept from the tiara on top of her white lace mantilla, down her white princess-style wedding gown to her satin slippers. He'd given her that same look as she'd started to get out of bed this morning. When she reminded him they should have been up an hour ago, he'd pulled her back on top of him and made love to her again with insatiable hunger.

It was embarrassing how much time they'd spent in the bedroom when there was so much to get done in preparation for the coronation. But obviously not embarrassing enough, because she was the one who always moaned in protest when Hector finally managed to convince Alex he was needed in the office or the queen's drawing room immediately.

Her husband kept squeezing her hand as they slowly made their way toward the great doors. In her heart she knew that if Neil and Cory were looking on, they would be happy for her.

She smiled at the guests standing on either side of the aisle. Everyone looked wonderful in their hats and wedding finery. Halfway down she caught sight of Mark and his parents. He made a little wave to Dottie and Zoe with his hand. It warmed her heart. Next she smiled at Bari and his family. Near the doors she spotted Hector, who beamed back at her.

When she and Alex emerged from the cathedral, a huge roar went up from the crowd in the ancient agora. Alex helped her into the open-air carriage, then assisted Zoe, who sat opposite them. Once he'd climbed inside and closed the door, the bells began to ring throughout the city.

Almost at once a chant went through the crowd for King Alexius to kiss Princess Dot. Somehow word had gotten out that Princess Zoe called her new mother Dot.

"Don't mind if I do," Alex said with a wicked smile before he kissed her so thoroughly her tiara slipped off. The crowd went wild with excitement. The horses began moving.

While Alex fit it back on her, taking his time about it as he stared at her, Zoe said, "Was the crown heavy, Daddy?"

"Very. Your Uncle Stasi wasn't kidding."

"Could Mark ride with us, Mommy?"

"Not today, but you'll see him tomorrow. There are hundreds of children lining the streets with their families. They'd all love to ride in this carriage with you, so wave to them. They're very excited to see you."

"They are?"

"Yes. Just think—today your country got a new king and he's *your* daddy. We need to start working on your K sounds."

Alex's chuckle turned into a deep rumble. He leaned over to give her another kiss that stirred her senses clear down to her toenails. It was a kiss that told her he couldn't wait until they were alone again. As they reached the palace and climbed out of the carriage, the limo carrying the queen and Stasio pulled up behind them.

As they all entered the palace together, Alex's grandmother said, "Really, Alex. Did you have to kiss Dottie like that in front of thousands of people? And you kept doing it! You realize it'll be all over the news."

He grinned at Stasio. "I don't know how to kiss her any other way, *Yiayia*. Worse, I can't seem to stop."

"Are we going to have a baby now?" piped up a little voice.

"Oh, really, Zoe!" her great-grandmother cried out. "You don't ask questions like that in front of people. There's going to be a reception in the grand dining hall and I expect you to behave like the princess you are."

Unabashed, Zoe turned to Hector. "Can Mark sit by me?"

While they were sorting it out, Alex pulled Dottie away from the others and led her to a deserted alcove. Before she could breathe, he kissed her long and deeply. "I needed that," he murmured after lifting his head a few minutes later. "You looked like a vision in the cathedral. Promise me you're not a figment of my imagination. I couldn't take it."

She kissed his hard jaw. "I'll convince you tonight when we're finally alone. I'm so glad I married royalty. I love the idea of going to bed with my husband and *my liege*. It sounds positively decadent and wicked, don't you think?"

"Dottie—"

* * * * *

GEORGIE'S BIG GREEK WEDDING?

BY
EMILY FORBES

Emily Forbes began her writing life as a partnership between two sisters who are both passionate bibliophiles. As a team Emily had ten books published, and one of her proudest moments was when her tenth book was nominated for the 2010 Australian Romantic Book of the Year Award.

While Emily's love of writing remains as strong as ever, the demands of life with young families has recently made it difficult to work on stories together. But rather than give up her dream Emily now writes solo. The challenges may be different but the reward of having a book published is still as sweet as ever.

Whether as a team or as an individual Emily hopes to keep bringing stories to her readers. Her inspiration comes from everywhere, and stories she hears while travelling, at mothers' lunches, in the media and in her other career as a physiotherapist all get embellished with a large dose of imagination until they develop a life of their own.

If you would like to get in touch with Emily you can e-mail her at emilyforbes@internode.on.net.

CHAPTER ONE

JOSH swung himself out of the ocean and onto the back of the pontoon. Slipping his dive fins from his feet and his mask from his face, he held them in one hand as he used his free hand to haul himself into a standing position. The air tank on his back was ungainly, making his balance awkward, but he was used to the sensation and after more than two hundred dives he knew better than to try to lean forward while changing position.

He dropped his fins, mask and snorkel into his dive bag and checked his watch, noting the dive time and depth. It had been a fairly standard dive, pleasant but certainly not the best. The visibility had been reasonable but aside from a few eels and one huge Maori wrasse he hadn't seen anything spectacular.

He was disappointed. He'd hoped the easy access to the world-renowned Great Barrier Reef dive sites off the coast of Cairns in northern Queensland would make up for the fact he'd had to transfer to this country town. He unclipped his buoyancy vest and slung it from his back. Okay, to be fair, Cairns was a large regional centre, not a typical Australian country town, but it definitely wasn't a big city. He'd spent the past two and a half years in Brisbane, a city of two million people, working his way up to a senior position, or so he'd thought, only to find himself banished to the sticks for six months.

But he'd survived smaller towns before, much smaller, all for the sake of experience, and he just hoped this move would pay dividends too. Besides, it wasn't like he'd had much of a choice. His six-month stint started tomorrow and he'd have to make the most of it.

He would take the opportunity to have one last holiday before he prepared to knuckle down and work hard to achieve the goals he'd set himself. He would be free to do as he pleased on his days off but once he returned to Brisbane he imagined days off would be few and far between.

Have fun, he told himself as he pulled his thin dive shirt over his head before running his hands through his hair to dry it off, but remember to think of the bigger picture and of what you stand to gain, that was the way to get through the next six months.

Georgie pushed herself out of the warm water and onto the ledge at the back of the pontoon that was moored permanently at Agincourt Reef. She removed her mask and snorkel as she dangled her legs in the ocean and watched the myriad holidaymakers splashing around, enjoying the beauty of the reef.

Her stomach rumbled as she basked in the afternoon sunshine, reminding her that she'd skipped lunch in favour of a longer snorkel. She pulled the flippers from her feet so she could stand and threw her borrowed diving equipment into the containers at the back of the pontoon. The deck was almost deserted now that most of the day-trippers had consumed their lunches and returned to the water, so she'd go and see what remained of the buffet.

She hung her life jacket on the rack and let her eyes

roam over the handful of people gathered on the pontoon. Her gaze lingered on the starboard side where a group of scuba divers had just emerged from the water and were now laboriously removing their equipment. She searched the group for her brother Stephen and his girlfriend, Anna, who were visiting from Melbourne and had come out to the reef to go scuba diving, but she didn't see any familiar faces. They must still be in the water.

They'd tried to talk her into doing an introductory dive and initially she'd been keen, but she'd chickened out when they'd reached the pontoon and she'd seen the huge expanse of empty ocean. Who knew what was lurking under there? She decided she felt safer splashing about with all the other snorkellers. Being able to lift her head out of the water and see the pontoon and the catamarans that had ferried them to the reef gave her a sense of security out in the middle of the vast Pacific Ocean.

She continued to watch the group of divers, smiling at their attempts to shed their equipment. They'd looked so graceful under the water when she'd seen them from her snorkelling vantage point but out of it they looked ungainly. She was glad she'd changed her mind about the introductory dive—she wasn't sure she could be bothered with all the paraphernalia and the air tanks looked awfully heavy.

There was one man, however, who managed to make the tank look as though it weighed no more than a sleeping bag. Georgie watched as he unclipped his buoyancy vest and slung it and his air tank off his shoulders before he removed his thin dive shirt by pulling it over his head. His torso was bare and she was treated to a rather attractive view of a smooth, lightly tanned back and rippling muscles as he stretched his arms overhead. His dark blond hair was cut short and when he ran his hands through it the salt water made it stick up in all directions. He had the physique of a man who worked out. He had broad, square shoulders that tapered nicely into his waist and the muscles on his arms were well defined.

He threw his shirt over his shoulder as her eyes travelled down his back. She could see the two small dimples at the base of his spine just visible above the waistband of his shorts. His shorts hugged the curve of his buttocks and were patterned like the Australian flag. If all divers looked like him, perhaps she would take up the challenge.

'Help, somebody, please, help us.'

Georgie spun around, her meandering thoughts interrupted by a woman's cries. The sound came from her right, out in the ocean. She searched the water and it took her a second or two to locate the woman. She was about fifty metres off the back of the pontoon in one of the snorkelling areas marked out by floating buoys. The woman was waving one arm and hanging onto someone else with her other hand. From the corner of her eye Georgie saw a flash of movement as someone dived off the starboard corner of the pontoon. She turned her head. The guy in the Australian flag board shorts had disappeared. In the time it took her to process the cries for help and to find the source of the sound he had dived into the water and was now swimming strongly towards the distressed woman.

A couple of crew members had raced to the back of the pontoon, one unhooking a lifebuoy and the other carrying a first-aid kit. Seeing other people in action galvanised Georgie. She made her way across the pontoon, past stunned tourists, to offer her assistance as the crewman with the lifebuoy jumped overboard and struck out towards the woman, trailing in the other guy's wake.

Georgie followed him with her eyes. She could see that the diver in the Aussie flag shorts had almost reached the woman but it was getting difficult to see everything that was happening as the swell had picked up and the small waves breaking on the top of the reef were obscuring her vision. With two more over arm strokes, the guy in the board shorts had reached the woman and taken over control of the person she was supporting. He had hold of the person's chin and Georgie could see him making his way back to the pontoon with a strong sidestroke action, dragging the person with him. The woman was doing her best to follow but she was being rapidly left behind. The crewman with the lifebuoy swam up to her, slipped the lifebuoy over her head and under her arms and started towing her back to the pontoon.

The guy in the board shorts was already back at the pontoon with the rescued man in his grip. One of the crewmen knelt down at the edge of the pontoon and hooked his hands under the distressed man's armpits and hauled him onto the deck.

'He's complaining of chest pain,' the diver in the board shorts told the crewman as he helped to lift the man's legs out of the water, 'and I suspect he's aspirated some salt water.'

What sort of person used the term 'aspirated'? Georgie wondered. It was a medical term but perhaps it was common in diving as well? She watched the diver as he hoisted himself up onto the deck. His biceps and triceps bulged as he lifted his weight clear of the sea. Salt water streamed from his body as he stood. His chest was smooth and tanned and despite having just swum a fast fifty metres while towing a heavy body, he was breathing normally. He didn't appear to be even slightly out of breath.

There were now several people gathered around the back of the pontoon and Georgie was able to blend into the crowd. The guy seemed oblivious to her scrutiny so she let her gaze travel higher.

She was pleased to see that he had a face to match his body. He had an oval face with strong features that complemented his chiselled physique. He had full lips set above a firm jaw, which had a day's growth of beard and perfectly symmetrical, sandy brown eyebrows that framed his eyes. His nose was straight and narrow and his teeth, when he spoke, were even and white. He was rather cute.

'Let's clear the area and get him comfortable. We don't want to encourage extra blood flow to his heart. I don't want to stress it more than necessary.'

The cute guy, as Georgie now thought of him, continued to issue instructions as he directed the crew to reposition the man where he wanted him. Because of the board shorts he was wearing she'd initially wondered if he was an overseas tourist but he spoke with a definite Aussie twang. Foreign or not, the cute guy was sounding more and more like he had a medical background. Which reminded her of why she'd crossed the deck in the first place. It hadn't been to ogle a complete stranger, she'd meant to offer assistance. There were more important things to focus on than an attractive scuba diver.

She took a couple of steps away from the cute guy and towards the crew member who was standing nearby, holding the first-aid kit.

'Have you got a towel or something we can use to dry him off and keep him warm?' she asked.

He nodded and Georgie took the kit from him so he could go and find what she'd asked for. She squatted down and spoke to the cute guy. 'I'm a paramedic. Can I help?'

He nodded in acknowledgement but kept his head down and directed his words at the patient. 'I'm a doctor so between us we should be able to get you sorted.' For a moment Georgie thought he was going to ignore her but when he finished reassuring the patient he looked across at her.

His eyes were an unusual shade of grey. Silvery grey, almost metallic in colour, they reminded her of the paint the Navy used on its ships. 'Can you have a look and see what's in the first-aid kit?' he asked.

She flipped the catches open as she listened to the conversation going on beside her.

'Can you describe your pain to me?'

'I feel like someone has punched me in the chest.' The man spoke with a British accent and he sounded out of breath, as though each word took great effort. He was going to have a holiday to remember, Georgie thought, assuming they managed to pull him through this crisis.

'Have you had chest pain before?' Cute guy had his fingers on the man's wrist pulse and his eyes on his dive watch, counting the seconds. His fingers were long and slender, his nails shortly clipped and nicely shaped.

The patient nodded but the woman, whom Georgie assumed was his wife, and who was now back on board the pontoon thanks to the efforts of the crew member, elaborated. 'His doctor said it was angina.'

'Is he on any medication?' Cute guy quizzed the man's wife.

Georgie made a concerted effort to turn her attention back to the contents of the first-aid kit and away from the cute doctor's hands.

'The doctor gave Nigel some tablets.'

'Have you got them with you?'

The wife shook her head. 'We forgot to pack them—they're in our hotel room.'

Fat lot of good they were going to do there, Georgie thought. She looked up from the first-aid kit and caught cute guy's eye. It was obvious from his expression he was thinking along the same lines.

'There's nothing useful in here,' she muttered as she

finished searching through the kit. The crewman had returned with a towel but Georgie had another assignment for him now. 'Do you have a medical cupboard that would have any drugs other than mild analgesics? Painkillers,' she clarified, when all she got was a blank look.

He nodded. 'Yes, we've got a sick bay. If you want to come with me, you can see if we've got what you need.'

Georgie stood and quickly followed him along the deck into the small sick room. She grabbed a portable oxygen cylinder that was hooked up against the wall as the crewman unlocked a medicine cupboard. She hunted through the cupboard and found some GTN spray and a mask to use with the oxygen. There wasn't much else that was helpful.

She returned to the back of the pontoon with her meagre supplies. 'Symptoms?' she queried, wanting to know whether the patient's status had changed.

'Pulse rate irregular and possibly slightly elevated,' cute guy said as she squatted beside him. He smelt of salt and sunshine and Georgie could feel the heat of the sun bouncing off him. 'Shortness of breath,' he continued speaking, 'but that could be exercise related. Left-sided chest pain but not extending into his extremities.' He turned to look at her and the movement made his abdominals ripple along his side.

'How long since his symptoms started?' she asked, forcing herself to concentrate.

He glanced at his watch. 'We've been out of the water for four and a half minutes and his pain's no worse.'

'Angina?' she queried.

He nodded in agreement. 'Most probably.'

'I found this.' Georgie held up the spray. 'I think it's our best option.' She expected the doctor to move over and let her administer the spray but he reached out and took it from her. She was a little bit taken aback. She had no idea what sort of doctor this man was but, as a paramedic, she was almost certain she'd have more experience in these situations than him and she wasn't used to playing second fiddle. But she wasn't going to have an argument about it—after all, it was a fairly simple exercise and he'd already given Nigel the spray. All that was left was to monitor him and hope his condition improved.

Georgie saw Nigel's wife waiting anxiously nearby. She swallowed her irritation. Someone needed to talk to the wife. 'I'll call QMERT and put them on alert but hopefully we'll get him stabilised,' she told the doctor as she stood up. 'And I'll explain what's happening to his wife.'

To save time she spoke to a crew member and Nigel's wife together so she only had to explain things once. 'Nigel's symptoms aren't worsening so hopefully it's just a case of angina,' she told them. 'He's been given medication and we'll monitor him for the next ten minutes. If it is angina, we expect his symptoms will have eased considerably in that time.'

'And if they don't? What do we do then?' Nigel's wife asked. 'We're out in the middle of the ocean.'

'I'm going to radio QMERT, that's the Queensland Medical Emergency Retrieval Team.' Georgie kept her voice calm as she wanted to stem the rising panic she could hear in the wife's voice. 'I'll explain the situation and get a helicopter on standby to evacuate him if necessary.' She didn't mention that she worked with QMERT, it wouldn't make any difference to anyone else.

Georgie got a few more details from Nigel's wife and put a call in to the Clinical Coordination centre in Brisbane to advise them of the situation. All calls to QMERT went through Brisbane. It was up to the central command to find the closest available crew from one of the bases located throughout Queensland. It was more than likely that Cairns, which was her base, or the Townsville crew would be put on standby.

She finished the call and returned to the patient. The cute doctor looked up at her with his gunship-grey eyes and Georgie forgot she was annoyed at him.

'He's recovering well, chest pain abating and respirations normal.'

'So you think we're okay to bring him in on the boat?' Georgie asked.

'How long will that take?'

Georgie frowned. Had she misheard him? Hadn't he come out to the reef on the boat? Was his cool grey gaze interfering with her concentration?

'About ninety minutes,' she replied, 'but it's not due to leave for another hour. There's time to alter plans if things change. I've put the QMERT chopper on standby.'

He stood up. 'Can I speak to you over here?' he asked, inclining his head towards the side railing of the pontoon.

Georgie wondered what he couldn't say in front of Nigel and his wife but she nodded anyway. He held out a hand. She reached for him and he clasped his fingers around her wrist to help her to her feet, but when his skin met hers a spark shot through her. It made her catch her breath. It made her heart race. It must have something to do with the adrenaline coursing through her system after the excitement, she thought. He let go of her hand and walked over to the edge of the pontoon, away from Nigel, his wife and the crewman, who was still hovering waiting for any further instructions. Georgie followed him, she didn't think she could do anything else. Her feet seemed to be behaving independently of her brain, following his lead.

He leant on the railing and Georgie could see each bony

prominence of his vertebrae where his spine curved as he bent forward.

'Are you happy to monitor him and make that call if necessary?'

Her frown deepened. 'Of course.' She had no problem with that but she wondered why he was handing total patient care over to her.

'I flew out to the reef on a helicopter charter,' he explained, 'and I've just been told it needs to take off as there's another chopper coming in onto the landing pontoon shortly. But I can stay to help monitor Nigel if you like. I need to know what you're comfortable with before I tell him what's happening. I could come back on the catamaran with you if you'd prefer.'

Did he think she couldn't handle things? Was that why he'd offered? He didn't need to do her any favours.

'Thank you but I can manage. I'm used to working in these conditions,' she said as she looked around the pontoon and the expanse of water surrounding it. 'Well, perhaps not these exact conditions, but I'm certainly used to coping outside a hospital environment. If I'm at all concerned I'll call QMERT in. They can do an evacuation from the catamaran if things get really dicey. It's fine. Go.'

Go and let me concentrate. She knew it would be better if she was left to work on her own. After all, she'd wanted to be in charge.

There was a stretcher fixed alongside the stairs that led to the upper deck, and she instructed the crew to bring it to her as she swapped places with the doctor. She watched him as he gathered his things and boarded the little dinghy that would ferry him across to the helicopter pontoon.

She watched him as he left her to monitor Nigel. That wasn't an issue. She was more than capable. She didn't need his help. She could work more efficiently without the distraction. But as the dinghy pulled away from the pontoon, she wondered where he was from and, as he raised a hand in farewell, she realised she had no way of finding out. She didn't even know his name.

CHAPTER TWO

GEORGIE parked her car beside the airport building that was the headquarters for the Cairns division of QMERT. She climbed out and pulled her white singlet top away from her body, looking for some respite from the heat. A quarter to eight in the morning and the north Queensland humidity was already stifling. She could feel the perspiration gathering between her breasts. She'd been in the tropics for months now but after moving from the cooler climes of Melbourne she still hadn't got used to feeling hot and sticky ninety per cent of the time. But despite the sometimes intolerable humidity she was thoroughly enjoying her secondment to the Queensland Ambulance Service and QMERT.

And the weather wasn't always so oppressive, she reminded herself. It had been remarkably pleasant out on the reef yesterday. It was only on the mainland that she noticed the humidity. The scenery yesterday had been very pleasant too, she recalled with a smile. It had been a pity the cute doctor had left before she'd got his name.

She still hadn't decided whether she was more annoyed or intrigued by him. She had to give him credit for his quick reaction to the crisis yesterday. Nigel had made it safely back to the Cairns hospital and he had the doctor to thank for that. She supposed he'd only been doing what he'd been trained for and she couldn't hold that against him. But, still, she wished she knew who he was.

She'd kept her eyes peeled last night when she'd gone out to dinner with her brother and sister-in-law, hoping she might see him wandering the streets of Cairns, but her search had been fruitless. She shrugged. She'd expected nothing less really, it had been a rather vain hope. But it had been her only hope. The only way she might see him again. More than likely he was just a tourist, just someone passing through Cairns, someone she was never likely to see again. But that idea was strangely disappointing.

She shook her head, trying to clear it. She had other things to think about than a perfect stranger. It was time to go to work. She searched through her bag for an elastic band to tie up her hair. The air was muggy, heavy with moisture, and having her hair hanging halfway down her back was making her feel hotter. She gathered her dark hair into a ponytail that hung in a thick rope between her shoulder blades, picked up her bag and headed for the air-conditioned comfort of the corrugated-iron and weatherboard building.

She walked past the helicopter that was the latest addition to the QMERT fleet. The night crew was obviously back at base and she wondered what kind of shift they'd had. She hummed show tunes as she crossed the tarmac, pushed open the door to the base and headed for the communications centre. Comms was always her first port of call as she always wanted to check what was happening.

'Morning, Lou, what have I missed?' she greeted the dispatch officer who was stationed at her desk.

'Nothing much,' was the answer. 'The boys have just got back from an IHT,' Louise went on, using the abbreviation for an inter-hospital transfer, 'but other than that it was pretty quiet overnight.'

Georgie pulled a face, her dark eyes flashing with good humour. She loved the pace and hype of busy days. Flying off in the helicopter to save lives was a huge buzz and while quiet days were good because they meant no one was getting injured, busy days meant the chance to put her skills to use.

'It's not all bad,' Louise added. She knew how Georgie felt about quiet days—everyone on the team felt the same. 'The new doctor starts officially today. Showing him the ropes should keep you out of trouble.'

'That's Josh Wetherly, right? The emergency specialist from Brisbane?' Georgie recalled some details from the bio that had been circulating about him.

Louise nodded. 'His experience looks pretty good on paper but, trust me, he looks even better in real life. I reckon you'll be more than happy to show him around the chopper and maybe even around Cairns.'

Georgie rolled her eyes. She was used to Louise trying to find her a man. Louise and her husband had been married for twenty-five years and she thought everyone deserved the same happiness. Georgie didn't disagree. Her parents were also a fine example of a happy marriage, but she didn't want to be reminded that at twenty-seven years of age people were starting to expect her to settle down. There were still things she wanted to do before she settled down to domestic life and she certainly didn't need another mother figure trying to find her a husband. Her own mother was perfectly capable of that! Besides, at fifty and almost twice her age, Louise's idea of a hot man was not quite the same as Georgie's. It took more than good manners and a nice head of hair to get her attention.

One of the reasons Georgie had moved to Cairns had been to get away from the pressure her family had been putting on her to find a partner but so far her plan wasn't working too well. Her family continued to show a tendency to send eligible bachelors her way and she'd lost count of the number of blind dates she'd been obliged to go on. She didn't need Lou on her case as well. She needed a project, something to occupy her time so she could legitimately say she was too busy to date. Showing Dr Wetherly around Cairns wasn't her idea of a suitable project. She'd have to find something else.

The phone on Louise's desk rang before Georgie could think of a smart retort. She waited for Lou to take the call, knowing it would probably mean a job for the team.

Lou jotted notes as she spoke to the clinical co-ordinator in Brisbane, nearly fourteen hundred kilometres south of their Cairns base. The information the retrieval team received was almost always third hand: the emergency call would be put through to headquarters in Brisbane and, depending on the location of the emergency, the Brisbane co-ordinator would pass the call on to the dispatch clerk in Brisbane, Townsville, Toowoomba or Cairns. They would then pass the information on to the retrieval team. QMERT was responsible for an area extending in a radius a few hundred kilometres around Cairns, including the waters and islands in the Pacific Ocean off the coast of Australia. The Royal Flying Doctor Service took over to the north up to Cape York and further inland into the Outback, while QMERT Townsville covered the area to the south.

Louise hung up the phone and relayed the scant information she had to Georgie. 'A four-month-old baby in respiratory distress. She's in Tully hospital, they've requested an IHT. I'll find Pat—'

'And I'll get changed and track down Dr Wetherly.' Georgie finished Lou's sentence. She knew she had time. Pat, the helicopter pilot on duty, would need to get details about the flight and landing, do his pre-flight checks and refuel if necessary. She only needed a few minutes to get changed and find the new doctor. A job this early in the morning wasn't going to be an ideal introduction for the new recruit on his first day but there was no way around it. She just hoped he was up to the challenge.

She headed for the change rooms to stow her bag and change into the navy and grey jumpsuit that was the retrieval team's uniform. As she pushed open the door and stepped around the privacy wall that screened the room from the corridor she was greeted by the sight of semi-naked men. The QMERT building was not overly large and the change rooms were unisex. There was a central changing area divided by lockers with male and female showers and toilets off to each side, which afforded a little privacy but not a lot.

The night-shift team was changing to go home. Sean, the duty doctor, was towelling his hair after his shower; she recognised his stocky build even though his face was hidden under a towel. And Marty, an intensive care paramedic like herself, was already dressed and was pulling his motorbike helmet from a locker.

'Morning, guys,' she said in greeting.

As Marty stepped away from his locker Georgie could see a third man at the end of the room. He was stripped to the waist, his jumpsuit top hanging on his hips. His back was tanned and smooth, muscular and strangely familiar. She could see two dimples at the base of his spine, just above his waistband, teasing her in a repeat performance. Georgie felt her heart rate increase. It couldn't be, could it?

He was turning around now at the sound of her voice and his abdominals rippled down his side. Did she dare move her gaze higher?

She lifted her eyes. Abdominals and then pectoral muscles came into view followed by full lips that were smiling, and above those a narrow, perfectly straight nose and grey eyes. Gunship grey.

Her eyes widened. Standing in front of her, semi-naked, was the cute doctor from yesterday. All that was missing were the Australian flag board shorts.

He was the new doctor?

She could feel her heart beating in her chest and she imagined everyone else could hear it too in the quiet of the room.

'You're Dr Wetherly?' She broke the silence but didn't apologise for bursting in on him while he was changing. Anyone who was at all self-conscious needed to learn to change in the bathrooms. Besides, she'd been treated to the same spectacular view yesterday and looking at this man's semi-naked body she couldn't think of a single reason why he might need to hide away. She swallowed hard, forcing herself to continue speaking. 'I'm Georgie Carides.' She took a deep breath and tried to relax.

'Please, my name's Josh,' he said as he extended his hand and stepped forward to meet her halfway. He was several inches taller than she was and as he closed the distance between them her gaze fell on his bare chest. Again. It took all her self-control to force her gaze up to his face. But even that was no great hardship. His grey eyes were watching her with amusement and she realised he was still holding his hand out, waiting to shake hers, while she stood there, staring at him. She couldn't believe he was the new doctor.

Quickly she clasped his hand, unprepared for the tingle that shot through her. It was the same reaction she'd experienced yesterday when he'd helped her to her feet on the pontoon. It felt as though he'd triggered a connection in her palm that led straight to her chest. Her breathing was shallow and rapid and her heart was racing. Again. Yesterday she'd put the feeling down to the adrenaline that had been flowing through her but that wasn't the case today. This time she knew it was all Dr Wetherly's doing. Josh.

'It's good to see you again,' he said. He appeared completely unflustered, calm and relaxed, behaving as though he was the old hand, while she felt completely disoriented. He let go of her hand and pulled a grey T-shirt over his head, before slipping his arms into the sleeves of his jumpsuit and zipping it closed. 'Small world.'

'Isn't it?' she replied, able to speak now that he'd let go of her and her breathing had returned to normal.

'You guys know each other?' Marty's voice came from behind her, startling her. She'd forgotten Marty and Sean were there.

'We met yesterday—' she told him.

'But I didn't know who she was.'

'You're in good hands, mate. Georgie's a good operator,' Sean said.

'We're going to be working together?' Josh's grey eyes hadn't left her face. He was watching her intently, almost as though he was committing her face to memory. But why he'd need to do that she had no idea. His gaze was intense and focussed but not obtrusive.

She nodded and remembered what had brought her in here. 'I'm the rostered paramedic today and our first call has just come in. A four-month-old girl in respiratory distress—she's in the Tully hospital but they're concerned her condition is deteriorating. Pat, our pilot, is just getting the flight details. We should be ready to take off in about ten.' That was better. If she concentrated on work, she could block out the image of a bare-chested doctor.

'The chopper's restocked and ready to go,' Marty said as he slammed his locker closed. 'Good luck, Josh.'

'Thanks, guys,' Josh replied as the night crew headed out the door. He turned back to Georgie, watching her with his grey eyes. 'So you drew the short straw.'

Georgie could see flashes of silver in Josh's eyes. The colour was striking. She forced herself to concentrate on speaking. Gazing into his eyes was not terribly professional. 'What do you mean?'

'You get to work with the new guy on his first day.'

'I don't mind,' she said with a grin. 'This way I can get you trained up just how I want.' And she didn't mind. She'd seen his CV and she knew he came with an excellent reputation, although she had expected someone older. Josh looked to be in his early thirties, pretty young for a specialist with his credentials, but that didn't bother her because this time she'd be in charge.

In an effort to stop ogling him, she opened her locker and threw her bag inside. She needed to get changed.

'I'll meet you outside,' Josh said as she slipped off her sandals and stowed them in her locker.

She turned to him and nodded. He was standing very close to her; she could have reached out a hand and touched him but she didn't.

As he stepped away she wondered if he was nervous about her disrobing in front of him? Surely not, she thought. He was a doctor, he'd have seen it all before. And he'd seen pretty much all of her just yesterday, she recalled. Her cheeks darkened a little as she remembered what she'd been wearing. Her black bikini hadn't seemed revealing out on the pontoon, not when everyone else had been dressed in a similar fashion, but now she felt her outfit yesterday may shown him more than she would have liked. She was glad of her olive complexion. Hopefully he hadn't noticed the blush staining her cheeks.

'See what other info you can get about the job,' she said

as she tried to quell her embarrassment. 'Louise should have a contact number for someone at Tully hospital.'

He nodded and said, 'No worries, I'll get onto it.'

He turned and left the change rooms, taking the image of Georgie Carides with him. Hearing her voice today and realising they were to be colleagues had been a surprise. A very pleasant surprise, he thought as he entered the corridor. Working with an attractive woman was always a bonus.

He could remember her features. Her face was round and almost perfectly symmetrical. Her dark hair was pulled back from her face and her widow's peak in the centre of her forehead further highlighted the roundness of her face. Her nose was small and straight and her olive skin smooth and tanned. Her almond-shaped eyes were the colour of chocolate and were accentuated by perfectly shaped black eyebrows. The only splash of colour on her face was the red of her lips.

Her natural demeanour seemed to be quite serious and solemn but when she smiled her whole face changed. Unsmiling, she was striking to look at but when she smiled she was beautiful. Her whole face came to life. Her teeth were brilliantly white against her skin tone and her mouth and eyes and eyebrows all lifted. It wasn't just her lips that smiled, it was everything.

He'd wanted to give her some privacy to get changed but it had been an effort to make himself leave the room. The room was unisex but it seemed wrong to stand around and chat to her while she was changing when they'd only just met. But when he recalled what she'd been wearing yesterday he'd been tempted to stay. He'd seen plenty of her in her black bikini and he could recall every detail.

Despite the fact they'd been working to stabilise a patient, he was able to recollect every one of her curves.

The curve of her waist as it had flared out to her hip. The curve of her bottom at the top of her thigh. The curve of her cleavage where the Lycra of her halter-neck top had pushed her breasts together.

He'd known he couldn't stand there talking to her while those images had been flashing through his mind, that wouldn't have been a very professional start to their working relationship. He had no plans to get involved with anyone during his six-month stint; but if there were more women like Georgie Carides in town, his time in Cairns was looking more promising.

Georgie swapped her singlet for a T-shirt with 'Paramedic' stencilled across the back and swapped her skirt for her jumpsuit, before pulling on socks and lacing her boots. Her hands were shaking as she tied her laces. She took a deep breath. Although she'd said she didn't mind working with the new recruit, she was nervous.

But it wasn't Josh that made her nervous. It was her reaction to Josh.

She knew plenty of cute guys but she'd never had the sense that they could affect her physically. She certainly hadn't expected to have such a strong reaction to him. Yesterday she'd put it down to adrenaline but today she knew it was more than that. She'd never experienced an instant, powerful physical attraction to a man and now it had happened twice in a matter of hours. It was unexpected and surprising, pleasant but scary—and it was making her nervous.

She wondered how she was going to be able to work with him. Would they work together smoothly? Would their styles be harmonious? Would she be able to concentrate? Questions buzzed through her mind as she zipped up her overalls. There was no way of knowing all the answers.

She'd have to rely on her skills and expertise. She was an experienced intensive care paramedic; Josh was an experienced emergency specialist. In theory she knew they should be fine. But in reality she was the one with experience in pre-hospital emergency medicine. She was the one who would need to take the lead, which meant she needed to be able to concentrate. Josh was used to working in a well-organised hospital environment and she knew, from her days as an emergency unit nurse, that hospitals were a long way from the chaotic, cramped, hot and dusty locations the emergency retrieval team often worked in. She needed to make sure she kept a cool, calm head. She couldn't afford to be distracted. A lapse in concentration could put her patients at risk. She couldn't afford to get sidetracked by cute doctors.

She closed her locker and headed out.

Josh was waiting. He held the door for her as they left the building and his stride matched hers as they crossed the tarmac and headed for the helicopter.

'Are you feeling okay? Ready for this?' she asked. She wondered if he was nervous, although he certainly didn't look it. He looked completely at ease. If anything, he looked calmer than she felt.

He nodded his head. 'Don't worry. I'm not a complete novice.'

He'd obviously guessed the reason for her question or knew what she was thinking. It would make her job easier if he had a vague idea of what he was in for. 'This isn't your first retrieval?' she queried.

'I've done a couple of transfers before but no primaries and no S&R.'

The most common retrieval for the QMERT team was

an inter-hospital transfer or IHT, which was what they were heading to now. Often, but not always, this was a fairly straightforward exercise and Georgie hoped that would be the case today.

Josh's prior experience of IHTs was a bonus and she was comforted knowing that his confident walk wasn't just window dressing, but, still, it was probably a good thing that their first callout wasn't for a search and rescue.

They were almost at the chopper now and she could see Pat in the pilot's seat, doing his pre-flight checks. Isaac, the air crew officer on duty, was stowing equipment. He closed the final hatch as they approached so it looked as though they were just about ready for take-off. She might just have time to introduce Josh to the rest of the crew but they'd have to check their equipment and run through their procedures in flight. She would have liked a little time to establish some rapport first before they were sent out on a job but, as often happened, the calls dictated their day and they'd just have to get on with it. She prayed it would go smoothly.

'Have you met Pat and Isaac?' she asked.

'Yep, first thing this morning,' he said as he raised a hand in greeting and Isaac nodded an acknowledgement.

'G'day, Georgie, Doc,' Pat greeted them, pointing backwards over his shoulder with his thumb, indicating they should board the chopper.

Georgie let Josh climb in first and she dragged the door shut behind them both, securing it with a flick of the lock. There were four forward-facing seats across the width of the chopper and another two rear-facing seats behind each of the flight deck seats. Josh had taken the third seat across. She could sit beside the door but she preferred one of the middle seats so she slipped into the seat beside him.

'Baptism by fire,' she commented as Josh strapped himself in.

She was relieved to see he was able to shrug into his harness, adjust the straps and snap it closed without difficulty. He seemed comfortable enough in the close confines of the chopper and she knew he'd flown before. Yesterday, in fact. She also knew he would have undergone the escape training course. All the rescue crews had to pass HUET— Helicopter Underwater Escape Training—because a lot of their flying could be over water. So transport wasn't a problem, but what she didn't know was how much medical experience he'd had outside a hospital situation. A few inter-hospital transfers wasn't much.

Pat had started the engine and the rotor blades were spinning. The noise made it impossible to continue a conversation until everyone was wearing headsets. She and Josh both grabbed sets and flicked the comms switch on so they could talk to each other and the air crew.

The chopper was lifting off its trolley. It tilted as it left the ground and the movement threw Georgie against Josh. There wasn't a lot of room to move and she could feel his thigh, firm and muscular, where it rested against hers. His body heat radiated through the fabric of their jumpsuits and into her thigh. She'd never experienced such a visceral reaction to someone before. It was as though her body recognised him despite the fact they were strangers. On some level she knew him. She could feel her knees trembling but she couldn't break the contact. There was nowhere to go.

There wasn't much room to move in the back of the chopper. She often felt as though she only just fitted in between all the medical gear and Josh was several inches taller than she was. He was really jammed in. She was five feet six inches. He'd be six feet at least. The stretcher was locked in place in front of them. It ran the width of the helicopter, from one door to the other, between their seats and those opposite. Josh's knees were crammed between the seat and the stretcher and now he had her practically lying on top of him as well. There was no escape for him, he was well and truly stuck.

'Sorry,' she said through the headset as Pat straightened the chopper and she was able to shift back into an upright position and away from Josh's firm thigh. Perhaps she should have taken a different seat. Squeezed up against him in the back of the chopper, she was a bit too aware of him.

'No worries.' He looked at her and grinned, apparently completely unfazed by the lack of room. Her stomach did a lazy somersault in response to his smile and the look of mischief in his grey eyes made her blush. Her body was overheating, from her thighs to her cheeks. She was stifling and she wondered if she could ask Isaac to turn the air-sconditioning up higher but everyone else looked comfortable enough. She'd just have to put up with feeling as though her cheeks were on fire.

'How did things go with Nigel yesterday?' Josh's voice was cool and relaxed, in sharp contrast to her flustered state. If he'd been surprised to find himself working with her he hadn't shown it, and if their close proximity in the back of the chopper rattled him he wasn't showing any outward signs of that either. Looking at him, one imagined that things were going exactly according to plan. 'Did he get back safely?'

She decided she needed to chill out. She nodded. 'No further dramas,' she said as she filled him in on the outcome of the English tourist's medical emergency from the previous day. 'He was admitted to the Cairns hospital overnight but when I checked on him this morning he'd had an uneventful night and they were expecting to discharge him.'

'The hospital doesn't mind you following up?'

Georgie shook her head. 'As you said, it's a small world.' She shrugged. 'Cairns isn't a big town, everyone seems to know everyone else and that's especially true in the medical field. I think the hospital staff expect us to ring. Most of the QMERT doctors work in the hospital too, and we all like to know what happened to our charges. Will you be doing any shifts at the hospital while you're here?'

He nodded. 'I'll do one or two a week but I'm in Cairns to get as much experience as I can with retrievals, particularly primaries. I imagine it's vastly different from working in a first-class A and E department.'

Georgie finally relaxed. This was her area of expertise and discussing this topic kept her mind focussed. 'You'll find you'll have to strip your medicine back to basics. The principles and the goals are the same, you just won't have the same state-of-the-art equipment at your fingertips or the specialist services you're probably used to. We become everyone from anaesthetist to scout nurse out here.'

'Luckily I like a challenge,' he said. 'So what should we expect when we get to Tully?'

For the remainder of the flight they ran through possible scenarios that might greet them on landing, including the possibility that they might need to intubate the baby. Together they checked the medical kits to make sure they had everything they might need. Small regional hospitals would have standard supplies but they might not always have the less commonly required equipment.

Josh was methodical in his checking but that wasn't surprising. It was a character trait attributable to most of the team—organised, meticulous and logical would describe almost all of them—and by the time they circled over the landing site in Tully Georgie was feeling confident that they would be able to work together comfortably.

She watched out of the window as Pat landed the chopper on the cricket oval. Tully had the highest annual rainfall in Queensland and light drizzle was falling as they climbed out of the helicopter and into the ambulance that was waiting to transport them to the hospital. Within minutes of landing they were walking into the tiny hospital.

The local doctor, who looked like he must only be just out of medical school, gave them a rundown on the patient's condition as they followed him to her bedside. 'Carrie is four months old but she was born eight weeks prem so her adjusted age is nine weeks. She's of Aboriginal descent and this is her third admission for breathing difficulties. The first two admissions we managed to control her and discharge her home with her mum. This time we can't get her oxygen sats up—they're actually falling.'

They were at her bedside now and Georgie and Josh both glanced quickly at the monitors showing Carrie's vital statistics. Her heart rate was 98 beats per minute, low for a baby, and her oxygenation was below 88 per cent. That was dangerously low. The medical staff had a tiny oxygen mask over Carrie's mouth and nose but the baby was listless and her chest was barely moving on inspiration. She was only just breathing.

'What were her oxygen sats when she came in?' Josh asked.

'Ninety two.' Even that was low, and if they hadn't been able to improve her saturation since she got to hospital Carrie was in trouble.

Josh checked the monitor again. Carrie's vital signs were unchanged. 'Right, we need to get some improvement in her vitals. We'll have to intubate to see if we can get her oxygen levels up and we'll have to take her with us back to Cairns. I'll need a straight blade laryngoscope, size one, and a 4.0 endotracheal tube,' Josh told her.

Georgie unzipped the medical kit she'd carried in with her. It included all the items they'd need for intubating an infant. As they'd had no way of knowing whether the hospital would have equipment that was small enough, it had been safest to bring it from the chopper. She passed Josh the items he'd requested and he deftly inserted the tube. Carrie was so sick she didn't resist and the moment Josh was happy with his positioning Georgie taped the tube in place and attached the ambubag. She would need to manually squeeze the air into Carrie's lungs and she'd need to do this all the way back to Cairns. But if it kept Carrie alive she was happy to do it.

As Georgie squeezed the air in they could see the baby's chest rise and fall with each pump. It looked like Josh's intubation had been millimetre perfect. She looked up from the infant and her gaze met his.

She was impressed with his skills—intubating a child of this age was no easy task. 'Nice work,' she said, and was rewarded with one of his heart-stopping smiles. He looked incredibly pleased with himself but not in an arrogant way. His grin was infectious and she had to smile back. Things were good. They'd succeeded. Carrie's oxygen sats and heart rate were climbing. She was stable enough to transport back to Cairns in the chopper. They would manage to keep her alive and get her to specialist care. Their first job together had gone smoothly.

By the time they were ensconced back at the Cairns base after transferring Carrie to the Cairns Hospital, Georgie had almost forgotten it was Josh's first day on the job. She'd ducked across to the Cairns airport terminal building to buy a drink and when she returned she could see Josh chatting to Louise in the comms centre. He was perched

on the edge of the desk, one leg swinging lazily, looking
quite at home.

Georgie walked slowly towards him, taking a moment
to admire the view. His jumpsuit was undone and his grey
T-shirt, the colour an identical match to his eyes, hugged
his chest. She could imagine the ridge of his abdominals
underneath that T-shirt. That image was burned into her
memory from the day before. He was rolling a pen through
his fingers and his biceps flexed with the movement, drawing her eye to his arms. She could remember how his arms
had looked as he'd pulled himself through the water, the
sunlight bouncing off his muscles as he'd swum out to the
reef. He was an impressive sight.

She was within a few metres before he noticed her
but when he looked up he greeted her with a smile. Even
though Louise was sitting right beside him Georgie felt as
though they were the only two in the building. How could
he make her feel as though the rest of the world didn't exist
with just one smile?

She was vaguely aware of the phone ringing as she
smiled back at him. She forced herself to watch Louise answer the telephone, forced herself to concentrate on what
was going on around her.

Louise was scribbling details onto a notepad. 'Male patient, early twenties, he's fallen from the back of a moving
vehicle, severe head and chest injuries, possible spinal injuries. He's on a cattle station about a hundred kilometres
south-west of here.'

Ten minutes later Georgie was back in the helicopter
beside Josh. This time she'd deliberately chosen to leave
an empty seat between them. She needed to concentrate.
They needed to work out their priorities for when they
reached their destination. The anticipated flight time was
thirty to forty minutes and every one of those minutes

would be spent making sure they had a plan of action so they could hit the ground running. A road ambulance was also on its way but travelling on dirt roads it would take closer to ninety minutes for it to reach the accident site. The QMERT team would be the first team on site. This would be Josh's first primary and Georgie needed to make sure they both had a handle on what they might be facing.

Through the headsets she could hear Pat checking the co-ordinates. They'd flown over the rainforest hinterland and the landscape below them was vast, flat and brown. From this height even the trees appeared two-dimensional, flattening into the dirt. Landmarks were few are far between. Thousands upon thousands of empty miles stretched into the distance, broken only by the occasional hill or river. Homesteads blended into the surroundings and were almost impossible to find unless the sun reflected off a shiny tin roof. They were searching for a couple of isolated vehicles on an unmarked dirt road. A task that was near impossible without the right co-ordinates. It was vital that they find the scene of the accident as quickly as possible. Every minute counted.

Pat had established radio contact with the station hands at the accident site and Georgie heard the radio come to life as a voice, crackly with static, filled their headsets.

'Is somebody there?' Despite the static, Georgie could hear the tremor of panic underneath the words. The station hand continued. 'He's not breathing. What do we do?'

'Can you feel a pulse?' Josh was calm under pressure and Georgie relaxed as her confidence in Josh's medical expertise grew. He hadn't put a foot wrong so far.

The reply came back. 'I think so,' said the station hand.

Georgie glanced at Josh. A more definite response would have been good.

'Can you get his mouth open?' Josh continued to give

instructions—keeping them busy would help to rein in any panic. 'Check that he hasn't vomited or that his tongue isn't blocking his airway. If he's vomited, you'll have to try to clear his mouth.'

'His mouth is clear but he's still not breathing.'

'Check his pulse again.'

'I can't feel it!' They could hear panic through the radio.

'You'll have to start CPR,' Josh said. 'Does someone know how to do that?' Despite the urgency of the situation his voice was still calm, his words and tone measured in an effort to decrease any further panic on the ground.

'Yes.'

Pat's voice came through the headsets. 'I can see the vehicles. We'll be on the ground in three minutes.'

'We're almost there,' Georgie emphasised. If they could hear them, if they knew help was close at hand, that would buoy them up. 'Can you hear the chopper?'

'Yes.'

Pat circled the accident. He needed to check the landing site before he guided the chopper down to the ground. As they circled Georgie could see two station hands kneeling in the middle of the dirt track as they performed CPR. Shredded rubber from a blown-out tyre was scattered along the road. The trailer attached to the back of the utility had jackknifed and was resting at an angle. A second utility and a quad bike were standing guard further along the road.

Josh slid the chopper door open the moment Pat gave them the all-clear. Georgie followed him out, running in a crouch to avoid the downdraught from the blades. She carried a medical bag in one hand and an oxygen cylinder in the other. Red dust billowed around them, kicked up by the spinning blades of the chopper. Georgie squinted as she ran in a vain attempt to keep the dust out of her eyes.

As they reached the scene of the accident the two station hands performing CPR stopped, obviously believing that since reinforcements had arrived they weren't required.

'Can you help him? Please, you have to help him,' said one.

'We had a tyre blow-out and Gus was thrown from the back of the ute. I think he landed on his head,' said the other.

'Keep going with the chest compressions while we do a quick assessment,' Josh instructed as he extracted a pair of thin surgical gloves from a pocket in his jumpsuit and pulled them on. 'You're doing fine. Keep going.'

Georgie also pulled on gloves, before kneeling in the red dirt beside Gus. He was lying on his back but there was a depression over his left temple and blood had seeped out of his ear. He must have landed on his head and hit the ground hard enough to fracture his skull. That was not a good start.

Josh was holding Gus's wrist, feeling for a pulse. He looked at Georgie and shook his head. Nothing. He quickly checked inside Gus's mouth, assessing the airway.

'I'll take over now,' he told the station hands, and they didn't argue about relinquishing their role.

Georgie worked with Josh, breathing through a face mask, breathing for Gus, but there was no change. During the flight they'd planned to establish an airway, make sure he had oxygen and get IV access. They hadn't planned on resuscitating him.

Josh continued with chest compressions. Georgie continued breathing. There was no change. He still had no pulse.

'I don't think chest compressions are going to be enough,' Georgie said. It had been more than three minutes and normal CPR procedure was getting them nowhere.

Josh nodded. 'I'll draw up adrenaline.'

On the assumption that doing something was better than nothing and knowing that chest compressions were more important than breathing, Georgie continued pumping Gus's chest while Josh searched through the medical kit. He drew up a syringe and felt for a space between the ribs before he pierced the left side of Gus's chest wall with the needle and depressed the plunger, injecting adrenaline directly into the heart muscle.

Georgie held her breath. Waiting. Her fingers on Gus's carotid artery.

There was a flutter of a pulse.

'We've got him.'

'Get some oxygen into him.'

Georgie started breathing air into Gus again while Josh pulled an endotracheal tube and laryngoscope from the kit. It looked as though they'd be doing another intubation.

Georgie did two breaths. She had Gus's head tipped back slightly and the fingers of her right hand were under his chin, resting over his carotid pulse. His pulse was barely evident. She stopped her breaths and shifted her fingers, searching for a stronger pulse. She couldn't find it.

'Josh, I've lost the pulse.'

CHAPTER THREE

'No, DAMN it.' Josh turned away from the kit and back to Gus, kneeling over him, checking for a pulse. He trusted Georgie's skill but he needed to double check for his own peace of mind. There was nothing. 'Resuming CPR,' he said as he began chest compressions again in a vain attempt to restart Gus's heart. If the adrenaline hadn't worked he knew it was unlikely anything else he did would have an effect, but he had to do something.

He worked hard for another minute. Another sixty compressions. There was no change.

He felt Georgie's hands over his.

'Josh, stop. His injuries are too massive. He's not going to make it.'

He didn't stop. He couldn't stop. He couldn't lose a patient today. He was in Cairns to get some pre-hospital experience but it was expected that he would be demonstrating his medical skills and performing well. Losing a patient on his first day was not part of his agenda.

He brushed Georgie's hands away and continued. Sixty-one, sixty-two. Another sixty and then sixty more.

'Josh, it's too late,' Georgie insisted. Her hands were back on top of his, stilling his movements. 'It's been too long.'

He listened then. He sat back on his heels, his hands

resting on Gus's chest, Georgie's hands covering his. He could feel her hands shaking. Or maybe it was his. He couldn't tell.

'We've done everything we can,' she told him.

He looked at her and he could see the bleakness of his own expression reflected in her chocolate-brown eyes. He could see she knew exactly how he felt.

'I know,' she said. 'We want to save them all but sometimes we can't. It's just the way it is.'

He rubbed his eyes and the latex of the gloves pulled across his eyelids. He stripped the gloves from his hands and tossed them onto the pile of discarded face masks and syringe wrappings, the detritus of the action. He breathed deeply. He could smell dust and heat and perspiration. He exhaled loudly and breathed in again and this time he could smell honey and cinnamon, an already familiar scent, and he knew it came from Georgie. Sweet and fresh, it competed with the smell of defeat.

The other station hands had moved back, giving Georgie and Josh some room. He looked up at them. They were gathered together, supporting each other. They knew the battle had been lost. He stood and went to them.

'I'm sorry. His injuries were too extensive. Even if you'd been closer to help, if we'd been able to get here faster, even then I doubt there's anything we could have done.' He knew his words would be of little consolation but he didn't want them blaming themselves or wondering if they could have done more. Today was just one day out of hundreds just like it. There would have been many times when someone had travelled in the back of the ute without incident but today Gus's luck had run out.

They stood in silence in the heat of the late afternoon. The bush was still, there was not a breath of wind and even the birds were quiet. Josh knew it was only the heat that was keeping the wild parrots mute but it felt like their silence was in deference to the situation.

In the distance he heard the sound of a vehicle approaching. First one. Then another.

An ambulance pulled up, followed by a police car, their distinctive markings almost obliterated by red dust.

Josh spoke to the policeman. He spoke to the paramedics. He was operating on autopilot. Gus was pronounced dead. His body would be put into the ambulance and transported to the morgue. There was nothing left for him to do here.

Pat and Isaac were helping Georgie load the equipment back into the chopper. He left the police and paramedics to finish up and went to help his team.

'Sorry, mate, tough day,' Pat said as Josh returned to the chopper. Josh appreciated his sentiment. Pat hadn't exaggerated the situation neither had he downplayed it, he'd said all that was necessary with those few words.

Josh climbed into the chopper and started securing the medical kits into position. The empty stretcher in front of his knees was a bleak reminder of what had happened. He unclipped one kit from a seat and strapped it onto the stretcher instead, partially covering the empty expanse. That was better. Less confronting.

The chopper lifted off the ground. As they banked to the east Josh could see the accident scene below them. The paramedics were closing the doors at the rear of the ambulance. The police were still speaking with the station hands. He closed his eyes, blocking out the tableau.

He should be saving lives in a big city hospital, with specialist help at hand and state-of-the-art equipment in place. He should be in control, not shooting adrenaline into a young man's heart on a dirt track out the back of beyond. What a bloody mess.

What the hell was he doing here?

He kept his eyes closed until he knew they were far away from the cattle station. Far away from the ambulance that held Gus's body. When he opened his eyes he kept his face turned to the window, his head turned away from Georgie. He didn't want to make eye contact. He didn't want to have a conversation. Not about what had transpired out in the red dirt. He knew he would have to think about it at some point. He'd have to fill in a medical report. A death certificate. But he didn't want to discuss it yet.

Georgie was quiet. Perhaps she was lost in her own thoughts. Whatever the reason, he was relieved she didn't seem to need to talk. Most women he knew would be attempting to have some sort of discussion, even if it was about nothing. The majority seemed to think that silence was there to be broken. He was pleased Georgie wasn't one of them.

The silence wasn't awkward. He knew she was there and knowing he wasn't alone was somehow comforting. He couldn't see her but he could feel her presence. He could smell her perfume, cinnamon and honey, warm and sweet.

He let the silence continue for the entire trip and it was after six in the evening and night had fallen before Pat started to guide the chopper down to the airport. In the distance Josh could see the lights of Cairns. They were almost home.

Cairns was a beautiful city by day and even more so by night, but it wasn't enough to lighten his mood. They were on their way home while Gus was on his way to the morgue. A young life extinguished. He felt the tension of the day in his shoulders. He sighed, a long, audible exhalation, trying to release the strain in his muscles.

He felt Georgie's hand on his. Her fingers entwined with

his in response to his sigh. Her hand connected him to the living. He knew her gesture was meant to give comfort and the warmth of her hand did exactly that. It warmed his entire body. He hadn't realised he was feeling cold but he was now aware of heat suffusing through him, bringing him out of his fog.

'Are you okay?' Georgie asked.

'I will be.'

'We did everything we could,' she said.

'Are you sure?' Today's events made him question his skills. He liked being in control of situations and, while he realised that was sometimes going to be difficult out in the middle of nowhere, what if things went wrong because of him? What if he didn't have what it took to work in this environment? 'It's our job to save lives. I'm no good to anyone if I can't do that.' What if he didn't have what it took to run an emergency department in a big city hospital?

'You said it yourself,' Georgie reminded him, 'Gus's injuries were too extensive. Even if we'd been able to reach him sooner, the outcome wouldn't have been any different. There was nothing else we could do.'

Losing a patient was never easy but Josh knew Georgie was right. He'd said those exact words to the other station hands. He and Georgie had done everything they could. But would others see it that way? He needed to prove himself. He needed to show he could handle working in this environment and losing a patient on day one wasn't an auspicious start.

He'd lost patients before, working in A and E it was inevitable, but today had felt very personal. He knew it was because it had been up to him and Georgie. A team of two when he was used to a team of three or four or ten or however many it took, and having greater numbers took the intimacy out of it. It didn't remove the responsibility but it did lessen the sense of failure.

As Pat guided the chopper down onto the landing trolley Georgie gave his fingers a gentle squeeze. 'Today was a bad day. They're not all like this. It'll be all right.'

He hoped like hell she was right.

Pat switched the engines off. The blades continued their revolutions but even the rhythmic thump-thump of the spinning blades didn't disguise the silence that enveloped the team within the chopper. Georgie unclipped her harness and Josh followed suit.

Georgie leant forwards between the pilots' seats. 'Dinner at my place when we're finished here?'

Josh heard her issue an invitation to Pat and Isaac. He was strangely disappointed not to be included yet there was no rule that said he should be. He was the new kid in town.

Their shift was over but it was their job to restock the supplies ready for the next crew and he knew following a routine would help to focus his thoughts. He got busy unloading the medical equipment they'd used and pretended he hadn't heard Georgie's words.

Georgie climbed out of the chopper and then turned and reached for the kitbags, preparing to carry them back to the QMERT building. 'The guys are coming back to my house for a feed. Would you like to join us?'

Yes, he thought. 'No,' he said, before thinking he'd better elaborate. 'Thanks, but you're not expecting an extra mouth to feed. I'll grab some dinner at the hotel.' He didn't like to feel as though he was imposing.

'Don't be silly. I wasn't expecting to feed Pat and Isaac either but we have a rule that we always have a meal or a drink together if we've had a bad day, kind of an unofficial debriefing session, and we certainly can't let you finish your very first day with us like this. There's nothing worse than going home alone with just your thoughts.'

'Are you sure?' After the day they'd had the prospect of his empty hotel room didn't appeal, neither did the idea of dinner for one in the hotel's restaurant.

'Positive.'

An evening in Georgie's company would be better than being alone in his hotel room. Looking at her now, even though she was wearing her QMERT overalls, which pretty well covered every square inch of her skin, he could picture her as she had been yesterday, in her black bikini, her olive skin darkly tanned, her petite figure perfectly proportioned. It seemed wrong, given the circumstances, to have that vision of her in his head, but he couldn't shake it. Perhaps he should take himself back to his hotel, he didn't need any distractions. But even as he had that thought he heard himself accepting her invitation. 'What can I bring?'

'Nothing. I've got a fridge full of food, I'm always feeding people.'

'She's not kidding, mate,' Isaac interrupted. 'Georgie's a great cook. Don't ever pass up one of her invitations.'

'I'm Greek,' she said with a shrug. 'It's what we do.' She smiled at him and her face lit up. It wasn't just her mouth that smiled, it was everything. Her smile had the power to make him forget about the day they'd had, just for a moment, and he knew that if he spent more time with her he'd eventually be able to forget the day for longer than a moment. And that had to be a good thing. He didn't want to forget about the boy they hadn't been able to save, but he did want something else to think about and he was more than happy for that to be Georgie.

'I'm going to have a quick shower here and then you can follow me to my place,' she said. 'Have you got a car?'

He nodded and twenty minutes later he was following

her little red car through the streets of Cairns and trying to block out the image in his head of Georgie in the shower. In his mind he could see the water running down between her breasts, her skin glistening wet, slippery and cool. Her long, dark hair was loose, slick and heavy hanging down between her shoulder blades, drawing his eye to the curve of her waist and buttocks. He told himself he was being ridiculous. He hadn't even seen her hair loose, it had been tied back both yesterday and today. He shook his head as he remonstrated silently with himself. He'd known her for barely twenty-four hours, he had to work with her, he had a job to do, he had no plans on starting a relationship. He pictured her in her black swimming costume instead. It was a little bit more demure, but not by much, but at least that picture enabled him to concentrate on navigating the streets.

He pulled into the driveway behind Georgie. Her house was a typical Queenslander. Constructed of weatherboard and raised off the ground, a section of the downstairs had been built in but the main rooms were upstairs. He followed her up the stairs and across the deck into the kitchen. She'd restrained her hair in a plait after her shower and it swung from side to side as she climbed the stairs, catching his eye and reinforcing the fact that her hair was tamed and not streaming down her back. His disappointment was almost palpable.

The house looked far too big for one person. When she'd said earlier that there was nothing worse than going home alone with your thoughts, he'd assumed she'd been speaking from experience. He'd assumed she was single. But perhaps he'd taken her words out of context, perhaps she'd been talking about him. Did she have someone waiting for her here? 'Are you sharing the house?' he asked.

She shook her head. 'No. I rented a large house because

I knew my family would all be visiting and would need somewhere to stay.'

'Visiting from where?'

'Melbourne. I'm from down south originally. I'm almost ten months into a twelve-month secondment to the Queensland Ambulance Service,' she said as she started pulling things out of the fridge. 'In the time I've been here three of my brothers and my parents have all visited. My last lot of visitors headed off to Port Douglas this morning. So you see, I can't share a house with anyone, it wouldn't be fair to subject them to my family.'

Hearing about the number of brothers she had distracted him from the realisation that Georgie wasn't from Queensland and she wasn't going to be here for much longer. 'Three of your brothers! How many have you got?'

'Only four.' She laughed and he knew she was laughing at him. The expression on his face was probably pretty funny. But he was happy to be laughed at, he thought as the sound resonated through him and lifted his spirits. 'I take it from your expression you don't have a big family?' she said as she passed him the salad ingredients, which he put on the counter.

'No, just one brother,' he replied. Who he didn't want to talk about. 'What can I do?' he asked, effectively changing the topic.

She passed him two beers. 'Can you open these for us? And there should be some onions in the pantry,' she said, waving her hand at a cupboard on the opposite side of the kitchen. 'You could chop them for me.' She pulled some meat from the fridge. 'I'll barbecue this. We can have yiros.'

Josh found a bag of onions and by the time he'd turned around from the cupboard Georgie had piled flatbreads next to the lamb and vegetables and had chopping boards, knives and beer glasses at the ready.

Josh twisted the tops of the beers and poured them into two cold, frosted glasses.

'Cheers,' he said as he handed one glass to Georgie.

He sipped his beer as he started chopping the onions. The cold lager quenched his thirst and he could feel the stress of the day ease slightly.

Georgie had slipped out to the deck to light the barbecue but when she returned he had more questions for her. 'What number are you in your family?'

'I'm the baby. And the only girl.'

'Does that make you a tomboy or a pampered princess?'

She picked up the tray of meat and looked at him with one eyebrow raised. 'I'm an intensive care paramedic, you tell me.'

'Tomboy, I guess.'

'You'd think so, wouldn't you? But I wasn't a very good tomboy. My brothers are a lot older than me and I was a bit...' she paused briefly, searching for the right word '...protected. Not pampered, mind, just discouraged from following in the boys' footsteps.'

'How much younger are you?' he asked as he traipsed to and from the kitchen to the deck carrying platters, crockery and food.

'Stephen is the closest in age to me, he's thirty-four so seven years older, the twins are ten years older than me and Tony's two years older than them.'

He couldn't imagine coming from such a large family but he supposed in many ways she'd been like an only child. Her youngest brother, Stephen, was the same age as him and he was keen to know more about her band of brothers, and about her, but the arrival of Pat and Isaac changed the direction of the conversation.

Pat opened more beers for everyone and proposed a toast. 'To Gus.'

They each raised their drink in respect.

'I hope some of his dreams came true. I hope he lived a good life,' Georgie said, touching her glass to Pat's before she turned back to the barbecue to baste the meat.

The aroma of garlic, onions and lamb teased Josh's sense of smell and his stomach rumbled. He moved closer to the barbecue, closer to Georgie, and leant on the railing of the deck.

'Did anyone find out anything more about him?' Josh asked. 'Did he have a wife? Kids?'

Georgie opened her mouth but hesitated before speaking and he saw her flick a glance in Isaac's direction. 'He got married about three months ago, one of the other station hands did tell me that, but I don't know anything further.'

'Poor devil,' Pat chimed in.

'I can't imagine what I would do if I lost Lani like that,' Isaac commented.

'Isaac is getting married in a few weeks and Pat is a jaded, cynical divorcé,' Georgie explained for his benefit.

'And what about you?' Josh asked Georgie. She'd said she lived alone but that didn't mean she didn't have a boyfriend somewhere. In Melbourne, if not here.

Pat laughed. 'It'd be a brave man to take Georgie on,' he said.

'Why is that?'

'She's got four older brothers, that's a lot of pressure for a potential partner to handle,' Pat explained.

'Why do you think I've run away from home?' Georgie asked as she scooped the cooked lamb off the barbecue and onto a platter. 'Isaac's fiancée is a nurse at the hospital.' She turned to Isaac as she placed the platter on the table.

'Josh is going to be doing some shifts there while he's in Cairns, you'll have to introduce him to Lani.'

Josh wondered at the very deliberate change in the direction of the conversation but he had no opportunity to question Georgie as she'd deftly shifted the focus onto him.

'You'll be working in A and E?' Isaac asked. When Josh nodded he continued. 'Lani's in ICU. Let me know when you're doing your first shift and I'll get her to introduce you to a few people.'

'Thanks, mate, I'd appreciate that.'

The conversation slowed as they all assembled and ate the yiros. Eating gave Josh a reason to stop talking, he didn't want to volunteer too much information. It was better to let them all think he was happy to be here and had joined their team at his own instigation. And by the end of the night he found he was actually enjoying their company. They were an easy group, welcoming and relaxed. Perhaps the next six months wouldn't be too onerous.

Especially not if he got to work with Georgie, he thought. His gaze fell on her again as she emerged from the kitchen, carrying yet another platter. Her plait fell over her shoulder as she bent forward to put the plate on the table and Josh had a wild urge to pull the elastic band from the end of her hair and loosen it. She straightened and flicked her plait back behind her shoulder and he had to be content with catching a whiff of her scent as she sat beside him. Cinnamon and honey.

'Who would like coffee and baklava?' she offered.

Baklava. That's exactly what she smelt like. But Josh knew the fragrance he could detect was Georgie and not dessert. He'd been aware of it all day.

Everybody requested dessert and Isaac had several pieces. 'Excellent, thanks, Georgie,' Isaac said as he popped another piece into his mouth.

'I've got a confession to make,' she said. 'My sister-in-law made this.'

'I don't care who made it, it's delicious,' Pat said, his mouth full of the sweet pastry.

Isaac finished another piece and drained his coffee as he stood up. 'Sorry, George, I've got to run. I'm off to collect Lani, she was doing a late shift.'

Pat followed suit. 'I'd better get going too. I'm flying you guys again tomorrow, I need to get a decent sleep.'

Josh stood too but after his initial hesitation to join them for dinner he was now reluctant for the evening to end. His lonely hotel room held even less appeal now than it had a few hours earlier.

'It's okay, Josh, stay and finish your coffee,' Georgie said as she put another piece of baklava on his plate. 'Eat that too 'cos the rest will get sent home with Pat.'

'You're a saint, Georgie,' Pat said as he kissed her cheek.

As Georgie wrapped up the remainder of the baklava and said goodnight to Pat and Isaac, Josh found himself wondering if Pat wasn't just a little bit enamoured with Georgie. If that was the case he then wondered how Georgie felt about Pat. Not that it was any of his business, he thought as he ate another piece of baklava. 'That dinner was delicious, compliments to you and your sister-in-law,' he said when Georgie returned to the table. 'Have you got as many sisters-in-law as you have brothers?'

'Nearly. Alek, one of the twins, isn't married yet.'

'Have all the sisters-in-law visited?'

Georgie shook her head. 'One to come.'

'So you've run away from home and almost all your family have followed.'

Georgie laughed and once again Josh found the sound of her laughter comforting. 'I didn't really run away. Not from my brothers anyway, they're harmless enough.'

He wondered what her reason for being here was. Something in her tone suggested there was more to the story than she was volunteering. What wasn't she telling him?

'So what are you doing here?' he asked.

'Same as you I guess, I came for the experience. In Victoria most people are within reach of a regular ambulance service so there's not nearly as much work for the helicopter team. It's mostly inter-hospital transfers and the occasional multiple-vehicle country accident. The distances in Queensland are so much bigger and the demand for the helicopter units is so much higher I can get twice as much experience in half the time up here,' she explained.

'So this is a career move for you? Work was the draw card?'

Georgie wondered how she should answer that question. The simple answer would be yes, but the honest answer was that she was escaping. Technically, she wasn't running away. She was planning on returning to Melbourne but she had needed to escape for a while. To escape from the life that was being mapped out for her. From her parents or, more correctly, from her parents' plans for her. All her life she'd played the part of dutiful daughter, baby sister or perfect girlfriend and she wanted, needed, a chance to find out who she was while she was on her own, away from the expectations of her family. 'Yes. It really is about maximising my experience in the shortest timeframe.' She went with an edited version of the truth. He didn't need to know more than that.

'And when you're not working? What do you do then?'

'When I'm not being a tour guide and chauffeur for my relatives, you mean?'

He nodded. 'What do you do in your spare time? You were out on the reef yesterday. Do you dive?'

'Was that really only yesterday?' Georgie shook her head in disbelief. It felt like days ago. 'That was me playing tour guide. My brother, Stephen, and his wife, were visiting. They are divers so I went out to spend the day with them. I was actually supposed to do an introductory dive but I chickened out. I had grand intentions of trying new things while I was here in Cairns but it turns out I'm not as adventurous as I thought.'

Josh laughed and his grey eyes flashed silver with amusement. 'Life is for living. You've got to experience it.'

'Believe me, as a paramedic I've seen what can go wrong when people try to experience things. I've decided I'd rather live to a ripe old age.'

'Come on, you must have done something slightly adventurous. You're a Victorian, you must have tried skiing, or have you done any travelling? Bungee-jumping in New Zealand perhaps?'

'I've been to Greece but that's about it,' Georgie said. 'Do you count being lowered from the helicopter by a winch as adventurous?'

'That's a good start.'

'A start! All right, tell me about your wild escapades.'

'What would you like to hear about, diving with Great White sharks in South Africa or heli-skiing in France?'

Georgie could feel herself growing pale just at the thought of those activities. Working as a paramedic, and prior to that as an emergency nurse, Georgie had seen the results of reckless behaviour too many times. There were some things she had no intention of attempting. 'You win. I'm not about to try to compete with that. Don't you realise life is precious?'

'Of course I do, I just don't think we should take it too seriously. We have to enjoy it. I went through a bit of a stage where I tried anything and everything with little regard for safety, but I've calmed down in my old age. Now I look for something middle of the road, somewhere between mundane and illegal but still fun. Could I tempt you to try something like that with me?'

Josh was grinning at her, his expression full of mischief, and Georgie could just imagine what trouble he'd got up to at times. All sorts of ideas flashed through her mind, most of which she wasn't about to share with him, but if he thought he could get her to agree to something dangerous just by smiling at her, he was mistaken. 'Like what?' she countered.

'Sky-diving?'

Not what she'd had in mind. She shook her head. 'No.' Definitely not.

'Scuba-diving?'

'Mmm, unlikely.' She'd hardly jumped at the chance to try diving yesterday. Josh might fancy his chances but she thought it was doubtful.

'White-water rafting?'

That sounded a little better. 'Maybe.'

'Excellent. A definite maybe!'

'That's a "maybe" maybe,' she said with a smile that morphed into a yawn.

'Okay, I'll work on your objections when I see you next but now it looks like it's time to call it a day.' He pushed his chair back from the table and stretched. His T-shirt rode up above the waistband of his jeans, exposing inches of toned abdominal muscles right before Georgie's eyes. She was tempted to reach out and touch him. She could remember how his thigh had felt when she'd fallen against him in the chopper earlier today, hard and warm and muscular, and she wanted to know if the rest of him felt the same. But while she was resisting reaching out to him he had lowered his arms and stepped away to push his chair under the table. 'Thank you for your invitation. You were right. I didn't want to spend the evening alone.'

She'd missed her opportunity. Not that she would have dared take it. Josh was a colleague and that meant he was out of bounds.

'And no one expected you to. I'm glad you came,' she said, remembering just in time to respond to his thanks as she stood and accompanied him down the stairs that led from the deck to the driveway.

'Can I repay your hospitality?' he asked. 'Can I take you out to dinner? I'd offer to cook but until I move into the apartment the hospital has organised for me I'm afraid the meal will have to come from someone else's kitchen.'

'I'd like that, thank you,' she said, meaning every word.

Josh pressed the button on his keyring and his car beeped as it unlocked. 'I'll see you tomorrow, then, and we'll make a date.' He opened the door but before he got in he leant down and kissed her cheek. His lips were soft and warm. She closed her eyes as his lips brushed her skin. 'Thanks again.'

It was just a thank-you kiss, she told herself as she watched him reverse out of her driveway. And his invitation to dinner was just a thank you as well. Josh was a colleague. And that was all he could be.

CHAPTER FOUR

JOSH was the first person she saw when she walked into the QMERT building the following morning. Through the viewing window in the wall of the comms room she could see him sitting at a desk, concentrating intently, not aware of her entrance at all. His head was tilted at an angle, he was propping his forehead in one hand, his elbow resting on the tabletop, and his biceps were bulging from the sleeve of his grey T-shirt. She could see the top of his head, his sandy blond hair sticking up in all directions; his face was obscured but she'd seen enough to know it was him. Seen enough to make her pulse race.

She wasn't used to this strange feeling of impatient excitement. She'd spent her life surrounded by men. Growing up, the house had been full of her brothers and their friends and now at work she was often the solitary female so she knew there was nothing special about men in general. She was used to all male company. They were just people. She'd never felt confused by them. Until now.

That was what was unfamiliar to her. Her reaction to him, the strong attraction she felt for someone she'd only known one day. Someone who, for all intents and purposes, was a perfect stranger. But he was someone who could set her skin on fire with one touch. Someone who could send her pulse soaring with one look. While there might be nothing special about most men, she wasn't sure if that description could be applied to Josh. Something about him was playing havoc with her senses. Something about him was constantly drawing her focus and she'd never felt so connected to someone she barely knew.

As she entered the comms room he dropped his pen onto the paperwork spread in front of him and rocked back on his chair. He ran both hands through his hair, a look of exasperation on his face.

'Good morning,' she said.

Georgie was pleased to see his look of frustration was replaced with a smile when he saw her. 'Hi. You have perfect timing,' he said as he retrieved his pen and pushed the papers across the desk towards her. 'Could you read through this and make sure I haven't missed anything?'

She glanced down at the paperwork. It was Josh's report regarding the cattle-station accident and Gus's death. That was what was bothering him. She wasn't surprised. Completing the form would mean reliving yesterday's events. It was a tough thing to do. 'How are you feeling?' she asked.

'I'll feel better once we get the autopsy results.'

'We did everything we could, Josh.'

'I know. I'd just like to have it confirmed by the pathologist's report.'

She sat at the desk and Josh moved his chair closer to hers, looking over her shoulder as she read through his words. He smelt clean and fresh, like peppermint, and she had to concentrate hard to make sense of the report. It was no easy task, reading with an audience, especially one who could distract her just with his scent. Eventually she finished. 'It looks right to me. Shall I witness it for you?'

'Thanks.' Josh passed her his pen and Georgie's heart

skipped a beat as his fingers brushed hers. Once again, just the briefest touch was enough to send a frisson of energy through her.

Get it together, she reprimanded herself. He's just a colleague. No different from anyone else. And she didn't want him to be any different. She didn't want to be attracted to someone. She wanted a break from all that.

But she had to concentrate hard to block him out as they were strapped side by side into the chopper, flying to Ingham for their first job of the day, a little later.

They were on their way to another inter-hospital transfer. The patient, Kevin, had come off second best when his motorbike had slammed into a tree on a wet road. He'd sustained multiple injuries, including spinal fractures and bilateral rib fractures, and his broken ribs had resulted in a flail chest and a haemothorax. He had chest drains in but he was critically injured and needed to be in a specialist unit. Ingham's small hospital wasn't equipped to manage his injuries.

Josh had completed his assessment of Kevin but as they started making preparations for the transfer, Georgie hesitated. Something didn't feel right and she knew neither of them needed another drama today. Not after yesterday's tragedy.

'Wait. I think we should intubate him before we move him to the chopper,' she said.

'Because?' Josh queried.

Because she couldn't cope with a second fatality on their shift in as many days. Because it was better to be safe than sorry.

'It's a two-hundred-kilometre flight back to Cairns,' she said. 'We'll be in the air for over an hour. If something goes wrong en route, we'll either need to land or try to intubate in mid-air. I don't know about you but I'd rather do that here.' In her opinion, intubating Kevin now would decrease the risk involved with the transfer and increase his chances of survival.

'Sounds reasonable.' Much to her relief, Josh didn't debate her suggestion. 'I'll give him a light anaesthetic so he doesn't resist the intubation.'

Once again, Josh made the sometimes difficult task of intubating a patient appear straightforward and Kevin was sedated, intubated and ready to transfer within a few minutes.

But ten minutes into the flight their treatment plan started to unravel. A high-pitched beeping rent the air. Something had set off the peak pressure alarm on the ventilator.

Georgie was closest to the machine. She checked the monitor. It was possible that Kevin wasn't getting enough oxygen. But the screen showed oxygenation at ninety five per cent, blood pressure 120/60. Both figures were falling but the machine looked to be working okay. It meant something was going wrong at Kevin's end.

'The ventilator's working—check the drain,' she said to Josh as she reset the alarm.

Josh was sitting opposite her and the chest drain was by his knee. He moved it. Nothing flowed out of it.

'It's either blocked or he's got a repeat haemothorax.'

The drain didn't appear blocked but a build-up of air or blood in Kevin's chest cavity could put pressure on the tube and prevent it from draining.

Josh removed a scalpel from the open medical kit beside him. The incision for the chest drain was visible on Kevin's chest wall above his arm. Josh enlarged the incision and inserted a finger to clear any obstruction in the chest cavity, but still nothing flowed through the drain.

The peak pressure alarm sounded again. The high-pitched noise was loud and intrusive, even against the background noise of the helicopter.

'Oxygen sats at ninety-four. His lips look blue,' Georgie reported. Kevin's condition was deteriorating before their eyes.

'I'll top up his anaesthetic,' Josh said. 'If he's starting to wake, he could be resisting the tube and that could set off the alarm.'

Georgie reset the alarm again while Josh topped up the anaesthetic.

'Pupils equal and reacting.' Georgie checked Kevin's eyes. She couldn't work out what was going on. Kevin was under anaesthetic and he hadn't lapsed into a coma, but his oxygen sats weren't improving and his lips were still blue. The drain wasn't flowing. Nothing was working. What had Josh said? 'Life is for living. You've got to experience it.' If they could save a life today, she was prepared to broaden her horizons and try a new experience. She was prepared to make a deal. 'If we get him through this, I'll go on one of your adrenaline-junkie escapades with you.' The words were out of her mouth before she could really think about what she was saying.

Josh finished injecting the anaesthetic into Kevin's IV and looked across at her with a raised eyebrow. For a moment she thought he was going to give her a chance to take back her impetuous offer but no such luck. 'You're on,' he said.

He looked at the monitor and then back down at Kevin. His concentration was unwavering. 'Right, what's going on with you, mate? I'm going to have to open him up some more.' Kevin's arm was lying alongside his chest. It hadn't prevented Josh from enlarging the incision slightly but he was going to need better access now if he needed to be more invasive. He moved Kevin's arm away from his body and with that slight movement blood began to gush through the drain. 'Would you look at that?'

Georgie could hear the relief in Josh's voice and saw him visibly relax into his seat as he checked the monitor. She followed his gaze. Kevin's blood pressure had quickly risen to 135/70 and his oxygenation was rising too. It looked like the crisis was over but she could still feel the adrenaline coursing through her veins. 'That was close.'

'We were not going to have a repeat of yesterday.' Josh replied. 'Not if I could help it.'

Georgie hoped Josh wasn't going to beat himself up over Gus's death yesterday. Thank goodness they'd managed to pull Kevin through. 'This is a tough gig, Josh. We're often working in difficult conditions with very little information. Things go wrong but luckily for Kevin things weren't worse.'

'Things came pretty close.'

'Yes,' Georgie admitted. 'But he'll make it, thanks to you.'

Josh still didn't look convinced.

Georgie frowned. 'Is something else the matter?'

Josh ran his hands through his hair as he let out a loud sigh. 'I'm not here for the experience alone,' he said. 'I do need exposure to pre-hospital medicine but I also need to show I have the necessary skills for this work. When I leave Cairns I'm hoping to return to Brisbane General as the head of emergency medicine but I was advised to have a stint up here first. I need to show I can work under this kind of pressure. I need to show I can save lives out of a hospital setting. I've already lost one patient and I don't intend to make a habit of it. I need to show I can do this.'

'Don't be too hard on yourself,' Georgie tried to reassure him. 'You've done an amazing job today. Kevin chose to ride a motorbike in wet and slippery conditions and you've saved his life. It's a good day.'

Josh was nodding. 'You're right. We won this round, didn't we?'

'We sure did,' she agreed. 'But being in this job and seeing some of the odd decisions people make is why I don't like taking chances.' Now that the drama was over she'd forgotten about the deal she'd made.

'Oh, no. You're not getting out of it that easy.' Josh grinned at her and his grey eyes flashed silver with humour. 'You have a choice to make. Sky-diving, scuba-diving or white-water rafting.'

Inadvertently she'd distracted Josh from his sombre thoughts but now she wondered why on earth she'd made such an impetuous call. 'There's no way I'm voluntarily jumping out of an aeroplane,' she said.

'Okay. On the water or under the water? What's your preference?'

It didn't look as though he was going to let her off the hook. 'Can we toss a coin?'

Josh patted the pockets of his jumpsuit. 'Don't seem to have one on me.' He grabbed an unopened syringe from the medical kit and hid it behind his back. 'Choose a hand,' he told her. 'If you get the syringe, you'll have to learn to scuba-dive.'

She took a deep breath and pointed. 'Left.'

Josh brought his hands to the front and opened both fists. The syringe was in his left palm. Georgie's heart plummeted. Seeing that syringe reinforced that she really didn't want to try diving.

'Can we try two out of three?' she pleaded.

Josh grinned at her. 'I guess that means you'd rather go rafting.'

She nodded. 'I guess so.' As much as she would like to

get out of the deal, she supposed going white-water rafting was a small price to pay in exchange for Kevin's life. And if she got to spend the day with Josh, she wasn't really about to complain.

A few days passed without Josh mentioning white-water rafting and Georgie allowed herself to hope for a reprieve. Today it looked as though she was still in luck. Josh was doing his first shift at the hospital, which meant he wasn't at QMERT reminding her about rafting. But it also meant she was working with Sean.

It was her first shift without Josh since he'd come to Cairns and it was strange to be working with Sean again. He was a funny guy with a dry sense of humour and Georgie enjoyed working with him. He and his wife and two young children had emigrated from the UK. He was a good doctor but Georgie missed Josh. She told herself it was because they'd developed a good working rapport but she knew that was only half the truth. She and Sean had a good rapport too, yet she hadn't missed him when their shifts hadn't coincided.

She enjoyed Josh's company and the buzz she got from being near him, and that element of excitement was missing today. Normally she would have thought her job was exciting enough but since Josh had arrived that level had increased. Even sitting in the lunchroom was more interesting when Josh was there.

She was flicking through the local paper when Louise's voice came through the intercom.

'Georgie, are you there? I've got Josh on the line for you.'

She hurried across the room to pick up the phone. She could feel her heart beating a little bit faster and as she picked up the receiver she felt herself panting. She was out of breath and feeling like she'd sprinted one hundred metres instead of just taking a few steps across the room. She breathed in deeply before she spoke. She didn't want to sound breathless.

'Hi, how's your day going?' she asked.

'Hi, yourself. It's okay, actually,' he replied. 'It hasn't been too busy. I had time to pop in and visit little Carrie to see how she's going.'

Georgie remembered the baby they'd brought back from Tully hospital on their first job together, and wondered if that was the reason for Josh's call. 'How is she?'

'She's doing well. She's had lots of tests done, there's nothing sinister, her chest is obviously just a weakness, most likely a result of her being a premmie, but her mum is expecting the all-clear from the specialist and she'll be taking her home soon.'

'That's good news. It sounds like you're finding your feet.'

'I'm doing okay, but I'm missing you guys. I feel like I'm missing out on the action.' For a brief moment Georgie thought he was feeling the same as her, off balance, but his voice sounded as though he was smiling and she could imagine his grey eyes sparkling as he spoke to her.

'You're not missing anything. It's quiet today and we're sitting around, twiddling our thumbs,' she replied. *And thinking about you.*

'I got the keys to my apartment today,' he told her. 'I've just been around there in my lunch break and although technically it's furnished there are a few things I'll need to get. What are you doing after work?'

'I probably should be going to the gym,' she replied. She tried to get to the gym three times a week; she needed to keep fit in order to cope with the physical demands of her job but at the end of a busy shift she often didn't have the energy. Today seemed like it was going to stay quiet so she should make an effort to exercise, but she wondered about the reason for Josh's call. 'Why?'

'What are you doing after the gym?' he asked. 'Would you come shopping with me? Point me in the right direction for the things I need. I'll buy you dinner afterwards.'

'I'd be happy to help you but I can't tonight.' She didn't have time to fit it all in. She had a previous commitment, one she wished she hadn't made, but it was too late to back out of it now.

'I'll take a rain check, then,' he said before he ended the call, leaving her wishing she hadn't agreed to tonight's blind date with a friend of her brother's.

'How did your date go?' Lou asked the minute Georgie stuck her head into the comms room at the QMERT base the next morning.

'Tedious,' Georgie replied. 'It was about as much fun as going to get my legs waxed. I've decided enough is enough. No more blind dates. No more dating at all. I'm staying single.'

'If you had a proper boyfriend, people would stop trying to set you up on blind dates,' said Louise.

'You stood me up to go out with a complete stranger?'

Georgie whirled around when she heard Josh's voice behind her. He stepped into the comms room and closed the door. He leant against Lou's desk and folded his arms across his broad chest. He was clearly waiting for her excuse.

'Sorry, it was a prior commitment, but if it makes you feel better it was a complete disaster,' she told him.

'You didn't tell me you had another option,' Lou reprimanded.

Georgie shrugged. 'Josh wanted me to help him shop for

his apartment but I'd already said yes to Costa. I couldn't cancel, my brother would have insisted I reschedule.'

'What has your brother got to do with it?'

'Costa has just been relocated to Cairns. He used to work with my brother Alek, and Alek thought I might like him.'

'Why are your brothers setting up dates for you? What's wrong with you?' Josh's grey eyes sparkled with silver lights as he grinned and baited her.

'Hey, watch it! There's nothing wrong with me!'

'There must be plenty of single men around if you want a boyfriend. What about Marty or Pat?' he continued.

'Don't you start!' she protested. 'Pat's forty! And Marty goes through women like a man possessed. Anyway, I'd have to be completely desperate before I dated a colleague. I've spent far too much time listening to them talk about women to ever want to put myself in the situation where I could be the one they discuss on a Monday morning.' She'd dated a colleague before and she'd hated it when everyone had known their business, sometimes before she'd known it herself. 'Besides, who said I even wanted a boyfriend? I'm perfectly happy on my own.'

'I just thought—'

She jumped in and cut him off. 'You thought you were helping but I don't need your help and I don't need a boyfriend. What I need is a project. Something to keep me so busy that I can tell my family I don't have time for dating. Actually...' She paused momentarily as a thought occurred to her. 'If you do want to help, you could be my project.'

'What?'

She nodded. 'I can tell my family I need to spend all my free time getting the new doctor up to speed. That might keep them off my back and it'll teach you not to meddle too.' She grinned and both she and Louise laughed at the shocked expression on Josh's face.

He held his hands up in surrender. 'I'm sorry, I didn't mean to give you a hard time. I promise to mind my own business from now on.'

'It's all right, I was just having a bit of fun.'

'Well, in that case, I'm sorry your date was terrible.'

'You don't look sorry,' Georgie argued.

'No?' He shrugged. 'I guess I'm not, seeing as it wasn't my fault. All I can say is you should have come shopping with me instead.' He laughed and Georgie was tempted to agree with him.

'I'll remember that next time,' she said.

'Here, I have something that might cheer you up,' he said. In his hand he held a stack of brochures and he passed them to her.

Every pamphlet had a picture of happy, smiling people wearing lifejackets. Happy, smiling people going white-water rafting. 'Where did these come from?' she asked.

'The tourist information counter in the main terminal building. Were you hoping I'd forget?'

'Yes,' she said. But she wasn't sure if that was true. She'd been planning on trying to avoid it but she had agreed to go. That was the deal.

She opened the top brochure. 'Which one looks good?'

'They're all pretty similar.' Josh took the rest of the pile from her and shuffled through it. He passed one brochure back to her. 'The girl at the tourist counter recommended this one. They've been around for a long time and have a good safety record. And it's on the Tully River, which has proper rapids.'

Georgie flicked through the brochure. 'What does that mean exactly?'

'It means you'll feel like you've done something challenging.'

Georgie pointed to the half-day option, 'So this one you think, "The River Challenge"?'

'No, that's for kids,' he said with a smile, almost daring her to argue. 'This is the one I think we should do.' He pointed to the full-day option.

'But that says "thrilling", not challenging.'

'I know. Sounds fun, doesn't it?' He was still grinning at her, his grey eyes flashing with amusement.

She raised one eyebrow in response as she read from the brochure. '"Level Three and Four rapids." That sounds okay if they're classed out of ten, not so fun if they're classed out of five. How are rapids rated?'

'Out of six.'

'Six!'

'It's okay. Only grade-six rapids have the warning "Danger to life or limb" so by the process of elimination that should mean that grades three and four are pretty safe.'

'Hmm.'

Josh wrapped his arm around her shoulders. 'I won't let anything happen to you, I promise.'

Georgie jumped when he touched her. She reacted as though she'd touched something hot when she hadn't expected to and that was how she felt, as though she'd been zapped by electricity. Why did he affect her like this? She needed to get away. She needed some distance, some perspective.

She stepped out of his embrace. 'We'd better go and get changed so we're ready if we get called out,' she said as she hurried to the change rooms.

But this wasn't one of her best ideas. In fact, it was downright idiotic. Because, of course, Josh followed her and the first things he did was open his locker and strip off his shirt. There was nowhere to hide in the unisex change rooms. Nowhere she could go to avoid Josh. And if she found it difficult to ignore her attraction to him when he was fully clothed, it was almost impossible to ignore it when he was standing beside her half-naked.

She put her bag in her locker, hiding behind the door to avoid ogling Josh's washboard abs. Not that it made any difference. She was perfectly capable of remembering what his body looked like: the image of him in his board shorts out on the reef was permanently imprinted on her brain.

'So are you doing anything on Saturday?' he asked. 'I know we're both rostered off.'

She pretended to be searching in her locker, looking for something. She found her hairbrush. That would do. 'Saturday? I don't have any plans.' She pulled her hairbrush out and turned away from Josh to look in the mirror and brush her ponytail but realised she could still see him in the reflection. He was pulling another T-shirt over his head.

'Excellent. Shall I ring the rafting company and book us on a trip this weekend?' he said as he tugged his shirt down to his waist.

Josh took his overalls from his locker and Georgie realised he was about to drop his shorts. Her breathing was suddenly shallow and she needed to look away. 'Okay. I guess I don't have an excuse not to do it. A deal is a deal.' At the moment she'd say anything just to get him out of the locker room so she could get her hormones under control. Her heart was beating like crazy and her mouth was dry. Her senses were fully charged. Why didn't she feel like that when she went on these blind dates?

She put her hairbrush away and plaited her ponytail, keeping her face hidden, using delay tactics until she was certain Josh had finished getting changed. Suddenly she wasn't sure how sensible this plan was, she'd be spending the day with Josh on the river and he'd be wearing next to nothing if the pictures on the brochure were anything to go by. She wasn't sure how she'd cope with that but it was too late to back out now.

'Come on, it'll be fun,' he said as he closed his locker. 'I'm sure I can be better company than your date last night.'

Once she heard his locker-door slam shut she dared to look again. He was dressed now and her breathing was under control again. She didn't doubt she'd enjoy Josh's company more than her blind date but she wasn't about to tell him that. It was bad enough that he seemed to know the direction of her thoughts. 'And if you're not?' She laughed.

'Then you get to choose the next adventure,' he said as he bent down to tie his bootlaces.

Once Josh left the change room Georgie collapsed onto the bench that ran in front of the lockers. She needed a moment to get her head together. She had to work out a way to cope with the feelings Josh evoked in her. She had to work out a way to get her responses under control when he was around.

CHAPTER FIVE

GEORGIE spent all the free time she had over the next few days cooking. Cooking normally helped her to clear her head but it wasn't having its usual calming effect this time. She alternated between trying to keep her mind off Josh and trying to work out why she was so affected by him so she could figure out how she was going to deal with it. But when he arrived to collect her for the drive to Tully she still hadn't come up with a solution.

He was wearing a grey polo shirt and camel shorts. He had good legs for shorts, muscular without being bulky. She glanced over at him where he sat in the driver's seat. His thighs where she could see them emerging from his shorts were tanned and covered with light, sandy blond hair. Strong and masculine.

She should have kept her eyes to herself because now she had to sit on her hands to stop herself from reaching out to touch him.

She concentrated hard to hold normal conversation as she tried to work out what it was about him that stirred her senses. She felt alive, alert and aroused. She realised he made her feel like a woman. It wasn't necessarily because of the way he treated her but more in the way she responded to him, to his masculinity. She was totally aware of him and, in response, she became aware of her own desires.

She'd have to accept that was how it was and deal with it. Ignore it. She certainly wouldn't act on it. She was taking a break from dating and she certainly wasn't about to date a colleague.

She managed to keep her hands to herself and her hormones in check until they reached the meeting point for the white-water rafting company. They left their car at the end point of their ride and were taken upriver by bus. At the launch site they were kitted out with lifejackets, aqua shoes and helmets. Josh took off his T-shirt and stood before her in his board shorts before he put the lifejacket on over his bare chest. Getting through that display without licking her lips was test number one. Test number two was when he helped her fasten the chin strap on her helmet and his fingers brushed against her throat, sending her heart rate soaring. She swallowed but managed not to hyperventilate. So far, so good. She hoped she'd get through the rest of the day as easily.

'I thought you said this was safe?' she said as she straightened her helmet and flicked her plait over her shoulder.

'It's just a precaution,' he replied. 'The company has an impeccable safety record. I checked.' He reached out to help straighten her helmet and her heart skipped a beat. 'You'll have fun, I promise.'

Georgie looked around at their group and suppressed a smile. The helmets they had to wear were most unflattering but she guessed she looked as bad as everyone else. The participants had been divided into four small groups and she and Josh followed their guide as he led them away for the safety briefing.

Their group, like the others, mainly consisted of young

backpackers, but fortunately most had enough command of the English language to be able to understand the instructions. Once they'd covered the basics regarding the commands, how and when to paddle or not to paddle and how to approach the rapids, they were allocated a position in the inflatable raft. Their guide, Darryl, sat in the rear, Josh was given the front position and Georgie found herself given a spot towards the back of the raft near Darryl. That wasn't quite where she wanted to be but she knew the raft need to be balanced and they couldn't choose their own positions.

Before they launched their raft Darryl instructed them to practise their war cry.

'Our what?' Georgie asked.

'Our war cry,' Darryl explained. 'Each raft has their own war cry. There are spots on the river where we compete to get to the next set of rapids and our war cry is part of the challenge,' he explained before he let loose with his catch cry. 'All for one…'

'And one for all,' his team responded.

From along the bank the other teams responded with their own cries and the bush reverberated with noise.

'You didn't warn me about this,' Georgie muttered to Josh.

He laughed. 'What's the matter? It's just a bit of fun. Just think of it as a team-building exercise.' Georgie's response was one raised eyebrow. 'You must have done things like this before?' he said. 'What about when you went to Greece, did you join any backpacker tours? Some companies are notorious for these types of stunts.'

'I went to Greece with my cousin and we stayed with relatives. I was barely allowed out of the house without a chaperone, so there's no way I would have been permitted to go off with a group of random twenty-somethings.'

She looked at the backpackers sitting all around her in the raft and thought how different her overseas experience was from theirs. But it was what it was.

'In that case, you'll just have to trust me,' Josh was saying. 'Let yourself go and yell, it's quite empowering.' To prove his point, he joined in with the rest of their group in a raucous 'And one for all' following Darryl's next command as they pushed off the bank and entered the water. Georgie had no option but to do as he said. The only way out of there was downriver and to reach the end they had to work together. She dug her paddle into the water, let go of her inhibitions and yelled with the best of them. Her reward was a big thumbs-up from Josh and a huge smile. The effort was worth it and made her determined to enjoy herself.

From her vantage point she could see Josh working hard, digging his paddle into the water, pulling strongly, his biceps flexing with the effort. He looked completely at ease. It was obviously something he'd done before and he seemed to relish the activity. She could imagine Josh alongside her brothers—they would enjoy rafting too. They were always on the go, always challenging each other to silly contests, always active. Josh was a lot like them, full of the joy of life.

She kept Josh in the corner of her vision as she concentrated on paddling and following Darryl's instructions. The section of the river they negotiated before lunch was relatively easy but they were still soaked when they stopped for a barbecue on the river bank. They dried out as they devoured the burgers but once they'd eaten Josh suggested taking another dip in the water.

'We've just eaten. What if I get cramp and drown?' Georgie protested.

'I'll save you.' Josh grinned as he reached for her hand

and pulled her to her feet. 'But if you don't trust me, put your life jacket back on and we'll just float about.'

Georgie picked up her jacket and slipped her arms into it. The river was wide and shallow in this spot and some rocks had formed a natural pool, cutting into the main channel. Georgie waded into the pool and floated on her back, drifting with the current.

Josh floated beside her. He turned his head and grinned at her, his grey eyes flashing silver. 'This is the life.'

She had to agree with him. This was perfect. There were no demands on her, there was nothing else she should be doing, and that was an unusual state of affairs. She was completely relaxed. And she had Josh to thank for that. She could be herself with him. He had no preconceptions about her. No knowledge of her as part of her large family. No knowledge of her as someone's daughter or sister or girlfriend. He was spending time with her because he'd chosen to and she was enjoying his company. But all too soon they were called from the water and directed to climb back into the raft for the post-lunch trip.

Georgie's confidence had increased and she was loving every minute of the experience. She laughed and yelled and occasionally screamed and she was still grinning and yelling encouragement as they approached the final rapid.

She couldn't believe how quickly the day had flown by. On the other side of this last rapid was the car park and kiosk that marked the end point of the day's excursion. One rapid remained to negotiate before the day was over. She couldn't believe how much fun she'd had. She'd expected to be totally out of her comfort zone, her sheltered upbringing and girls' school education hadn't prepared her for this. Perhaps she was really an adrenaline junkie. Perhaps, thanks to Josh, she'd discovered something about herself today.

They were neck and neck with one of the other rafts as they headed towards the final, narrow opening.

'Paddle hard, all for one,' Darryl yelled at them.

'And one for all,' they responded as they dug their oars into the water and tried to inch their nose in front of the other raft.

'Left side only,' was the next command, and those sitting on the right took their paddles out of the water, but their reaction time was slow and the other raft shot past them, taking first place into the final rapid.

As they emerged from the rapid in the wake of the first raft they could see the victors celebrating downstream. They had their paddles raised above their heads and were chanting their war cry. In the excitement of the celebration one boy stood up and his movement unbalanced the vessel. Because everyone had their hands and paddles in the air, no one was holding onto the ropes that ran around the inflated sides of the raft. As it tipped three rafters fell overboard into the river.

The raft righted itself as the weight distribution corrected and continued to drift down the river. Two heads emerged quickly from the water and those boys struck out for the raft where eager hands waited to pull them back on board.

The river wasn't particularly deep and the water here was relatively calm but the third boy hadn't reappeared. They all scanned the water, searching for him.

There. Georgie saw the red of the boy's lifejacket pop up behind a boulder. She pointed in his direction as she saw him trying to grab hold of the rock but the boulder was smooth and slippery with no purchase.

'I'm going in,' Georgie heard Josh yell to Darryl even as he was already slipping over the edge of the raft and into the river.

'What the——?'

Georgie heard the confusion in Darryl's tone. He was sitting near her, and she turned to explain to him. 'It's okay, he's a doctor—an emergency specialist.' She had every confidence in Josh's ability to get the situation under control. She'd seen him do it before. In fact, watching him swim away from her now gave her a sense of déjà vu. There was something immensely attractive about a man who didn't back away from a challenge, a man who was prepared to leap to the rescue and who had the skills to pull it off.

He'd reached the boy now. She could see Josh talking to him and, as Darryl and the other guide steered their rafts into the bank, Josh floated the boy on his back and pulled him to the shore but not out of the water.

'We've got trained first aiders, I'll get one from the office,' the guide from the other raft called out to them as Darryl gave orders for disembarkation from his raft.

Georgie was agitated as she waited for the others to climb ashore before her. As soon as she was able to, she hurried off to assist Josh, though she knew he was perfectly capable of managing on his own. There was no doubting his skill and medical expertise. She couldn't believe she'd joked about having to help him get up to speed with pre-hospital emergency medicine, he was totally in control of the situation, but she wanted to help. She wanted to be a part of it. It wasn't in her nature to be a spectator in these situations.

'Hi.' He didn't waste time with pleasantries. 'We need to get him out of the water but we'll need to be careful. I suspect he has fractured ribs and he's twisted his knee. There doesn't appear to be any spinal damage. His name is Ulrich.'

One of the rafting company's employees arrived with

a first-aid kit and a stretcher. Together Georgie and Josh rolled the boy onto the stretcher and with the help of the guides lifted him onto the bank.

Josh unclipped the boy's lifejacket. The jackets were cushioned at the front and back but along the sides, under the arms, the fabric was only thin. Georgie could see a large bruise already forming under the boy's left armpit. Ulrich grimaced in pain as Josh moved his arm but told them it was his chest that was sore.

Josh undid his own life jacket now that they were out of the water and slid it from his body. Georgie knew he'd want to get rid of its cumbersome bulk to give him freedom of movement.

He was bare-chested, his back tanned and smooth as he leant forward and extracted a stethoscope from the medical kit. He bent over the boy and placed the stethoscope on the boy's chest. 'Can you try to breathe in through your nose and out through your mouth for me?' he asked the boy. Ulrich did as he was asked but complained when he attempted a deep breath. He spoke perfect English but Georgie could detect an accent, possibly German, which fitted with his name.

'I know it hurts but try once more for me,' Josh instructed as he moved the bulb of the stethoscope.

'Equal air entry,' he said to Georgie. With fractured ribs she knew Josh would have been concerned about a pneumothorax but equal air sounds meant that was one thing the boy had escaped.

'He's not going to be going anywhere in a bus, you'll need to call an ambulance to take him to Tully hospital.' Josh was speaking to the rafting guide. He was issuing instructions, taking control of the situation, as Georgie had known he would, and everyone was running around doing his bidding, happy to have someone take responsibility.

Georgie helped Josh to sit the boy up so they could remove his wet lifejacket. She then carefully dried his upper body with a towel before covering him with a space blanket to keep him warm. Satisfied that the boy was able to breathe and hadn't sustained any serious chest trauma, Josh moved his attention to the boy's knee.

'It looks as though you've just twisted your knee. Nothing's broken,' he announced as he finished his examination. Darryl arrived at that moment with the news that the ambulance had been called but would take half an hour to reach them. The boy's friends trailed in Darryl's wake.

'Do you want anything for pain relief?' Josh asked Ulrich. A thirty-minute wait with fractured ribs would seem like a long time. When Ulrich nodded Josh searched the rafting company's medical kit. 'There's nothing really suitable, or strong enough, that won't interfere with the paramedics when they arrive,' he said to Georgie. 'In my car is a medical bag and there should be an analgesic inhaler in there. Do you think you could get my keys from our locker and find it?' Josh turned back to Ulrich. 'You don't have any medical conditions, do you? You're not diabetic?'

Ulrich shook his head and Georgie went to find their things and retrieve the car keys. She was familiar with these inhalers. They were carried in all the ambulances for short-term pain relief, and she found the box and slotted the cylinder into the bright green inhaler and returned to Josh.

Ulrich seemed much more comfortable once he'd self-administered the analgesic and the wait for the local paramedics became easier to bear. One of his friends travelled in the ambulance with him and Georgie and Josh stood side by side and watched as the ambulance made its way down the road towards Tully.

'I suppose that's the end of our foray into uncharted waters for you, then?' Josh asked her. 'You won't believe me next time I tell you something's safe.'

Georgie laughed. 'I'm pretty sure things wouldn't have gone haywire if Ulrich had kept his seat. He's only got himself to blame.'

'You haven't written me off altogether, then?'

'Not completely, but whether or not you get a second chance will depend on what you have in mind.'

'How about dinner? If we leave now we'll be back in Cairns in time for me to take you out somewhere.'

'Are you okay to drive all the way? You're not too tired?' It was a two-hour trip back to Cairns, a long way at the end of a busy day.

'Would you rather stay in Tully overnight?'

'No!' Georgie panicked. 'I was just going to offer to share the driving.'

The two of them, staying overnight in Tully. Together! Not that he'd actually suggested they spend the night together but she knew her resistance would be minimal at best if she found herself alone with Josh, away from home, overnight. Staying in Tully would only complicate matters. She needed to rein in her crazy fantasies.

'We're heading home, then?' he asked.

She nodded. Spending a couple of hours in a car with Josh would be enough to test her willpower and she thought even that might be a struggle. She couldn't be expected to stay away overnight with him and behave.

'All right,' Josh continued, 'let's head off so we can shower and you can choose somewhere for dinner. You will have dinner with me?'

Did she want to? She wasn't tired after the day of rafting. Adrenaline was still coursing through her system and if she was honest she'd admit she didn't want the day to end. Dinner would help to stretch out the day. 'Dinner would be lovely.'

Josh's grey eyes gleamed as he smiled at her and despite the streaks of dust and dirt on his face he looked fresh and alert, not in the least bit exhausted. Georgie wasn't sure where he got all his energy from but his smile was enough to give her a second wind and she looked forward to dinner with eager anticipation.

He took her hand as they walked to the car. His touch made her skin tingle. It felt alive, as though she could breathe through her pores. She felt as though she was floating and it was several moments before she even wondered about his easy, casual manner. She shouldn't be holding his hand but it felt so natural and so good she didn't want to let go.

On the drive back to Cairns Josh kept glancing at her even as he was driving and he would occasionally reach over to touch her arm or her knee as he talked. His touch was enough to keep the adrenaline coursing through her system and she was on the edge of her seat by the time they reached Cairns.

She hurried through her shower once he dropped her home. She was keen for their time together to continue. He was good company, he knew how to enjoy himself and he made her feel attractive, intelligent and amusing.

Which was exactly why she should keep her distance, she knew she should. She was supposed to be using this time in Cairns to find her independence, to find her own identity, and she couldn't do that if she was spending time with someone else.

So in an effort to attempt to keep Josh in the box marked 'colleague' she chose The Sandbar on the esplanade for dinner. It was a new restaurant and bar, not far from the hospital, and Josh's apartment, and it was super-trendy and busy so there was little danger of an intimate dinner for two. Georgie figured there was safety in numbers and she knew if she was going to be able to resist Josh she needed to avoid being alone with him. Every time she was alone all she wanted to do was touch him and taste him but she knew there was no point.

The bar was busy, as Georgie had hoped, but she hadn't counted on it being so busy that they wouldn't be able to get a table in the restaurant.

'If you don't have a reservation then I'm sorry but we're fully booked,' the hostess told her when she requested a table.

Josh intervened.

'If you could manage to swing it, I'd really appreciate it.' He focussed intently on the hostess and Georgie knew she'd be feeling like the only woman in the room. She knew that feeling all too well herself. Then Josh played his trump card. He smiled at her and Georgie saw the hostess cave in.

'I'll see what I can do. Come this way,' she said as she led them to a table on the very edge of a balcony overlooking the Cairns foreshore.

Josh held Georgie's chair for her as she sat. He ordered drinks for them and then proposed a toast.

'To new experiences.'

'Thank you for organising the rafting,' Georgie said as she joined in the toast. 'I really did enjoy it. I think maybe I am an adrenaline junkie in disguise.'

Josh laughed. 'Of course you are—you're a paramedic. I just can't believe it's taken you all this time to discover that side of you. What were your brothers doing when you were growing up? Why weren't you out with them, pushing boundaries?'

'I'm so much younger than them they didn't want me tagging along after them and my parents certainly didn't encourage it. I was, am, a good Greek daughter. I spent my time in the kitchen with my mum and Nonna. I wasn't out climbing trees and terrorising the neighbourhood with the boys. But after today I think I might be a little more adventurous.'

'Sky-diving?'

'Still unlikely.' She laughed. 'I know I told you I came to Cairns for the career experience but it was also my chance to try to discover who I am, away from the perceptions and expectations of my family, and today I learnt a bit about myself. I tested myself physically and I survived. I even enjoyed it, so thank you.'

'It was my pleasure.'

The waitress brought their order but as soon as they were alone again Josh continued the theme of the previous conversation. 'I'm intrigued. How do your family see you? Is their version very different to the one I see?'

Georgie shrugged. 'I'm the baby, the only girl with four big brothers. They all think I need looking after. That's why they're all looking for a partner for me, they see that as part of their responsibility, making sure I'm taken care of.'

'They're still searching for boyfriends for you? I thought you were going to tell them you're happy being single?'

'I haven't said anything yet. It's not that I mind the idea of marriage,' she explained. 'I'm just not ready for it. I need to work out who I am first. I just hope I can do that before my time here is up and I find myself back in Melbourne.'

'You're braver than I am. The idea of marriage frightens the life out of me.'

'Why?'

'Spending your life with one person, that takes a lot of commitment, a lot of trust. I think it's a lot to ask. A lot to expect.'

She smiled. 'Don't let Isaac hear your opinions. Their wedding is only a fortnight away.'

'I'm not against marriage for other people,' Josh clarified. 'It's just not for me.'

'Why not?'

'You're lucky to come from a stable, supportive family background. That immediately gives you a different perspective. Naturally you think the institution of marriage is a good one. Not everyone is as fortunate.'

Her family was immensely important to her and she couldn't imagine feeling differently, but it was clear that Josh didn't have the same rosy view of family life. She wanted to know more, she was desperate to know more, but something about Josh's tone stopped her from questioning him. Before she could think of another topic of conversation to break the awkward silence that had fallen, the waitress came to clear their plates.

The trade-off for securing a table for dinner was that they needed to vacate the restaurant by nine o'clock for another booking. Georgie still wasn't ready for the day to end; she didn't think she ever would be, but because she'd parked her car at Josh's apartment the day stretched further still. They walked along the esplanade together.

It was a beautiful North Queensland evening, warm and humid, but once the sun had set the humidity became pleasant rather than stifling. Josh took her hand as they crossed the street and instantly Georgie felt her temperature rise even further. His hand was warm and the heat, his heat, flooded her body. Their steps were unhurried but still she felt they reached her car all too soon.

Things had changed today. Despite her best intentions, her awareness of Josh had increased and her resistance was weakening. Every glance, every touch, every smile had gone straight to the heart of her, making her pulse race, her stomach flutter and her nerves spark. She wasn't sure exactly what had happened, she just knew that she wasn't ready for the day to be over. She wasn't ready to say good-bye.

She raised herself up on her toes and kissed his cheek. Her lips pressed against his skin, so close to his mouth that if he'd turned his head a few millimetres she would have kissed his lips.

'Would you like to come up for coffee?' His voice was soft and she could feel his words brush her cheek in little puffs of air.

She hesitated, running the different scenarios through her head, letting her imagination take flight before she replied. 'I really need to get home, I'm working tomorrow.' It had nothing to do with tomorrow, it was all about her lack of resistance to Josh. A coffee could mean so many different things. She'd learnt to take risks today but she didn't think she was ready for another one quite so soon.

'It was just a coffee.' He was smiling at her and his grey eyes were full of amusement.

'Stop doing that!'

'Doing what?' Now his eyes were a picture of innocence.

'Reading my thoughts.'

'Let me see if I read them correctly.' He leant towards her.

He was so close she could feel the heat radiating from him. Their faces were inches apart. He moved his head towards her, closing the gap.

Was he going to kiss her?

He stayed where he was for what seemed like for ever. How could he remain so still?

He was watching her, studying her, and then he moved another fraction closer, his head tilted slightly to one side.

Georgie shut her eyes as she waited for the caress she was sure was coming.

Josh's lips brushed over hers, the gentlest of touches, so soft she wondered if it was nothing more than her imagination. His mouth met hers again. His touch was firmer this time, more definite. Her lips parted involuntarily and she tasted him. He tasted of mint and she heard herself moan as his tongue explored her mouth. The outside world receded; it was condensed into this one spot, this one man.

CHAPTER SIX

Her heart raced in her chest and she could feel every beat as Josh's lips covered hers. She closed her eyes, succumbing to his touch. She opened her mouth and Josh caressed her tongue. She felt her nipples peak in response as he explored her mouth. His hand was on her bare arm and she could feel the heat of his fingers on her skin. She wanted his hand on her breast but she didn't dare move it there. She pressed herself against his chest instead as she kissed him back. Where was the harm in that?

Her skin was on fire as Josh ran his fingers up her arm. She melted against him. She was aware of nothing else except the sensation of being fully alive. She wanted for nothing except Josh.

She felt his hand move to her back. Her skin was bare between the straps of her sundress and her flesh burned under his touch. She felt her nipples harden further as all her senses came to life and a line of fire spread from her stomach to her groin. She deepened the kiss, wanting to lose herself in Josh, but a car horn tooting shattered the silence, interrupting the moment and making her jump. Her eyes flew open as Josh straightened up. Too late, she remembered where they were, standing beside her car in the middle of the street, behaving like a couple of hormone-fuelled teenagers. Her heart was racing in her chest and her breaths were shallow. She could hear herself panting.

Josh was studying her face as if committing each of her features to memory. His fingers trailed down the side of her cheek, sending a shiver of desire through her.

'Now would you like to come up to my apartment?'

She hesitated. The kiss was magical but it couldn't lead anywhere. Hadn't he made it clear at dinner he wasn't looking for commitment? It would be a one-night stand. That wasn't what she wanted.

She pulled back, breaking their connection. 'I can't.'

'Why not?'

'It's a bad idea.'

'It was just a kiss.'

Just a kiss! Maybe to him, but it had set her world on fire and she knew she couldn't be trusted if she followed him to his apartment. No, this was definitely a bad idea. 'You're a colleague. You're off limits.'

'Are you sure?'

She nodded. She couldn't speak.

'Okay. But let me know if you change your mind. No strings attached.'

No strings attached. It wasn't her style but it was tempting.

If he could play it cool, so could she. She smiled, striving for a casual tone, and said, 'I'll get back to you,' as she pushed the remote on her car keys and unlocked the door.

He bent his head and kissed her softly on her mouth, a brief brush of his lips, a gentle goodbye kiss, but her reaction was every bit as strong as when he'd kissed her more thoroughly. She used every ounce of willpower to make herself get into her car and drive away. But she watched him in her rearview mirror as he stood in the street and she knew she wouldn't be able to avoid him or pretend he didn't exist. She knew she couldn't pretend she wasn't attracted to him and she suspected he would become her forbidden apple, a temptation too strong to resist. One way or another she would need to get him out of her system.

Josh had got to work early and was chatting to Louise when they saw Georgie struggling through the door, carrying two large baking trays. She pushed the door open with her hip and nodded in their direction as she headed for the QMERT kitchen.

Louise watched her go before she turned to Josh and said, 'Something's bothering her.'

Josh wondered how on earth Louise had figured that out. Georgie had seemed perfectly okay to him. In fact, she'd seemed perfectly okay for the past few days, ever since he'd kissed her. He, on the other hand, had been completely rattled. Despite what he'd told Georgie, their kiss had rocked his world. It hadn't been 'just a kiss'. It had shocked him, surprised him, to his core. The moment he'd kissed her he'd had the sensation that he'd been waiting all his life to find her, all his life to have that kiss, and ever since then he'd been wondering how to persuade her to date him. What was the difference between him and any of the blind dates she was prepared to go on? The only difference he could see was that they already knew they had chemistry. But she refused to date a colleague and she'd refused to discuss it any further and he had no idea what he could do about that.

But why did Louise think something was wrong? What had he missed? What did Louise see that he didn't?

'How do you know something's wrong?' he asked.

'She's been cooking.'

Josh frowned. As far as he could tell, Georgie was always cooking. 'Don't forget we're all going to her place this weekend for Pat's birthday. Maybe she's run out of room in her fridge.' To his ears that sounded like a perfectly reasonable explanation.

'I'm telling you, something's bothering her. Go and find out what's wrong.' Lou glared at him and he half expected her to shove him out the door.

'Okay, okay, I'm going,' he said, fighting the urge to laugh. With a sharp salute in Lou's direction he followed Georgie into the kitchen.

Her back was to him as she slid the baking trays into the fridge. He dragged his eyes off her rounded backside as she stood up and turned around.

'Hi. Is everything okay?' he asked.

'I guess.'

Josh felt his heart drop to his stomach. She wasn't sounding like her normal chirpy self. Something was wrong. He wondered if he could fix it.

He crossed the room and put his hand on her arm, connecting them. 'What is it?'

'My parents arrive tomorrow.'

'I thought that would be good news.' In the time he'd known her she'd only had nice things to say about her parents and she seemed more than happy to have visitors.

She nodded. 'But they're meeting up with some friends here too.'

'And?'

'These friends have three sons.' She paused. 'Three single sons.'

'Let me guess, they're your next string of blind dates?' he smiled.

'It's not quite that bad. I don't think the boys are coming, but my parents think it's time for me to settle down and they're getting desperate. If it doesn't look like I'm going to find my own husband, I think they're not averse to helping me.'

'An arranged marriage?'

'That's not very twenty-first century,' she said, and finally he saw her smile. 'I don't think they'd call it that but they seem happy enough to send a few eligible bachelors my way. Or the bachelors' parents.'

'Why haven't you told them you're happy being single?'

'Because that's easier said than done. You haven't met my parents. That excuse would only work for so long and then they'd feel obliged to "help" me again.'

'Well, tell them you've already got a boyfriend.'

'Josh, they're coming to Cairns, they're coming to visit.' Georgie sighed. Hadn't he been listening? 'They'll expect to meet my fictitious boyfriend. What do I do about that?'

'Introduce me.'

'You? Why?'

He shrugged. 'You have a problem, that's one solution. I'll be your surrogate boyfriend. It'll give you your freedom back. Your parents can stop setting you up. It'll take the pressure off you.'

It wasn't a bad idea—in fact, she rather liked the sound of it—but she knew she liked the sound of it for all the wrong reasons. 'You don't want to do that. The experience could be a bit traumatic.'

'That doesn't matter,' he said. 'How long are your parents staying? A week? I can keep the charade going for that long.'

'Thanks for the offer but I wouldn't subject you to that.' She smiled and added, 'It's for your own protection.'

'What does that mean?'

'My last relationship ended because of my parents. Trust me, you do not want that level of expectation.'

'Didn't they approve?'

'No, quite the opposite. They loved Peter. So much that they wanted him to join our family. They started asking when we were going to settle down, offering to help us buy a house. Peter decided he wasn't ready for that commitment and headed for the hills. If you told my parents that's what happened, they'd be horrified. I don't think they're aware of what they did, but I don't want to subject each and every boyfriend to the same treatment. I don't want someone forced to marry me.'

'That's why I'm the answer to your problems. There'll be no forcing me to marry anyone! I'm offering my services and I guarantee I can handle parental pressure.'

She wished he was the answer to her problems but she doubted it was that easy. It was his fault she'd spent hours in the kitchen cooking, trying to clear her head. Her parents' expectations were nothing to cope with compared to her reaction to Josh. If she'd relived the kiss they'd shared once, she'd relived it a hundred times. She'd never spent so much time obsessing over a man, let alone one she barely knew, but she couldn't get that kiss out of her mind. She could remember how he'd tasted and felt and how the kiss had made her blood flow like molten gold and warmed her insides. For every second the kiss had lasted she'd spent as many hours thinking about what she should do, but when Josh walked into the kitchen she still hadn't made up her mind. Just the sight of him got her all flustered again. Her heartbeat kicked up a notch and her skin tingled when his fingers caressed her arm.

She shook her head. Her parents were definitely the least of her problems.

'They'd know something was up. They wouldn't be expecting you.'

'What does that mean?'

'You're not Greek.'

'You're kidding? You have to date Greek men?'

She shrugged. 'Pretty much.'

'Surely you've dated men who aren't Greek before?'

'Yes,' she admitted, 'but I've never seen the need to introduce them to my parents. It's never been anything serious and it would just make everyone uncomfortable. I don't need a pretend boyfriend. I don't even need a real one. I don't need to be rescued but I appreciate your offer.'

He shrugged. 'Okay, but let me know if you change your mind. I'm happy to help.'

'Thanks, but I'll manage. I'd better go and get changed.'

She appreciated his offer but it wasn't one she could imagine accepting. As if the kiss wasn't enough for her to ignore, now she had to ignore the image in her head of Josh as her boyfriend. The idea was delicious. He was delicious. But therein lay the danger. He was offering to be a fake boyfriend and she knew she might have trouble remembering that.

No. She was positive she could handle having her parents' friends here. Surely that would be easier than handling Josh. But knowing she had his support gave her some comfort.

Twenty-four hours later Josh was surprised to receive a frantic phone call from Georgie. Her parents had landed in Cairns that morning and he hadn't expected to hear from her at all today.

'Josh, it's me. Can you talk?'

'Why are you whispering?'

'I don't want my parents to hear. I have a favour to ask you. Remember when you offered to be my surrogate boyfriend?'

'Yes.'

'Does your offer still stand?'

'Why?'

'Mum has just told me that Con and Anastasia, the friends with the three sons, were making noises about bringing one of them up to Cairns to meet me. I kind of panicked, I'm definitely not ready to be set up by two sets of parents, so I took your advice. I told them I have a boy-friend and now they expect to meet him tomorrow at Pat's birthday barbecue!'

'And you want me to be your boyfriend?'

'Just for a week or so. Unless you've got any other ideas? Please?'

He had no intention of refusing, especially as it had been his idea in the first place. 'All right.' He was happy to do it, not least because he knew there would be some enjoyable perks to accompany the position of Georgie's boyfriend. 'I'll come over a bit early tomorrow and you can introduce me to your folks.'

'Thank you. You're a lifesaver. I owe you.'

Josh kept his word, arriving half an hour earlier than the other guests, and Georgie tried to get her heart to slow down and stop its frantic pounding. She was nervous and anxious. She hoped their plan wasn't a disaster.

He was carrying a large cardboard box, which he de-posited on the kitchen table before kissing Georgie. His spontaneity startled her and she could feel her mother's eyes watching every move.

'Relax,' Josh whispered, and Georgie willed herself to stay calm. She knew Josh was keeping up appearances and she needed to do the same.

She introduced him to her parents, George and Sofia, and Josh pulled gifts out of the box, champagne for Georgie and flowers for Sofia, and then he set about helping with last-minute preparations, setting up the bar, putting out glasses, turning on the barbecue. He obviously remembered his way around the kitchen, he looked right at home, and his casual assistance lent authenticity to their charade.

When their QMERT friends began arriving, Georgie introduced them to her parents as Josh slipped into the role of host. As she watched Josh pouring drinks and handing around nibbles, Georgie realised she hadn't properly thought through their story.

What would happen if one of their colleagues alerted her parents to their fabrication? What would happen if her parents found out about their deception? What would their colleagues think? If she'd known she'd worry so much, she would have thought of a different plan.

She pulled Josh aside to ask him what they should do, only to find he'd already filled Louise in on their scheme and she'd told the others. Their secret was safe.

But the one thing she hadn't thought about was physical contact. Josh was very demonstrative and she realised she hadn't given this side of things any consideration. She didn't want to appear cool and aloof but she jumped every time he touched her. Which was often. Every brush of his fingers, every touch of his hand sent her pulse racing, and she grew more and more self-conscious.

Eventually, when she thought she was going to go crazy, she dragged him aside again and begged him to stop.

'Don't think you're overdoing it just a little?' she asked.

'Overdoing what?'

'The touching, the kissing, the looks.'

'The "looks"?'

He was laughing at her now. 'Stop it,' she said, trying to glare at him, but he'd made her smile. 'I think you've convinced my parents enough for one day.'

'Don't be a spoilsport, I'm enjoying myself.' He reached for her hand and hooked his fingers through hers. 'This is what people do when they're in a new relationship, when they can't get enough of each other. Before it all goes pear-shaped. Don't you remember a time when you couldn't keep your hands to yourself?' He brought her hand to his lips and kissed her fingers. Georgie had to clamp her lips together to stop herself from sighing out loud. 'I'm making sure we look authentic,' he said. 'I'm having fun.'

'I think you're having too much fun. Can you try keeping your hands to yourself? Please.'

'That's the first time I've had that request,' he said just before he leant forward and kissed her lips. It was just a quick kiss, timed to perfection so she couldn't resist or complain, and then he winked at her. 'I'll do my best.'

He walked away then and left her standing, rooted to the spot, looking after him as he did another round of the party, topping up people's drinks.

She took a deep breath. Her fingers were still warm from his touch and her lips were still tingling from his kiss. She needed to relax.

She went to find her glass. Perhaps another drink would help.

She finished her drink and tried to forget about Josh but she couldn't help wondering whether she'd made a mistake by asking him to do her this favour. She couldn't help wondering if it was all going to end in tears.

But the rest of the afternoon went smoothly. Her father was enjoying himself, mingling with the guests, but Sofia was spending most of her time in the kitchen. Georgie tried to get her to leave the dishes and go outside to enjoy the party, but she resisted.

'I'm happy in here and everyone pops in eventually either for more food or on the way to the bathroom. I'm fine,' she said as she started to assemble coffee cups and saucers on the kitchen table. 'So Josh is the one who took you white-water rafting?'

Georgie nodded in reply.

'I thought you weren't going to date co-workers after what happened with Peter,' Sofia said.

'Peter was a paramedic, Josh is a doctor.' It was all semantics but Georgie could hardly tell her mother it was irrelevant because it was only a charade. Fortunately Sofia had moved on to more important matters.

'His surname is Wetherly?' she asked. 'He's not Greek, then?'

Georgie suppressed a smile. 'No, Mum, he's not.'

'Well, your father seems to like him anyway.'

She looked across the deck to the barbecue, where Josh and her father were deep in conversation. She realised then it was too late to change her mind. Josh was doing her this favour and it was working. Her parents liked him and hopefully he'd buy her some time.

She wondered if she should rescue Josh but before she had a chance, guests began to say their farewells and she didn't get a moment alone with Josh until everyone had left, the dishes were done and her parents had gone to lie down.

Georgie made more coffee and took it out to the deck to Josh. 'Thank you for your help,' she said as she handed him a cup.

'My pleasure,' he replied. 'It went well. Pat enjoyed himself. It was a really nice thing to do for him.'

'He gets a bit lonely, I think. I wish he would find someone, I'm sure he'd like the companionship.'

'You're not planning on matchmaking, are you?'

Georgie shook her head. 'No. He says he's happy on his own and I'm the last person who'd interfere in that case. I hate that interference myself.' She sipped her coffee and asked the question she'd been dying to know the answer to. 'What were you talking about with my dad?'

'Your ex-boyfriend, Peter.'

'Peter! What about him?'

'Your dad was just saying that it was good to see you happy again after Peter broke your heart.'

'What? He didn't break my heart.'

Josh held his hands in the air. 'Don't shoot the messenger. They were your dad's words, not mine.'

'That's probably my fault,' she admitted.

'How so?'

'After Peter and I broke up I pretended to be more distraught than I actually was because it gave me a reason to escape Melbourne. I wanted to take the twelve-month posting up here but Dad would have argued against it—his single daughter moving to the other end of the country—but he gave in when I said it would help me to get over Peter. We worked together. He was—is—a paramedic too, and I over-emphasised the discomfort I felt at work after we broke up. But my move wasn't so much to do with Peter as it was to do with me. I wanted a chance to find my own identity, away from being a daughter, a sister or a girlfriend. This move was about a journey of self-discovery.'

'You can handle going back to your old job? Even though Peter is married?'

'He wasn't married when I went out with him. He got married three months later.'

'Sorry, that's not what I meant, but I thought he broke it off with you because he wasn't ready for a commitment?'

'That's what he said, but it turns out he just didn't want to commit to me.'

'And you're okay with that?'

'Yes, perfectly okay. Despite what my parents were hoping for, I didn't want to marry him either.'

'You weren't in love with him?

'No, and he didn't break my heart. I'm twenty-seven years old and still waiting to fall in love,' she said as she finished her coffee and took a piece of birthday cake from the plate in front of her. 'Have you ever been in love?'

'Yes,' he said.

Georgie was surprised at the wave of disappointment that flowed through her when she heard his answer. She wasn't sure what she'd expected him to say, he was thirty-four years old so it would be unrealistic to think he'd never been in love, but she hadn't realised she'd hoped he was in the same romantically barren situation as her.

'Was it a long time ago?'

He nodded.

'Was it the loveliest thing in the world?' She sighed. Despite being in no hurry to get married, she did want to experience her own very traditional, romanticised idea of being in love.

'Yes and no. I gave her my heart but it ended badly.'

'What happened?' She asked the question before she realised it might not be something Josh wanted to talk about.

'She was killed in a car accident.'

'Oh, Josh, I'm so sorry.'

Georgie felt mortified, as though she'd had the wind knocked out of her. She was so shocked she could barely talk. She sat in silence for a moment and then remembered he'd told her that that he didn't plan on marrying. 'Was she your soul mate? Is that why you said you won't marry?'

'No.' He was shaking his head. 'We were engaged but a few months before the wedding she came to me and said there was something she needed to tell me. It turned out she'd been having an affair. She told me because she was worried I'd find out anyway. I think if she thought she could keep it a secret she would have. We had a huge fight. That wasn't unusual, we had lots of ups and downs and usually I gave in, but not this day.' He paused slightly and Georgie wondered how long ago this had happened. It was obvious it still affected him deeply. 'I couldn't believe she'd behaved that way. I told her it was over, the engagement, us, everything. I told her I didn't want to see her again. I should never have let her get in the car but I didn't stop her and then she was dead. And it was my fault.'

'You weren't to know what would happen.'

'Maybe not but I should have stopped her. She was upset when she left, she was in no state to drive, but I was so angry I let her go.'

'When was this?'

'Eight years ago.'

'You're still blaming yourself?'

'No, eventually I realised that a lot of what had happened was beyond my control but it took me a long time to process it all and it made me think differently about relationships. I decided that I needed to be in control of my life and being in a relationship, to me, seemed to require giving up control. When my parents were still married there was a lot of arguing in our house, lots of yelling and screaming, lots of crying, lots of broken promises. I thought that was how families were. But to keep things together, someone always gives in. Tricia and I had a similar pattern but I was the one backing down. I didn't want to live like that again. I didn't want to be one of those people who spend their life fighting and arguing. I promised myself I wouldn't solve problems that way.'

'And have you changed?'

'I hope so but I don't really know. I avoid serious relationships, I don't want to put myself in that position again. I don't want to lose control. That's why I'm the perfect fake boyfriend—you know I won't fall in love with you and make things difficult.' He finished his coffee. 'But now it's time for me to go.' He stood and came around to her chair. He leant over her and kissed her softly on the lips. Georgie was surprised again, thinking this time it was a spontaneous gesture on Josh's part, but that was before he explained himself. 'Kiss me back, your mum is watching.'

He pulled her to her feet and tipped her face up to his. Georgie closed her eyes and waited for his lips to meet hers. His mouth brushed across hers very gently before he deepened the kiss. She tried to pretend she wasn't enjoying the experience but as his tongue teased her lips apart she sighed and opened her mouth and she knew she'd just given him part of her heart.

CHAPTER SEVEN

GEORGIE had seen Josh every day for the past week, at work or after work or both. He was playing the role of the perfect boyfriend perfectly. Her parents thought he was fantastic and Georgie had to keep reminding herself that he was acting. His acting skills were beginning to rival his medical skills.

She was dressing for Lani and Isaac's wedding but it was taking her twice as long as usual. Her hands shook as she zipped up her dress, as she applied her makeup, and they were still shaking as she tried to slide a silver clip into her hair to keep it out of her eyes.

Josh was coming to collect her to take her to the wedding and no matter how many times she told herself otherwise it felt like she was waiting to go on a real date. She was full of nervous anticipation and she was finding it hard to keep a clear head.

He had everyone convinced that he and Georgie were a serious item. If he hadn't told her about Tricia, even she might believe there was a chance he could feel something for her. But Georgie had the impression that Josh was quite content living his solitary life and was not planning on giving it up. But if she thought she had a chance to change his mind, would she take it?

Josh arrived just as she finally got the hairclip into place. Her breath caught in her throat when she saw him standing before her. He was wearing a light grey suit with a white shirt and he looked divine. The suit fitted his broad shoulders perfectly, the cut was exact, and Georgie guessed it had been tailor-made for him. The colour of the suit was a perfect match for his grey eyes.

'You look beautiful.' She thought he was reading her mind again before she realised he was complimenting her.

'Thank you,' she said as she smiled at him.

'You both look gorgeous,' Sofia gushed. 'Let me take a photo before you go.'

Georgie took her camera from her handbag and handed it to her mother. Josh wrapped his arm around her waist as she stood beside him and her stomach did a lazy somersault of desire. As she posed for the photo she reminded herself not to forget it was all make-believe. She was worried that the invisible line between friendship and something more was disappearing. She'd have to be careful to make sure she didn't blur the boundaries between their pretend relationship and their real one.

The wedding and reception were being held in one venue, the yacht club overlooking the Cairns marina, and there were plenty of guests already assembled when Georgie and Josh arrived. Isaac was mingling with the crowd, showing no sign of pre-wedding nerves as he waited for his bride, but Georgie only had eyes for Josh.

She'd felt a million dollars when she'd walked into the room on Josh's arm and that feeling stayed with her even when they became separated as they mixed and chatted with other guests while they waited for the ceremony to start. But even when he was on the opposite side of the room she had no difficulty finding him. It seemed she could find him through osmosis, almost as though she could channel his energy and feel where he was.

He was chatting to Marty but he must have felt her gaze. He looked across at her and winked and as the music started for the ceremony he made his way back to her side. The guests began taking their seats and with his hand resting lightly in the small of her back Josh guided her towards two empty chairs. As they sat he removed his hand from her back and held her hand instead. She thought she should tell him he didn't need to, her parents weren't there to see, but because he'd never listened to her before and because she was enjoying the contact she kept quiet.

Josh's attentiveness didn't waver throughout the evening. They were seated together at a table with their QMERT colleagues and even though they all knew the story behind their 'date' Josh continued to play his part. He held her chair for her, kept her water and champagne glasses filled and constantly touched her knee or arm to get her attention. Each touch of his hand made her blush and she was finding it difficult to concentrate on the conversation as his touch was so distracting. As Isaac led Lani onto the dance floor for the bridal waltz Georgie finally decided to let Josh off the hook.

'It's okay, Josh, everyone knows it's just pretend, you don't need to worry about me.'

'I don't mind,' he replied. 'It's easier to stay in character.' He leant back as he spoke and rested his arm across the back of her chair, brushing his forearm against her bare shoulder. 'I think it's becoming a habit.'

Georgie wasn't sure if she liked the sound of that but she didn't argue any further, content to sit and enjoy his company, and if he was happy to continue playing his role she wasn't going to stop him. But as other guests joined the bride and groom on the dance floor, Josh stood. He leaned over her shoulder and his voice was soft in her ear as he asked, 'Would you dance with me?'

She looked back at him and smiled. 'Of course.'

Josh pulled Georgie's chair out for her and smiled when she slipped her hand into his and let him lead her onto the dance floor. He'd been waiting for this moment all night. Waiting for an excuse to have her in his arms.

She was beautiful. He'd grown so accustomed to seeing her in her work overalls that seeing her in a formal dress was a revelation. It was as if he'd met her for the first time all over again. All evening he'd found himself distracted. Distracted by her and distracted by the sequins shimmering on her silver dress.

He took her in his arms and her cinnamon and honey scent wafted over him. He wondered if he'd just made a mistake. Would he be able to dance with her in his arms? He feared he might suddenly discover he had two left feet. But then she looked up at him, her dark eyes luminous, her lashes thick and long, and his feet began to move of their own accord as he lost himself in the depths of her eyes.

The band was playing a waltz and he pulled her in closer, letting the music wash over them. His right hand rested at the base of her spine, his left held her fingers. She fitted perfectly within his embrace. Her heels gave her enough extra height to make her the perfect dance partner for him and he guided her around the floor, his arm wrapped around her waist, her head just below his. Every time he breathed in he inhaled her perfume and he knew the scent of cinnamon and honey would always remind him of her.

Her dress clung to her curves. Its neckline was demure but the exposed skin on her arms was smooth and soft and delightful. Her hair was pulled back on one side and caught in a silver clip but it cascaded down her back in soft curls and all night he'd been longing to run his hands through it, to feel its weight in his palms. On the dance floor he could slide his hand under her hair and as far as he was concerned that was the next best thing.

He knew he was supposed to be playing a role but it was becoming more and more difficult to remember that. Her scent, her red-lipped smile and her soft velvet skin were becoming part of him and he had to fight to recall that their relationship was just a pretence. It was starting to feel real.

Georgie was getting under his skin. It was dangerous. He should be wary but he was positive he could keep things under control. He hadn't made a mistake so far. What was the harm in satisfying their desires? He'd promised not to fall in love; he hadn't promised not to try to seduce her.

He was sure the attraction wasn't one-sided but he had to make certain. He bent his head to hers, burying his face among the soft curls of her hair, and whispered, 'You look amazing.'

He was pleased to see he was able to make her blush. If he hadn't been so close to her he wouldn't have noticed the deepening colour of her cheeks. It was hard to see with her olive skin, but from a few inches away there was no disguising it.

'Thank you.' She smiled and her eyes sparkled and her teeth were bright against her dark red lips.

The song ended and the band began to play a more up-tempo tune. Josh couldn't keep Georgie in his arms but he wasn't ready to let her go. He led her onto the balcony overlooking the marina. It was his chance to get her alone, away from their colleagues. There was something he wanted to ask her.

'What are you doing after the wedding? Am I taking you home or would you come home with me?'

'Why?' She looked up at him and her eyes were twin pools of midnight, inky black and shining.

He knew this was dangerous. If she came home with him he would be mixing physical intimacy with emotional intimacy and that was something he didn't do. He should stop now, before it was too late. He should leave her alone, but as he looked at her in his arms he knew he wouldn't. He couldn't. He liked the way he felt when she was with him.

It had been a long time since he'd had a relationship that wasn't just about sex. It was dangerous but something about Georgie made him want to try it.

'Let me show you something.' He took her hand and pulled her close. The moment he touched her he could feel her soul. He could see her react to him. Her face was like an open book—every thought flashed across it and he knew his touch stirred her in the same way hers stirred him. He placed her hand over his heart. They were alone on the balcony but he wouldn't have cared if there was a room full of onlookers. Her hand was cool through his thin shirt. 'Can you feel my heart beating?' She nodded. 'Its rhythm is your rhythm. We have a spark. I want you to imagine how we could make each other feel. There is something real between us. It's not all make-believe. Don't ignore it. Don't fight it.'

'What do you want me to do?' Her voice was a whisper.

'Come home with me. Explore our connection, see where it takes us. Don't deny yourself that pleasure.' His heart throbbed with longing where it beat under the touch of her palm. He lifted her hand from his chest and kissed her fingers, slowly, deliberately, one by one, drawing out the moment of intimacy. Her eyelids fluttered closed and he knew she was thinking about his proposal. 'We can have a night to remember.'

He bent his head. He had one last chance to convince her. He put his fingers under her chin and gently tipped her head up. She didn't open her eyes and she didn't resist. His lips met hers. Her mouth was soft, warm, pliant. She moaned a little as he teased her lips apart. His tongue darted inside her mouth and she welcomed him, opening to him. He had one hand behind her back and he pulled her in closer, deepening the kiss. Her hands slid up his back and pressed through the thin fabric of his shirt. Her breasts were flattened against his chest. He could feel her nipples through her dress, hard and erect against his body, and he knew their attraction was mutual.

She was holding onto him as tightly as he was embracing her. Her hips pushed into his groin and he knew she must be able to feel his response to her touch. He let her kiss him back. Let her feel their connection.

'Come home with me,' he repeated.

'No.' She was shaking her head. Her soft, black curls bounced around her shoulders and cascaded down her back, distracting him. 'I'm not denying we have chemistry but I see no point in complicating things. This is make-believe. We are make-believe. Remember?' She gave a slight shrug that sent the sequins on her dress shimmering again.

'I remember. But it's only one night, it doesn't need to change anything. There's nothing to worry about. Nothing to be afraid of. No strings attached.'

Before he could beg, plead, argue or cajole any further, they were interrupted by the master of ceremonies. He was summoning everybody to the dance floor to say farewell to the bride and groom.

'I'm sorry, Josh, one-night stands aren't my thing.'

Georgie pulled her hand from his and moved away. It appeared the discussion was over.

He watched her go.

At least one of them had the sense to fight this attraction. He'd been mad to propose the idea.

He let her go. He couldn't have followed her even if he'd wanted to. He needed to wait for his desire to abate. It was several moments before he was able to leave the balcony, by which time the women had gathered around the edge of the dance floor ready for the traditional tossing of the wedding bouquet. He threaded his way through the throng to the peace and quiet of the far side of the room, away from the women, away from Georgie. But from the opposite side of the room he had a clear line of sight to where she stood. She was right in the centre of the crowd, surrounded by other women.

Lani turned her back to the female guests and lofted the bouquet over her head. The bouquet hit Georgie solidly in the chest. It was a natural reflex to catch it.

She could feel everyone's eyes on her but she could feel one pair in particular. Across the dance floor a pair of gunship-grey eyes watched her as she caught Lani's flowers. Over the delicate bouquet of frangipani flowers she met his gaze.

She stood still, holding the bouquet, as Josh turned and raised one eyebrow.

She wanted to go to him but she held her ground. She couldn't give in.

She had no doubt they would have had a night to remember and even though she could imagine in minute detail how the night would have proceeded, she couldn't do it. She was afraid she wouldn't be happy with just one night, and it could be nothing more.

He'd offered her sex with no strings attached but that was the trouble. She couldn't trust herself to handle that. It would be like playing with fire and she knew she'd be the one to get burnt.

They were too different. He was a confirmed bachelor, focussed solely on his career with no strong family ties and no plans to ever settle down. She wanted to fall in love, she wanted to be married one day, she wanted a family of her own. Their backgrounds, their views on life and love, they were all different. She wished for the chance to get him to open his heart but she didn't think she was up to the challenge. He wasn't going to change for her or anybody else.

She wished she could have gone home with him. She wished he was offering her more than one night but that wasn't going to happen.

He'd told her there was nothing to be afraid of. But he was wrong. She was afraid of getting her heart broken and in her mind that was plenty. He had promised not to fall in love. She'd made no such pledge.

She didn't think she could.

I could have danced all night and still have danced some more. Georgie couldn't remember the right words but it didn't matter, she knew exactly how Eliza Doolittle had felt.

She climbed the steps leading to her deck and twirled around, reliving the feeling of being in Josh's arms, of being swept around the dance floor. Since the moment the music had begun she'd imagined how it would feel to be in his embrace but her imagination hadn't been able to capture the delight; the sensation of floating on air, the warmth of his hand where it had rested in the small of her back, the firmness of his shoulder muscles under her fingers or the soft brush of his breath as his words had caressed her cheek.

She could have quite happily stayed in his arms until the sun came up. But she would have been a fool to take that option. A fool to open herself up to those feelings. She'd have to be content with the memories. And if that was all she was going to have, she was determined to hold onto them.

She held the bouquet of frangipani flowers in one hand as she opened the back door. She was still humming the tune as she walked into the kitchen.

'You sound as though you had a good night.' Sofia's voice greeted her as she closed the door.

'Mum! What are you doing up?'

'Your father can't sleep. I got up to make him a warm drink and now I'm wide awake so I thought I'd wait up for you. How was the wedding?'

'It was lovely.' Georgie sighed. 'Isaac and Lani were so happy and their mood was infectious. Lani looked gorgeous. I took more photos,' she said as she put the bouquet on the table and removed her camera from her evening bag. 'Would you like to see?' Georgie had planned to come home and take her memories of Josh to bed with her as some form of comfort but she couldn't ignore her mother.

They sat together at the table as Georgie scrolled through the photos. There were several of Lani and Isaac exchanging vows and several more pictures of the QMERT team, which Georgie had taken during dinner, and a couple of Isaac and Lani during the bridal waltz. Georgie thought they were the last photos but her mum continued to go forward and the next photo was one of her with Josh. She must have left her camera on the table when he'd asked her to dance and, unbeknown to her, someone had picked it up and snapped a picture.

She was wrapped in his arms as they danced. He was smiling down at her as she gazed up at him. To anyone who didn't know better, they looked like a couple in love. The camera had captured a moment in time when they had been unaware of anything or anyone else around them. They looked like they were in their own little world and Georgie realised that's how Josh made her feel. In his company she was content. She didn't want for anything else when he was with her. Thank goodness she hadn't gone back to his apartment tonight. Seeing the expression on her face in the photograph, she knew now she was in big trouble. She'd have to watch herself. She was falling under his spell.

'That's a lovely photo, I didn't realise it was quite so serious between you two.' Her mum employed her favourite tactic, make a comment sound like a question and see what information was forthcoming, but Georgie recognised the technique and kept quiet. She wasn't going to give her mother anything to speculate about; she'd learned long ago how to play that game. Besides, she didn't know what she could say.

After what seemed like a short lifetime her mum gave up. 'I'll just go and check on your dad. I'll be back in a minute.'

Georgie put her camera away while her mum was out of the room and took the opportunity to change the subject when she returned. 'Is he okay?'

'He's asleep. He hasn't been sleeping well recently so that's good.'

'Is something the matter?' Georgie frowned. She hadn't noticed anything.

'He's been very tired lately. He's blaming the lack of sleep but what I don't understand is why he isn't sleeping well. He's not worried about anything, he's relaxed, but he says he finds it hard to breathe.'

Now that her mother had mentioned it, Georgie remembered that her parents had been having afternoon rests, her dad especially, which was something he'd never done before, but Georgie had just assumed it was because he was on holiday and could lie down. Now she wondered what she'd been missing. 'Has he complained of shortness of breath at any other times? With activity? Have you noticed anything?'

Sofia shook her head.

'Has he been to the doctor?' Georgie asked.

'He's made an appointment for when we get home from this trip.' Sofia paused. 'Perhaps it's been bothering him more than he's let on,' she mused, 'especially if he's made a doctor's appointment. You know what he's like about going to the doctor.'

'Has he got any other symptoms?'

Sofia frowned. 'Like what?'

'Chest pain, dizziness, that sort of thing?' Georgie was worried. Her paramedic training made her assume the worst, even though she hadn't actually noticed any worrying signs herself.

'No. He reckons it's just old age. He's been talking about getting old a lot lately. I think that's why he's keen to see you settled down.'

And with those words Georgie had to rein in her fantasies once more. On her way home from the wedding she'd imagined what would have happened if she'd gone home with Josh. Now that she knew what it was like to be in his arms, what it was like to feel as though they were the only two people who existed, her imagination had been able to conjure up all sorts of fantasies.

She'd imagined the touch of his fingers on her knee as

they sat in the taxi, the warmth of his hand as he led her into his building, the heat that emanated from him as he pulled her against him in the lift, the taste of his lips when he closed his apartment door and kissed her, the breeze over her bare skin as he lifted her dress over her head, and finally the look in his eyes as he took her to his bed.

She could sleep with Josh to satisfy her curiosity and desire but nothing more would come of it. She remembered the photo of them dancing and she knew she wouldn't be able to sleep with him without exposing herself to heartache, she would be leaving herself wide open. She'd never had a one-night stand and she wasn't going to start now.

Maybe she should put a stop to this fake relationship before she got any more involved. Before it was too late.

CHAPTER EIGHT

GEORGIE was flat out for the next couple of days and it had nothing to do with work. She'd spent a pleasant day with her parents following Isaac's wedding, although she found herself watching her dad carefully, looking for any sign that he was unwell. Her parents were only in their mid-sixties and it was the first time she'd really thought about them getting old. Her dad was semi-retired; he was a builder and he'd worked hard and always been in good physical shape, but perhaps the years had taken their toll on him. It wouldn't be unusual. But Georgie had never imagined her life without her parents. Keeping a close eye on him while trying not to make him aware of her attention was difficult but thankfully she didn't see anything that concerned her.

Con and Anastasia arrived the next day and Georgie found herself playing tour guide to not one elderly couple but two. She'd organised to take them up to Kuranda, a town in the rainforest hinterland inland from Cairns. Travelling by a combination of cable car and old steam train, it was an extremely touristy thing to do but Con and Anastasia seemed to enjoy the outing and were appreciative of the effort Georgie had made.

But the combination of looking for anything untoward with her father's health and being a shining example of a perfect daughter meant she was exhausted by the end of the day and she was looking forward to returning to work.

Until she got there.

The first thing she saw on the noticeboard in the kitchen was photos of Isaac and Lani's wedding. That was fine, except that when she got closer to the board she saw that most of the photos were of her with Josh. Lou was in the kitchen, making herself a coffee, and Georgie knew she was watching her, waiting to see her reaction.

'Who put these up?' she asked.

Lou stirred milk into her coffee. 'Marty. He's taking bets on whether your relationship with Josh is happening for real now.'

'He's doing what?'

'He seems to think that you and Josh are dating seriously now.'

'And what about everyone else? What do they think?' She'd been off work for two days and this was what had happened? She couldn't believe what she was hearing.

'I think they'd be quite happy to believe it. You do make a good couple.'

'Not you as well, Lou?'

'Don't worry, I haven't put any money on you either way, I value my life too much.'

That was why this whole fake relationship was a dumb idea. She didn't want to be gossiped about. She'd conveniently forgotten all the reasons why she hadn't wanted to do this but Lou was rapidly reminding her. 'What about Josh? What has he said?'

'He said nothing's going on but it seems most people are choosing not to believe him.'

Georgie was mortified. 'Is he working today?' She had to find him.

Lou was nodding. 'He came in just before you. He should be in the change room.'

Georgie didn't bother saying goodbye to Lou, she bolted for the change room and hoped and prayed she'd find Josh alone. He was just coming out as she got there. She grabbed him by the arm. 'Can I talk to you? Somewhere private?'

'Sure. What's this about?' he asked as she dragged him outside. She took him around the QMERT building, on the opposite side to the helicopters—that way she was pretty sure they wouldn't be interrupted.

'Do you know what Marty's doing?'

'Running a book?' He nodded. 'Yeah, I know. Pretty funny, don't you think?'

'No, I don't think.'

He was frowning now. 'What's the matter?'

'This is just what I didn't want, people gossiping about me. This is why dating a colleague is a bad idea.'

'Fair enough, except we're not dating.'

'We know that but it seems everyone else thinks otherwise. All because I caught the stupid bouquet.'

Josh didn't think that was why people were talking. He'd seen the photos. He'd seen the way they'd looked when they'd been dancing together. Even in a photo their chemistry was obvious. It wasn't surprising that people were putting two and two together and he couldn't blame them for jumping to conclusions. He knew he and Georgie were acting the part convincingly, so much so that they were also in danger of believing the illusion.

'So what do you want to do about it?

'We should just cancel the whole thing. It was a dumb idea in the first place.'

'And what will you tell your folks?'

Georgie shrugged. 'I'll think of something.'

'No. We may as well keep going. How much longer are your parents in town for?'

'Three days.'

'And their friends are here too now, aren't they?'

Georgie nodded.

'I think we should stick with the plan. Everyone here will draw their own conclusions anyway. I don't think they'll believe we've called it off for a minute if they don't want to.'

'Are you sure you don't mind?'

'That people think we're getting down and dirty?' He grinned.

'No! Are you sure you don't mind being a surrogate boyfriend for a little bit longer?'

'It's fine. It's probably only a matter of one more dinner and everything will go back to normal.' Georgie's parents would leave and this would all come to an end then. But until then he needed to remind her, remind them both, that this wasn't real. Could never be real.

'If you like, I can tell Marty and the others exactly why I'm the perfect fake boyfriend. I can tell them why I'm never getting married, why I won't commit.'

'You're going to tell them about Tricia?'

He was positive he could make everyone believe it was all a show, Georgie included, but he needed to tell her his whole story.

'There's more to it than what I've told you. The others don't need to hear the whole story but I think you do.' It would ensure she wouldn't imagine their relationship to be anything other than the charade it had started out to be.

'My parents got divorced when I was a teenager. My dad worked for a big international corporation and he travelled a lot. Mum was bored, and lonely too, I suppose, and she had a few affairs. I think my father turned a blind eye the first few times and despite lots of fighting they managed to stay together, but I guess at one point he decided not to accept it and they split up. My brother and I were sent to boarding school. Dad was still travelling and I think Mum either didn't want the responsibility of looking after us or the reminder of what she'd done to the family so she chose a new life. Scott, my brother, was...' he paused and corrected himself '...is a couple of years older than me. He was the only constant in my life. I depended on him, trusted him, and that was pretty significant because trusting people wasn't something that came naturally to me. When I started dating I always expected my girlfriends to either leave me or betray me. I was always suspicious and that wasn't conducive to healthy relationships. I can't remember now whether I chose to trust Tricia or whether she convinced me but, in my mind, she was my first serious, committed relationship until she betrayed me. But her betrayal wasn't the worst of it. It was Scott's betrayal that almost destroyed me.'

'Scott's?'

Josh nodded. 'Tricia had been sleeping with Scott. That's what we were fighting about when she drove off, when she was killed.' He paused and took a deep breath. He never discussed the incident that had changed his life and made him into the man he was, the man who couldn't commit, but Georgie needed to hear this. She needed to understand him.

'She'd been having an affair with your brother?' Georgie's dark eyes were wide with surprise. 'How could they do that to you?'

'I don't know. I couldn't understand it and I certainly couldn't accept it. Scott and I were always very competitive, as I think most brothers are, but I never expected him to steal my fiancée. He was my big brother. I thought he'd look out for me. I thought we'd look out for each other, but I was wrong. I went a little bit crazy after that. I took time off university, went travelling, looking for the most dangerous activities and situations I could find, the more outrageous the better. I was feeling sorry for myself, testing my own mortality, trying to decide if life was worth living.'

'And you decided it was?'

'Yes, but I promised myself I'd never put myself in a situation like that again, so I concentrated on work and avoided my brother and relationships in general.'

'Do you see your brother now?'

He shook his head. 'No. My experience of relationships has all been about arguing, fighting and betrayal. That's why I don't plan on getting married. I have nothing left in me to give anyone. If I can't trust, what's the point? But I can tell everyone about Tricia. That'll give them something else to gossip about instead.'

'No.' Georgie shook her head. Three days, that's all it was. She could manage three more days. 'You don't need to tell them about Tricia. I'd rather let everyone jump to conclusions for a few more days than make you divulge your secrets.' Marty could take bets but she wouldn't give him any more fodder for gossip. 'My parents will be gone soon and this will all be over. If you can manage one more dinner, that'll keep my parents happy and then things will be back to normal.'

Only two more days now, she thought the next morning as she parked her car outside the QMERT building, but even so she found herself automatically searching for Josh's car as she locked hers. Just thinking about seeing him again made her heart race.

Georgie disagreed about his assessment that he had

nothing to give but she knew it wasn't her place to say so. He was doing her a favour; he hadn't asked her to interfere in his life. In two days there would be no need to have any extra contact with Josh.

She'd let herself get carried away with their charade but hearing Josh's story had reminded her of the truth. She suspected that's why he'd told her and she knew she had to keep her feelings under control. She had to remember their relationship wasn't going anywhere. Had to remember they didn't actually have a relationship and they definitely didn't have a future.

She waited for her heart rate to return to normal, waited until she was sure she could behave normally around Josh, before she gathered her things and went into work, only to find he was doing a shift at the hospital. But at least with him out of the way she knew she'd be able to keep her mind on her job.

But he wasn't completely out of contact. The crew was on their second run of the day, a routine inter-hospital transfer, when Louise patched a phone call through to the chopper.

'Georgie, I have an urgent phone call for you. It's Josh.'

Louise's message immediately sent her into a spin. She wondered what Josh could possibly want that would require him to go to the trouble of tracking her down in the chopper.

'Josh, what's up?'

'Where are you guys?'

His tone was short, abrupt even. His phone manner left a lot to be desired but as the call was coming through the helicopter radio she gave him the benefit of the doubt. Maybe it was because he knew everyone in the chopper could hear the conversation through their headsets.

'We're heading to Dimbulah,' she told him.

'You're on your way there now?'

'Yes, we're about twenty minutes east of town.'

'I have something I need to tell you.' He paused very slightly and Georgie frowned. There was complete silence through the radio and it felt as though minutes had passed before she heard his next words. 'Everyone is okay but your father has just been brought into Emergency with chest pain.'

Immediately Georgie recalled her father's shortness of breath. 'Is he having a heart attack?' Why hadn't she insisted that he have a check-up with a doctor while he was in Cairns? Why had she been content for him to wait until he got home to Melbourne? Even though she'd seen no sign of any problems she still berated herself. Her mother had told her of the episodes—why had she ignored her?

'We're running tests now,' he said.

'It'll be a few hours before I'm back in Cairns. How serious is this?' She could hear the panic in her voice. Was there more that Josh wasn't telling her?

'It's okay, Georgie, you can relax. We've got things under control.' Hearing him say her name calmed her nerves. He sounded so assured and confident. He'd tell her straight, wouldn't he? 'If I thought it was critical I'd tell you,' he continued. Even over the radio it seemed as though he could follow her thoughts. 'The ECG isn't showing any signs of cardiac arrhythmia but we'll keep testing until we find out what's going on. I'll take care of him but come in when you get back.'

She breathed out, concentrating on expelling the air, releasing the tension. If Josh said he'd take care of things she trusted him to do just that. 'Have you seen Mum? Is she okay?'

'She seems to be. She's with Con and Anastasia.' He knew who they were and now he'd met them, but it was still strange to hear him mention her parents' friends. It was as though they had no secrets, as though he knew all the intimate details of her life, but fortunately he didn't disclose anything further. He hadn't forgotten that the rest of the crew could hear their entire conversation. 'Don't worry, everything will be all right. I'll keep you up to date. See you when you get back.'

'Thanks, Josh.'

She worked hard to keep her focus and concentration on the job and fortunately the IHT was straightforward and the return to Cairns went smoothly. Josh phoned with another update as they were returning to Cairns. Her father's condition had stabilised and he'd been transferred to one of the cardiology beds, and this news helped to settle her nerves.

It was nearing the end of her shift when the chopper landed opposite the hospital to transfer their patient. Sean suggested that Georgie stay behind and she gratefully accepted.

'Pat and I will get your car back to you somehow,' he said. 'And Louise can call Marty and see if he can come in a bit early in case we need a paramedic. Don't worry about us, go and see your dad.'

She didn't need to be asked twice. She and Sean transferred their patient to the hospital but Georgie didn't return to the chopper, heading instead for the cardiology ward. Her mum was in a chair beside her father but Georgie was pleased to see there were no other visitors. Con and Anastasia must have returned to their hotel.

'Dad! How are you feeling?' she asked as she kissed both her parents.

'Completely fine,' George said. 'If I wasn't hooked up to these monitors I'd walk out of here. It was just a bit of indigestion, I'm sure of it.'

'You don't have any pain? Any discomfort?'

'None. I feel like a fraud.'

Georgie's gaze flicked to the monitor. According to the figures George was okay. His oxygen sats, blood pressure and heart rate were all within normal limits. But that didn't explain why he'd been admitted.

'Tell me what happened this morning.'

'Your mother and I had breakfast with Con and Anastasia and then we went for a walk along the esplanade so they could have a look around Cairns. I had a bit of chest pain, which I'm sure was indigestion—'

'There was a bit more to it than that, George,' Sofia interrupted her husband. 'You felt a bit dizzy too.'

'I'm not used to the heat, that's all,' George insisted. 'I didn't have any arm pain or anything else.'

Sofia ignored him and turned to her daughter. 'We were right by the hospital so, in view of his other recent complaints about shortness of breath, I thought he should get checked out.'

'That was the right thing to do,' Georgie responded. With chest pain, dizziness and a history of shortness of breath, it was no surprise her father had been admitted to the cardiology ward. There was definitely something abnormal going on. 'What have the doctors told you? What have they found?'

'I think they said the major arteries are okay but they're going to do more tests tomorrow.'

Movement in the doorway distracted George, and Georgie turned to see what, or who, her father was looking at.

It was Josh.

'Hello, you're here,' he said as he entered the room, and with those few words he managed to make it sound as though he'd been counting the minutes until she arrived. He made it sound as though he'd missed her.

His eyes locked with hers and he smiled. His grey eyes sparkled silver and his smile said he was there for her. His dark blond hair was sticking up and he had a slight shadow of beard darkening his jaw. He looked good. She smiled in return and took a step towards him before she hesitated. She wasn't sure how she should be behaving. But Josh didn't hesitate. He stepped forward and took her in his arms.

'What are you doing?' she whispered.

He leant down and his lips pressed against her hair. 'I'm comforting you, I'm supposed to be your boyfriend, remember?'

She closed her eyes as she hugged him back, savouring the feel of him, the solid, dependable sense of wellbeing he gave her. They'd had no physical contact since the wedding, since she'd turned down his invitation to go home with him, and she'd missed it. Being in his arms gave her a sense of belonging, which was silly because she didn't belong to him, but that was how he made her feel.

'You have perfect timing. Dad's a bit vague with the details. Can you give me a bit more information?' she asked as she stepped backwards, out of his embrace.

Josh was nodding. 'He's had several tests today and the results in most of them were normal but the echocardiogram showed a problem with the mitral valve.'

'You left out that bit of information, Dad,' Georgie reprimanded her father.

'Josh interrupted,' he countered.

'The cardiologist will do some more tests tomorrow to see how serious the problem is. I'll give you a heads up, George, just so you don't get any nasty surprises, but you may need surgery.'

'I thought my arteries were fine and I didn't have a heart attack. Why would I need surgery?'

'The valves in your heart regulate the blood flow. If they're not opening or closing properly, you get insufficient blood pumped around your body and your heart will work harder to compensate for it. That stresses your heart and can lead to a heart attack down the track,' Josh explained. He kept the details simple and Georgie knew her parents would be able to follow his summary. 'The breathlessness and dizziness you've already experienced can be symptomatic of heart disease. But the severity of the symptoms doesn't always indicate the severity of the disease so the cardiologist will investigate further, and that's why I've said you may need surgery. It's a possibility, that's all. Does that make sense?' Josh waited for everyone's agreement before continuing. 'Now George needs to rest and I'm sure you two need to eat,' he said, preparing to bustle them out.

'Well, if you think it's okay to leave him?' Sofia was deferring to Josh.

'You don't need to worry. You can come back in the morning,' he told her.

Her mother turned to Georgie. 'I guess it would be okay to go home. Anastasia offered to cook dinner for us. She's at your house. I hope you don't mind.'

'I don't mind,' she said.

'Have you finished work for the day, Josh?' Sofia asked. 'Would you like to join us?'

Josh looked at Georgie. She tried to keep her face blank; she knew how well he could read her mind. She gave him just the tiniest shake of her head and then held her breath as she waited for his reply. She doubted her parents would be leaving in three days as originally planned and, if that was the case, Josh was going to have to continue to play the part of her boyfriend for a bit longer. But she needed time to digest this thought, they probably both did, and if she was going to survive until her parents left and life returned to normal, she needed to keep everyone in their own little compartments. Which meant only seeing Josh when absolutely necessary. Which meant not tonight.

'Thanks,' he said in response to Sofia's invitation, 'but I've got some other things I need to take care of. I'll catch up with you all again tomorrow. I'm back at QMERT then, but if you have any questions about what's happening speak to the staff here, and if you need further clarification don't hesitate to call me.' He turned to Georgie. 'Are you working tomorrow?'

She nodded and let out the breath she'd been holding.

'I'll see you then,' he said before he left the room.

'Josh?' Georgie called out to him and he turned, stopping in the corridor. She left the room and took a few steps towards him. She reached out, putting one hand on his arm. It was a reflex movement but the moment she touched the bare skin of his forearm and felt the tingle of awareness race through her she realised what she'd done and removed her hand quickly, as though it had been burnt.

'Thank you for taking care of my parents today. Knowing you were here helped when I was stuck out in the chopper.'

He glanced down at his arm, at the spot where her hand had touched him, and when he looked at her his eyes were dark grey, darker than she'd ever seen them before and unfathomable. 'Don't mention it. It was my pleasure. I'll see you tomorrow.'

'Mum and Dad might be here for a bit longer, depending on what dad's tests show. You were expecting to be my surrogate boyfriend for only a couple more days. What do you want to do, what do we say?'

'Don't worry. I'm happy to do this for as long as you need. I won't let you down,' he said. Then he was gone with just a brief nod of his head.

Georgie watched him disappear along the corridor, wondering if he was okay. He seemed upset. She wished she could read his mind as easily as he read hers. She had no idea what could be wrong. She stood looking after him as she tried to figure it out and then realised that nothing was wrong with Josh, something was wrong with her. She was feeling let down because he hadn't kissed her goodbye. She'd come to expect it. But no one had been watching so why should he kiss her?

Her mum joined her and Georgie let her distract her from Josh as they headed for the lifts. 'How are you coping, Mum? This must have come as a bit of a shock.'

'It was quite frightening, not knowing what was wrong. Your dad makes it sound like nothing but, believe me, he looked dreadful. He went quite grey and I thought he wasn't going to make it into the hospital. Thank goodness for Josh,' she said as the lift doors slid open and they stepped inside. 'He was fabulous. He was so good to me, to both of us. He kept checking on me, making sure I knew what was happening. He's quite something, isn't he?'

Georgie kept her gaze averted, avoiding eye contact. She didn't want her mother to read her opinion of Josh on her face, that wouldn't do. Her mother was going to take the news badly when Georgie and Josh had their inevitable 'breakup' and she didn't need her mother to know how much she really liked him—that would only make things harder. 'Mmm,' she replied, hoping that some sort of response would be all that was expected before her mother continued talking.

'I wouldn't have coped nearly so well without him,' Sofia added. 'It's a pity he couldn't join us for dinner.'

Sofia's chatter kept them occupied until they reached the taxi rank and climbed into a cab for the short trip home. Once there, conversation flowed easily between Sofia, Anastasia and Con, and Georgie wasn't required to contribute much at all, which suited her. The others made excuses for her, assuming she must be tired after such a long, exhausting and emotional day, but the reality was that she was quite happy to sit quietly and think about Josh. About how smoothly he'd taken care of all of them, her included. He'd single-handedly turned what could have been an extremely scary, stressful situation into something that seemed manageable. She'd seen his calm, confident approach when they'd worked together but to be on the receiving end of his bedside manner really made her aware of his compassion and ability to read a situation. It appeared that being able to read her mind wasn't his only talent. Her mother was obviously totally impressed by him and it wasn't difficult to see why.

The next few days were a whirlwind of activity, all revolving around her family. The cardiologist determined that George had a diseased mitral valve, which was more serious than his symptoms indicated. He advised George not to fly and advocated immediate valve-replacement surgery, which sent Sofia and Georgie into a spin. In the space of a couple of days George had gone from a fit and active man to one who required heart surgery.

Georgie didn't have many opportunities to think about Josh and their fake relationship, she was too busy concentrating on what her parents needed, but Josh didn't disappear. He worked quietly and tirelessly in the background, taking care of the little tasks that didn't seem important in the bigger picture but still needed to get done. Georgie hadn't asked him to help out but he seemed to be able to sense when things needed to be taken care of, and he did it without any prompting and without seeming to expect any thanks. He was just Josh, doing the things no one else had the time or energy for. He organised for Marty to swap shifts with Georgie so she could keep Sofia company while George was in surgery. He replenished the food in her fridge, filled her car with petrol and even managed to get George and Sofia's flights home to Melbourne changed. Georgie didn't know how he did that, considering he wasn't family, but Louise told her that Josh had gone across to the airport terminal in his QMERT uniform with 'Doctor' embroidered on the chest and had charmed the customer service officer into doing his bidding.

It must have been a female on the counter at the time, Georgie thought, but just picturing the scene made her smile. She didn't care how he'd managed it, she was just grateful for his help. It meant one less thing for her to worry about.

In fact, with Josh's help she found she had very little to worry about. Nothing was too much trouble for him. And it wasn't just Georgie he was taking care of.

He was constantly popping into the hospital to check on her father too. They'd started a regular evening game of backgammon to pass the time and he even helped to entertain Con and Anastasia. His efforts with them gave Georgie more time to spend time with her parents and it was another one of the selfless gestures that benefited her.

She couldn't believe she'd initially wanted to keep their contact to a bare minimum. She now wondered how she would have managed at all over the past few days without his help.

Five days after her dad's surgery Josh and Georgie were in the chopper, heading to Cooktown, two hundred kilometres north of Cairns. Georgie was tired. It had been a stressful few days and while her dad was making a good recovery she was feeling emotionally drained, even with all Josh's help. She'd been trying to keep several balls in the air—updating her brothers, looking after her mother and Con and Anastasia, plus keeping on top of dad's medical condition and working—but Josh had been effectively holding down two jobs and helping her, while somehow managing to remain his usual upbeat, enthusiastic self. Typically for an emergency doctor, he seemed to thrive on challenges. She wasn't quite sure how he'd managed it, but it left her feeling a little incompetent. But things were slowly getting back to normal. Con and Anastasia were leaving today and then it was just a matter of waiting for her dad to recover enough to head home to Melbourne. And then her life would return to normal and she and Josh would go their separate ways.

Georgie didn't actually want to think about that so in an effort to keep her mind occupied with other things she immersed herself in checking the medical kits. She told herself it was imperative that she know exactly what they were carrying, but the reality was that if she kept her head down she didn't need to watch Josh and she knew that's what she would do. It was far safer to sort through the medical kits, even though they didn't need sorting, but she could feel Josh watching her as she worked.

'You've checked that kit three times. Are you going to tell me what's on your mind?' he asked.

'You mean you don't know?' She'd become so used to Josh being able to read her thoughts that to hear him ask her what was wrong was a surprise.

He laughed and the sound cheered her up. 'I could guess but it would be quicker if you told me.'

Georgie flicked the communication switch on her headset to the 'Off' position. She didn't need Pat and Isaac listening to this conversation.

'I'm not sure if I'm ready to go back to Melbourne.'

Josh switched his headset off too before he answered. 'Why don't you stay in Cairns?'

'My parents expect me home and I promised I'd go back at the end of my twelve months. I've always done the right thing but I'm not sure I'm ready to go back to being the Georgie I was when I left. I've changed but I don't know if I've changed enough to avoid slipping back into the role of the dutiful daughter.'

'You'll be all right,' he replied. 'The Georgie I knew first isn't so different from the Georgie I see now. Being you parents' daughter has shaped you into the person you are, someone who embraces other people wholeheartedly and without reservation or judgement. Someone who is compassionate, unselfish, loyal and strong. There is nothing about you that you should want to change.'

'You think I'm strong?'

Josh nodded. 'And capable and confident.'

'I haven't felt very capable this past week. I don't know how I would have managed without your help.'

'You would have been perfectly fine. I didn't do anything you couldn't have done. Have faith in yourself. You can do anything you want to do, be anyone you want to be. Here or in Melbourne.'

Georgie wanted to ask Josh what else he saw in her. What could he see that she couldn't? But Isaac was leaning back between the seats, pointing at his headset, signalling to them to switch their communication on. They flicked the comms switches and Pat's voice came through their headsets. 'There's some rough weather coming—make sure you're buckled in nice and tight.'

The sun disappeared as Georgie checked her harness

and the cabin was cast into semi-darkness. They were over the ocean, heading east away from Cooktown and the Queensland coast. They were searching for a yacht, and were planning to evacuate a sixty-year-old woman who'd slipped and fallen and had a suspected broken leg.

Georgie looked out of the window, lost in her thoughts. Josh saw someone who was strong and confident. She wondered how much of that was due to his influence. She didn't think she would have been nearly as capable over the past week without his help. But perhaps the Georgie she was discovering was those things. She just hoped she could continue to be that person once she was back in Melbourne. Once she was without Josh.

'We should get a visual on the yacht in the next five minutes,' Pat said and as they approached the location they'd been given Isaac, Georgie and Josh all began scanning the ocean for the sailing boat. Away to the west Georgie saw a mass of dark clouds, chasing them over the ocean. The storm was heading their way and she hoped they could outrun it or find the yacht before the bad weather hit.

Ten minutes passed and there was no sign of the yacht. Not one boat could be seen.

'This is Victor Hotel Romeo Hotel Sierra to QMERT Cairns, do you read me?' Pat radioed Louise.

'This is QMERT Cairns, go ahead, Pat.'

'Can we check those coordinates please? I'm overhead now and there's no sign of a yacht.'

Louise read out the coordinates she had been given.

'Confirm that's our current location,' Pat said. 'But, I repeat, I do not have a visual on the yacht. Can you confirm with the vessel and get back to us?'

The clouds were closing in quickly now as Pat circled the chopper over choppy seas while they waited for Louise to confirm the yacht's position.

'QMERT Cairns to Victor Hotel Romeo Hotel Sierra.'

'Go ahead, Lou.'

'I have new coordinates for you, they read them out incorrectly.' Louise relayed the new location and Isaac repeated the coordinates back to her.

'That's thirty nautical miles north-north-west of where we are,' Pat said. 'Please confirm our ETA of fifteen minutes with the vessel and remind them to have their medical assistance flag flying for identification.'

'Will do,' Louise replied.

'This extra flying is going to make fuel pretty tight and the weather's not going to help as we'll be heading into the storm. We'll have to assess the situation when we find the vessel and determine if we can do a safe evacuation.' Pat filled the crew in. Being out over the ocean in bad weather when they were low on fuel was certainly not an ideal position to be in.

'We'll need to be ready to go as quickly as possible,' Georgie told Josh. 'We're not going to have the luxury of time.'

Isaac would lower them to the yacht on a winch. One would go with the stretcher and the medical kits, the other would follow. It was always a tricky manoeuvre as there were so many variables and the weather was only going to complicate matters. They would need to move quickly. 'Let's get the kits strapped onto the stretcher.'

Isaac spotted the yacht on their starboard side as Georgie and Josh finished arranging the equipment. Pat did a flyover and Georgie and Josh peered out the windows.

The sails had all been lowered in preparation for the storm, which had made the yacht more difficult to locate but gave them a good view of the deck. A woman was lying on the lower section of the deck at the foot of a short flight of stairs. They'd expected her to be in the cabin but this was preferable as access was easier. A man was squatting beside her, waving to the chopper.

'I'll go down alone. It'll be faster to evacuate if we only need to do one retrieval,' Josh said.

If only one of them went, it would mean two winch operations instead of four, something that would save precious time.

'That sounds sensible,' Georgie agreed, 'but can you manage to get the patient onto the stretcher on your own?' If the diagnosis was correct and the woman had suffered a broken leg, there was no great need for both of them to attend. The issue wasn't the medical care but the transferring of the woman.

'I should be fine but if it's difficult, her partner will have to lend a hand. If I find things are more complicated than we expected, I'll call you down then.'

Georgie shrugged. 'Okay.'

Isaac was out of his seat and had climbed into the rear of the chopper. He attached all three of them to safety lines.

'The wind is picking up and the forecast is for increasing wind speeds ahead of the storm so we're only going to get one shot at this,' Pat said.

Isaac slid the door open and the wind buffeted them inside the chopper.

'Your call, Josh,' Isaac said.

Georgie watched Josh's face. It was up to him whether he wanted to attempt this evacuation or whether he thought it was too dangerous. His expression was calm, his grey eyes steady and he didn't hesitate.

'Let's do this.'

Josh fastened himself into the harness and together Isaac and Georgie hooked him and the stretcher to the winch before disengaging him from the chopper's safety line.

Isaac directed Pat above the yacht. Pat was flying blind. In order to lower Josh directly onto the yacht, he had to position the chopper above it, meaning he couldn't see either the yacht or Josh on the winch. Isaac became his eyes; he was in charge of the descent. He swung Josh out of the chopper and waited for his signal before he pressed the button and the winch began to lower its load. Josh's head disappeared from view and Georgie watched as he dropped towards the sea.

Georgie was nervous. The yacht looked tiny, bobbing about on the waves beneath them. The sea was rough and it was a difficult exercise; trying to manoeuvre a heavy load on a wire suspended from a moving object onto a moving target was no easy task in calm seas, let alone in rough conditions. Georgie didn't like being in a situation where she had no control. She would have preferred to have been the one going down to the yacht rather than the one sitting, watching and waiting. If she was occupied she wouldn't have time to think of the danger.

Isaac slowed the winch down, trying to get his timing right. He had to lower Josh carefully to avoid crashing him onto the deck if the boat was lifted up on the peak of a wave.

Georgie saw Josh's feet touch the deck, saw him take his weight but then the deck fell away from him as the yacht fell into a trough. Josh was suspended again, his weight hanging on the winch line.

His feet touched the deck for a second time but the yacht tipped. Georgie saw Josh lose his footing and her heart was in her throat as he slipped and fell to his knees. For a second she forgot Josh was securely attached to the chopper, for a second she could imagine him sliding off the yacht into the sea, but then the yacht levelled out and he was on his feet.

He was on the deck now. He'd laid the stretcher out beside him as he knelt and waited for the winch line to give him some slack before unfastening the hook from the strap around his chest. He gave Isaac the signal and Isaac began to pull the cable in as he gave Pat the all-clear to move away, Josh didn't need the downdraught from the chopper to add to the already difficult conditions.

Pat guided the chopper far enough away to avoid the downdraught but close enough to still have visual contact. Georgie could see Josh working quickly, taking observations, talking to the woman's companion, assessing the situation. She wished she'd been able to go with him. Having two of them there would have made his job easier, but the extra time used might have been critical. Neither the weather nor their fuel situation was on their side.

Josh was putting a canula in the woman's vein and, Georgie assumed, giving her something for pain. They had radio communication but there was no need to use it. The others were of no assistance while they were in the chopper but Georgie still wished he'd say something. The silence was making her uneasy.

She saw him quickly splint the woman's leg before rolling her onto her side to get her onto the stretcher. He was working flat out. There was no time to wait for the pain relief to take effect, they needed to get her evacuated and get away from there before the storm hit.

Josh had fastened the straps on the stretcher and was repacking the medical kit. He was kneeling on the deck, his knees spread wide for stability. The woman's partner was bending over the stretcher but was supporting himself against the cabin wall with one hand. The waves had picked up and it seemed he could no longer keep his feet without support.

Josh crawled around to the top of the stretcher to fasten

the protective cage over the woman's face. He was kneeling at her head, reaching for the cage, when a rogue wave slammed into the side of the yacht. The vessel was thrown onto its port side and anything that wasn't tied down went sliding across the deck. Including the stretcher. And Josh.

Georgie watched as though it was happening in slow motion. She saw the woman's partner fall forward, slamming onto the deck. She saw the stretcher sliding towards the sea. She saw Josh's hand on the side of the metal cage.

'Josh!' she yelled, but she was too late. The stretcher had collided with the edge of the deck, trapping Josh's hand. The weight of the stretcher pinned him in place.

CHAPTER NINE

'JOSH!'

Georgie didn't know why she was yelling. There was nothing she could do.

Josh was trapped, pinned between the stretcher and the edge of the deck. She could see him trying to pull the stretcher away from the edge but with only one free hand he couldn't apply enough pressure.

The seconds seemed like hours. He needed help. He needed her. She should have been there.

In reality it was only moments before the wave subsided and the yacht righted itself, but the stretcher still didn't move. Josh was still trapped. Georgie could see him trying to shift the weight of it by moving from one leg to the other but because he was kneeling he couldn't get enough force. If the stretcher hadn't been loaded it wouldn't have been a problem, but he had close to one hundred kilograms pinning him to the side of the yacht. He needed help.

What was the other man doing? Georgie looked across the deck. The other man was on his knees and there was blood pouring down his face from a gash on his forehead.

'Isaac, I need to get down there now!' Georgie grabbed a second harness as Pat brought the chopper back over the yacht and Isaac organised the winch.

'Josh, I'm coming down.'

The wind whistled in her ears and her eyes watered as Isaac lowered her to the yacht. She narrowed her eyes, peering down to see how Josh was faring. The waves were tossing the yacht about but the movement of the boat had finally enabled Josh to push the stretcher off his hand. By the time Georgie reached the deck he had locked the protective head cage into place over the stretcher.

'Are you okay?' Georgie asked.

'Yes, I'm fine.' He nodded as he answered, emphasising his point. 'Can you see to Brian?'

The woman's companion, Brian, was now sitting on the deck, looking quite dazed. Blood was still streaming from a cut above his left eye but on examination he didn't seem concussed. Georgie opened a medical kit, looking for swabs, and was cleaning the wound to assess how to treat it when Pat spoke to them from the helicopter.

'Decision time, guys. We've got about fifteen minutes before we need to be heading back for fuel. I can leave now and come back for you but the storm is going to complicate matters. There's no guarantee I'll be able to get back or that we'll be able to get you off the boat. Are you ready to load up now and get out of here?'

Georgie checked Brian again. His head wound wasn't deep, she could see to it on board the chopper but to do so would mean leaving an unmanned yacht bobbing on the Pacific Ocean. Another option was treating Brian and leaving him behind on his own, on a yacht in the middle of a storm. A third option was for one of them to stay behind with Brian.

She looked over at Josh. He was looking pale and she knew he was hurt too. If one of them stayed behind, it would have to be her. She didn't like option two or three.

'I agree we need to get everyone on board the chopper now but what do we do with the yacht?' she asked.

Pat answered. 'I'll alert the coastguard, they'll come out and tow the yacht back.'

'All right,' Georgie replied. 'Let's get going.'

Quickly she taped a dressing over Brian's wound as a temporary fix as she explained to him what was going to happen. She told him to keep some pressure on it and went to help Josh. Isaac was lowering the winch cable and Georgie could see Josh trying to grab it with one hand. Somehow he'd managed to secure one medical kit to the stretcher but he was protecting his left hand, holding it against his chest.

Concern flooded through her. Was he badly injured?

She reached out to him, careful to make sure she didn't knock him off balance. 'Do you need some help? What have you done?'

'I'm okay. It's only a knock to my fingers. We'll worry about it later.'

She didn't have time to argue but she knew he was hurt, which meant they were going to do this evacuation her way. 'You take Brian up first—he's just got a nasty gash on his forehead that'll need stitching—and I'll come up next with the stretcher.'

Josh nodded, surprising her with his easy acquiescence. 'This is Meredith, fractured NOF, no LOC, no other injuries.' Josh gave Georgie a basic summary of Meredith's condition as Georgie fixed a harness around Brian and strapped him to Josh. Isaac winched them to safety and Georgie tried not to watch them every inch of the way.

She attached herself to the stretcher and waited for Isaac to lower the cable for Meredith and herself. Finally, he dragged them into the chopper and the moment they were inside Pat turned for the coast.

Georgie secured the stretcher and she could see Isaac helping to secure Brian and Josh. She wanted to check Josh but he couldn't be her priority. She checked Meredith's vital signs. Her BP and heart rate were slightly elevated but within acceptable limits and her oxygen sats were normal. When she was satisfied that Meredith's condition was stable she attended to Brian. Then, and only then, could she see to Josh.

'Your turn,' she said.

'I'm okay. It's just a couple of fingers.'

He was right, it was only a couple of fingers, but Georgie knew it could have been worse, much worse, and she'd hated the feeling of helplessness and fear that had overcome her. Josh had been in danger and there'd been nothing she could do about it.

'We should have both gone down to the yacht in the first place,' she said, still convinced that somehow she would have been able to keep him safe.

'It was an accident, you couldn't have stopped it,' he replied, still reading her thoughts. She wouldn't have thought she'd smile again today but hearing him voice the words that were in her head made her think everything would be okay.

He was sitting opposite her. She stretched out her hand, reaching for his. He didn't argue any further. He held his left arm out to her. The third, fourth and fifth fingers were already blue and swollen.

'Can you make a fist?' she asked.

He shook his head. 'No.'

She applied gentle pressure across the phalanges of his middle finger. Josh grimaced as she touched the intermediate phalanx. She got the same reaction on his fourth finger.

'Two broken bones, I suspect. Do you want something for the pain?' It had to be hurting regardless of what he told her.

He shook his head. 'No. I don't want anything affecting my judgement. Not while we've got patients on board.'

Georgie could have argued that being in pain could just as easily cloud his judgement but she knew that wasn't the same. 'Okay. I'll strap your fingers for you for now but you'll need to get an X-ray when we get home.'

Josh surrendered his hand again and let Georgie tape his fingers together.

'Georgie?' Pat's voice came through their headsets.

'Yes, Pat.'

'Our fuel's pretty tight. We're going to have to refuel in Cooktown and then head home. Are our patients okay for that?'

'Yes, all three are stable,' Georgie replied with a smile.

It took a long time to get home. Their shift had well and truly ended by then, but fortunately there were no further emergencies. When Pat landed at the hospital Georgie saw an opportunity to get Josh to the radiology department.

'Do you want to go into the hospital? Get your fingers X-rayed before we head to The Sandbar for today's post-mortem?'

He shook his head and made no move to follow the hospital gurneys. 'I'll come back after we knock off.'

'I'll take you, then,' Georgie offered. She wanted to make sure he got seen to. She hadn't been able to prevent the injury but she was going to ensure that he was properly taken care of now. 'I'm going to see Dad before I head to the bar. Mum was going to pick me up but if I drive your car it'll save her the trip.' Georgie knew that if she made it sound as though Josh would be doing someone else a favour he'd be more likely to acquiesce.

Her argument worked and she drove Josh from the QMERT base back to the hospital and delivered him to the radiology department before heading to the cardiology wing.

'Is everything all right, Georgina? You looked exhausted,' Sofia asked her as she entered her father's room.

'Yes, I'm fine,' she told her parents as she kissed them both. 'We just had a rather dramatic day at work,' she said, and proceeded to fill them in on the day's events.

'Do you think this is the right job for you, darling? It sounds terribly dangerous,' Sofia asked once Georgie had finished.

Her parents hadn't loved the idea when she'd told them she was going to retrain as a paramedic and quit nursing, although they had eventually got used to it, but Georgie knew they still had concerns. But ninety per cent of the time the job was routine and risk-free and Georgie loved it. She had no plans to give it up, not even once she was married with kids. But today she'd been frightened, not for herself but watching Josh and being unable to help him had been terrifying. But she didn't tell her parents of her fears neither did she tell them about running low on fuel. The worst hadn't happened, they'd made it home safely, and there was no reason to scare them with hypothetical situations. She was tempted to cross her fingers as she told them, 'I wasn't in any danger today.'

'Well, I'm relieved to hear that,' Sofia said.

Georgie kept her visit brief. She wanted to get to The Sandbar, and she was eager to check on Josh.

Sofia was staying at the hospital to keep George company in Josh's absence but she walked with Georgie to the exit. 'The surgeon had some good news today, darling. He's hoping to discharge your father the day after tomorrow. Dad would like to get home to Melbourne as soon as possible to recuperate there and the surgeon expects to give him medical clearance to fly a day after discharge. Which brings me to a favour I want to ask of you?'

Georgie listened, knowing she was going to agree, but there was one thing she needed to do before she granted her mother's request. And she'd have to do it quickly, as soon as an opportunity presented itself, or perhaps she'd have to create the opportunity. She ran through the possibilities in her head as she walked along the esplanade to The Sandbar.

Josh had beaten her there. He was talking to Isaac and laughing, looking like he didn't have a care in the world. As Georgie watched them, Isaac finished his drink and headed to the bar. Josh was alone.

She went to him. 'How's your hand?'

'Your diagnosis was one hundred per cent correct. Two broken fingers.'

'Are they sore?'

'Not now. I've taken something for that.'

'Are you able to work or do you need some time off?'

'I'm fine. I'm going to go into the physio department tomorrow and get a proper splint made. That should take care of things while they heal. It's no big deal.'

No big deal. He had been lucky to escape with just two broken fingers. Georgie remembered how she'd felt as the yacht had tipped on its side. She'd been terrified it was going to go over. Terrified it was about to drop Josh into the ocean. She had no idea whether capsizing a boat was easy to do, she hadn't had much experience with boats, but she did know she'd never been as frightened as she had been then.

It was time to face facts. There was no point denying that Josh sent her crazy with desire. That the touch of his hand sent her hormones wild, that his smile made her heart race or that his kisses made her want to leap into bed with him. She did. And sometimes it felt like it was all she could think about. She wanted Josh and if she didn't do something about it now, tonight, she was going to miss her opportunity. She hadn't forgotten how it felt to be in his embrace and she was having a hard time letting that memory go.

The team was celebrating the safe evacuation and return to Cairns but to Georgie tonight was about more than that. Tonight was about Josh.

'You haven't got a drink. Can I get you something?' he asked, seeing her empty hands.

It was now or never. 'That depends,' she said.

'On what?'

'On whether or not you're ready to go home.'

Josh looked at his watch. His left hand and fingers, what she could see of them where they emerged from the strapping, were swollen and bruised. 'But you just got here and it's still early,' he said.

'I know. But I thought I'd come home with you.' She looked up at him through her lashes and gave him a half-smile. She saw him read between the lines.

'Just the two of us?' he asked.

She licked her lips and smiled fully now. 'I thought that might be fun,' she said.

'Why now?'

Had she missed her chance already? Had he changed his mind? Given up?

'I'm tired of trying to fight this attraction,' she admitted. 'It's not going away. Pretending it doesn't exist hasn't worked. Ignoring it hasn't worked. I can't pretend I don't want you. I want to know what it's like to make love with you. I want to know how it feels. I've never seen the point in spending just one night with someone but it was so hard today, watching you in danger, and I realised that one chance, one night, is all I might have, and I know I'll regret it if I don't take it.'

'Are you sure?'

'This is what I want. No strings. No promises. Just this night.'

'But—'

'I know our relationship is an illusion,' she interrupted. 'I know it's not real and I don't expect a real relationship but you were right, our chemistry is real and all I'm asking for is just one night. You've taught me to take chances. You've given me the confidence to try new things. This is something I want. But if you're not feeling up to it…?' She let the question tail off into thin air.

Josh grinned at her, his grey eyes shining with excitement. 'A couple of busted fingers won't slow me down.' He drained his drink in one swallow and put his glass on a table. 'Ready when you are.'

'Down, boy.' Georgie laughed. 'Meet me out the front in five minutes. I don't want everyone to see us leaving together. They don't need any more fuel added to the fire of speculation.'

Georgie went to the ladies' bathroom to freshen up. Beside the hand dryer, directly opposite the door, was a condom vending machine. It was the first thing she saw as she walked in. She crossed the room and stood in front of it. She studied it. Was she really going to do this?

It would just be one night, she told herself. It didn't have to change anything.

She couldn't deny she'd spent many hours imagining just what it would be like. There was nothing stopping her. Nothing would change except she would know how it felt to let Josh love her.

She turned to her right and looked in the mirror. Her eyes were dark and shining. Her cheeks were flushed and her lips were bright red. Her blood vessels were dilating in anticipation. She wanted this.

She searched her purse for coins and inserted them into the machine. She twisted the knob and caught the little packet as the machine dispensed it and she stashed it in her handbag. She wanted this more than she'd wanted anything in a long time.

She left the bathroom and went to meet Josh.

He was waiting under a palm tree, leaning against the trunk looking calm and relaxed. She was a bundle of nerves. It had been a long time since she'd been intimate with a man, but she wasn't apprehensive. She was excited. She reached for his right hand and pulled him away from the tree.

'Are—?'

'Shh.' Georgie pressed her fingers against his lips. She didn't want to talk, she didn't want a discussion, she just wanted to get to Josh's apartment and make love.

Josh had left his car at the hospital and they didn't speak as they walked. The heat from Josh's hand was searing her palm, threatening to ignite her entire body. She could imagine how his hands would feel running over her naked skin, how her body would respond to his touch.

He pressed the button for the lift and Georgie was grateful he lived so close to The Sandbar. She didn't think she could make it much further. He held the door for her and followed her into the empty lift, pushing the button for the seventh floor on his way past. She stood in the corner and pulled him to her. She wasn't going to wait any longer. This was part of her fantasy. This was what tonight was about, satisfying her curiosity and their desire.

She reached her arm up and cupped her hand around the back of his head, guiding his mouth to hers. She kissed him hard and he kissed her back. His hands were on her hips, holding her to him. Her hands were behind his head, keeping him with her.

She felt the lift stop, heard the doors open. She didn't care if more people were getting into the lift, she didn't care if they were surrounded, she had no space in her head for thoughts of anyone else.

Josh was holding her hand, pulling her out of the lift. They were at the seventh floor. He unlocked his apartment door and they turned left, heading for the bedroom, not pretending this was about anything more than desire, lust and longing.

Georgie dropped her bag on the bed and went straight back into Josh's arms. She ran her hands under his shirt. She trailed her fingernails lightly over his skin and heard him moan. She grabbed the bottom of his shirt and pulled it over his head, exposing his flat, toned stomach. He started to undo his belt but Georgie stopped him.

'Let me,' she said. It would be difficult for him to undress with three fingers strapped together, though not impossible, but Georgie wanted the pleasure of doing it. She undid his belt and snapped open the button on his pants before sliding the zip down. She could feel the hard bulge of his erection pressing into her, straining to get free.

Josh stepped out of his shoes, not bothering to untie the laces, as she pushed his trousers to the floor. His pants joined his shoes and shirt in an untidy heap. He was naked except for his boxer shorts. Georgie looked him over.

He was glorious.

CHAPTER TEN

HE GRINNED at her and raised one eyebrow. In reply she put a hand on his smooth, broad chest and pushed him backwards until the bed bumped the back of his knees and made him sit. It was his turn to wait for her now.

She picked up her bag and opened it. Retrieving the condom, she placed it on the bedside table. Josh watched every move she made.

She stepped back from the bed. Out of his reach. He could watch but he couldn't touch. She wanted to tease him. She reached for the zip at the side of her dress and undid it slowly. She slipped one strap from her shoulder and then the other and let the dress fall to the floor. Josh's eyes were dark grey now, all traces of silver vanishing as he watched and waited for her.

She reached her hands behind her back and unhooked her bra, sliding it along her arms and dropping it to the floor. She lifted her hand to pull the elastic from her hair.

'Let me do that.' Josh's voice was husky with desire. Lust coated his words, making them so heavy they barely made it past his lips.

Georgie dropped her hand, leaving her hair restrained. She slid her underwear from her hips and went to him. She was completely naked but she didn't feel exposed. She felt powerful.

She sat on the bed beside him. He reached for her with his right hand, running it up her arm. His fingers rested at the nape of her neck before he flicked her plait over her left shoulder and pulled the elastic from her hair. He wound his fingers through her hair, loosening the plait as he spread her hair out, letting it fall over her shoulders before burying his face in it.

His thumb rested on her jaw. It was warm and soft, his pressure gentle. He ran his thumb along the line of her jaw and then replaced it with his lips. He kissed her neck, her collarbone and the hollow at the base of her throat.

His fingers blazed a trail across her body that his mouth followed. Down from her throat to her sternum, over her breast to one nipple. His fingers flicked over the nipple, already peaked and hard. His mouth followed, covering it, sucking, licking and tasting.

He pulled her backwards onto the bed.

She reached for his boxer shorts and pulled them from his waist. His erection sprang free, pressing against her stomach.

His fingers were stroking the inside of her thigh. She parted her legs and his fingers slid inside her, into her warm, moist centre. His thumb rolled over her most sensitive spot, making her gasp. He kissed her breast, sucking at her nipple as his thumb teased her. She arched her back, pushing her hips and breasts towards him, wanting more, letting him take her to a peak of desire.

Still she wanted more. She needed more.

She rolled towards him and pushed him flat onto his back. She sat up and straddled his hips. His erection rose between them, trapped between their groins. Georgie stretched across him, reaching for the condom, and her breasts hung above his face. He lifted his head, taking her breast into his mouth once more. She closed her eyes

as she gave herself up to the sensations shooting through
her as his tongue flicked over her nipple. Every part of her
responded to his touch. Her body came alive under his fingers and his lips and her skin burned where their bodies
met.

She felt for the condom, finding it with her fingers. She
picked it up and lifted herself clear of Josh, pulling her
breast from his lips. Air flowed over her nipple, the cool
temperature contrasting with the heat of his mouth. She
opened the condom and rolled it onto him. Her fingers en-
circled his shaft as she smoothed out the sheath.

She put her hands either side of his head and kept her
eyes on his face as she lifted herself up and took him inside her. His eyelids closed and she watched him breathe
in deeply as her flesh encased him, joining them together.

She filled herself with his length before lifting her
weight from him and letting him take control. His thumbs
were on the front of her hips, his fingers behind her pelvis
as he guided her up and down, matching her rhythm to his
thrusts, each movement bringing her closer to climax.

She liked this position. She liked being able to watch
him, she liked being able to see him getting closer and
closer to release. His eyes were closed, hiding their silver
flecks, but his lips were parted, his breathing was rapid
and shallow, his thrusts getting faster.

She spread her knees, letting him in deeper inside her
until she had taken all of him. Her body was flooded with
heat. Every nerve ending was crying out for his touch.
'Now, Josh. Now.'

He opened his eyes and his grey gaze locked with hers
as he took her to the top of the peak.

Her body started to quiver and she watched him as he
too shuddered. He closed his eyes, threw his head back and
thrust into her, claiming her as they climaxed together.

When they were spent she lay on him, covering his body with hers. Their skin felt warm and flushed from their effort and they were both panting as he wrapped his arms around her back, holding her to him. She could feel his heart beating under her chest. She could feel it as its rhythm slowed, gradually returning to normal.

'Wow.'

Josh's prediction had been right. Their chemistry made for amazing sex. Georgie had never been so overwhelmed by an experience. It was a pity she wasn't going to be able to get used to it.

'Wow indeed,' he said as he kissed her shoulder. 'Do you think we could improve on that with practice?'

Georgie laughed. 'I'm not sure it gets much better than that.'

'Give me a minute and we'll see.'

A minute! She needed longer to recover than that. 'I can't stay. Mum was expecting me home after dinner.'

'We haven't had dinner,' he said.

'She doesn't know that.'

Josh's fingers were running along her spine and Georgie would have been more than happy to stay right where she was. But that wasn't part of her plan. She didn't want to go, she wanted to spend the night in Josh's arms and forget about the world, but she couldn't stay. The longer she stayed, the harder it would be to make herself leave.

Tonight was about the present. It was a once-in-a-lifetime opportunity. They didn't have a future. She would have her memories but she wouldn't have Josh.

God, she was a fool, she thought later as she climbed into her own bed. Her sheets were cold and clean. They smelt of detergent and sunshine but she wanted them to smell of

Josh. She never should have slept with him. Now she had to walk away from the best sex of her life.

But it shouldn't matter. Great sex was just great sex. She could appreciate it for what it was and move on. Great sex wasn't a basis for a lasting relationship and that was what she wanted, the one thing Josh couldn't give her.

She was looking for a relationship based on respect, shared values and companionship, not on great sex; but she knew that, at the moment, she'd trade respect and shared values for another night with Josh.

Josh wasn't at work the following day as he had a physio appointment but he arrived at the hospital for his regular game of backgammon with her father just as she was leaving. He was waiting for her in the corridor.

He was wearing jeans and a green T-shirt, his hair was spiky and he looked just as he'd looked last night when she'd left him all rumpled in his bed. The only difference was that he was dressed and the fingers of his left hand were encased in a splint.

He was smiling at her. She wanted to tell him to stop, it was messing with her equilibrium and with her resolve, but she couldn't speak—her mouth was dry, her knees were weak and her heart was racing. Her body reacted even before her brain had fully registered that he was there. Last night couldn't be repeated. They wouldn't share another night. She'd have to get over it but her body seemed to have other ideas.

'Hi. I was hoping I'd catch you here.' He stepped towards her and reached for her hand. His eyes were dark grey but as their hands touched she saw silver flecks flash in his irises like little lightning strikes and she felt the flash race through her. 'Can you sneak away tonight?' he asked.

No, she meant to say, but when she opened her mouth to speak that wasn't the word that came out. 'Yes,' she said.

'My place? Eight-thirty?'

She nodded and tried to tell herself that when she got there she'd explain why she couldn't stay, why they couldn't have another night. But then Josh leant forward and kissed her lips and she felt her resolve crumble into a pool of rampant desire.

She smelt of cinnamon and honey. He closed his eyes and savoured her scent as he kissed her in the hospital corridor. In ninety minutes she would be in his arms once again but first he had an appointment to keep.

'Evening, George,' he said as he entered the room. George was sitting out of bed, looking a picture of health, but the room was bare. The flowers, cards and magazines that had been cluttering all the horizontal surfaces of his room and giving it some personality were gone. 'What's going on?' he asked as he looked around.

'I'm being discharged in the morning,' George explained.

'That's great news.'

George was nodding. 'I'll be glad to get home, that's for sure. This wasn't how I planned to spend my holiday. Not that I'm complaining, it could have been a lot worse, it could have been my last one.' George stood and crossed to the table and picked up a small case that was lying there. It was his backgammon set and it was the only personal item that hadn't already been packed away. 'Have you got time for one final game?'

'Of course,' Josh said, 'but I'll warn you now, this time I'm going to win.'

George laughed. 'Give it your best shot, but if you couldn't beat me when I was medicated up to my eyeballs following surgery, I don't fancy your chances now.' He flipped the catches on the case and opened it out, quickly positioning the checkers. They sat on the edge of the bed, the table between them, and started to play. As had become their habit, Josh went first.

'You've been given medical clearance to fly?' he asked as he shook his dice in their cup and rolled them out.

'Yep. I had another echocardiogram today and a stress test and apparently it's all looking like it should. I've got my piece of paper and the flights are all booked. I was a bit nervous about flying but the specialist says it's fine and Georgie's coming home with us.'

Josh was about to move his checkers but he hesitated. 'Georgie's going with you?'

George was watching the board, waiting for Josh's move, but he looked up quickly. 'She hasn't told you?'

Josh shook his head, afraid to hear what George would say next.

'She's taking holidays and coming home.' George threw his dice as he spoke.

Josh didn't like the sound of that. 'So she's coming back?'

'I'm not sure. You'd have to ask her,' George said as he moved his checkers. 'What are your plans? You're only in Cairns temporarily too, I understand. What's next for you?'

Josh wondered if it was a deliberate change in the direction of conversation. Was there more George wasn't telling him? But George had always called a spade a spade and Josh couldn't imagine him keeping something from him now. 'I'm waiting to hear about an appointment at Brisbane General,' he answered.

'For what position?'

'Head of Emergency.'

'That sounds important.'

'I've been working towards a position like this for years. As you can imagine, they don't come up all that often. The current head of emergency suggested I come to Cairns to get some more experience in emergency retrievals. He's due to retire when I finish here and I'm hoping to be able to step into his role. That's where I'm headed.'

'You've no plans to come to Melbourne?' George asked.

Josh shook his head, aware that George was watching him closely. 'No.'

'Georgie knows of your career plan?'

'She does,' Josh replied, thinking that he'd at least been honest with her about his future direction. He wondered when, or if, she was going to tell him about her departure and whether or not she was planning on returning.

'Well, if you ever find yourself in Melbourne, be sure to come and see us,' George said as he moved his last checker into the home position, victorious in yet another game of backgammon. 'You'll always be welcome.'

It was close to midnight and Josh knew Georgie would be going home soon. All evening he'd been waiting for her to tell him about her plans to return to Melbourne but she'd said nothing. Not before or after they'd made love. They were lying in his bed, naked. He knew his bed would feel cold and empty when she left. She was tucked in against his shoulder. He had his arm around her and the top of her head was resting under his chin. Her skin was soft under his hand and he was surrounded by the scent of honey and cinnamon. He closed his eyes and let her scent invade his senses. He could get used to this.

No. He didn't want to get used to this. That was a dangerous thought.

He needed to keep his defences up. He had to get on

with his future. He couldn't get caught up in Georgie. Her parents would be returning to Melbourne and his life would return to normal. While he had enjoyed this interlude, it was only ever going to be temporary. That was their arrangement and that was the way he operated. He would keep his memories but he would move on.

He opened his eyes and moved his head slightly so that Georgie's head was no longer under his chin, trying to avoid her scent of honey and cinnamon so he could concentrate. 'Your dad told me he's going to be discharged tomorrow. That's good news.'

She nodded.

'And you're going home with them?' Josh asked, even though he already knew the answer. What he didn't know was what would happen next and it seemed that unless he asked, he was never going to find out.

'He wants to go home to Melbourne to recuperate but he's nervous about flying. They've asked me to fly with them,' she explained.

'When will you be back?'

'I'm not coming back.'

Josh frowned and wondered if that's what George had been keeping from him. 'What do you mean? You've still got another month on your contract.'

'I've applied to take annual leave. We leave the day after tomorrow.'

He'd known she was leaving, just as he was, but he hadn't expected it to be so soon. He'd thought she'd come back, give them time to say their goodbyes. He was ready to move on but he hadn't expected to start the process tonight.

He tried to be pleased. He should be pleased. Surely this was a good thing.

* * *

Georgie was lying in Josh's arms. She'd hoped to resist him but it had been impossible to forego her one last opportunity. He'd opened his apartment door for her and kissed her senseless before he'd started undressing her with his eyes, and she known then she'd end up here, naked, in his bed. He hadn't needed to say a word. In fact, he hadn't spoken, he'd just looked at her and her heart had pounded so hard in her chest she'd thought it would explode. Her hands had been shaking as he'd held them and pulled her to him. She'd stepped into his arms and kissed him, followed him to his bed and made love to him. Now she was lying in his arms, her head nestled in the curve of his shoulder, her cheek resting on his bare chest, her ear pressed against his heart, listening to it beating.

His words vibrated in his chest when he spoke, reverberating under her ear. It wasn't quite where she'd planned to have the conversation about leaving Cairns, leaving him, but he'd opened the discussion and she couldn't put it off any longer. She didn't have any more time.

'I've applied to take annual leave. We leave the day after tomorrow.' Accompanying her parents on the flight back to Melbourne was the favour her mum had asked of her and it had given her the perfect escape clause. And she was going to take it. She knew she had to get away from Josh quickly before it became impossible. She was going to Melbourne and she wasn't coming back. She'd decided that the way to get over Josh was to have a quick, clean break.

'So that's it? You're leaving now?'

'It's only a bit earlier than I'd planned. It's not going to make any difference in the scheme of things.'

She wanted Josh to tell her that it would make a difference to him. She wanted him to ask her to come back. Or not to go. But of course he didn't. She was a fool to hope for that. He didn't want a relationship, he'd told her that. 'Your life can return to normal. No more pretending,' she said.

'I thought...'

'What?'

He shook his head and she could feel his shoulders shaking with the movement. 'Never mind.' He paused briefly and she was left wondering what he'd been going to say. 'So what was last night all about? And tonight?' he asked.

'It was about you. Us.' She shrugged. 'Your philosophy has rubbed off on me. I was being adventurous. This was sex with no strings attached. That was what you wanted.'

He didn't argue.

She wished he would.

But he didn't protest and as she lay in his arms she knew he would keep quiet. He wasn't going to beg her to stay.

What on earth had she expected? Had she thought he was going to tell her he loved her and he couldn't live without her?

She'd made a mess of everything. She should have left him alone. She should never have crossed the invisible line they'd drawn. But she hadn't been able to resist.

The old Georgie would have resisted. The old Georgie hadn't had casual sex but she knew that was also true of the new Georgie. She was kidding herself if she thought going to bed with Josh could be considered casual sex. She'd known exactly what she was doing. The question was, why had she done it? Why had she crossed that invisible line?

And she knew the answer too. She'd crossed the line both physically and emotionally.

She'd fallen in love with him.

She had come to Cairns to find her independence. To find herself. She hadn't expected to fall in love but that's what had happened. She had begun the process of her metamorphosis from dutiful daughter to independent woman; she'd engineered the move away from home; and Josh had helped her to complete it. He'd helped to complete her. She was now the person she wanted to be but would she be able to continue to be that person without Josh by her side?

She would have to do it, she thought, she had no other option. But that meant the sooner she got away from here the better, before she lost herself in Josh.

She was leaving for Melbourne tomorrow. Part of her couldn't believe it. She knew she would find it hard to leave but she had no other option. She'd told everyone of her decision and nothing had happened to change her mind. Or, more specifically, no one had tried to convince her to stay.

Her last shift with QMERT was an ordinary day. She was working with Sean and they were called out for a couple of routine inter-hospital transfers, nothing dramatic, nothing difficult. Without realising it, she'd shared her last shift with Josh the day they'd evacuated Meredith and Brian from the yacht off the coast of Cooktown. But she would see him tonight. She was on her way to The Sandbar for her farewell dinner and drinks, and Josh would join them there after his hospital shift.

This was going to be the last time she saw him and she was determined to put on a happy face. She was trying to be brave. Trying to pretend she was happy to be going home. Pretending she was ready. Pretending she didn't mind that he hadn't asked her to stay. Or come back.

Pretending she hadn't fallen in love.

But, of course, nothing in the world of emergency medicine ever went to plan when she needed it to.

Her mobile rang as she walked into the bar and Josh's name appeared on her screen. As she answered she could hear sirens in the street. This was only going to be bad news.

'Georgie, it's me. I've been held up. There's been a fire at one of the backpacker hostels and it's all hands on deck while we wait to see what the ambos bring us. I have no idea yet how bad it is or how long I'll be.'

Disappointment surged through her but there was nothing she could do. 'It's okay.'

'I'm sorry. I really wanted to be there.'

'I understand, Josh. I know how it goes. Hopefully we'll see you later.'

She would have a drink with her other colleagues but Josh was the one she really wanted to see. The night dragged from that point on.

She waited and waited but Josh didn't show. She checked her mobile phone constantly but it was hours before she heard it beep, signalling a text message. She pulled it out of her handbag.

Can't get away. Working at QMERT 2mro, will c u at terminal.

'Is something wrong?' Louise was standing beside her. 'You've been looking at your phone every five minutes.'

'Everything's fine,' she lied. 'That was Josh, he's still at the hospital. I was waiting to see him, to say goodbye, but if he's not going to make it I think I might go home. There are still some things I need to do before we leave tomorrow.' That wasn't true either. She'd packed and the removalists had collected her boxes and her car. All she had to do was get up and go to the airport but she didn't want to be at the bar any longer without Josh.

'I'll give you a lift home,' Louise offered. 'It's past my bedtime too.'

Louise drove down the esplanade and along the sea-front. 'We're going to miss you,' she said as she drove. 'You've been a breath of fresh air around the place.'

'I'm going to miss all of you too. I've loved my time here,' Georgie replied, but her heart was heavy with the knowledge that there was one person she was going to miss most.

'Why don't you come back?' Louise asked as they passed the hospital.

Georgie couldn't help looking through the emergency entrance, hoping for a glimpse of Josh, but of course she saw nothing except for a couple of paramedics standing by their ambulance. Her heart ached in her chest, knowing that Josh was just a few metres from her but unreachable.

'Because there's nothing for me here,' she answered. Josh was leaving too, there was nothing to bring her back to Cairns. She sighed with longing and the sound escaped from her and broke the silence.

Louise slowed the car and turned her head to watch Georgie. 'Did you want to go in and say goodbye?'

Georgie looked at her, wondering how much she thought she knew. 'No, he'll be busy.'

'I'm sure he'll stop for you.'

Georgie didn't think so. She shook her head.

'Have you told him how you feel?'

Georgie heard her own sharp intake of breath. 'What do you mean?'

'Marty was right about the two of you, wasn't he? Your relationship isn't pretend any more,' Lou said. 'Does Josh know how you feel?'

Georgie didn't bother denying Lou's assessment but she wasn't about to announce it to everyone and especially not to Josh. 'No. And I won't tell him.'

'What if he feels the same way? What if both of you are too stubborn to be the first to admit your feelings?'

She wished she was brave enough to take that chance but although she was more confident than she'd been a year ago, she wasn't that brave. 'He has a totally different view of it. He doesn't want a proper relationship.'

'He's a man,' Lou scoffed with the voice of experience. 'I doubt he has any idea what he really wants. You need to tell him.'

'No.'

Louise turned the corner and the hospital receded into the distance. 'Have you thought about moving to Brisbane? You'd get a job there.'

Georgie shook her head again.

'Why not?'

'Because Josh hasn't asked me to.' She knew it wouldn't take more than that to get her to pack her bags and move again. All he had to do was ask. But that wasn't going to happen. 'It's okay, Lou, I'm okay,' she said before her friend felt she had to offer counselling. 'Josh and I had a deal. This whole thing was make-believe, I just forgot that temporarily.'

To her relief Louise didn't question her further. She probably realised that Georgie had a point. No matter what she or Louise thought, there wasn't anything they could do to change the situation. It was what it was. Life would go on. Without Josh.

Georgie had made it through her last night in Cairns by consoling herself with the idea she'd see Josh at the airport before she left. He'd told her he'd get across to the airport terminal. She wanted to know she would see him one last time, it would make it easier to leave, but as the taxi drove her and her parents along the entry road she saw the helicopter taking off from the QMERT base. Her heart sank in her chest. Josh would be on board, on his way to an emergency, which meant he wouldn't be meeting her at the terminal. He wouldn't be saying goodbye.

Disappointment and frustration left a bitter taste in her mouth. She'd prepared herself to say goodbye but she hadn't prepared herself not to.

Perhaps it was for the best, she thought as she started piling luggage onto the trolley. There was always the danger that if she saw him again she might just tell him she'd fallen in love with him. And there was no need for him to know that. It was better this way. She needed to move on.

CHAPTER ELEVEN

IT WAS a glorious spring day in Melbourne. One of those perfect days that made up for the many bleak, grey wintry days the city seemed to exist on. Or perhaps that was her perception. In the two months since Georgie had been back in Melbourne every day had seemed grey and wintry.

Today was her parents' fortieth wedding anniversary, a day her parents had been looking forward to celebrating, but she was having trouble mustering up any enthusiasm. She was pleased for her parents but every time a wedding was mentioned it just served to remind her of her own situation.

She was still single but dating, and for the past few weeks had been seeing Con and Anastasia's son Michael. She knew Michael was more into the whole idea than she was and it was getting to the stage where she'd have to do something about that. She knew everyone was hoping for some sort of announcement and while he was nice enough they had no chemistry, no spark. Maybe that would come, but all she could think of was the instant connection she'd had with Josh. He'd been a perfect stranger yet they'd had an immediate, physical attraction, an awareness, a connection, and it hadn't dissipated. If she was honest, it was still overpowering her, making everything else seem paler, less significant, weaker.

She couldn't bring herself to get excited about anything at the moment. Least of all Michael. But that wasn't his fault. She wanted Josh and she couldn't imagine wanting anyone else the same way.

Georgie knew she should be focussing on her future. Josh was history. She hadn't heard from him since she'd arrived back in Melbourne but it was proving impossible to forget about him.

'Are you looking forward to dinner tonight?' Sofia asked her as they sat at the hairdresser together. The official party that had originally been planned to celebrate the anniversary had been replaced with a small dinner for the immediate family due to George's surgery. The big celebration would now take place in two weeks' time but Sofia had decided that a family dinner was enough of an occasion to warrant a trip to the beautician and the hair salon.

Georgie looked across at her mother. Today was such a special occasion for her that she would have to try, at least, to pretend to be happy. 'Of course.'

'Are you sure you don't want to invite Michael? You know he's welcome.'

'I'm positive. It will be nice to have dinner with just the family. I feel like I still haven't caught up with all the boys properly since I got home from Cairns,' Georgie said, making excuses. 'Michael doesn't need to come.'

She could feel her mother's watchful gaze on her but she avoided eye contact. 'How are things going with him?'

'Fine.'

'What does that mean exactly?'

Georgie didn't need to look at her mother to know she'd raised her eyebrows and was giving her a questioning look. 'Fine means fine. It means there are no problems, no dramas. There's no anything really.' She sighed.

There was a brief silence and Georgie knew her mother was weighing up her next words. 'Can I ask you a question? When you picture your own fortieth wedding anniversary, who do you see by your side?'

Georgie didn't respond. She didn't know what to say. How honest to be.

Sofia didn't wait for an answer. 'It's not Michael, is it?'

Georgie shook her head.

'Is it Josh?' Sofia asked.

She risked a glance at her mother. 'Why do you ask?'

'For the twenty-seven years that I've been lucky enough to be your mother I've never seen you look like you do when Josh is around. You glow from within, as though something about him gives you an extra boost, makes you complete. Are you in love with him?'

Georgie swallowed hard. 'It doesn't matter if I am. We don't have a future together.'

'What makes you say that?'

'He doesn't want to get married. He doesn't want a relationship. His future is about his career.' Hot tears gathered in her eyes as she remembered that Josh hadn't chosen her. 'His dream is to be head of the emergency team at Brisbane General. His dream isn't me.'

'Have you heard from him?'

Georgie shook her head.

'It's going to make it difficult for you to find someone while you're still in love with Josh.'

'I'll get over him.' She was not going to admit to her mother that she was right. It wasn't going to do her any good to acknowledge her feelings. She wished she was brave enough to admit she loved him, but the confidence that Josh had seen in her, the confidence he believed she had, seemed to have forsaken her. Somehow he'd helped her believe in herself. 'I don't want to spend the rest of my life alone. I'm sure you and Dad can find someone for me, seeing as I haven't done a very good job of that myself. Maybe an arranged marriage isn't such a bad idea. It worked for you.'

'Ours was a slightly different proposition.'

Georgie frowned. 'What do you mean?'

'Our families came to Australia from the same village in Greece. Your father and I practically grew up together, but when we fell in love we decided the best way to ensure that we were able to get married was to let your grandparents believe they were arranging our marriage.'

'You fell in love and then got married?' This version of the story was different from the one Georgie had grown up hearing.

Sofia was nodding. 'Your father sowed the seeds of the idea and then we let our parents work it out. That arrangement suited everybody. We all got what we wanted. Your grandparents believed they had final approval and your dad and I got each other. Your father wants to see you settled and happy but we don't want you getting married because we think it's the right thing for you to do. We would never encourage you to marry someone you don't love. We want you to be happy.'

Georgie wanted to be happy again too, but right now she was miserable. She wanted to feel complete but she knew that was impossible. She'd gone to Cairns on a mission to find herself. The irony was Josh had helped her to discover her true self, but she couldn't maintain it without him. She needed him. Part of her had remained behind with Josh and she knew she'd never be complete again without him.

Josh took the coffee pot off the stove as he tried not to think about the free Saturday that stretched emptily in front of him. It was the first free day he'd had in the past eighteen since he'd moved back to Brisbane General to take up his new position as Head of Emergency. The role had been offered to him earlier than expected and he'd jumped at the chance. Not only was it the job he wanted but it gave him a reason to leave Cairns.

He'd thought leaving Cairns was the answer. He'd thought it would help him get his life back in control. After all, taking up this position meant he was achieving his goals. And leaving Cairns should help him to forget about Georgie. It would remove him from everything they had in common, from all the familiar places they'd shared. But, of course, he took his memories with him and even taking on the new job didn't keep him busy enough to forget about her.

Last weekend he'd chosen to spend his days at the hospital, finding his feet, he'd told himself, rather than spending the days alone. His own company wasn't something he normally minded but he wasn't particularly enjoying his solitude at the moment. He wasn't particularly enjoying anything.

He thought about what he'd shared with Georgie—sex with no strings attached. It was what he'd asked for and what he'd been given, but it hadn't been the answer either. Too late he'd discovered that it wasn't what he truly wanted. He wanted the strings. He missed the strings.

The phone rang, interrupting his sombre thoughts. He recognised the QMERT Cairns number as he answered.

'Hi, Josh, it's Lou. How are you? How's Brisbane? How's the new job?' In typical Lou fashion she barely paused for breath.

'Good.'

There was silence. Josh had expected her to jump straight in with her next question but she was obviously waiting for him to elaborate and he had nothing more to say. The job was good, it was everything he'd expected, but it wasn't enough. He had the job he wanted but he didn't have the girl. And he wasn't about to tell Louise that.

'I've got some mail here for you.'

Louise had his forwarding address. Why was she ringing to tell him about random mail?

'It's from Georgie's parents,' she said. 'I got one too. It's an invitation to their fortieth wedding anniversary celebrations. I'll send it down to you.'

'Thanks. When's the party?'

'In two weeks,' Lou said. 'But why did they send the invitation here? Don't they know you're in Brisbane? Haven't you spoken to Georgie?'

Ah, her phone call made more sense now. 'No. Why would I have?'

'I just thought you might have called to tell her you'd got the job and were back in Brisbane. I'm sure she would be pleased for you.'

'Have you spoken to her?' he asked. Maybe Louise could tell him what he wanted to know. 'Is she—?' He cut himself off. He couldn't ask the questions he wanted to. Is she seeing anyone? Is she happy? It wasn't up to Louise to tell him the answers. Lou was right, he should have called Georgie himself. But he couldn't do that. Somehow that would feel as if he'd be losing control. He changed his words. 'Is she enjoying being back in Melbourne?'

'I think she's taking some time to settle back in. You should call her, tell her you'll go down to Melbourne for the party.'

'No. I don't think I will.'

'Why not? I thought you'd want to catch up with her. I still don't understand why you let her go.'

'Because I'm not the man she's looking for. I'm not what she needs.'

'Did she tell you that?' He could hear the surprise in Lou's voice.

'No. She didn't need to. I'm not cut out for relationships, for commitment. I'm no good at it.'

'What a load of rubbish. You've obviously just never been in the right relationship.'

'My relationships always end in disaster. She's better off without me.'

'There's always the chance that the two of you would be better off together than apart. Georgie wants someone to love. What if that someone was you? Have you thought about that? Unless, of course, you're happy alone?'

No, he wasn't happy, he thought as he hung up the phone, but being alone meant having complete control over his life.

But he didn't feel like he was in control of anything. His career was supposed to be all he needed but it was no longer enough.

He missed her.

He wanted to know how she was. He wanted to hear about her day. He wanted to be able to come home and share his day with her.

But he had his reasons for not calling. He'd been speaking the truth when he'd told Lou he was no good at relationships. Georgie wanted a happy ending and she wasn't going to get it from him. It was better for him to be miserable and alone than to make Georgie miserable.

But he missed her.

And she wasn't coming back. She was hundreds of miles away from him. Waiting for someone else to sweep her off her feet.

The realisation hit him that this was it. This was going to be his life. Georgie wasn't coming back to him. He hadn't really imagined what his life was going to be like without her. He couldn't imagine it.

But what if she loved him like he loved her? What then?

He loved her.

He was an idiot.

He loved her.

Why hadn't he realised that?

Why did love always make such a fool of him?

The first time he'd been in love, Tricia and his brother had made a fool of him. This time he was doing it without help from anyone else. But this time it wasn't too late. Or so he hoped. He loved Georgie and this time he had a chance to change the outcome.

Georgie wanted to fall in love. What if she could love him? What if she did love him?

He stirred his coffee as an idea took hold. He figured he had one last chance. He was supposed to thrive on challenges, wasn't he? He'd taught himself to see challenges in a positive light and this might be his biggest challenge yet. He wasn't going to let it beat him. It wasn't over. He had one last chance and he had to take it.

Josh paced nervously in front of the lounge room fireplace. He'd spent the entire flight from Brisbane to Melbourne rehearsing what he'd say, only to arrive in Melbourne to find Georgie wasn't home. He had left Brisbane after speaking to Lou, once he'd made his decision he hadn't waited, but apparently he'd arrived on the actual day of George and Sofia's fortieth wedding anniversary and Georgie was at the hairdresser with her mother.

Despite his timing, George was pleased, but not overly surprised, to see him. Apparently he and Sofia had been discussing him and trying to work out how to entice him to Melbourne—hence the invitation to the forthcoming anniversary celebrations. His early arrival was greeted with enthusiasm, particularly when Josh explained why he'd appeared on their doorstep.

Now all that remained was to see if Georgie was similarly enthusiastic. If their chemistry was as powerful as he remembered. If she loved him like he loved her. If he could persuade her to follow her heart.

He and George heard the garage door opening, signalling the return of Georgie and her mother. George left Josh in the lounge and would send Georgie in on a pretext without alerting her to the fact that Josh was waiting.

Josh froze as he heard the doorhandle turning. He held his breath as he waited to see who was coming into the room.

Her scent reached him first.

Honey and cinnamon. It washed over him in a wave of memories.

The fireplace where he stood was on the same side of the room as the door and he knew she hadn't noticed him yet, so he took a moment just to look at her. Her tan had faded since she'd been away from the tropical Queensland sun, but her skin was still smooth and golden and her hair was still glossy and thick. It wasn't constrained but hung in a thick, straight shiny sheath over her shoulders.

She still hadn't noticed him but he'd seen her now and his feet were moving without direction from him, taking him towards her.

Georgie opened the lounge room door to retrieve her father's glasses. Movement to her left made her jump. There was someone in the room. There was someone moving towards her.

'Josh?' For a moment she wondered if her imagination was playing tricks on her. He'd been in her thoughts so much. Was she now starting to have visions? But it was him, in her parents' lounge room. His familiar gait, his familiar figure, his broad shoulders, his spiky sandy blond hair, it was definitely him.

He smiled at her and the silver flecks sparkled in his grey eyes. Her heart skipped a beat and she was halfway across the room, meeting him in the middle, halfway into his arms, before she remembered she didn't have the right to be there any more.

She stopped in her tracks. 'What are you doing here?'

She'd spent the afternoon talking about him and now he was here. In her house. This made no sense.

He didn't share her hesitation. In two strides he'd closed the remaining distance between them. 'I came to see you,' he said as he gathered her in his arms. She clung to him. It felt so good to be back in his embrace. She could feel his heart beating next to hers, echoing the rhythm.

She looked up, turning her head to him, lifting her mouth to his, and that was all it took for Josh to claim her. His lips covered hers, hungrily, passionately. There was nothing soft and gentle about this kiss. It released all the longing that had built up in the days they'd been separated. This kiss brought them home.

It left her feeling light-headed and weak-kneed and, as usual, Josh could read her thoughts. He took her hand and led her to a sofa.

'Why are you here?' Georgie couldn't remember if she'd asked him that or if he'd already told her. Her thoughts were completely chaotic and confused.

'I didn't get to say goodbye.'

'You came all the way to Melbourne to say goodbye?'

'No. I came all the way to Melbourne because I couldn't say goodbye. I don't want to say goodbye. I came to see you because there are some things I need to know.'

He was still holding her hand. His touch sent shivers of desire through her and made it impossible for her to speak. She sat beside him, mute with surprise.

He leant forward and lifted her hair in his palm, burying his face in it and inhaling deeply. Georgie closed her eyes as she felt his breath on her neck. Her heart was pounding in her chest and she could feel herself leaning in towards him, yearning for his touch. 'I remember your scent perfectly,' he said. 'And I needed to know if our chemistry was real or whether my memory has been deceiving me. Can I still read your thoughts? Do you miss me like I've missed you?'

'You've missed me?'

He nodded. 'Every minute of every day.' He reached up again and tucked her hair behind her ear. 'And I have to know, have you missed me too or has Michael made you forget all about me?'

'You know about Michael?'

Josh nodded. 'Your father told me. Does he make you happy? Is he the one for you? If he is, I'll leave now. You just have to tell me.'

His arrival had totally confused her but she did know one thing. She shook her head. 'Michael isn't for me.' This was her chance to be honest with Josh. Something had brought him to Melbourne, to her. She wanted no regrets. 'There's no spark,' she said. 'Before I met you I thought it didn't matter but now I think I need more. I want more. I want passion, excitement, exhilaration, all those things I said weren't important. I want fireworks and everything that goes with them. I want to fall in love.'

'Do you think you could love me?'

She wasn't sure she was planning on being that honest. Did Josh need to know her heart already belonged to him? She hesitated but Josh didn't wait for her reply.

'I came to ask you to marry me.'

'Marry you?' Georgie couldn't understand what was happening. She felt as though she was watching a movie of someone else's life but she'd missed the beginning. 'But you don't want to get married.'

'I didn't want to but I've changed my mind. You've changed my mind.'

Georgie was more confused than ever. 'What happened to the man who was focussing on his career? Who didn't need relationships?'

'I have the job I wanted and it's fantastic, but it's not enough. It's challenging, it's rewarding, it's keeping me busy. At the end of the day I don't want to go home, but that's not because I can't bear to leave work—it's because I don't want to go home and find that you're not there. There's more to my future than my career. You are my future. I want you. I need you.'

Georgie waited but the words she longed to hear didn't come. If he didn't love her then what was he doing here?

'Are you sure I'm not just the next challenge in your life?'

He frowned and the silver flecks in his eyes darkened to grey. 'What do you mean?'

'You thrive on challenges. You set yourself a goal and when you achieve it you need a new goal. For the past eight years that goal has been your career. Now that box is ticked. You've avoided relationships ever since Tricia died and now that your career is on track suddenly you're ready to get married?' She didn't want to be his next challenge. This wasn't what she'd been dreaming of. 'Are you sure this is what you want? Have you really thought about this?'

'This is not about Tricia,' Josh argued. 'It hasn't been about her for a long time. When she died I lost two relationships, one with her and one with my brother, and I admit it did change my view of the world. I made a decision to put my energy into my studies and my career. I wanted to concentrate on things I could have some degree of control over. I decided not to invest time and energy into relationships but that was a conscious decision. I recovered a long time ago but, until recently, I haven't had any reason to change my mind about relationships. Until I met you.

'You have opened my eyes and opened my heart. Everything has changed for me since I met you. I tried to tell myself it was Cairns affecting me, making me see things differently, but it wasn't. It was you. You showed me how to let people back into my life. I had closed myself off and you opened me up.

'The night before you left Cairns I could have made it to The Sandbar but I chose not to. I was afraid I might not be able to say goodbye. I didn't want you to go but I couldn't ask you to stay because I was afraid of what that might mean. I was scared that I might fall in love. I didn't realise I'd already fallen in love with you.'

He loved her.

'You do challenge me but you are not a challenge. You challenged the way I saw myself and you made me reassess my life. I can't ignore my feelings. I can't pretend I want to be alone any more. Everything is better when you are with me. I am better.' He got off the couch and knelt beside her on one knee. 'I want to share my life with you.' He picked up her hand. 'I know you. You exist here…' he touched their hands to his forehead '…and here…' He touched their hands to his heart. 'You're part of me,' he said as he kissed her hand. 'I love you, Georgie, and I want you to be my wife. Will you marry me?'

He loved her and he wanted her to be his wife.

But could she marry him? There was so much they'd

never discussed, so many differences. But were they big enough to stop her from having the one thing she wanted?

'What is it? What's wrong?' he asked, and she could hear the worry in his voice. She needed to find a way to make this work. He loved her and she was determined to make sure they got their hearts' desires.

'My parents—'

'Want you to be happy,' Josh interrupted. 'Your father has given us his blessing. He's told me the decision is yours.'

'He has?'

Josh nodded. 'Your father is on our side and you can let me worry about your mother.'

Georgie knew he'd have no problem there. She smiled at him. She knew exactly how her mother felt about Josh and if her parents were prepared to give their blessing she knew she could have what her heart desired. 'My mother thinks the only thing wrong with you is that you don't want to get married. Now she'll believe you're perfect.'

Josh grinned and his eyes flashed silver again. 'So that just leaves you. Do you love me?'

Georgie nodded. 'I've only ever loved you.' She never would have believed that she could love someone so completely. 'I've been waiting for you my whole life.'

'And will you marry me?'

'Do you trust me with your heart?' She had to know he could trust her to love him completely and only him. 'Do you believe I will love, honour and keep you? When I say you are the only man for me, do you know that I mean it?' She had to know that he didn't doubt her words, that he believed her promises.

Josh nodded. 'I know how you feel about your family. If you love me and if you will marry me and make me part

of your family, that's all I need. You are all I need. I have
faith in you and me. I trust in us.'

'And you realise what you're getting yourself into?' she
asked. She had to be sure. 'A big Greek family and everything that goes along with that?'

'Why do you think we're going to live in Brisbane?' He
was smiling at her but he'd never looked more serious. He
held both her hands, holding her to him. 'I promise to keep
a spare room ready for your family and to fly your parents
up to visit whenever they want. I will immerse myself in
all of it if you'll marry me.'

She had seen how he'd cared for her parents. She'd seen
how he'd looked after her. She trusted him. She loved him.
She belonged to him. They belonged to each other. Fate
had brought them together and she knew he'd keep his
promises. She knew he'd do anything for her, just as she
would for him.

'I love you more than I ever imagined it was possible to
love someone,' she told him. 'I will marry you. I am yours.
Now and for ever.' She leant forward and kissed him, sealing their commitment, sealing their love. 'I love you now
and I promise I will love you just as much on our fortieth
wedding anniversary and on every one before and after.'

EPILOGUE

JOSH saw his wife as she came out of the house and crossed the grass. Her hair was loose, caught behind her ear on one side with a clip, and he thought how amazing it was he never grew tired of watching her. He couldn't believe how much his life had changed in the past two years. How fortunate he was.

He crossed the lawn and went to meet her. Georgie smiled at him as she saw him approaching and his heart swelled with love and satisfaction. 'Is she asleep?'

She nodded and her hair swung in a thick, glossy curtain around her shoulders.

He slid his arm under the heavy sheath of her hair and pulled her close to him, breathing in her scent of cinnamon and honey.

'I can't believe our daughter is one year old already,' he said as he hugged her.

'I know. Soon she'll be running after her cousins and getting into all sorts of mischief.'

Josh looked over to the pool where most of Georgie's nieces and nephews were mucking about. Her parents were keeping a watchful eye on their grandchildren and her brothers and sisters-in-law were scattered around the garden, having all travelled up from Melbourne to celebrate the baby's birthday. Despite Georgie living in Brisbane,

her family kept in touch and they all made a special effort
to get together for big celebrations. But Josh knew that,
for his daughter, seeing her cousins on an irregular basis
was no match for growing up surrounded by family.

'Do you miss Melbourne or are you happy here?' he
asked.

Georgie took his hand from her shoulders and held
it. 'Come with me.' She smiled at him. 'I want to show
you something.' She led him into the house. 'I don't miss
Melbourne. Sometimes I miss my family,' she admitted,
'especially after we've had weekends like this, but I have
you and I have our family.'

She opened the door to their daughter's room and
led him to Alexandra's cot. Alexandra was lying on her
back, arms thrown wide, spread-eagled in her favourite
position, clutching one of her soft toys in her chubby fingers. Georgie stood in front of him and wrapped his arms
around her waist, resting them on her stomach. 'I have everything I want right here.'

Josh rested his chin on the top of his wife's head as he
watched his sleeping daughter. This was another vision
he'd never grow tired of. 'What about Alexandra? Do you
think we're depriving her of her cousins and grandparents?'

'She'll be okay. Don't forget, she won't know anything
different,' Georgie assured him. 'We'll just have to have a
big family ourselves so the kids can keep each other company.'

'More kids?' He raised an eyebrow. 'Should we start
today?' he asked with a grin.

Georgie laughed. 'We've already started,' she said as
she squeezed his fingers and turned her head to smile at
him. 'I'm nine weeks pregnant.'

'What? You are?'

Georgie nodded. She'd planned to tell him the news when her family had all returned to Melbourne as she'd wanted it to be just between them for a while, but once she'd had a positive pregnancy test she'd found it very difficult to keep the news from Josh. She knew that if she didn't tell him soon, he'd guess. His ability to read her thoughts hadn't diminished since they'd married but, for once, if the stunned look on his face was anything to go by, she'd managed to surprise him this time. 'Is that okay? Not too much to deal with?'

'Are you kidding?' His eyes were shining silver and he was grinning like the Cheshire cat. 'Being married to you, being a father, has been the best thing that's ever happened to me. Adding to our family can only make things better,' he said as he smoothed his fingers over her stomach. 'It's fantastic news.'

The gentle pressure of his fingers sent a shiver of desire through Georgie. She'd never imagined she could love someone so completely. She turned to face him, careful to stay within his embrace. 'I love you. Thank you for sharing your life with me.'

'Our life together is still only just beginning,' he said as he bent his head and kissed her softly on the lips. 'I am going to love you for ever.'

And as he claimed her lips a second time there was not a trace of doubt in her mind that he would do just that. She had everything she'd ever wished for.

* * * * *

GREEK DOCTOR
CLAIMS HIS BRIDE

BY
MARGARET BARKER

Margaret Barker has enjoyed a variety of interesting careers. A State Registered Nurse and qualified teacher, she holds a degree in French and Linguistics, and is a Licentiate of the Royal Academy of Music. As a full-time writer, Margaret says, 'Writing is my most interesting career, because it fits perfectly into family life. Sadly, my husband died of cancer in 2006, but I still live in our idyllic sixteenth-century house near the East Anglian coast. Our grown-up children have flown the nest, but they often fly back again, bringing their own young families with them for wonderful weekend and holiday reunions.'

CHAPTER ONE

TANYA hurled the mop with the spider still clinging to it straight out of the window. It was a trick she'd learned from her grandmother when she had been very small and absolutely petrified of the giant spiders that had scurried along the floor of her bedroom.

"Just pick up a mop, dangle it over the spider and it will cling on, thinking it's found a friend," Grandmother Katerina had told her all those years ago, and it was still a good solution.

"Ouch!"

The sound of a deep masculine voice muttering a few choice Greek expletives rose up from the courtyard below her window. Tanya leaned out so that she could see the swarthy man beneath her and for a brief moment she thought she might be dreaming. It couldn't be…no, the low evening sunshine was playing tricks with her eyes…Manolis Stangos was in London, not here on the island…wasn't he?

"Tanya?"

"Manolis?"

"For a moment I thought you were Grandmother Katerina moving back into her old house."

He was speaking rapidly in Greek as if to a stranger, none of the smooth, silky tones he'd used when they had been together all those years ago. Tanya ran a hand over her long auburn hair. She was sure her afternoon cleaning session had done nothing to help her jet-lagged appearance. A cobweb was still clinging to her hand but thankfully the large scary spider was now scuttling away across the courtyard.

"Thanks very much! I know it's a long time since you saw me but I can't have aged all that much. Anyway…" Tanya swallowed hard as she rubbed a dusty hand over her moist eyes "…Grandmother—Katerina—died a few months ago…"

"I'm sorry. It's just that you were the last person I expected to see here."

His voice was softer now. Tanya took a deep breath as she tried to remain calm. This unexpected encounter was playing havoc with her emotions.

"Considering it's now my house, I feel I've every right to be here."

"I'm getting a crick in my neck looking up at you. Aren't you going to come down and check if you've fractured my skull with that mop, Dr Tanya?"

He smiled, and she could see the flash of his strong white teeth in his dark, rugged face.

"News filtered through to me in London that you'd qualified. I always knew you would in spite of…in spite of everything that might have stopped you."

She looked down at Manolis and found herself relaxing.

"I'll come down and check you out, although you could surely do that yourself, Dr Manolis," she said as she turned away from the window, taking her time to negotiate the narrow wooden staircase.

By the time she'd reached the tiny, low-beamed kitchen, Manolis had come in through the open door. Nobody ever closed their doors on this idyllic island of Ceres where she'd been born. Doors were closed when you went out. That was to make sure a stray goat or donkey didn't wander in and help itself to the food in the larder, but the key to the house was always left in the lock on the outside so that friends and neighbours would be able to get in if they needed to.

Meeting up with Manolis again after six long years had almost taken her breath away. She'd forgotten how handsome he was. Eight years older than her, he must be…what? Quick mathematical moment…thirty-six, because she was twenty-eight.

She remembered them celebrating her twenty-second birthday together. She'd just told him she was pregnant. She remembered how shocked he'd looked, how confused she'd felt.

"OK, are you going to check whether you've cracked my skull?"

"Sit down, Manolis. You're too tall for me to check it when you're towering above me, and you make me nervous."

"Nervous?" Manolis laughed. "When were you ever nervous of me?"

He pulled a chair out from under the check-clothed table and sank down, spreading his long legs out in front of him. She remembered that as a child when the impossibly tall Manolis had come into her grandmother's tiny kitchen he'd seemed to fill the whole room. She'd tried so hard to get his attention in those far-off days but he'd barely seemed to notice her.

"Keep still, will you?"

Her fingers were actually trembling as she smoothed back the thick black hair that framed his dark, rugged face. How many times had she run her fingers through his hair? And yet her reaction had always been the same. That sexy frisson she got from simply touching him. It travelled all the way down through her body and before she knew it her legs were turning into jelly, and as for her insides—well, that was almost impossible to cope with at such close quarters.

She sat down quickly on a chair. Her eyes were almost level with his.

"I can't see anything wrong with your forehead. Not a mark on it. You're just making a fuss about nothing."

If she continued using her bantering tone she could cover up the fact that she was so deeply moved she wanted to give in to her impossible desire. She wanted to laugh and cry at the same time. She wished she could turn the clock back to the time when they'd been so deliriously happy, so madly in love.

Manolis stirred on the small hard chair, unable to believe that he was so close to Tanya again. He had to clench his hands to stop himself reaching out and pulling her into his arms. Desire was rising up inside him, that familiar stirring in his loins that wouldn't cease until they'd made love again. But that would never happen. He'd known when she'd turned down his proposal of marriage for the second time that he would never try again. She was lost to him for ever and they couldn't go back.

"I think you'll live," Tanya said as she resisted the temptation to place her lips on his forehead in the pretence that she was kissing it better.

For a moment she wondered how he would react if she gave in to temptation. She could try…but he had a hard look on his face now. The moment had passed.

"I've got to go," he said evenly.

"Does your mother still live on the end of the street? Are you visiting her?"

He hesitated. "She still lives there. But actually I bought the house next to yours when I came back to Ceres a couple of years ago."

"Next door? In Villa Agapi?" She drew in her breath. Agapi was the Greek word for love. She had just come to live in Villa Irini, which meant peace. Love and peace next door to each other.

"Manolis, are you here on holiday?"

"I work here on the island again. I wanted to return and it was better for…"

He broke off as the sound of a child's voice came from the street.

"Papa, Papa? Where are you?"

Manolis hurried through the courtyard and stood by the open door that led to the street.

"Papa!" The little girl flung herself at him. He lifted her high into the air. She was laughing and screaming with delight as he lowered her into his arms.

Tanya remained absolutely still as she watched the joyous reunion of a little girl with her father. Her hands were clenching the side of the table to steady herself as she listened to the rapid non-stop Greek words that flowed from the child as she told her father she'd had the most exciting day. It emerged that she'd brought her papa a picture she'd painted at school but she'd put it down on a stone at the side of the path as she'd bent to take her shoes off because she hated wearing shoes when it was hot and the wind had blown it away and she wanted to paint another one now as soon as they got home because…

The story came out in one long breath. As she listened to the chatter, Tanya felt tears prickling behind her eyelids. This child, this beautiful little girl, couldn't be much younger than the child she'd lost. Their child. She and Manolis should have had a child like this one but…

"Chrysanthe, *agapi mou*," Manolis said, setting his excited daughter down on the cobbles of the courtyard. "Come inside and meet an old friend of mine. Tanya, this is Chrysanthe."

The little girl hurried across the small courtyard and through the open door of the kitchen, smiling, friendly, totally trusting.

Tanya tried to swallow the lump in her throat. This wasn't what she'd thought would happen today. It was all too poignant. Her confused emotions were draining her strength away. She reached out a hand towards the child.

Chrysanthe smiled as she placed her hand in Tanya's. A pretty little dimple had appeared in the adorable child's cheek. Who did she get that from? Must have been from her mother. The unknown woman who'd obviously taken Tanya's place so soon after they'd split up. How could he have met up with someone and conceived a child so quickly?

"Do you live here, Tanya?" Such a lovely lilt to the lisping childish tone.

Tanya cleared her throat. "Yes. I've just moved in today."

"I like your hair." The little girl took her hand out of Tanya's and reached up to stroke her auburn hair. She looked up at her father. "Daddy, why couldn't my hair have been this colour?"

Oh, no, please don't say things like that!

Tanya heard Manolis's swift intake of breath.

"It's very…unusual," he said quickly. "You can't…er…choose which colour your hair will be when you're born. Sometimes the colour comes from your daddy and sometimes from your mummy."

"My mummy's got blonde hair but she says it's out of a bottle. Could I get some of this colour out of a bottle, Tanya?"

"You probably could, but I prefer your hair the colour it is."

"Like Daddy's?"

Tanya swallowed hard. "Yes, like Daddy's." Her eyes met Manolis's and she turned away to avoid the poignancy of this discussion.

"Did you have a good journey, Tanya?" Manolis said quickly, breaking the uncomfortable silence.

"I'm always relieved when I get here because it seems to take for ever."

"Where did you come from?" Chrysanthe asked.

"Australia."

"Australia? My daddy used to live there, didn't you, Daddy?" The little girl had started to speak English now. "He told me all about it. It's a long way from here, isn't it? It's got lots of croccy… What are they called, Daddy?"

"Crocodiles."

Tanya noticed his voice was husky. He was reaching down and hoisting his daughter onto his shoulder.

"Your English is very good, Chrysanthe."

"My mummy's English. Are you English or Greek, Tanya?" The little girl looked down at Tanya from Manolis's shoulders.

"I'm both—like you. English mummy, Greek daddy. But I was born here on Ceres."

"I was born in England but I like living here best. Daddy used to bring me out to stay with Grandma Anna and all my cousins. I love being in my grandma's house. It's such fun playing with my cousins. Look, I can touch the ceiling! Daddy, I can touch the ceiling!"

"Tanya, I'll take Chrysanthe away and we'll leave you in peace. I'm sure you've got lots to do still."

Peace! How did he ever think she could be at peace when there were so many questions to be answered? She'd come back here to escape her stressful life in Australia but had never imagined she would have to face the turmoil of the past. Yes, she'd come to find peace but that wouldn't happen now, not while she was living next door to Manolis.

Manolis cleared his throat. "I know you've had a long journey, Tanya, but would you consider coming out for supper with me this evening?"

She'd never heard him sound so nervous. As if he was expecting her to squash the idea as impossible. Well, she had turned him down just before they'd split, only to bitterly regret it when it had been too late to change things.

"That would be after I've settled Chrysanthe with Mother. She stays with her when I'm on call. My mother has a huge bedroom—with plenty of room for her grandchildren—and they all love to stay there. We're a very close family, as you know, and…"

His voice trailed away. He was looking down at her, his eyes betraying how much he wanted to see her again that evening.

"Yes, I'd like that. There are so many questions I want to ask."

"Me too. So, I'll call in about eight. We could go to Giorgio's."

"How is he?"

"His health isn't too good but he sits in the corner and watches the rest of his family do all the work." He turned away, one hand still holding onto the child on his shoulders. "Bend your head, my darling, as we go through the door."

"Goodbye Chrysanthe. Come again to see me." She meant it wholeheartedly.

"Ooh yes, I will. Daddy, I'm still taller than you. When I'm grown up I might really be taller than you. When you're an old man I'll put you on my shoulder and…"

The voices became indistinguishable as father and daughter made their way down the street. Chrysanthe was a beautiful little girl, but Tanya had never imagined that Manolis could have moved on so quickly after they had split up.

He'd moved on. She mustn't dwell on it. She would remember only the happy times. She found herself wishing that little Chrysanthe was her child but stopped herself as soon as the thought occurred. No regrets. She had to move on with her life and not spend time wishing for the impossible.

Upstairs again, she ran hot water into the half-size hip bath in her tiny bathroom. As a child she'd loved to be bathed by her Grandmother Katerina when she'd been staying with her. She'd never dreamed that her grandmother would leave this house to her. Katerina must have realised how much Tanya loved it.

Tanya stripped off and stepped into the warm water. Mmm, it was bliss to lie back with the bath foam she'd bought in the airport shop in Sydney only yesterday. It hadn't occurred to her that today she would be preparing to go out for supper with Manolis. Once more she had to remind herself that nothing had changed between them. And now that Manolis was a married man, the gap between them must remain wide.

She closed her eyes and smoothed some more foam over her skin as she leaned her head against the back of her bath…

Tanya woke with a start and her arms flapped around in the cold water as she heard someone calling her from downstairs. Above the bath she could see moonlight shining through the tiny little window.

Manolis stood downstairs with his hand resting on the wooden banister. "Tanya, are you OK up there?"

"Yes, yes, I'm fine." She hauled herself out of the bath, spilling water onto the tiles. "I must have fallen asleep."

Manolis heard the splashing water and had a sudden mental image of Tanya's slim, lithe figure emerging from the tiny bath where Grandmother Katerina had often bathed him when he had been a small child and his mother had been too busy to cope as she'd fed the latest baby. He was sorely tempted to ask if he could join her upstairs but he knew what the answer would be. Still, a man could dream, couldn't he?

He put on his sternest voice so that Tanya would have no idea how much she'd already affected him. "That's a dangerous thing to do—fall asleep in the bath. You should never do that!"

Tanya was already climbing the narrow wooden steps up to her bedroom, clutching the towel around her. If it slipped and Manolis looked up through the rungs of the wooden stairs that connected the kitchen with the top floor… She glanced down as she stepped off the stairs into her bedroom but couldn't see him below her.

"I know it's dangerous but the bath's so small my knees were up to my chin so it's unlikely I could have slipped under the water," she called breathlessly, as she searched for something to put on. Not the smelly travel clothes…how about these trousers? She pulled them out of her case along with new, lacy black knickers. They were to make her feel good, nothing to do with the fact that she was going out with the sexiest man on the island—in the world.

It took her barely five minutes to emerge from her room fully clothed in three-quarter cut-off denims, white T-shirt and flip-flops. She'd spent a lot of time swimming and running at the beach near the hospital just outside Sydney and rarely used make-up for a casual night out. She would blend in with the tourists in Giorgio's taverna. And she knew for a fact that Manolis preferred a natural-looking face—not that it was any concern of hers!

He turned as she came down the stairs and in spite of his resolutions he whistled. "Mmm, you scrub up well, Tanya!" he said in English.

She laughed. "You haven't lost the Australian accent you picked up, Doctor. Are you trying to make me feel at home?"

"Something like that." He moved to the bottom of the

stairs, placing his hands, which seemed to have a mind of their own, on her shoulders. For a brief moment he hesitated before pulling her gently against him and kissing her on both cheeks.

"Welcome home," he said in the sexiest, most unplatonic tone. He hadn't meant to inject all that warmth and innuendo into his words but spending five minutes waiting for Tanya, knowing that she was first naked, then semi-naked then… well, it had played havoc with his intentions.

She tried to move backwards to escape his arms but she was pinned against the end of the banister.

She took a deep breath as she prepared to ask the big question. "Manolis, is your wife with you here on the island?"

"We're divorced. My ex-wife is in London," he said evenly.

She pushed her hands against his chest, making it quite clear that she wanted to escape this potentially dangerous embrace. There were too many questions that needed answers before she could begin to relax with him. But the fact that he was a free man made the situation a little easier…no, it didn't! Her emotions were already in turmoil.

"Let's go," she said quietly. "I'm looking forward to being back in Giorgio's."

She stepped out into the narrow cobbled street, terribly aware of Manolis's huge frame close behind her. She wasn't small by any means—her legs were long but she was quite short—so she'd always felt that Manolis towered above her. Glancing up at him as they walked together over the uneven cobbles, she missed her footing. He put out a hand to prevent her falling as she stumbled.

"Careful!" He took hold of her hand. The touch of his fingers unnerved her completely. "This part of the street is so dark," Manolis said as he waved his other hand upwards towards the light at the bend in the street. "There! That's better."

White light flooded down over them. "I know every stone along this street. You'll soon get used to it. How long do you intend to stay, Tanya?"

She gave a nervous attempt at a laugh. "Good question. The shortest answer is I don't know. It all depends…"

"On what?"

"On how I feel after I've had some time here."

There was a comfortable silence before Manolis spoke again. "The only thing is, if you didn't have any plans to return to Australia in a hurry, I was going to put a proposition to you."

She took her hand out of his. No! He wouldn't propose to her again, would he? The clock could never be turned back.

As if reading her mind, Manolis said, "That was perhaps an unfortunate phrase to use. This is a professional proposition. You see, I'm medical director of the hospital here and we need another doctor because it's the beginning of the tourist season."

He paused and took a deep breath before continuing. "There is a hospital board of governors who have the final say when a doctor is appointed but I'm the one who assesses the medical credentials of a candidate."

She was still listening, even appearing slightly interested. Well, he could but ask. "Would you like me to put your name forward?"

Tanya remained silent as she reviewed all the implications. Manolis walked on beside her, making absolutely sure that he didn't touch her. He wanted to tell her that he would never propose marriage to her again. Two proposals, two rejections from the love of his life was more than any man could suffer. But they did need a good doctor at the island hospital and he did want to have her near him as much as possible while she was here. He had no plans beyond that.

CHAPTER TWO

THE emotional warmth given out by the revellers, tourists and islanders in Giorgio's Taverna welcomed and wrapped around Tanya as if she'd never been away. As a small girl she'd been carried in here many times by her parents, elder brother, uncles, cousins and had often fallen asleep on somebody's lap, the music lulling her to sleep as the evening progressed. She would wake up in her own bed either at home with her parents or at Grandmother Katerina's, wondering how she'd been transported there.

Her brother Costas, who like his friend Manolis was eight years older than she, would sometimes tell her the fairies had carried her home in a special coach that ran over the cobbles without a sound. She'd liked to think that was true and whenever she found herself falling asleep at the table she'd made an effort to stay awake so that she could enjoy the journey home. But, however she'd tried, sleep had always got the better of her.

Manolis was trying to guide her to a table, one hand gently in the small of her back, but many people wanted to talk to them as they passed by.

"Dr Manolis, come over here! There's room on my table."

"Thank you… I'll see you later on…" Manolis was

smiling as he repeated his friendly phrase and moved on between the tables.

"I'm heading for that table in the corner," he whispered as he stooped down towards her.

Tanya was aware of the many glances in their direction. One middle-aged lady put out a hand to detain her.

"It can't be!" she said in Greek. "You're Katerina's granddaughter, aren't you? You're the absolute image of her when she was young and beautiful like you. Apart from the colour of your hair. You got that from your lovely mother, didn't you? I remember when she arrived here from England. Very soon she was going out with your father, our young Dr Sotiris. Ah, he was such a handsome man." She giggled. "All the girls fancied him. Including me!"

The giggle turned into joyful laughter.

Tanya smiled, wanting to give the lady her full attention even though Manolis was making his impatience to move on very obvious

"How is your father? Still living in Australia?"

Tanya swallowed hard. "He died of cancer five years ago."

"Oh, I'm sorry. How's your mother?"

"She's married again to an old friend. She's happy."

She felt Manolis's hand putting pressure on her to escape if she could.

"Lovely to see you again!" Tanya moved away, still smiling as she and Manolis finally reached the corner table.

Giorgio's son had seen them making their way through the crowded taverna and was already standing over the table they coveted, fending off potential occupants.

"*Efharisto*. Thank you, Michaelis," Tanya said, as she sank down on to the seat that was being held out for her.

"Good to see you back, Tanya. Have you come to work with Dr Manolis in the hospital?"

She hesitated. "I'm not sure what I'm going to do. First I need some holiday and then...who knows?"

Manolis smiled. "I'm trying to get her interested in applying for the newly vacant position."

Michaelis shrugged his shoulders. "What is there to think about? Tanya, you would be ideal as an island doctor. We have a beautiful hospital now. Not like the old days when your father had to cope with a small surgery and not enough medical help. Come into the kitchen to decide what you want to eat. Mama has got everything laid out on top of the ovens. The chicken in mataxa brandy is very good!"

"Did your mother make it?" Tanya asked.

"Of course!"

"Then I'd love to have some."

"Me too!" Manolis said. "And bring us a small selection of meze to start with, *parakalor*."

The sound of Giorgio playing on his accordion drifted over the happy voices. In spite of the general clamour, as she looked across the table at Manolis she felt as if they were the only two people in the room. It was almost as if they were back in their favourite Greek restaurant on the outskirts of Sydney.

A bottle of wine was placed on their table. "On the house," Michaelis said. "It's from my father to welcome Tanya back to where she belongs."

Tanya looked across and mouthed her thanks to Giorgio. He raised a hand from his accordion.

"What a welcome!" Manolis said as he poured the wine. "Does it make you want to live here permanently?"

"As I told you, I have no plans at the moment," Tanya said. Her words came out more sharply than she'd intended.

Manolis reined in his enthusiasm. Tanya had always had a mind of her own. "I didn't intend to upset you," he said evenly.

"I'm not upset. I just need time to think. I came here for a holiday and I don't want to have to make any decisions while I'm still jet-lagged."

"Of course you don't. It was just an idea. Take all the time you need regarding the vacancy at the hospital. The post has already been advertised and we've had a couple of applications. The current doctor is returning to England to take up a post in London. He's not going until the end of the month but we're expecting an influx of tourists very soon."

Michaelis poured wine into Tanya's glass. Manolis put a hand over his. "I'm on call tonight, Michaelis, so would you bring me a bottle of still water?"

Michaelis called the order to a young waiter who threaded his way through the tables and poured a glass of water for Manolis.

Manolis was anxious to return to their discussion about the vacant position but he waited until they were alone before continuing.

"We particularly need someone who knows the islanders and someone like you who was born here is absolutely ideal. In the past we've had outsiders who didn't really understand what working on Ceres involved. So, at the last meeting of the hospital board it was decided that if we could find an islander with good medical qualifications, that would be the candidate we would take. As I say, you would, of course, be ideal but it has to be your decision. I know you have a mind of your own."

He gave her a wry smile as he said this. For a few moments neither of them spoke. Tanya knew what he was referring to. She remembered that fateful day when she'd turned down his second proposal. How different her life would have been if she'd said yes.

She looked across the table. He lifted his glass towards

her. "Here's to your stay here on the island, whatever you decide."

She raised her glass and took a sip. "I would have to be approved by the hospital board as well as you, wouldn't I?"

"Of course. We now do more operations than we used to. We're licensed to perform emergency operations when it would be counterproductive to try to get the patient over to Rhodes. And we do some elective surgery as well. So I'm still able to make use of the surgical skills and qualifications I needed in my previous London job as head of surgery. Our hospital grew from a very small surgery not so many years ago, as you will remember, so our rules here have to be more fluid than on Rhodes or on the Greek mainland."

He could feel his hopes rising as he saw the expression of increasing interest on her face. "But knowing the excellent grades you got in your finals and the fact that you're an islander born and bred, I know—"

"You know an awful lot about me." She looked across the table, her gaze unwavering. "Did you check my exam grades?"

He leaned back against his chair. "I contacted Costas around the time I knew you should have finished your finals. I wanted to make sure that…you were OK after…after everything that had happened. I knew you wouldn't have dropped out of medical school altogether but you might have needed to take some time off."

"I didn't take much time off."

"I think it would have been a good idea. Your health had suffered."

"Yes, yes." She looked around her. Nobody could hear what they were saying because of the noise. "You were probably right when you advised me to take a year off."

She swallowed hard as she remembered how confused she'd been after the miscarriage. She'd realised too late that her hormones and emotions had been all over the place. Still feeling that a baby was on the way and yet having to come to terms with the fact that she was no longer pregnant.

"I chose to continue and, of course, I didn't drop out of medical school. It had always been my dream to qualify as a doctor. All my life. Especially when I was very young and you and Costas were making fun of me or ignoring me completely. I thought to myself, One day I'll show you big boys and my dad I'm not just a silly little girl who enjoys playing with her dolls."

Manolis stared at her. He'd never heard her say anything like that before.

"I didn't know you felt like that." He paused and took a deep breath. "Were we awful to you, Costas and I, when you were growing up?"

Tanya attempted to shrug it off, wishing she hadn't been quite so vehement about something that had bugged her for years.

"Oh, you were OK," she said, lightly. "You were behaving like boys do when girls are around. Trying to be macho. Sometimes you even noticed me."

"We were only teasing you, Tanya," he said gently. "When you came out to Australia to begin your medical training I could see you were a force to be reckoned with. Ambitious, clever, full of potential. Wow, I wouldn't have dared to tease you then."

She smiled to try and lighten the mood she'd created. "Oh, you were wonderful with me—really supportive. I never felt patronised by the fact that you were a qualified doctor and I was only a student. It was just something I wanted to do for myself at that point in time. I suppose I was ambitious. I was one of the generation of girls who wanted everything. I didn't want to miss out on anything."

She lowered her voice. "When I found out I was pregnant

I still wanted to continue with my studies. As I told you at the time, my mother had agreed to help me. You probably remember she was actually delighted at the prospect of her first grandchild."

Her voice cracked as she reached her final heart-rending words.

He leaned across the table and took hold of her hand. She remained very still but she could feel the prickly tears at the back of her eyes waiting to be released.

"I couldn't understand why you wouldn't take time off," he said gently. "Why you wouldn't let me take care of you, why you turned me down when—"

"I think my hormones were jumping around too much. I wasn't sure if you were proposing because…well, because you thought it was the dutiful thing to do."

"Was that why you turned me down for the second time?"

"Manolis, let's defer this discussion, shall we?" she whispered. "I can see people looking at us."

"Of course."

She knew now she'd been mistaken to turn down his proposal. In the agonising weeks after they'd split up she'd realised how stupid she'd been. She'd destroyed the most essential part of her life. The love of the person she'd admired as a child and desired when she'd become an adult. And by the time she'd come to her senses it had been too late.

She swallowed hard, very aware of the big hand holding hers.

One of the young waiters put more meze on the table. Taramosalata this time to add to the kalimara and the Greek salad, all of which remained largely untouched.

Manolis held out a plate towards her. "Try some of these Ceres shrimps. You used to like them when your parents invited me for supper, I remember."

She removed her hand from his and took some of the tiny

pink shrimps. "Delicious as always." She chewed slowly. "Some things never change."

"And some things do. You, for instance," he said gently.

She leaned back against her chair. "How have I changed?"

"Well…you always were stubborn but—"

"Stubborn? I suppose you mean when I didn't agree with something you wanted?"

He smiled. "Possibly."

She nodded. "I have to admit that some of the ideas I had when I was younger have changed. I don't think I would be quite so…well…stubborn, as you put it, now."

He wondered if he was in with a chance now with this older, wiser woman. No, of course not! If they were ever to become close again and he was to raise the question of marriage she would dash his hopes again. What did she mean when she'd questioned if his proposal had been merely dutiful? When the time was more convenient he'd quiz her further.

"So, you got all your information about me from Costas?"

"Mostly. We rather lost touch when he went to South America to work in that rural area. He hasn't answered any of my letters for ages!"

"He's chosen to live in a remote hospital near the Amazon. Sometimes he doesn't get his mail for weeks, months or at all. Often he can't get his letters sent out of the area. He's very dedicated to his work and doesn't have much spare time to worry about the outside world. My mother worries continually about him, of course, but she's adamant that he'll tire of this difficult life when he's had enough deprivation."

"He had a relationship in Australia that went wrong, I believe," Manolis said, quietly.

"Yes." She sighed. "These things happen."

Their eyes met and Tanya saw the moistness in Manolis's

gaze before he looked down at his plate and began crumbling a piece of bread.

"You haven't drunk your wine."

Tanya took a small sip. "The jet-lag is getting to me. I'd better not drink it. It might make me sleepy and I want to stay awake. I feel that we…well, we're getting to know each other again."

"I was completely surprised when you turned up here today. I'd had no news of you for ages."

The people on the next table had now gone. He waited before he dared to broach the subject of their disastrous break-up again. He'd been so unhappy, so completely devastated and depressed that he couldn't imagine how Tanya had suffered when her physical health had been at an all-time low and she'd had to cope with the emotional confusion as well.

"I was so proud that you coped by yourself after I left Australia. It couldn't have been easy after…"

"After I'd lost the baby?" she said quietly.

"Yes. Costas said you went straight back to medical school."

"I was still in a state of shock, I think. As I said, I now know I should have taken some time off but I was very confused. Keeping busy kept me sane—or so I thought. You must have done something similar when you went off to England and almost immediately married."

She tried but failed miserably to disguise the bitterness in her tone of voice.

"Tanya! I…"

The young waiter was placing the main course plates in front of them, having removed the scarcely touched meze dishes.

"Tanya, it wasn't like that!" he continued when they were alone again. "You'd made it clear that you didn't want me.

My old tutor in London had already contacted me about a newly created post as head of surgery which he said would be perfect for me. I was holding off discussing it with you because I wouldn't have gone over to London without you. When you virtually sent me away I decided to go for it. There was nothing to keep me in Australia any more. Victoria and I were old friends and we just happened to meet up again."

"How convenient!" She couldn't hold back the jealous anguish she'd experienced when she'd heard that he'd gone straight into the arms of another woman.

She took a deep breath. "And then married and had a baby very shortly after."

"On the rebound, I suppose," he said quickly, regretting how much she must have been hurt when she'd found he had a child. "But in mitigation…I'm not trying to sound as if I'm in the dock being tried for something…"

She watched him, anguished about what he'd done but still unable to crush her feelings for him.

"Go on, Manolis, tell me why you're hoping to be forgiven for jumping from one bed to another in double-quick time."

His eyes flashed. "You'd turned me down, told me to go away, said I was making things worse for you by staying, didn't you?"

"Yes, I did," she said quietly.

"So, Victoria being an old friend helped to salve my wounds. Somehow the comfort she gave me turned to sex. She fell pregnant. We married in haste and repented at leisure, as the old saying goes. It didn't take us long to realise that we would drive each other mad if we stayed together. We split up when Chrysanthe was six months old. Victoria was busy with her career and agreed with me that Chrysanthe would be brought up well on Ceres with the extended family

here. My mother was overjoyed to add another granddaughter to her brood, and I came over as often as I could. I was
on a long-term contract at the time so I had to wait before I
could give in my notice. When a vacancy came up here on
Ceres I applied and was accepted."

"They must have been delighted to have you here."

He nodded. "Yes. After a while I was offered the newly
created post of Medical Director. We've had to expand in
recent years because of the long tourist season from April to
November. Better boats, more tourist facilities…"

His voice trailed away. He hoped he'd helped to justify
what had happened since he'd walked away from her. She'd
asked him to go, but maybe, just maybe she hadn't meant it.

He gave a deep sigh. There he went again, giving himself
hope that he could turn the clock back to the time when
they'd been so idyllically happy together.

"Dr Manolis." The young waiter was standing beside his
chair. "There's a lady in the kitchen who wants to speak to
you. She's climbed all the way up the *kali strata* to find you.
Her granddaughter is having a baby in her house and there's
some problem that I…"

The young man paused in embarrassment. Manolis was
standing now, his hand on the young waiter's shoulders.

"I'll come and see her. In the kitchen, you say?"

Tanya was also on her feet. She'd heard what had been
said and her medical training was taking over. She was
holding her jet-lag in check as she followed Manolis up the
three worn old stone steps that led from the main restaurant
part of the taverna into the ancient kitchen with the moussandra platform in the high ceiling where Giorgio and his
wife had first slept when the taverna had been their home
before the six children had arrived.

The agitated elderly lady was sitting on a chair sipping a
brandy that Giorgio had poured for her.

It took only a couple of minutes to elicit the medical information they needed. Manolis ascertained that there was someone with the woman who was in labour before telling the grandmother to stay where she was. Someone from the hospital would come to collect her later. Yes, he knew the house where she lived.

As they hurried down the *kali strata*, Manolis was on his mobile phone, speaking to the hospital maternity section, giving them instructions, telling them to send a midwife, a stretcher with a couple of porters, and have an ambulance standing by at the bottom of the *kali strata* in case an immediate transfer to hospital was required, as well as the medication and instruments he would require if that happened.

Tanya was trying desperately to keep up with him but the ancient cobblestones beneath her feet were treacherous and slippery and the moon was covered in clouds again. Manolis, sensing her difficulty, took hold of her hand.

"Nearly there," Tanya said in a breathless, thankful voice. "I know the house where this family lives. My father used to say the houses in this area are in the worst place to get to for an emergency. Neither up nor down."

"Exactly! And yet nobody around here has a phone," he said in exasperation as he reached for the old brass door knocker.

The door was opened almost immediately.

"Doctor! Thank goodness you are here. My daughter…"

Manolis and Tanya stepped straight into the living room where the patient was lying on a bed. A low moaning sound came from her as Manolis gently placed his hand on her abdomen.

"It's OK, Helene. I'm just going to see how your baby's doing."

Tanya had immediately recognised Helene as an old friend from her schooldays. Helene smiled through the pain as she recognised Tanya, holding out her hands towards her.

One of the hospital porters arrived shortly afterwards, carrying the Entonax machine that Manolis had ordered. He explained briefly that the maternity unit was very busy and they weren't able to send a midwife yet but that one would arrive as soon as she was free.

Manolis nodded. "That's OK. Tanya will assist me."

While he was examining the patient Tanya fixed up the machine and placed the mask over Helene's face.

"Breathe deeply into this mask, Helene," Tanya said in Greek. "That's going to help the pain. No, don't push at the moment, Manolis will tell you when. I know it's hard for you. You're being very brave."

Helene clung to Tanya's hand as if her life depended on it.

Manolis began whispering to Tanya in English. He was totally calm and in control of the situation but she recognised the urgency in his voice.

"The baby is in breech position. I'm going to have to deliver it as soon as possible because it's showing signs of distress and the heartbeat is getting fainter. Take care of Helene and don't let her push yet. I've tried to turn... No, it's too late, I'll have to deliver the baby now. Ask Helene to push now so I can get the baby's buttocks through... Yes, that's fine... No hold it for a moment—I'll need to do an episiotomy. Pass me that sterile pack." He took out a scalpel and some local anaesthetic injection and performed the procedure.

It seemed like an age as Tanya, almost holding her breath, kept her cool with the patient.

"Manolis has everything under control, Helene."

Please, God, she thought. Don't let her lose this baby. She knew the anguish of losing her own baby and wouldn't wish that on anybody. Helene had carried this baby to full term and she couldn't imagine anything worse than losing it at this late stage.

"The baby's buttocks are through, Tanya," Manolis said. "You can ask Helene to push. One last push should… There, brilliant!"

As he lifted the slippery baby up it gave a faint mewling cry, rather like a kitten that had been disturbed from its warm, cosy sleep.

"Let me see, let me see my baby!" Helene held out her arms.

"In a moment, Helene," Tanya said, gently. "Manolis will—"

"Tanya, will you cut the cord while I put a couple of stitches in?" Manolis said quietly.

Tanya quickly scrubbed up. Taking the surgical scissors from the sterile pack, she cut the cord and wrapped the protesting infant in a clean dressing towel.

"You've got a little boy, Helene," she said gently as she put the baby in her arms. Tears sprang to her eyes as she saw the wonderful first meeting of mother and son. She dabbed her eyes with a tissue and held back the tears. She had to stay professional and think only of her patient. But she sensed that Manolis was looking at her. He was standing beside her now and had put a hand on her shoulder.

She looked up into his eyes and saw they were moist and knew he was thinking of their baby. She swallowed hard. How could she have hardened her heart and told him to leave her? Why had he not understood in the first place what a miscarriage did to a woman? Would they ever recover from what might have been? Would it ever be possible to repair the damage they'd done to each other?

The future was impossible to predict. She would take one day at a time, but she knew without a shadow of a doubt that she wanted to stay here on Ceres for a long time, whatever happened. This was where she belonged.

She looked around the room, which had become rather

crowded during the time that she and Manolis had been
taking care of their patient. Standing near the door that led
straight out on to the *kali strata* was a midwife, two porters
and a young man who now identified himself as Lefteris, the
baby's father. The midwife had held him back when he'd
arrived a few moments ago.

"Baby's father is here, Manolis," Tanya said. "Is it OK
if…?"

Too late! The young father had already sprung forward
to embrace Helene and his son.

"We'll need to do some tests on your baby, Lefteris,"
Manolis said gently after a short while. "He had a rough
passage into the world and we need to check him over." He
smiled. "Although from the way he's crying, there doesn't
seem to be anything wrong with him."

The midwife came forward and said that someone from
the postnatal team would do the tests as soon as they got baby
and mother settled into the hospital. The ambulance was
waiting at the bottom of the *kali strata* for them now.

As they emerged from the crowded room into the cooler
night air Tanya took a deep breath.

"It's such a relief that we got here in time," Manolis said,
taking her hand in what seemed to have become a natural
instinct again. "It could have been otherwise."

His hand tightened on hers as he became animated about
a subject close to his heart. "It's so strange here on the island.
On the one hand we've got the latest technology at the hospital
and on the other we've got people who haven't even got a
phone living in a difficult place to reach, yet within minutes
of help."

He broke off in frustration at the situation. "Sorry, Tanya.
I don't want to offload my problems on you." He let go of
her hand and turned her to face him.

In the moonlight she could see his eyes shining with happiness as he looked down at her. "We could be such a good team you and I—I'm talking professionally, you understand," he added quickly. "It felt so right working together just now. We seemed to sense that."

"Yes, I felt the rapport between us was...natural," she said quietly.

He lowered his head and kissed her gently on the mouth.

Oh, those lips, those sexy, wonderful lips. She'd never thought she would ever feel them on hers again. She'd cried with frustration when she'd realised how much she wanted him and he was never coming back. But here he was.

He raised his head and murmured against her lips. "So, do you want me to put your name forward as a candidate, Dr Tanya?"

Shivers were running down her spine. "Let's talk about it later," she murmured as she looked into his eyes.

She was making it patently obvious that she wanted him to kiss her again...

CHAPTER THREE

FROM somewhere in the distance Tanya could hear a cock crowing. She was hotter than usual. Where was she? She stirred in the strange bed and opened her eyes. Wooden rafters above her…where was the window?

The mists of her mind suddenly cleared. She was at Grandmother Katerina's, snug in the big bedroom at the top of the house. For several seconds she went back in time. She couldn't remember the end of the evening. She'd been in Giorgio's and… It was almost as if she'd been transported back here in the mythical fairy coach. There was a feeling of happiness tinged with sadness in the air.

And then she remembered. That kiss…that wonderful kiss! She'd murmured something to Manolis, held her face ready for another kiss, practically thrown herself at him. What did a woman have to do to make it obvious she would be putty in his hands? Oh, no! How humiliating to be rejected like that. Like what? She couldn't remember the details. Only the feeling that she'd expected Manolis to take her in his arms and…

She squirmed with embarrassment as she remembered how he'd made it clear that the kiss had been a one-off, the sort of thing that happened between old friends when they met again after a long time. Oh, he hadn't said that, in so many words. As far as she could remember, he hadn't said anything apart from suggesting they should get back.

At that point, the jet-lag she'd been holding off while she'd assisted at the birth of Helene's baby came back with a vengeance and she'd found herself agreeing with him. He'd held her hand but only in a courteous way so that she wouldn't slip on the treacherous cobblestones. As they'd reached Chorio, the upper town, they'd passed the door of Giorgio's Taverna where the door was closed but the revelry was continuing as always well into the night, and she'd found herself hoping Manolis would suggest they go in and join in the fun.

But they had kept on walking until he'd delivered her to her door and said goodnight. Not even a peck on the cheek! She told herself it was best they hadn't got emotionally involved. Too much too soon. Yes, Manolis had been very wise and she'd been stupid to think they could turn back the clock. There was too much between them to jump straight into any kind of relationship other than professional.

She began to doubt now whether she'd been too negative in her reaction to the idea of working at the Ceres hospital. She hoped that Manolis would put her name forward as soon as possible because, having worked with him last night and having had time to reflect on the proposition, she realised it would be ideal.

Her thoughts swung back to that idyllic period in her life when she and Manolis had lived together in Australia. The key stages of their relationship came flooding back to her. Their initial friendship when they'd first met again in the hospital, she a medical student, he a well-respected doctor. He'd asked her to have a coffee with him so she could tell him what she'd been doing since he'd last seen her on Ceres when she'd still been a schoolgirl of sixteen and he'd just qualified as a doctor at the grand old age of twenty-four.

She'd looked around her as they'd entered the staff common room she remembered. Seen the envious glances of the female staff as she was escorted in by this fabulously handsome, tall, athletic, long-limbed, highly desirable doctor. She and Manolis had seemed to be on the same wavelength right from the start of their new adult relationship. That evening he'd taken her out to a Greek restaurant near the hospital, wined and dined her, and she'd fallen hopelessly in love.

Four weeks later, at his suggestion, she left her hospital accommodation and moved into his apartment. It was pure heaven! Somehow she managed to keep her mind on her medical studies and clinical work during the day but, oh, the nights! In that amazingly luxurious bed that always looked as if a herd of elephants had trampled over it in the morning!

She never really worked out why the contraceptive pill she was taking at the time failed. Whatever had caused it, she was totally unprepared when she realised her period was late. She remembered the shock as the result of her pregnancy test came out positive.

She experienced the awful conflicting emotions of wanting a baby with Manolis, yet wanting to plough on unencumbered to reach her goal of becoming a doctor as soon as possible. And then she realised that she could have both of these dreams. Many women had careers and children as well. She went to talk it over with her mother, who was truly delighted at the prospect of becoming a young grandmother.

She remembered the characteristic way her mother ran her hands through her still beautiful, shiny, long, auburn hair and pulled a wry face. "Not very good timing, Tanya, with your medical exams to get through, but don't you dare tell me you're not going to have my first grandchild! I'll take care of him or her while you're studying and working in the hospital. There won't be a problem..."

She saw the tears of happiness in her mother's eyes as she hugged her. When they separated her mother dabbed at her eyes with a tissue. "You go for it, my darling, and I'll be with you every step of the way."

"What will Daddy say?" Tanya asked tentatively.

"Oh, don't you worry about your father. I can handle him. He's a pussy cat really, although he may find it a bit irregular. Now, you run along and get back to that wonderful man of yours and tell him…well, break it gently. Men can be a bit strange at times like this but he'll come round to the idea if you give him time. I've known Manolis since he was a child and he's a good man. He'll stand by you. After all, it's not as if you got pregnant by yourself. It takes two to tango…"

When Manolis arrived back that evening she waited until after supper, having cooked one of his favourites, a chicken casserole. Then she told him the news. Oh, the shock on his face! She told him to sit down because he looked like he might faint. Then she joined him on the sofa. She told him she was definitely going to go through with it.

He said, "Of course you are!" Then he paused as if he was weighing his words. "And, of course, we must get married."

It was his tone of voice that had made her think he was simply doing the dutiful thing. He was still in a state of shock. She remembered her mother's words. *He's a good man. He'll stand by you.* Did she really want someone who was simply being dutiful?

"I don't think we should rush things," she told him.

"Are you saying you don't want to marry me?"

She took a deep breath before saying, "It's not as straightforward as that. I'm going to have a baby. Let's do one thing at a time. For the moment I want to make my preparations for being a good mother and also I need to get on with my studies."

But nothing prepared her for the agony of her miscarriage at fourteen weeks. It was all such a blur now. The sudden bleeding, Manolis driving her to hospital, being told she'd lost the baby, rushed into Theatre for a D and C.

She stifled the sob that rose at the back of her throat and looked out at the bright sunshine beyond the bedroom window, breathing deeply to calm herself again.

She had a sudden vision of Manolis standing by her hospital bed, telling her that he wanted to take care of her until she was well again. He was again asking her to marry him, to be his wife so that he could look after her. His voice had been so tender and kind. But she remembered the feeling of panic. Her hormones had been in control of her body, not she. She couldn't make decisions at a time like this when she was grieving for the baby that had died inside her. Couldn't commit to anything so life-changing as marriage.

So she'd looked up at Manolis and said she couldn't marry him. That it was best they separate until she didn't feel so confused. They'd only been together for a few months and everything had happened so quickly.

She turned her head to look around Grandma Katerina's bedroom, her bedroom now, and decided that was enough reminiscing for today. Time to get back to the present and continue with her new life.

No time for nostalgic reflection now! It was high time she got herself moving and sorted out her clothes. Just in case Manolis phoned to say she should go down to the hospital for an interview.

In the house next door Manolis stared up at the ceiling. He couldn't believe he'd passed up the opportunity of a night with Tanya. How often had he dreamed that she'd come back to him, that they were together again?

She had obviously been aroused by his kiss last night. Or

had she just been pretending so as not to hurt his feelings? He could never be sure with Tanya. He'd lived with her for a few months, loved her, conceived a child with her and mourned with her when their unborn child had died in the womb. But he still couldn't understand her!

He remembered the night she'd told him she was pregnant. The shock of it had almost taken his breath away. He'd felt so guilty at giving her an added burden to the load of getting through her studies and exams. He had been so worried it would all be too much for her that it had only been in the next few weeks that he'd had time to begin anticipating how wonderful it would be to have a child with Tanya. She'd seemed so happy, and so capable of handling the situation that he'd begun to relax with her again.

She'd made it quite clear this was what she wanted, a child and a medical career. He'd realised that life was going to be wonderful when they were a family and not just a couple.

Then had come the awful evening when she'd started to bleed. She had been fourteen weeks, he remembered. He'd driven her to hospital, made sure she was admitted immediately but there had been nothing anyone could do to save their baby.

He swallowed hard as the awful sadness of their loss hit him again. His grief had been almost impossible to bear. But he'd forced himself to stay strong for Tanya. He wanted to protect her, to take care of her while she'd been weak and vulnerable. That was when he'd made the mistake—he realised it now—of again asking to marry her. He'd told her that he wanted to look after her, to make sure as a doctor that she had the best treatment until she was strong again. He'd told her not to rush herself with her answer. He would wait until she was stronger.

But she'd looked at him as if he was a stranger. Her eyes had been blank, he remembered. This wasn't the girl he knew and loved. He'd worked in obstetrics and witnessed how hormonal a woman could be when she'd lost a child. But it would pass—surely Tania would realise that her current situation was temporary.

He looked up at the ceiling as he tried to bring his emotions back under control. He hadn't been prepared for her rejection of him. She'd asked him to leave her.

He remembered going out through the ward door. Her mother had been coming towards him down the corridor. She'd put out her hand and taken hold of his. "It's best you leave Tanya alone for a while, Manolis. She's very confused. We're going to take her home for a while until she's strong again."

After she'd sent him away, rejecting the love he wanted to give her for the rest of his life, he'd felt he would never understand her. Not in a million years!

But last night, as he'd kissed her, he'd felt the desire rising in him as she'd snuggled against him and he'd felt that it might be possible to take this embrace to its obvious conclusion. But the old fears of rejection had nagged him. No, he'd been deluding himself, elated by the successful conclusion of a working partnership when they'd safely delivered Helene's baby together.

Oh, yes, she might have gone to bed with him. But he wanted more than a no-strings relationship with Tanya. But he could tell she valued her freedom. He could understand that now. She'd worked hard to become a qualified and now experienced doctor. She didn't need marriage.

Not like he did. As a young man he'd had two ambitions—one, to become a doctor and, two, to raise a family with the woman of his dreams. He'd had several no-strings relationships before he'd gone to Australia to take up a post in the hospital where Costas had been working. Meeting up with Costas's sister Tanya again when he'd been twenty-eight and she was a promising medical student of twenty-two had been like a bolt of lightning.

He'd been amazed when he had seen her for the first time for six years. The last time he'd seen her had been just before her father had taken the family out to Australia. He'd just spent his first year as a qualified doctor in the London hospital where he'd trained and had come over to Ceres for a short break. Tanya had been with Costas one time when they'd all walked down from Chorio to the harbour for drinks together as night fell.

He'd noticed she was growing into a very attractive young lady. But she had just been his friend's sister and far too young for him. But when he'd met her again six years later in Sydney he'd realised she was mind-blowing, with her fabulous, flowing, long auburn hair! Beautiful, attractive, intelligent, everything he'd ever dreamed of.

He remembered looking into her eyes, realising that she admired him too. Four weeks later he'd asked her to move into his apartment with him. They'd been idyllically happy until she'd told him she was pregnant. He'd been so worried about her, but he'd come to terms with it and relaxed, finally beginning to look forward to being a father. Then she had miscarried and their lives had changed completely. He had been totally rejected by the woman he adored at a time when he'd wanted to give her all his love and take care of her for ever.

The only way out of the impossible situation had been to start a new life and try to forget her.

"Papa!"

The sound of his daughter's voice brought him back to the present. She was downstairs, having come from his mother's house to see if he could take her to school. He always took her to school if he wasn't already working at the hospital. The school wasn't far away and the path was perfectly safe, but he liked to go with her.

"Chrysanthe, I'm coming, my love!"

* * *

The pile of clothes Tanya had brought from her suitcase to the bedroom could wait until she'd had some breakfast. She'd hardly eaten any supper at Giorgio's. She set off to walk round to the baker's to get some bread. As she stepped into the street, she caught a glimpse of Manolis turning the corner and the sound of his daughter's chatter. If she hurried she could catch him up before he reached the main street. No, she needed to cool down. She wasn't sure how she was going to face him today.

She lingered a while to make sure he was well on the way to Chrysanthe's school. She wasn't ready to face him just yet. Not until she'd made a cafetière of strong coffee and had some breakfast. He would probably phone later from the hospital and ask her down to discuss the job. At least, that was what she was hoping.

But he didn't! She spent the entire morning doing more cleaning, organising the kitchen, organising the bedroom, hanging up clothes, neatly placing her pants and bras in one drawer, her T-shirts in another, her swimwear in another...

"He should have phoned by now!"

She realised she'd spoken out loud. Maybe that was what happened to people who lived by themselves. She needed to get out more! The sun was shining outside. To hell with him! She wasn't waiting around any longer. She knew she really wanted this job now and so if he wasn't going to contact her she would go to the hospital and ask for it herself. Her father had been one of the founders of the new hospital, for heaven's sake! She would go in there with her head held high and ask to see the chairman of the board, whoever he might be these days.

Choosing the right clothes when you wanted to impress had always been a problem, because she preferred a casual look. Somewhere in the middle? Her cream linen suit? With a pale pink silk shirt underneath in case the heat got to her? Yes, that looked fine.

She sat down at her grandmother's dressing table. Looking in the mirror, she smiled at herself to remove the worry lines that had appeared on her forehead. At twenty-eight she needed to take care not to get real wrinkles settling there. The light tan she'd had since she'd gone to live in Australia needed very little makeup. A little foundation cream and a dash of lipstick was all she'd use. There!

Several strokes of the hairbrush smoothed out the long auburn hair and made it shine. She was glad she'd taken the time to wash it that morning. She could, of course, coil it up so that she looked more professional. Yes, that would definitely impress the chairman of the board, the old boy she was going to see. He was bound to be old, wasn't he? These types always were.

She piled her hair up on top and stuck it in place with several pins and grips. Over the years she'd practised this so often that it wasn't difficult for her. She immediately felt more efficient, intelligent, a better doctor, somebody that the chairman would take seriously.

"In short, Dr Tanya," she told her reflection, "you are the perfect candidate we've been looking for. The job is yours."

She smiled. "Thank you, sir. I accept."

Outside, the midday sun was stronger than she'd realised and the smart court shoes were hardly conducive to the cobblestones. Still, by the time she'd gone through the upper town and tried to persuade a taxi to collect her it would be quicker and easier to simply make her way on foot down the *kali strata*.

Halfway down, the door to Helene's house was wide open. Helene's grandmother was standing on the step and called out to her.

They chatted together. Tanya explained that she was on her way to the hospital and wouldn't come in for a drink. Yes, she would try to see Helene at the hospital and was glad that all was well with her. With praise ringing in her ears about the way that she and Manolis had delivered the baby, she continued on her way.

It was marginally cooler as she walked through the narrow streets of Yialos, the town by the harbour. The hospital, referred to by everybody as the New Hospital, was set back from the harbour near the church. It had started off as the doctors' surgery, she remembered, and had then been extended a great deal to qualify as a real hospital. It had certainly grown since she was last here.

She walked in through the front doors that led from the area where a couple of ambulances were parked. The reception area was very smart and, luxury of luxuries, it was air-conditioned! She really hadn't expected anything quite so grand here on Ceres. She began to feel slightly overwhelmed. And definitely overdressed. And the fact that she'd assumed she could just walk in and demand to see the chairman of the board was perhaps a little…

"Can I help you?" an English voice asked.

She moved forward to confront the white-uniformed receptionist who, unsmilingly, didn't seem as if she wanted to help at all.

"Actually, I was hoping to see…I'd like to make an appointment to see the chairman of the hospital board."

The young woman frowned. "Could you give me some details, Miss…?"

She cleared her throat and straightened her back. "I'm Dr Tanya Angelapoulos."

"Tanya!"

She turned at the sound of Manolis's voice—his most welcome voice! For a moment she felt like the young girl who'd craved his attention. No, she was all grown up now and didn't need his help—did she?

He came towards her, looking so handsome in his theatre greens, a mask still dangling round his throat, that she was sure her heart missed a beat.

"I've been in Theatre all morning. I was going to call you when I got a moment to spare about the job. I haven't been able to contact any of the board. Wheels run slowly out here and now everything closes down for lunch. Why are you here?"

"I just happened to be down in the town, shopping, and I thought I'd drop in to…er get the feel of the place, see if I might like to work here," she improvised.

He looked taken aback, she thought, and wished fervently that she hadn't arrived unannounced. He didn't seem at all pleased to see her.

"Look, come along to my office. I'll fill you in on what's involved with the job." He turned to looked at the reception-ist, who was desperately trying to find out what was going on. "It's OK, Melissa, I'll look after Dr Tanya."

He put a hand on her back as he guided her out of Reception. He hadn't even noticed she was smiling.

Tanya could feel the gentle, soothing touch of Manolis's hand in the small of her back as they walked along the corridor. He was pushing open a door that led into a spacious room. He was obviously very important here. She'd noticed the sign on the door that read "HOSPITAL DIRECTOR." He was the one who'd got her interested in this job. Surely he could bypass the usual rules and sign her in?

As if reading her mind, he said, "If you've come about the job, I have to tell you we'll have to go by the book—at least in principle."

He waved an arm toward the seat at the other side of his desk. "There are only three men on the board, mainly chosen for their influence on the island. Two are retired doctors and worked with your father—so that's a definite plus. The other used to be mayor and can be a bit difficult."

"Manolis, I want to be appointed to this job on my own merit, not because the doctors on the board worked with my father."

"Of course you do, and you will be. You have brilliant qualifications, hospital experience and background. I'll get on the phone as soon as everybody wakes up from lunch and siesta which, as you know, is obligatory on Cercs."

"I'd forgotten about the routine here on Ceres. I've been away for twelve years and the routines you follow here…"

She looked up into his dark brown eyes and saw them twinkle with amusement. "It's not so much routine as necessity, Tanya. After a long morning in Theatre I need a break. Some lunch—why don't you join me?"

He managed to make it sound like he'd only just thought of it, although he'd been wondering how he could drag it into the conversation without eliciting a negative response. Playing hard to get was more difficult than he'd thought it would be this morning. Trying to hold down his feelings for this woman was almost impossible.

She hesitated, just long enough to make him think she was considering her answer.

"Yes, I'd like that," she said, giving him a cool little smile, not too much, not too little. Hopefully, just cool enough to make him forget how she'd looked up into his eyes last night, practically begging him to kiss her again.

"OK. I'm going to have a quick shower. Help yourself to a magazine from the patients' waiting area over there. I'll be with you in a couple of minutes."

He was actually three minutes because she was timing him. She'd got a magazine open on her lap but the sound of the shower coming from his bathroom next door was tantalising her. She couldn't help thinking about that wonderful muscular body that had been hers all those years ago. Hers to snuggle next to in the night after they'd made wild, passionate love.

She remembered the way he would move languidly round to hold her in his arms again. And even though she'd thought she was exhausted she'd felt herself reviving, the whole of her body alive to his touch. She breathed deeply as she felt that even here. As she waited for him to finish his shower, she was becoming aroused. The thought that she could just walk across, open that door and—

"Hope you're not getting bored out here."

He stood at the other side of the room now, a white towelling robe covering his magnificent body, one hand furiously rubbing his thick dark hair with a towel.

"No…you were very quick, really." She stood up, hoping she didn't sound too eager to agree with him.

He strode across the room.

How could he stand next to her dressed like that? She only had to reach out and take hold of that belt, give it a tweak and…hey, presto, they would be on the carpet in no time at all!

"Are you OK, Tanya?"

"I'm fine. Hungry, I think. Been a long morning."

She turned and deliberately moved into the patients' area to replace the magazine. She heard him close his bathroom door again. When he returned he was wearing hip-hugging jeans and a T-shirt. Now she really did feel overdressed!

They walked out through the deserted reception area. Everybody, it seemed, was on their lunch and siesta break.

"No doubt somebody is still in the hospital to take care of the patients and deal with any emergencies," she said as they moved down the busy street outside.

"Oh, we're all in touch by phone. And there are nurses in

the wards, taking care of the patients. At the back of the hospital the accident and emergency unit is functioning as normal. But as much as possible we like to keep the work down in the afternoon."

They'd reached the harbour. Manolis slowed the pace as people milled around everywhere, tourists stopped in small groups chatting before deciding where to have lunch.

"Everything gets back to normal from five o' clock, doesn't it?" Tanya said. "I'd forgotten what life was like on Ceres."

"Yes, shops are closing now but they'll reopen when people begin to emerge for the evening. You'll soon be back in the swing of Ceres again."

He looked down at her and unable to contain himself any longer he reached for her hand. She looked up at him questioningly. For an instant she thought she'd glimpsed the old Manolis, the man she now suspected might have been totally committed to her. But she'd killed that commitment, hadn't she?

It would obviously be emotionally safer if she didn't try to resurrect what they'd had between them. Just get on with her life here on Ceres. Or should she tell him how, only weeks after she'd lost their baby she'd felt strong again and had come to her senses? Should she tell him that she'd regretted asking him to leave and missed him with an ache in her heart that was almost physical and wouldn't go away?

He'd dropped her hand again. She followed him to the table he'd selected outside Pachos Taverna. She remembered coming here with her family for evening drinks.

"Is Pachos still here, Manolis?"

"He retired a few years ago. His son has now taken over and he does delicious snacks at lunchtime. It's near enough to the hospital for me to pop out in the middle of the day if I'm not working. Would you like a glass of wine—or an ouzo perhaps?"

"A glass of retsina," she said, boldly. "Then I shall really feel I'm back on Ceres."

"I've got to work again this evening so I'd better stick to water."

A waiter came to take their order. They ordered Greek salad and Ceres shrimps.

"Nice and light, so that I can go out again for supper," she said, hoping that didn't sound like she was angling for an invitation.

He hesitated. He'd been holding back long enough. "I'm working late tonight, otherwise I could have joined you." He hesitated, sure that she seemed disappointed. "I'm due for a day off at the end of the week. Would you like to come out in the boat with me?"

"You've got a boat?"

"Don't sound so surprised! I'm not as impoverished as I was when I was a junior doctor. It's my pride and joy, as you'll find if you come with me. How about Saturday? Are you free?"

She hesitated just long enough. Was she free? What a question!

"I think so."

"Well you can let me know. I'll be going anyway—and probably Chrysanthe. She loves the sea. We can—"

"Manolis!" A tall, distinguished-looking man was standing by their table. "So this is the mysterious young lady you've been keeping to yourself."

"Demetrius!" Manolis was standing, holding out his hand to shake the older man's. "I was going to phone you this morning but I've been tied up in Theatre. Dr Demetrius Capodistrias, let me introduce you to Dr Tanya Angelopoulos."

"Not Sotiris's daughter? Yes, of course you are. With that wonderful hair, you're the image of your mother."

Tanya felt a firm grasp as she extended her arm towards Demetrius.

"Do join us, Demetrius." Manolis was pulling up a chair. "Let me get you a drink."

"Thank you. What did you want to speak to me about, Manolis?"

"I was hoping you could convene a meeting of the hospital board fairly soon. Tanya is interested in applying for the post that's soon to be vacant."

"That's why I'm here. News travels fast on Ceres and when I heard that Sotiris's daughter had helped to deliver Helene's baby last night I knew I had to suggest she apply for the post. We need someone like you, born and bred on the island with a medical background." He smiled at her. "And rumour has it that your own qualifications are excellent."

"Actually, Manolis said there would be a vacancy for a doctor in the hospital soon so I've already given it some thought. I'd like to be considered if—"

"Splendid! I'll get in touch with the rest of the board this afternoon. Could you be free for an interview about six, Dr Angelapoulos?"

"Yes, of course."

"And you, Manolis. We'll need you there in your capacity as medical director."

"Yes, I'll be there."

Demetrius raised his glass towards Tanya. "I used to be a junior doctor when your father was in charge here. He was a great man to work with. We were all saddened, everybody who'd known your father, when we heard that he'd died."

"Yes." She swallowed hard. It still hurt.

"And your mother?"

"She's fine. Did you know she'd married again?"

"No, I hadn't heard that."

"An old friend of my father's. I'm glad my mother is content again."

Manolis's mobile was ringing. She could tell it was an emergency by the way he was speaking.

He stood up. "Sorry, I'll have to get back to the hospital. There's been a crash on the waterfront. One of the cars has gone into the sea and the passengers are being brought in."

"I'll come with you, Manolis."

Manolis hesitated. "I suppose it's OK for Tanya to help out before she's been appointed to the staff, isn't it, Demetrius?"

"In an emergency, we're relieved to get all the help we can. We have to be totally independent here on our small island. Our emergency rules have to be flexible." Demetrius turned to Tanya. "Thank you. I'll see you at six, Dr Angelopoulos."

She was glad to be busy in the hospital during the afternoon, with no time to worry about the interview in the evening. The first thing she did was to change out of the smart, inappropriate suit and put on a white short-sleeved coat.

The small accident and emergency unit was crowded with relatives and friends of the drivers and passengers of the two cars that had collided on the narrow waterfront road. The driver of the car that had gone into the water and the woman who'd been sitting in the passenger seat were being treated already by a couple of nurses.

Manolis immediately took over the treatment of the driver while Tanya tried to revive the unconscious woman whose lungs were waterlogged. Tanya turned her on her side and gently but firmly tried to remove the water from her lungs with an aspirator. Seconds went by before a loud gurgling sound indicated that the lungs were disgorging water. She started to cough and water now came up from her stomach.

She opened her eyes. "Where am I?"

"It's OK. You're in hospital." Relief flooded through her as she raised her patient to a sitting position and held a bowl under her mouth.

Meanwhile, she could see that Manolis had also been successful with his patient. The driver was already talking quietly, fretting about his wife, hoping everybody was going to survive. And how was the car?

Manolis gave his patient a wry smile. "Several metres under the sea, but everybody's alive, which is the main thing."

The two nurses took over from Manolis and Tanya, who were now required to deal with a patient whose leg was causing him a lot of pain. It wasn't difficult to diagnose that there was at least one fractured bone.

"We'd better have an X-ray of that leg. I'll do that because I know we haven't got a radiographer in the hospital this afternoon. Will you organise the plaster unit over there, Tanya?"

He put a hand on her arm. "Welcome to the real world of an island hospital! This is going to seem very different to the hospitals you've worked in."

"I know the score, Manolis. I used to watch my dad, remember. It was even more impromptu in his day."

By the time Manolis had X-rayed the distorted leg, he'd decided he would have to operate.

"It's worse than I thought," he told Tanya quietly. "I'll need to put in a steel plate and some screws in the tibia, which is shattered in several places. How much experience have you had in orthopaedic surgery?"

"I've assisted in Orthopaedic Theatre several times and passed my orthopaedics practical and theoretical examinations—with distinction," she added, just to set his mind at rest. "It won't be a problem."

"Excellent. The sooner we can get this leg in the right

position again, the better will be the outcome for the patient. Check when the patient had his last food. I'll see you in Theatre when you've scrubbed up. The anaesthetist I've contacted should be with us shortly."

Minutes later she was standing across the other side of the operating table waiting for Manolis's instructions. The patient was anaesthetised and the anaesthetist was satisfied with his breathing. Tanya glanced at the monitor. Blood pressure was normal.

Above his mask Manolis's eyes registered calm. She'd never worked in Theatre with him before but she felt they were already a good team.

"Scalpel..."

CHAPTER FOUR

TANYA could feel the intense pressure under which the quickly assembled team was working. In this sort of emergency situation, where most of the team had expected to be off duty, the concentration required by them was paramount.

She watched as Manolis was cutting through the skin and outer layer of tissue to expose the tibia. As she'd seen on the X-ray, it was badly shattered. The front of the bone would require plating and other less damaged sections could be aligned with screws. In any case, whatever Manolis did, everything would depend on the healing process. If the bone didn't heal, amputation would be the only option.

As if reading her mind, Manolis began to explain to the team what he was doing and why. Whenever he was operating he tried to remember to pass on his skills to the team. He firmly believed that continual teaching was necessary in the operating Theatre. That was how he had learned. Textbooks were helpful but the real skills were learned by assisting and listening in the operating Theatre.

"We've got a young, otherwise healthy man here," Manolis concluded as he indicated to Tanya the steel plate he was going to insert. "There's no obvious reason why the bone shouldn't heal but always, in orthopaedic surgery, we cannot take anything for granted. Infection is always a possibility."

There was a murmur of assent from everyone. Manolis glanced across the table at Tanya. Beneath his mask she could tell he was smiling at her. The smile had reached his eyes. He was calm, totally in control, doing the job he was born to do—like she was.

For a brief instant she remembered the interview. She mustn't be too complacent about it. She wanted this job more than ever now she was actually working in the hospital. But now she had to concentrate on the work in hand. They had to save this young man's leg from amputation…

Three hours later, she pulled down her mask and breathed a sigh of relief. She was standing in the scrub room with Manolis, who was peeling off his gloves. A nurse and porter had just taken the patient to the orthopaedic ward. He was conscious now and Tanya had already removed his airway as his breathing was normal again.

"I'm quietly confident he's going to be OK," Manolis said, as he dropped the gloves in the nearest bin.

Tanya reached forward and released the Velcro fastening at the back of Manolis's gown. It was an automatic gesture which she'd done many times for whoever she'd been working with in Theatre.

Manolis swung round as he tossed the gown towards the large bin near the door. "It's a long time since you helped me to undress," he said, his voice much too husky and suggestive. He regretted the remark as soon as he'd made it. He waited for Tanya to retire into her shell again.

To his delight she smiled up at him. Her rich auburn glossy hair had tumbled down onto her shoulders as she'd removed the theatre cap that had been holding it in place. He remembered how it used to fan out on the pillow in the morning, all rumpled after a particularly fantastic night of sheer passion, love and…

"Purely second nature to me to assist the chief surgeon," she said, pleasantly but without a hint of sexual innuendo.

Good thing she couldn't read his thoughts! He reined in his feelings and physical arousal with great difficulty. They were standing so close now. Surely she could feel the emotional tension between them.

"I've got to go and see Helene in the postnatal unit," she said in the same tone. "I promised her grandmother I would."

He cleared his throat to remove all possibility that he would sound husky and provocative. "Don't be late for the interview."

"Of course not."

As she turned away she wondered how much longer she should put up the pretence that she wasn't interested in renewing their old relationship. They'd been standing so close just now. It had been all she could do not to take hold of his hand just to feel contact with him again. He'd had such a tense expression of control on his face.

As she walked out through the door she knew he was watching her. She could feel his eyes on her every movement. The door swung back again behind her and she walked away quickly before she had time to reveal her true feelings.

It wasn't going to be easy working with Manolis but she was determined to get this job. The old ambition was back. She still wanted to show him what she was made of!

She walked purposefully along the corridor towards the postnatal unit.

Helene was sitting in an armchair by her bed, feeding her tiny baby boy.

"Tanya! Grandmother said you were going to come in."

Helene patted her baby gently on the back as he finished feeding. A welcome burp came from the tiny mouth and she handed him to Tanya. "They checked him over but I'd like you to give your professional opinion."

Tanya ran her experienced eyes over the little body while she was changing his nappy to check that everything was in working order. As she removed his nappy a fountain of urine spurted into the air. They both laughed as Tanya narrowly missed being showered.

"He seems extremely healthy to me," Tanya said as she fixed a clean nappy and placed him back in his cot. "Have you got a name for him yet?"

"Lefteris, after his father."

They chatted together in Greek, both trying to fill in what had happened to them since they'd been together at school. Tanya was deliberately vague about her life in Australia, and managed not to mention that she'd had an affair with Manolis.

Helene began to tell Tanya about how difficult it now was that she and Lefteris were living with her grandmother. "It's kind of her to take us in but we're very cramped—it will be even more so now that our baby is here. You see, my parents don't approve of him. We're not married and unmarried lovers don't live together on Ceres, as everybody knows. When I found out I was pregnant my parents were furious. It was OK for me to live at home, even at the ripe old age of twenty-eight, but scandalous to get pregnant. We had a big row and Lefteris and I moved in with Grandmother."

"Do you know why your parents don't approve of Lefteris?"

"They think he's a drifter, never had a proper job. He's worked on the boats for a low wage for years and now he earns very little as a casual builder and labourer. My parents have forbidden me to marry him. They say he'll leave me when he wants to move on again."

"Perhaps they'll change their minds now that your baby is here."

"I doubt it! We could go ahead and have a quiet wedding

without spending too much money but I don't want to disobey my father."

Tanya put her hand over her friend's. "I'm afraid I've got to go now. I'm due for an interview with the hospital board at six o' clock and I need to change out of this white coat into something more presentable."

"Are you going to be working here permanently?"

"I hope so."

"So do I. You'll come and see me again, won't you? They're going to keep me in for a few days in view of the difficult living conditions at my grandmother's."

"I'll come and see you again as soon as I can."

The hospital board was assembled in a large office near the reception area. Manolis went into the room first and introduced Tanya to the three men, before taking his place behind one of the desks. As he'd explained to her, there were two doctors—Demetrius, who she'd already met, and another retired doctor. Alexander Logothetis, the ex-mayor who still had a great deal of influence on various committees, the island council, the school board and the hospital, was the third man.

Manolis had told her that Alexander Logothetis might be a tough nut to crack.

"We'll have to play down the influence your father had when he was doctor in charge of all medical services on the island." Manolis had told her just before they'd entered the room.

"Alexander is not much younger than your father and I believe they didn't always see eye to eye when Alexander was trying to climb the ladder of success in the property world here. There were several disputes between them before the new hospital project got off the ground."

She had looked up at him with confidence she didn't

entirely feel. "Don't worry about me, Manolis. I intend to get this job on my own merits."

"I'm sure you will," he said, quickly.

The interview lasted almost an hour. By the end of it Tanya was feeling very tired. It had been a long day and she could feel the tension in the room getting to her. As Manolis had predicted, Alexander Logothetis was the most difficult member of the board to convince.

He'd asked questions about her qualifications, experience, health and stamina, hinting that it was a tough job for a young woman, with long hours and a flexible attitude required to every situation.

She'd answered all his questions at length and hoped she'd convinced him she would be totally committed to her work. The medical questions put to her by Manolis and the other two doctors were easier to handle. She had a wide range of medical and surgical experience and rarely had a problem with the questions that examiners put to her.

At last the board members started shuffling their papers around and Manolis stood up to signify the end of the interview.

"Thank you, Dr Angelopoulos," he said in a formal voice. "If you would like to go along to the waiting room, I'll call you back when the board has reached its decision."

He escorted her to the door and opened it. She stepped out into the corridor and he closed it without even looking at her. Oh, dear, was that a bad sign? Had she fluffed it? She walked along to the small waiting room. There was a drinking-water dispenser. She felt in need of something stronger to calm her nerves. How long would they be in there?

She sipped her water slowly.

In the interview room Alexander Logothetis was making his views abundantly clear. He pointed out that there were two candidates who'd been interviewed by the agency in London who hadn't yet travelled out to Ceres. They seemed keen to settle on the island.

"They're both straight out of medical school, without the experience of Dr Angelopoulos," Manolis pointed out succinctly. "Tanya's qualifications are at a higher level than theirs."

He'd already given a glowing account of her medical qualifications and experience, which had been of great interest to the two doctors but seemed to bore the ex-mayor. "Also, they haven't yet experienced life on this island. How do we know they will be able to improvise and adapt to difficult conditions as Tanya, having been born and bred here, knows extremely well?"

"Only yesterday Tanya helped Manolis to deliver a breech baby in a small house halfway up the *kali strata*," Demetrius put in. "That's when her ability to improvise was fully shown."

"I have heard about that incident," Alexander said icily. "And also it's come to my ears that this young lady doctor was actually assisting in an operation here this afternoon. Has anybody looked into the irregular insurance situation? You, as Medical Director of this hospital, Manolis, should have known better than to allow such a thing to—"

"When it's a question of a patient's welfare I will be the judge of whether to worry about insurance," Manolis countered vehemently. "In actual fact, I have already made provision with our insurers and ensured that a clause has been inserted in our policy for each emergency case to be taken on its own merits. Don't forget, Alexander, that you are the only non-member of the medical profession in this room. I will defend my right to improvise in situations of life and death without worrying about unimportant issues."

This time it was Alexander who remained silent. Manolis

could see that he was seething with anger. He had to convince him that Tanya was the best candidate they were every likely to get on the island.

"Tanya went to see Helene and her baby here in hospital just now," Manolis continued evenly. "Helene and Tanya were friends at school. From what Tanya has told me, the baby is in excellent health and Helene is extremely grateful that Tanya helped to deliver her baby. As for the operation we performed this afternoon, without her help it would have been—"

"OK, Manolis," Alexander interrupted impatiently. "Let's take a vote on it. You've made it quite clear how you will vote. I shall vote that it would be better for us to see the two candidates who—"

"And meanwhile have Manolis run the hospital without the full complement of staff!" Demetrius interjected furiously. "And have to pay the expenses of the two young, inexperienced men who may prove just as unsuitable as the present outgoing doctor."

Demetrius banged his fist on the table. "He's resigned apparently because of what he calls the difficult working conditions on the island. Alexander, doesn't this prove the case for appointing someone who was born and bred here and totally understands these so-called difficult working conditions?"

Manolis knew this was the moment he had to play his trump card. "My secretary was making an important phone call when I had to leave her to attend this interview. She'd been notified earlier today that there was a possibility that the two other candidates may withdraw their applications. If we could hold off taking the vote a little longer until she's had time to—"

"It's time to take a formal vote, Manolis," Alexander said dismissively. "We shall know where we stand when everyone has voted."

A formal vote was taken. The outcome was a foregone conclusion. Manolis and the two retired doctors voted in favour of Tanya. Alexander Logothetis voted to postpone the appointment until all candidates had been seen.

There was a knock on the door. Manolis leapt to his feet. His secretary was standing on the threshhold with a piece of paper in her hand. "I've written out the details of the phone call, Dr Manolis."

"Thank you!" He glanced down and scanned the page before turning round, trying hard not to sound too triumphant. "Basically, gentlemen, it appears that both candidates have taken the jobs they'd previously applied for in London."

He paused for dramatic effect to give them time to let the news sink in. "Alexander, would you like me to re-advertise the post?" Another pause, still trying not to sound smug. "We could spend yet more hospital money on finding some other non-islander who is toying with the idea of working on a beautiful Greek island where they can spend their off duty sunning themselves on the beach…"

"OK, you've made your point, Manolis," Alexander conceded. "Under the circumstances I suppose—"

"The vote is carried in favour of Dr Tanya Angelothetis," Manolis declared, trying hard not to show how delighted he was, both on a professional and a personal level.

The sun was setting over the water down in the harbour as Manolis raised his glass of sparkling water towards Tanya. They'd both been busy after the interview, finalising plans for the work that Tanya would be expected to do.

Tanya sipped at her glass of wine, feeling excited about the outcome of the interview but apprehensive about the work she would be expected to do. She couldn't afford to let Manolis down when he'd been so supportive. She watched him now as he phoned his mother to find out if Chrysanthe was all right.

Even across the table, with the noise of the early evening chatter and laughter from the other tables outside the taverna, Tanya could hear the excited childish voice coming through on Manolis's mobile.

"Chrysanthe wants to speak to the pretty lady," he said, handing her the phone.

"When can I come to your house again, Tanya?"

She swallowed the lump in her throat. "You're welcome any time that Daddy says you can come. I've been very busy since I arrived but I'd love to see you again soon."

"*Daxi.* OK, Tanya! *Avrio?* Tomorrow?"

She looked across the table enquiringly at Manolis. He nodded. "Tomorrow's fine. I shan't expect you to work tomorrow after all the extra work you've done already. So…"

She waited for him to continue. He reached across the table and took hold of her hand. It seemed the most natural gesture to make but the touch of his fingers grasping hers was affecting her emotions deeply. Why was he looking at her in that whimsical manner?

"So if you happen to be at home after school, maybe Chrysanthe could drop in?"

Tanya smiled her assent as she continued chatting to Chrysanthe. "Did you hear that, Chysanthe? Daddy says it's OK if you come to see me after school."

The squeals of delight made her feel happier than she had in a long time. She looked across the table at Manolis, her heart too full for words as she handed back the mobile. It was almost as if the baby that they'd so wanted had materialised in this lovely child.

No, she mustn't fantasise! She must stay in the real world. This child wasn't hers—but this was what it would have been like if fate had allowed them to keep their baby, to move on and become parents.

Instead, Manolis had started another baby with someone

else, just months after the trauma of losing their own, which was something she'd not been able to understand. How could he have resolved his emotional turmoil so quickly? It had taken her years—and it was still unresolved. She could never really trust him again—could she?

Oh, it was all so confusing…just like it had been when the miscarriage had happened. She should have got her emotions sorted out by now, shouldn't she? How long did it take to get over an ex-lover?

Deep down she knew she could never get over Manolis. He was the only man she'd ever really loved. Yes, she'd had other relationships. But nothing to compare with the intensity of emotion she'd felt for Manolis. He'd been her life, her love, her reason for living, the centre of her universe. She stifled a moan of anguish at what she'd demolished by asking Manolis to leave her by herself all those years ago.

She'd wanted to sort out her emotions, to grieve for their baby by herself without any pressure about the future being put on her.

Some of the anguish she'd felt at that time was coming through to her again. She sighed as she realised she was going to have to work through this and decide if she dared give rein to her true feelings or…

"You're looking very solemn all of a sudden, Tanya." He frowned. "Are you having second thoughts?"

"About what?" she said sharply. It was almost as if he'd been able to see into her mind!

"About having Chrysanthe round to your house tomorrow? I'll try to get back early from the hospital to help you because I don't want to overload you with my family responsibilities."

"Oh, don't worry. It won't be a problem. Do get back early if you can. Obviously, it would be more fun the two of us looking after Chrysanthe. I'm sure she would enjoy having her dad and…me…at the same time…"

She leaned back against her chair, her eyes locking with his.

"You're a good father," she said quietly.

He hesitated. "I try to be." His husky voice trailed away.

They continued to look at each other, both instinctively knowing that the other was thinking about that other child which should have been theirs.

Manolis reached across the table and took her hand in his. "Are you thinking about…?" He couldn't finish his sentence.

She nodded. "Are you?"

He nodded, not trusting himself to speak.

Tanya leaned forward. "We need to talk about…what happened…when we split up."

Manolis squeezed her hand. "I think we should…if only to clear things up between us. Sort out where we go from here now that we're going to be working together."

"Exactly! So…"

He stood up. "I've got to get back to the hospital this evening. I'm doing a general practice surgery in a few minutes."

"I gathered you were going to be on duty when you ordered sparkling water."

He nodded. "But if you're going to stay down here by the harbour, I could meet you in a couple of hours for some supper."

"No, I've got to get back." Her words came out in a rush.

For a moment she'd panicked at the thought of the discussion about the past. She'd suddenly got cold feet. Was she really ready to face it head on with all the problems that needed to be resolved?

He was standing beside her now, looking down with an enigmatic expression, waiting for her to elaborate about why she had to get back, no doubt. She couldn't think of one reason why she couldn't enjoy a couple of hours here by the harbour so she remained silent. The thought of her empty house suddenly filled her with dread. But she really needed time to work out what it was she wanted.

To have him tell her he wanted to take care of her for the rest of her life? That she need never worry again if only she would play the little woman and let him do her worrying for her...as he had told her before? Well, not in so many words but that was how she'd worked out what he'd meant in her confused mind during and after her miscarriage.

Manolis looked down at her, his eyes troubled. He sensed she was going through some kind of emotional turmoil but he felt powerless to help. He'd been unable to reach out to her when they had both been trying to come to terms with the awful trauma of losing their baby. He hadn't understood what it was she'd wanted then and six years on he still didn't know! She must be the most complicated woman in the world!

"OK, I'll see you tomorrow, then, and we'll talk—yes?" He turned and strode off into the crowded harbour-side, back towards the hospital.

His hard, determined tone was ringing in her ears as she watched him until the crowd swallowed him up. The holidaymakers were still laughing and carefree but she felt a wedge of ice lodging on her heart. Once again she'd somehow managed to send Manolis away just when their troubled relationship was beginning to thaw out.

She made her way through the crowds towards the bottom of the *kali strata*, the steep cobbled climb that was the connection between Chorio, the older town at the top, and Yialos at the bottom. So many times she'd climbed this as a child, holding firmly to a grown-up's hand. She'd always belonged to somebody older and wiser than she.

But tonight she felt like a little lost girl with no hand to hold—and nobody waiting for her at home.

Reaching the top, she turned along her street and made her way over the cobbles to her house. From the end of the street she could hear the sound of laughter and chatter coming from the open door and windows of Anna's house. Manolis's mother was never alone. Always surrounded by her family, her children leaving their children in her care for a while or overnight.

She hadn't had time to go and visit Anna yet. She would make time tomorrow because she'd always loved her. As a child she'd always been welcomed into her house and treated like part of the family.

"Tanya!"

Chrysanthe's voice was, oh, so welcome at this moment of solitude as she was about to go into her empty house. She turned back into the street. The little girl was running over the cobbles, a beaming smile on her face, laughing for the sheer joy of living.

"Grandmother Anna wants to see you."

She had just time to glimpse the still good-looking older version of the Anna she remembered from her childhood before Chrysanthe grabbed her by the hand and began to tug her down the street.

"Grandma! I've found her."

Anna began walking up the street, her arms outspread. "Tanya! You haven't been to see me!"

"I've been busy, Anna."

The older lady hugged her. "I know, my child. Manolis told me about your job interview. How did it go?"

Tanya smiled. "Well, Alexander Logothetis was a bit difficult but—"

"Oh, that old goat! I hope you took no notice of him."

"I was polite but Manolis managed to convince him I was the right person for the job."

"I knew you'd get it! You clever girl. Passing all those

medical exams. Manolis is so proud of you and so happy you are back here on Ceres."

Anna lowered her voice, even though Chrysanthe had already darted off into the house to rejoin her cousins. "I never did understand why you and Manolis split up in Australia. What was the problem? You were made for each other, you two! He came back home for a little while after you'd broken up. Devastated. Inconsolable! But he wouldn't tell me what had happened. Me! His own mother! So…?"

Tanya could feel tears threatening to roll down her cheeks. "These things happen," she managed to say in a choking voice.

Anna, as if sensing she'd gone too far, put an arm round her waist.

"Come inside. You need a drink, my girl. Now, let me introduce you to some of my grandchildren. This little one is Rafaelo. He's Diana's first child. She's working in the pharmacy this evening. This is her baby son, Demetrius, and I was just going to feed him."

Anna picked up the feeding bottle from the bottle warmer.

"Let me do that Anna," Tanya said quickly. "You must be very busy with all these children around you."

Anna beamed. "My children are my life! What else would I do but look after my family? Here! Sit in this feeding chair. I've fed all of them on this chair—even Manolis. He was a handsome baby. I'll be in the kitchen, cooking, if you need me. You'll stay to supper, won't you? Keftedes tonight."

Anna smiled as she settled herself in the chair with baby Demetrius sucking contentedly on his bottle.

"Keftedes! How could I resist your home-made meat balls?"

She was totally absorbed into family life. Almost three hours had elapsed since they had all assembled around the large wooden kitchen table to eat supper. Baby Demetrius, who also needed some solid food, had sat on Tanya's lap while she'd spooned the semi-solid mixture of mashed potatoes and carrots into his mouth.

After supper Tanya had helped wash the children and put them down in their beds or cots. Chrysanthe had fallen asleep almost immediately.

"Will she sleep here tonight, Anna?" Tanya asked as she walked down the winding wooden staircase.

"I think it's better she does. Sometimes Manolis lifts her out of her bed and carries her back to her own bedroom, but tonight I'll suggest he leaves her."

"I must get back," Tanya said quickly.

"No hurry, child. Manolis will be home soon and you can— Well, talk of the devil!"

Tanya's heart skipped a beat as he appeared in the open doorway.

His face lit up.

"How was the surgery tonight?"

"Nothing too disturbing. I had to admit a patient with abdominal pains but I've checked him out thoroughly and the night staff are going to monitor his progress and call the doctor on duty if necessary. Which, fortunately, isn't me!"

"Well, I'll say goodnight."

"No, you won't!" He reached forward and put his hands on her shoulders, looking down meaningfully into her eyes.

"Chrysanthe is asleep," Anna said quickly. "I don't want you to disturb her. Leave her here till the morning, Manolis."

"In that case, Tanya, would you like to come back to my place for a nightcap?"

She looked up into those brown, melting, seductive eyes and all her resolutions disappeared.

How could she resist?

CHAPTER FIVE

MANOLIS closed the door behind them and for a brief instant he leaned against it, breathing heavily. He hadn't expected Tanya to agree to come back home with him. He hadn't expected her to now be looking up at him expectantly. If he took her in his arms now, would she vanish back into the dream he'd held onto for the past six years? He had to take that risk because he couldn't believe this was happening. But at the same time he had to consider her feelings. He knew how vulnerable she was. If he came on too strong, she would move away...

Oh, to hell with it! He was fed up with treading on egg-shells around her! He reached forward and more roughly than he'd meant to he pulled her into his arms. To his excitement and utter amazement he heard her give a gentle moan. She was actually going to stay there in his arms while he...while he what? Dared he...dared he...?

He bent his head and pressed his lips against hers. She was so wonderfully pliant. He'd never thought she would ever mould herself against him as she was doing now...

Tanya moved to feel the maximum intimacy she could achieve without total abandonment. She had no idea why she'd thrown caution to the wind and she didn't care any more. She wanted so much to regain that wonderful relationship they'd had all those years ago. If only for a short time she would allow herself to pretend that they were both six years younger. She hadn't lost their baby, they hadn't had that awful row, she hadn't lost him, as she'd thought, for ever.

He was here with her now, his arms enfolding her, his body hard, muscles taut against her, needing her. Oh, she was so sure of how he needed her right at this moment! His manhood pressed hard and rigid against her own desperate body as his hands caressed her tenderly.

"Tanya?" he whispered as he held himself away from her for a brief moment.

She looked up into his eyes and saw that wonderful expression of total commitment that she'd once cherished so much, and had then destroyed.

She was aware that he was carrying her up the narrow wooden stairs. Once he bumped his head on the low ceiling of the ancient house. They both laughed and the tension relaxed. They'd been taking each other too seriously. Their previous relationship had been full of laughter, lightness, enjoyment.

She knew she could relax now. There was nothing serious about this romantic moment. They would make love…oh, yes, they would make love. Nothing mattered except this exquisite moment in time.

He put her down gently on the wide bed in the centre of the room. She was briefly aware of the moon shining through the window. A profusion of twinkling stars added to the mystery of the dark velvet sky. And then she saw it. A shooting star seemed to be coming to land in the bedroom before it disappeared without trace. She held her breath as she made the only wish possible.

"Tanya?"

He was leaning over her, his eyes full of concern. "Are you still with me? For a moment I thought I'd lost you."

"No, you hadn't lost me," she whispered. "There was a falling star and I was making a wish."

"What did you wish?"

"I couldn't possibly tell you or it might not come true." She reached forward to unbutton his shirt.

"One day perhaps?" He was gently removing her bra with one hand, the other straying inside to tease her rigid nipples.

"Who knows what the future holds?" She sighed as she anticipated how it would feel when their vibrantly excited bodies merged together…

She had no idea where she was when she awoke. Through the strange window a dark cloud was half obscuring the moon. The stars had vanished. But she'd made a wish some time ago…hadn't she? Or was that years ago? Now she remembered! She'd just repeated the wish she'd made a long time ago in Australia after they'd made wonderful, mind-blowing love…just like they'd done before she'd gone to sleep.

Manolis gave a soft moan in his sleep.

"Manolis?" She touched him on his shoulder, still hot and damp from their love-making. "Are you awake?"

He opened his eyes and smiled as he stretched his long muscular limbs like a tiger waiting to pounce.

"I am now," he murmured huskily as he wrapped his arms around her, holding her so close that it was immediately obvious why he'd moaned in his sleep.

As he thrust himself inside her she echoed his moan of pleasure. Why had she ever doubted him? Why had she denied herself of a lifetime of love that was too precious to have been destroyed?

They slept again after their love-making, this time with their arms around each other as if making sure that nothing could ever change between them again.

The sun was creeping over the windowsill when she awoke again. She stretched herself gently so as not to awaken him and also to make sure she still had arms and legs of her own! She seemed to have spent the night absorbed by this hunky, magnificent body which had taken over and melted inside her.

She lay back against the pillows, staring up at the ceiling, and suddenly reality hit her…and hit her hard. Where should they go from here? She had to be completely sure of her feelings this time around, now that she was older and wiser and had suffered the agony of separation from Manolis. She also had to be sure of how he felt about her. Oh, it had been wonderful to spend the night with him. But passion aside, she had to think clearly about the future.

Manolis was waking up slowly. He felt wonderfully happy but the old worries were crowding in on him again. Their love-making had been out of this world, just as he'd always remembered it had been. But now he had to tread carefully so as not to frighten this fragile girl away. He knew that in some way he'd been too demanding when they'd been in Australia. He'd possibly tried to take over her whole life. She was like a delicate butterfly who needed to be handled with care or she would fly away from him.

She'd been totally abandoned during the night, just like when they'd been together before their split. But now that it was the morning, would she have put up her guard again, decided she needed her independence and didn't want to commit herself to anything with him? He thought about it for all of two seconds.

One little kiss wouldn't frighten her, would it? He would test it out very gently.

Before the thought had barely formed in his mind he'd drawn her gently into his arms, his lips seeking hers. Oh, yes, they were still as soft and moist as he remembered during their love-making. Her lips parted as he kissed her.

He checked the temptation to make love again. Later, he promised himself as he raised himself on one elbow, looking down at her lovely face.

"We decided yesterday we needed to talk," he said gently. "About what happened to us the last time we were together. I think we both need answers."

She took a deep breath. It was now or never. "Yes, we do. Er…you first."

He swallowed hard. "Why did you send me away when I came to see you in hospital? I was so hurt by the way you treated me. You'd had a terrible ordeal, but I was also grieving for our baby. I couldn't understand why you were being so…" He broke off, unable to put into words the horror of his rejection.

"I'm sorry, I'm so sorry." She was trying to hold back the tears as the memory of their last few moments together came flooding back to her.

He gathered her into his arms. "And I'm sorry if I was too pushy with my ideas for our future. When I asked you to marry me it was only because I wanted to take care of you."

"I know, I know…and I think that was one of the things I was scared of…losing my independence. We'd only been together for a short time. I was still very naïve. You were my first real lover—older and much more experienced than me. I'd never been on the Pill before and I managed to get unintentionally pregnant within the first few weeks of our relationship."

She gave a nervous laugh. "Then when I got used to the idea of having a baby I managed to make a mess of that. I was so confused by the speed at which my life had changed since I'd met you. And then you asked me to marry you. I realise now that my hormones were all over the place, adding to the confusion I felt about whether I wanted to commit to marriage."

"You make it sound like a life sentence."

"Well, that was how I saw it at the time." She softened her tone. "It was something I wanted eventually in my life, but there were so many things I had to do before I made an important commitment like marriage. But I didn't want to lose you. I wanted everything to revert to the way it had been between us." She paused. "And I never dreamt that you would go off and marry somebody else so quickly!"

"Tanya, I was devastated when you asked me to leave you alone. In effect you made it clear you didn't want any contact until you were ready to make it. I waited, heartbroken, for the girl I knew to come back to me and—"

"You didn't wait long. Six weeks after you left I went back to the hospital medical school to hear that you were working in London."

"Six weeks! You didn't want to know about me for six weeks!"

"You've no idea how ill I felt during that time! Then shortly after I started studying again I heard you were in a relationship with an ex-girlfriend. At that point I decided I had to try to forget you."

"Which was what I'd decided to do when you sent me away and didn't try to contact me. I saw no reason to stay in Australia when you didn't want me so I applied for and got the job in London."

"And who should you meet as soon as you arrived but your ex-girlfriend!"

She moved out of his arms so she could watch his expression.

He lay back on his pillow, looking up at the ceiling. "Victoria was actually on the interview panel."

"I don't believe it! How convenient! No wonder you got the job. No, I'm sorry. I shouldn't have said that. I'm sure you got it on your own merits. So what happened after the interview? Did you take her out for dinner, wine and dine her, like you did with me?"

She could feel jealousy rising up inside her. "How could you? So soon after…"

"You'd rejected me, told me stay away, you were better off without me! I was on the rebound. Victoria and I were friends and went out for dinner a lot. One night we both had too much to drink. We got a cab back to her place…"

"Fell into bed?"

"Something like that. First I'd drowned my sorrows in drink, then tried to forget you in the oblivion of another woman's arms. Classical situation for the rejected male. It was only when I woke up the next morning the regrets crept in. Then we discovered she was pregnant and…"

Both of them were trying to ignore the shrilling of Manolis's phone. With a groan of frustration Manolis reached out towards the bedside table.

"I'd better answer it. It might be Chrysanthe."

"*Kali mera*, Papa!" squeaked a delighted voice at the other end. "Are you awake?"

For the second time, Manolis said, "I am now."

"Good. Because I'd like to come and have breakfast with you. Will that be OK?"

He ran a hand through his damp, rumpled hair as he tried to get his thoughts together. "You mean now?"

Chrysanthe was laughing now. "Well, of course now! What's the matter with you, Daddy? I'll have to have breakfast now or I'll be late for school. Grandma says she wants to give me breakfast with my cousins but I want to see you. I missed you last night because you didn't wake me up when you came home. Why didn't you wake me up?"

"I'm sorry, darling. We thought it best not to wake you. Grandma said you were very tired. Yes, come now for breakfast. Give me five minutes to take a shower."

Tanya was already out of bed, shrugging into her clothes. She would have a much-needed shower later but for the moment she wanted to make sure that she didn't shock Chrysanthe.

Manolis put out a playful hand to halt her from buttoning her shirt.

"Manolis, I have to go!"

His spirits sank as he withdrew his hand and went into the bathroom, deliberately closing the door so that he couldn't see how wonderful she looked half-dressed in the early morning light.

Five minutes later she was out of the door into the street, almost bumping into Chrysanthe who was eagerly skipping along over the cobbles to her door.

"Hi, Tanya. You're out early."

"Yes, I just came round to borrow something I need for my breakfast. Lovely to see you. I'll see you later this afternoon. Don't forget you're coming to my house after school."

"Oh, I won't forget. I'm looking forward to it."

"So am I."

She really meant it, but not right now! Not now when her body needed a good soak in the bath to remove the lingering odour of sex. As she hurried away she felt guilty at having spent the night with Manolis. This dear little innocent child. She didn't want to do anything that would upset her.

She closed the door behind her and made her way through the little courtyard into her kitchen and up the stairs as quickly as she could. Not until she'd peeled off her clothes and climbed into the bath did she begin to relax. She poured in some of her expensive bubble bath.

What a night! What a wonderful night! And she was glad they'd had their talk. At last they were beginning to understand each other again. So much had happened to both of them. It was essential they brought it out into the open. There had been far too much misunderstanding for far too long. She lay back amid the suds and simply wallowed in that wonderful post-coital, rapturous feeling that always came over her when she and Manolis had made love.

After a long soak and an effort to return to normality she'd continued sorting out the house, doing more cleaning and trying to get the place organised enough for her to entertain a five-year-old when she arrived after school.

The sound of a childish singing voice and the clattering of skipping feet outside in the street made her glance at the clock. Good heavens, was that the time?

"I'm here, Tanya!"

Breathless and excited, the little whirlwind was holding up her arms for a hug. Tanya bent down and lifted her up into her arms. She was warm and smelt of pencils and paint.

"Have you had a good day at school?"

Was that the sort of question children liked?

"It was OK. I've brought you a picture of my mummy. We had to paint one and take them home for our mummies to see but as my mummy's in London I thought I'd give it to you. Oops, it's got a bit crumpled. It'll look better when I've straightened it out...there! What do you think?"

Tanya put Chrysanthe gently on the worn rug that covered that part of the kitchen. Taking a deep breath, she held up the picture to the light coming in through the small window.

"Let's take it out on to the terrace, shall we? It looks beautiful to me. You're good at painting, Chrysanthe."

"My teacher said it was a good effort." Chrysanthe screwed up her face as she looked down again at her work, now a bit crumpled and grubby. "It was difficult to make it look like Mummy, you know."

"Is she very beautiful?"

"Oh, yes! I'm going to spend two weeks of my school

holiday with her during the summer. She lives near a big park in London—I've forgotten the name of it but it has a lake in it and we go and feed the ducks."

"That must be lovely! Would you like a drink, Chrysanthe? Orange juice perhaps or…?"

"Orange juice, please."

Tanya went back into the kitchen while Chrysanthe settled herself on a chair by the small wrought-iron table in the middle of the terrace.

"You must be looking forward to going to see your mummy in London," Tanya said as she placed two glasses of orange juice on the table.

Chrysanthe smiled happily. "Yes, I love going over there. But I'll miss Daddy, of course—and Grandma, and all my cousins. But Daddy takes me there and brings me back and I love being on the boat and the plane with him and— Daddy!"

Tanya had only just noticed that Manolis had come through the kitchen and was standing on the edge of the terrace.

He smiled at the two of them as Chrysanthe leapt down from the table, knocking over her glass.

"Oops, sorry!"

"It's OK. I'll get a cloth."

Tanya pushed past Manolis as he lifted his daughter into his arms.

"May I have an orange juice?"

"Of course. Or something stronger?"

She was selecting a cleaning cloth for the dripping table and rinsing it before screwing it out. Manolis watched and thought she'd never looked so desirable to him. His heart ached for her to tell him that she wanted to start all over again.

"Something stronger?" she repeated. "I assume you're off duty for the day."

He gave her a wry smile. "Never assume anything when you're working at the island hospital. I'd better have an orange juice, please. I've got to go back in half an hour."

She handed him a glass of orange juice and put a fresh glass on the terrace table for Chrysanthe.

Chrysanthe was sitting on the floor, looking at one of the picture books that Tanya's grandmother had kept for her in the bookshelves by the kitchen door. Having discovered this treasure trove, the little girl was now oblivious to what the grown-ups were talking about.

Tanya sat down beside Manolis and took a sip of her orange juice. "I have to say the working hours seem very flexible at the hospital."

Manolis laughed. "You could say that. We have to cover any and every eventuality on the island. So one minute we're working as GPs in the outpatient surgery and the next we're scrubbing up for Theatre." He paused. "Talking of which— Theatre, that is—I'm operating this evening on Alexander Logothetis."

Her eyes widened. "Not our less than friendly ex-mayor? He seemed OK yesterday when he had all guns blazing at me during my interview. Did my appointment upset him too much?"

"He's had a suspected problem in the lower abdomen that could suggest appendicitis. A couple of times when he's been in pain I've taken him into hospital and given him a thorough examination, kept him in hospital for forty-eight hours, did all the tests that needed to be done. But after a couple of days or so the pain disappeared and I let him go home, calling him back into hospital every couple of months to be re-examined. He came to me last night when I was doing the GP surgery."

"Was that the patient you said you'd admitted?"

He nodded. "I kept him in overnight but I found his condition had worsened by this afternoon. He's now running a high temperature. I'm going to operate this evening."

Once more he paused. "I need another doctor with surgical experience. My surgical junior doctor has been on duty for nearly twenty-four hours. He's willing to assist me but really I need somebody who's not been working all day. Will you assist me, Tanya?"

"Of course! Oh, but what about Chrysanthe?"

The little girl looked up from her book at the sound of her name. "What about me, Daddy?"

She raised herself from the floor and pulled herself up onto Manolis's lap, still carrying the book. "Can you read this story to me?"

"I'm afraid I can't, darling. I've got to go back to the hospital."

"Do you need me right now, Manolis, or do I have time to read the story to Chrysanthe?"

He glanced at his watch. "I'll need you at the hospital to scrub up in half an hour. I'm leaving now."

"All right. Would you like to come here onto my lap, Chrysanthe? Daddy and I have to work tonight. If I read to you for ten minutes now, I'll finish the story tomorrow. Will that be OK with you?"

"Well, if you have to work at the hospital it'll have to be OK. Yes, thank you, Tanya." She snuggled closer to her nicely scented new friend. "I know that doctors have to work hard whenever they're needed. Daddy's told me that lots of times when he's gone back to the hospital. I'll go to Grandma's in ten minutes so let's get started, shall we? It's this story here, Tanya. Bye, Daddy."

"This was one of my favourites when I was a little girl. My grandma used to read it to me."

"Did you have a grandma in this house?"

"Yes, it was her house when I was small."

"What was her name?"

Manolis smiled to himself as he let himself out and began to sprint along the street. Ten minutes would pass too quickly for his little daughter, who had obviously formed a close bond already with Tanya. If only…! He daren't allow himself to think of what might have been if their own child had survived.

As he hurried down the *kali strata* he turned all his thoughts to the operation ahead of him. He hoped the anaesthetist he'd contacted had got himself back to the hospital. He hoped the results of all the tests he'd ordered would be back. He hoped the operation was going to be a success. It made no difference that this was a man who'd always been difficult with him. This was a patient who needed all the surgical expertise he could offer him.

Manolis stopped briefing Tanya as they scrubbed up side by side in the antetheatre. "I'm impressed you made it here in half an hour. Was it difficult to get away?"

"No, you've trained your daughter very well to accept the inevitable."

"She takes after her father," he observed dryly.

She decided to ignore that remark. "You were telling me about Alexander turning up at your clinic last night. What were his symptoms then?"

"High temperature, pain to the right of the groin around the appendix area. Just like on previous occasions. This time the pain was worse and the temperature was higher. I suggested we arrange to have him taken by our helicopter ambulance over to Rhodes to be under the care of a surgical consultant. He refused, saying that it would be just the same as last time. It would go away in a couple of days. So I admitted him here."

A nurse put her head round the door. "We're ready for you now, Doctor."

"I'm coming now. Tanya, final briefing."

"I've just checked the ultrasound and there appears to be an abnormality with the colon. I think we may find that the appendix is tucked behind the colon. Could be tricky to remove the appendix if it's stuck to the colon. That's why Alexander has been having recurrent pain and all these false alarms. I may have to take out some of the colon, depending on what we find when I open him up."

"Will you have to do a colostomy?"

"It may be necessary—I hope not. Alexander isn't the sort of man who would tolerate having to deal with a colostomy."

A nurse pushed open the swing doors that led into Theatre. Tanya could feel all eyes on them as they took up their positions on either side of the patient.

She'd never felt so nervous in a hospital before! She looked across the table at Manolis and saw the crinkly lines around his eyes. And suddenly she felt totally calm, completely at peace with her chosen vocation. Her patient was safe with her. Manolis's hands were as steady as a rock. So were hers.

She cleared her throat. The Theatre was silent. No sounds except those made by the anaesthetic machine.

Manolis looked at the anaesthetist. "Everything OK with the patient, Nikolas?"

He nodded. "Yes, Manolis. Breathing excellent. Blood pressure slightly raised but not at a dangerous level. I'll let you know if a problem arises."

"Fine." Manolis turned back to look across the table again. "Then let's begin. Scalpel please…"

Three hours later they were finally able to relax. The patient was settled in a room with intensive care equipment right next to the night nurses' station.

Tanya leaned back against the cushion of the wicker

armchair on her terrace and looked across at Manolis, who was relaxing in the other armchair by her table, drinking the strong coffee she'd just made.

"I'm glad you agreed to hold our debriefing session back here," he said.

"Well, I decided if we stayed any longer in the hospital somebody would find something for us to do. At least this way we get to relax in comfort."

When Manolis had suggested they discuss the operation at his house she'd been adamant that it should be at hers. The memory of last night's love-making wouldn't help her concentration while they still needed to check out the details and make a report on the operation they'd performed that evening.

"I think we could say the operation was a success." Manolis was checking some notes he'd made earlier and adding to them. "I've given the night staff a detailed report already. I just want to make everything clear for all of us."

"It was a relief that we didn't need to do a colostomy. You took a large section of colon, didn't you?"

"I had to in order to get at the appendix, which was tucked behind it as I thought, and I didn't want to try to separate the organs in case there was some malignancy there. If there's a trace of cancer it could spread to other areas of the body. You did put those biopsies into the path lab for checking tonight, didn't you?"

She nodded. "Of course. The pathologist on call was none too pleased when I phoned him, but he's agreed to come in and get on with the tests."

"Good. The sooner we can rule out malignancy, the sooner Alexander will be happy. And he can be an impatient man, as we both know."

"And irascible, cantankerous, difficult…"

He laughed. "Can't think why we saved the old—"

"Manolis! How can you say such a thing?"

"Only joking! A patient is a patient and they all get the same excellent treatment whatever we think about them. Will you go in and see him first thing in the morning, Tanya?"

"How first thing? It's nearly midnight now."

"Oh, eight o' clock, if you can make it. I'll be in by half past. I need to take Chrysanthe to school. Her teacher wants to see me about something." He paused. "Now, that's the end of our working day so no more talking shop. And I've made sure that we don't get called out again tonight by designating one of the surgical team to stay on the premises and be on hand for any eventuality. And I've got absolute faith in our excellent night sister."

He picked up both coffee cups and went into the kitchen. "I'll go and get a bottle of wine from my fridge."

Manolis disappeared next door. She felt totally exhausted but when he reappeared she came to life again.

"Where do you keep your corkscrew?"

"I don't know. In the knife drawer by the sink, I suppose, although I doubt if Grandma drank wine at home."

She joined him in the kitchen and found him already searching where she'd suggested.

"I'll have to get the kitchen sorted out. Oh, look, here it is—in with the clean dusters. Funny place to put it."

She turned round triumphantly, holding it in her hands. "Da-dah!"

He'd been right behind her, leaning over her, in fact. They were so close again.

He reached for the corkscrew and put it down on the draining board while with his other hand he drew her even closer, lowering his head to kiss her, gently at first but when he felt her responding he became daring again. Memories of their previous night of passion were bringing him hope that their relationship might be moving on. It hadn't been just a one-off for old times' sake.

A sigh escaped her lips as he released her from his arms and looked down at her quizzically, trying to gauge her mood. Deftly, he began to unbutton her shirt, his fingers unsure of how quickly to move, however, as he willed her to feel some of the excitement that being close together always generated.

His tantalising fingers were on her breasts, gently coaxing her into a state of impossible arousal. She could feel herself melting as her desire rose. Her heart was winning the contest. She was going with the flow, entering that well-remembered paradise in which there was no yesterday, no tomorrow, just the present…

She could tell she was in her own bed as she came round from a deep sleep. Her limbs felt delightfully relaxed. In fact, her whole body had a fluid feeling, as if she'd been swimming in a warm tropical pool all night.

She turned her head. In the early morning light coming through the tiny window beside the bed she could see the outline of Manolis's features. Oh, he looked so wonderfully desirable even though she should be feeling satisfied after their passionate night of love-making. Even when they'd been six years younger they'd never had such a night together.

She couldn't turn her back on such love. She had to trust it could continue. But she didn't want to look too far into the future. Making plans might jeopardise their happiness.

She touched his face gently. He opened his eyes and smiled as he reached out to draw her into his arms, skin against skin, breasts against his hard chest, damp bodies entwining with each other, exciting each other, arousing the senses so that they turned into one body that moved slowly, rapturously, until both of them cried out together as they climbed to the highest peak of their paradise...

Some time later, Tanya made a determined effort to escape from Manolis's arms and climb out of bed. She felt his restraining fingers on her thigh as her feet reached the floor.

"Manolis, I've got to go. I promised the boss I'd see this difficult patient at eight o'clock and I'm going to need a long soak in the bath before I can face the world."

He gave her a wry smile, "How about I help you bathe? That would make it much quicker for you and you could come back to bed now for a few minutes while I outline the patient's treatment."

She laughed as she shrugged into her robe. "The best plan is for you to go home in case your daughter arrives early."

"Spoilsport!" He pretended to sulk as he climbed out of bed and searched among the clothes strewn across the floor.

She gave one last fond look at the handsome hunk on his hands and knees.

"Duty calls," she said, as she slipped out of the door. Minutes later she heard him pattering down the stairs on his bare feet. She held her breath, expecting he would call into her bathroom to say goodbye. Her lips moistened at the thought of his lips on hers but she could hear his footsteps continuing to the ground floor.

Their idyll was over—for the moment.

CHAPTER SIX

HURRYING down the *kali strata* she still found time to pause and admire the view at the first corner after the initial descent from the upper town. She'd always stood right here since she'd been a child, holding her father's hand tightly so as not to slip on the well-worn cobbles.

The view of the harbour with the people on the boats beginning to wake up was spectacular as always. One tiny boat was making its way out to sea already. From this height, it looked like the blue boat she'd played with in her bath when she had been small.

She mustn't linger. She had a patient to see. He wasn't in any danger—she'd just checked again with the night sister but apparently he was being impatient about seeing her again.

A difficult patient, Night Sister had said. "You're telling me!" she'd replied, as she'd switched off her mobile. For a brief moment, she allowed herself to lift her eyes up to the horizon where an early morning mist had settled over the sea, making it difficult to figure out where the sea finished and the sky started.

And over there across the water on the hills of Turkey the morning glow of the newly risen sun had bathed the grass of the hills in a special light. Mmm, she loved this island.

She was so glad she'd come home again, especially now that she'd made her peace with Manolis.

Moving swiftly down the steps, she realised it wasn't so much making peace with him as allowing herself to be honest. She hadn't really had time to get to know him during the weeks they'd been lovers in Australia. Yes, they'd had a wonderful heady, sexy relationship. But now, six years on, she was beginning to find out so much more about what this wonderful man was really about. She realised that she loved him so much still! She could never let him go again. They needed to rediscover each other and find out exactly what each of them had been through during the last six years.

She turned the corner at the bottom and made her way through the wide terrace of tables outside a taverna where people were drinking their first coffee of the day.

"*Kali mera*, Tanya."

"*Kali mera*, good morning." She smiled as she greeted friends she remembered from her childhood.

She wended her way through the narrow streets, past the church and in through the front door of the hospital. It was still quiet. Nobody had dashed up to tell her she was needed yet. She checked with the night staff gathered round the nurses' station. Night Sister was giving her report to the newly arrived fresh faced, clean uniformed day staff.

She broke off to tell Tanya that nothing had changed since they'd spoken on the phone a short time ago. Alexander's condition had improved steadily throughout the night and he was asking to see her again now.

Tanya nodded. "Thanks, Sister. I'll go in and see him now."

Alexander's door was wide open, as it had been all night so that the night staff could keep a constant check. A young nurse was washing Alexander's face and hands, while her patient protested that he wasn't a baby. He didn't need all this fuss.

"Go away, Nurse. I want to speak to Dr Tanya."

He flapped a wet hand at the terrified nurse and indicated she should remove the bowl of soapy water from his bedside table.

"And close the door! Doesn't a man deserve a little privacy in this place? Do you realise who I am? In case it's escaped your notice, I'm Chairman of the Board of Governors at this hospital and I used to be the mayor of Ceres!"

He tried to raise himself up but flopped back against the pillows.

"Tanya, do I need all these tubes and things sticking in my hand?"

"That's your morphine line, Alexander. I told you last night before I left. You can press that little knob at the end of this tube if you are in pain and—"

"Oh, I've been doing that all night. I feel as high as a kite!"

The elderly patient gave a little giggle and held out a still damp hand towards Tanya, indicating that she should hold it in hers.

"I'm deeply grateful to what you and Manolis did last night. I hope I wasn't too difficult with you in the interview, my dear. My wife is always telling me I'm cantankerous. But it's just my way of dealing with my own nerves, you know. I'm actually quite shy so I like to make people feel frightened of me—yes, I do! It means they won't walk all over me."

He broke off, looking confused. "I don't know why I'm telling you all this."

"It's the morphine. It loosens the tongue—a bit like alcohol."

"Oh, alcohol! I don't suppose you could smuggle in a small glass of ouzo, could you? Not even for medicinal purposes? No, I thought not."

"Give it a few days, Alexander. You've been through a big

operation. We removed half your colon, your appendix, a couple of abscesses and—"

"You'll let me know when that pathologist man has done his tests, won't you, Tanya? I hope he gives me a clean bill of health. I don't want to die just yet. I enjoy life too much. Always have!"

"Now, I need to examine the wound."

"Never! Wait until Manolis comes. Lady doctors have their place but I don't want you fishing around under my sheets."

He gave another uncharacteristic giggle. Tanya let go of his hand and checked the oxygen flow from the cylinder by his bed. "You won't need this much longer," she said, indicating the tube with the oxygen flowing into his nostrils.

"Thank goodness. Stop fiddling about, woman, and sit down on the bedside where I can look at you. Yes, you're beautiful like your mother and stubborn like your father. We got on so well, Sotiris and me, especially when I was mayor. Everybody thought we were deadly enemies but it was all an act, you know. We used to sink a few drinks after we'd been together in a public meeting, both taking different sides just for the hell of it. Well here the boy comes…at last! Close the door behind you, Manolis! I've just sent out for a bottle of ouzo so we can celebrate."

Manolis shot a glance at Tanya and she gave him a wry smile and a tiny nod of amusement.

"Alexander's been overdoing it on the morphine, Manolis. He—"

"Just listen to the woman! Get her out of here, my boy, before I drag her into my bed and show her who's boss around here." He started muttering incoherently. "Never could resist a pretty woman."

Manolis put his hand on Tanya's arm and spoke quietly. "I'll take over, Tanya, if you'd like to start on the patient round, please. I think this is our most difficult patient so I'll deal with the wound."

"I heard that, young man! I'm not senile yet. Get this oxygen tube out of my nose and be quick about it or…" He continued ranting to himself.

Manolis moved over to open the door for Tanya. She looked up into his eyes. For a few seconds neither of them spoke.

"Come and have a coffee in my office when you've finished your rounds, Doctor."

"I will, Manolis," she promised quietly.

"You make a lovely couple," came the now calm voice from the bed. "You'd better snap that beauty up before anybody else gets her. It was the same with her mother. I fancied her rotten but Sotiris got in there first. Mark my words, Manolis…"

Tanya closed the door on her patient's musings and headed for the obstetrics unit to check on Helene.

"Great to see you, Tanya!" Her friend was sitting in an armchair by her bed, cradling her newborn son. "I've just finished feeding so we can have a chat. I'll put Lefteris back in his cot."

"Let me do that, Helene. I need to check him out."

"Why?"

"Oh, just routine," Tanya said, as she placed the small baby on his cot and began her checks. "I'm on my rounds at the moment and I'll have to write a report on everybody I'm able to see so that the nurses know how to continue with their treatment today, what medication needs changing…that sort of thing."

"Well, can you put me down to go home? I'm getting bored in here and I'd love to be back at my grandmother's house with baby Lefteris's daddy."

"Well, as far as baby Lefteris is concerned, there are no

problems. He's in excellent health. And as far as I can see from your chart, you've made an excellent recovery from your unscheduled home birth. You look great!"

Tanya settled the little boy in his cot and sat down on the edge of the bed. "I can't stay long. I've got to get round most of the patients and then spend the rest of the morning in Outpatients. Just wanted to see how you were doing."

"I really do want to go home!"

Tanya smiled. "Of course you do! It's only natural to want to be at home rather than be stuck in here. I'll recommend you're discharged today and if Manolis agrees…"

"Oh, thank you, Tanya! You know, I'm glad you're working with Manolis. When you were delivering my baby I could tell there was a spark between you two. It would be absolutely perfect if—"

"We're just a good team, that's all."

"Huh! Pull the other one!"

Tanya stood up. "I'll arrange for one of the nurses to go home with you later today to check that you settle in OK and have everything you need. Then a nurse will come in every morning for the next week to help you get used to being a mother. I think you'll be excellent."

"Can't wait to get started!"

Tanya smiled as she stood up. "I'll call in and see you later this morning when I've made the arrangements."

"So you're sure Manolis will accept your recommendation that I go home?"

"Of course! I mean, we seem to see eye to eye on most of our professional responsibilities," she added hastily.

Helene grinned. "Sounds perfect to me. See you later, then."

Tanya continued on her rounds. She had two more patients to see in Obstetrics. The nurses had reported that one of these patients wasn't enjoying breastfeeding and found it difficult.

"My baby just doesn't suck, like she's supposed to," the young mother said. "She either falls asleep or starts screaming. The nurse had to give her a bottle last night to keep her quiet so we could all get some sleep."

"According to your chart, the nurse gave baby Rosa a bottle because she was worried she wasn't getting enough nourishment."

"Same thing!"

"Do you want to keep on with breastfeeding, Lana?" Tanya said gently.

The young mother pulled a face. "Not particularly. My mother told me I should breastfeed like all mothers on Ceres do. But to be honest I'd prefer to put her on the bottle so my husband can help with the feeding in the night. I need my sleep—I get really tired if I don't sleep enough."

"Well, let's give it another couple of days, shall we? You're staying with us till the end of the week because you had a hard time at the birth."

"It was awful, Doctor! I'm not going through that ever again. I thought I was going to die—and I actually wanted to when there was all this pain. Ugh!"

Tanya took hold of the young mother's hand. She'd skimmed through the notes and realised that her patient's blood pressure had been way too high and she'd been suffering from pre-eclampsia, a dangerous condition that, if untreated, could sometimes cause the death of the mother, the baby or both.

"You know Lana, for you to suffer as you did during your first labour must have been very frightening. It will take a while for you to regain your strength and feel as if you want to care for your baby."

"Actually, Doctor, I feel it was my baby's fault I've suffered so much. And it's hard to feel love for her when she was the cause of everything. She just cries all the time and I want to rest."

"You've had a very difficult time, Lana. Your beautiful little Rosa didn't ask to be born, did she? It's not her fault you had a bad time. You wanted her so much when you were strong. I'll get the nurses to see that you can rest more so that your strength returns. I'll ask them to give Rosa the occasional bottle but we'll also give you more help when you're trying to feed her."

"Thanks. I'd like that."

"You're so lucky to have such a healthy, beautiful baby. You might find you enjoy feeding her when you're feeling more rested and start getting to know Rosa. I'll come back and see you at the end of my morning."

By the end of her morning she was beginning to wish she hadn't promised to give so many patients a second visit. Fortunately, there were fewer outpatients than usual and those who came in weren't in a serious condition.

Amongst the patients she treated were a couple of tourists with mild sunstroke who only needed reassuring that if they stayed out of the sun till the end of their holiday, and applied the cream she gave them they would survive.

A small boy who'd fallen down in the school playground required a couple of stitches in his head and Tanya gave him a glass of milk and a biscuit because he said he hadn't had time for breakfast.

Another bigger boy required her to set his arm in a cast, having fallen from a tree and fractured his ulna. The four friends who'd come with him wanted to sign his cast immediately and then the patient wanted Tanya to sign it and the two nurses who'd helped her.

She hurried round the patients requiring second visits. As she came out of the orthopaedic unit where she'd given a second visit to reassure the young man who'd been admitted during the night with a fractured jaw that he was first on the list in Theatre that afternoon, she saw Manolis heading towards her down the corridor.

"We never did get that coffee," he said, looking down at her as they both paused.

"Later," she said.

"Much later. I've just scheduled Thomas for two o' clock. Has he been starved?"

"He's complaining he's had no food since yesterday evening. Difficult to tell what he says with that fractured jaw but—"

"He shouldn't even be trying to speak."

"That's what I told him. I gave him a notepad and a pencil so he can write instead of speaking."

"Good!" He paused. "I need an assistant in Theatre this afternoon."

"I thought you might."

"Let's take a break."

"Not now. Manolis, I need to—"

"Whatever it is, delegate it. We need a break together before we spend the afternoon and possibly the evening in Theatre."

She gave him a whimsical smile. "So I'm included in your schedule today, am I?"

"If I had my way…" He paused and took a deep breath while he stopped himself before he spoke his innermost thoughts. He mustn't say it—yet. He wanted to be absolutely certain of her feelings for him. He mustn't say that he wished she would be part of his whole life. He mustn't frighten her away again.

"Yes?"

"If I had my way, we wouldn't have so many emergency operations." He moved closer. "It would make life so much easier. But, then, we wouldn't have chosen to be doctors if we wanted an easy life."

He cleared his throat to get rid of the huskiness that had developed suddenly. Putting on his professional voice, he told her they would have a break together so that they could discuss the patient they were going to operate on that afternoon.

There was no one in the staff canteen when they arrived. A young waitress appeared from the kitchen and took their order. Manolis led the way to one of the small tables by the window, overlooking the harbour. He held the back of a chair until Tanya sat down on it. They looked at each other across the table.

Tanya had so many questions she wanted to ask Manolis about the six-year period in their lives when she'd tried to forget him. But now wasn't the time. Later, she hoped, there would be a real opportunity when they were alone and really off duty.

They discussed their patient, Thomas, while sipping their strong black Greek coffee as they waited for food to arrive.

"Apparently he was in that new nightclub on the edge of the harbour road. He was coming down from the roof terrace when he missed his footing and fell head first onto the ground floor. He took the full force of his weight on his chin which, from the X-rays, looks as if it's shattered. I'll need to put a titanium plate in to keep the shards of bone from disseminating into the surrounding tissues, I think. But I'll decide exactly what needs to be done when I operate."

"Will you have to cut through the tissue at the front of the chin?"

"I'm going to try to approach it from the lower palate. As I say, it will become more obvious when I've got the patient under sedation."

He reached across the table and took her hand. She felt her body quiver imperceptibly at his touch. Even in the middle of a professional discussion her body could awaken with desire by the least physical contact.

"Thanks for agreeing to assist me. We work well together, don't we?"

She smiled, still very much aware of his fingers now stroking her hand. "It's my job to assist you when I'm needed."

The waitress had arrived with their food and was waiting to place it on the table. Manolis leaned back in his chair and simply looked across the table at the wonderful woman from his past who'd materialised in this unexpected way. He'd never thought he would get a second chance. He mustn't blow it this time.

Tanya looked at the Greek salad and kalimara they'd ordered. She watched as Manolis dressed it with oil and vinegar, before serving some onto her plate together with a few of the battered and deep-fried baby squid.

She smiled. "You remembered just how I like it."

"It was a long time ago but I seemed to remember automatically. It was that restaurant by the sea in Darling harbour, wasn't it?"

She laughed. "No, it was when we used to go to that Greek taverna by Bondi beach. Spend the whole day swimming. We always had Greek salad and kalimara because it was light enough for us to go in the water during the afternoon—after we'd had a short siesta under the trees."

"Yes, I remember now."

His eyes had taken on a distant look as his memory became nostalgic for those wonderful heady days of sun, sea, surf and sex with the most wonderful woman in the world. It could be like that again if…

"And now we're having the same meal because it's light enough to eat before a long afternoon in Theatre," Tanya said. "I'm enjoying the work here but I'm looking forward to the weekend to spend our off duty with you and Chrysanthe."

Manolis put down his fork and looked across the table. "There's been a change of plan, I'm afraid. We're expecting a large tourist vessel to be anchored off Ceres for the weekend. The tour company has informed us that the passengers are going to spend the whole weekend on the island." He hesitated. "I had to make the decision to cancel all weekend off duty."

She pulled a wry grin. "Oh, well, I suppose it was a wise decision. I'm disappointed but—"

"That's the problem with being in charge. I have to make wise but unpopular decisions. We'll get away one weekend soon. But now that the tourist season is in full swing, our off duty times will be a little unpredictable."

"I understand."

She did, she really did. But she longed to have more time with him. To sort out where they were both going together. A whole weekend together would have helped to cement this new uncertain relationship they were trying to sort out between work assignments.

She pushed her plate to one side and took the bold step of reaching across the table to take his hand in hers. "We'll just have to make the most of the time we can spend together."

He smiled across at her. "Always the pragmatic one. That's one of the things I like about you."

She smiled back. "Come on. We'd better get moving."

He glanced up at the clock. "Yes. The anaesthetist will be here in a few minutes and I want to fill him in on the patient's condition. He's got a history of high blood pressure…"

The operation was long and difficult but with the expertise of the surgical team it was a success. Manolis put two small titanium plates in the chin, which would ensure that the tiny fragments of bone were contained within their boundaries. The fractured jawbone required screws to hold it in place and he'd had to extract four molars, which were badly smashed and posed a danger at the back of the mouth.

Then he'd put four little hooks into the patient's gums so that he could fix elastic bands around them to limit mobility of the mouth. Thomas was put on a high-protein-fluids-only diet for the next six weeks until the bone healed.

As she settled their patient in his bed after several hours, Tanya breathed a sigh of relief.

"Am I OK, Doctor?" Thomas murmured.

"You're going to be fine. But don't try to talk yet. There's a nurse sitting here beside you and she'll be there all night. So, anything you want, just scribble it on your notepad. I'll be in tomorrow morning to see you."

Her patient's grateful eyes told her all she needed to know. He was a tough young man and would pull through very well.

"Your girlfriend's just arrived and I've told her she can stay the night here so you've got a nurse and a girlfriend to take care of you. The morphine will help you to sleep."

Manolis held her hand as they walked up the *kali strata*.

"Let's stop here for a moment," Tanya said, feeling slightly breathless. "I always like to admire the view and catch my breath. It seems ages since I was here this morning. Such a difference now that Ceres harbour is bathed in moonlight. The twinkling lights on the boats and the tavernas— and the club where Thomas fell down the stairs last night. Poor Thomas! He's a good patient."

He turned and drew her into his arms. "And you're a very good doctor, Tanya."

She looked up into his eyes, seeing his tender expression that seemed so poignant in the moonlight.

"I always longed for the day when you would say that, Manolis."

His expression turned to one of surprise. "Did you?"

"That was one of the reasons I worked so hard to become a doctor. So that you would take me seriously."

"I've always taken you seriously."

"Yes, you have, since I grew up. But you did used to tease me as a child, didn't you?"

"Boys always believe girls are there to be teased. Your brother was just the same, wasn't he?"

"Exactly. But, yes, you're right. I shouldn't have taken it to heart as I did. But that's the way most young girls react."

"But you must admit I took you seriously when we met again and I realised you were grown up."

She smiled. "Yes, you certainly took me seriously then."

"I'd noticed you when you were a teenager but at that time the age gap was too much. But when I saw you that first time in Australia, I was absolutely blown away!"

He bent his head and kissed her lips as they parted to welcome him. For several idyllic seconds they remained locked in an exquisite embrace before the sound of footsteps threatened to disturb them.

"Let's go home," Tanya murmured as she tried to gather her strength for the final climb.

"Your place or mine?" he whispered.

Tanya was the first to waken. They'd both slept after making exquisitely wild passionate love on the soft feather mattress of her bed. It was a hot night and Manolis had thrown the sheet on to the floor where it lay entangled with their hastily discarded clothes. As she looked around her bedroom, with the early morning light filtering through the window, she felt glad that she'd suggested they sleep at her place last night. She loved waking up in her own bed with Manolis by her side.

She turned to look at him and her heart filled with love—

real love this time, she realised. Had she experienced real love all those years ago when she had still been rather naïve about her emotions? Maybe. But not like she felt now.

He stirred beside her and opened his eyes, reaching for her, pulling her into his arms.

"Why are you looking so serious?"

"I was just thinking how inexperienced I was when I moved in with you in Australia."

His eyes, so tender, locked with hers. "I didn't notice," he said huskily.

"Oh, I'm not talking about when we made love. That was just…just…"

"Wonderful? Out of this world?"

"Yes, it was, but emotionally I wasn't ready for the big commitment I was expected to make."

He leaned up on one elbow and stared down at her. "I hadn't realised that."

She swallowed hard. "When you asked me to marry you…I wasn't ready. It was such a big step. I wanted to be with you but…" Her voice trailed away.

"I'm sorry you felt…hassled?"

"Manolis, I didn't feel hassled. I just found that I had too many decisions to make all at once. My life had changed so completely in the space of a few weeks. When I told you I was pregnant and you proposed, I wondered if you were simply doing the dutiful thing and—"

"Of course I wasn't doing the dutiful thing! I wanted you to marry me so that we could bring up our child together!"

"And then again in the hospital after the miscarriage, I was in such a weakened state I couldn't think straight. I simply wanted time to sort out all my feelings." She took a deep breath. "If I could turn the clock back I think I would have done things differently. I wouldn't have asked you to leave like that. I just wanted you to go away for a while so

I could sort out my confused feelings. I didn't think I might never see you again—"

He held her closer in his embrace. She was trying to hold back the tears. Between sobs she began again. "I remember the awful day, just a few weeks after I'd miscarried, when reality hit me and I realised how I'd mismanaged everything and you'd gone away for ever."

"I really thought that was what you wanted. Your mother had advised me not to contact you. I thought the best thing for everyone was if I started a new life and tried to forget you."

He was still holding her close as if to reassure himself that she wasn't going to vanish. This precious person, the only woman he'd ever really loved, was actually here with him and he had to tread carefully not to destroy his dreams.

"I was devastated when you sent me away," he said hoarsely as the memories came flooding back. "I don't even remember what I said to your mother when she advised me not to contact you. She asked me if I was OK, I remember, but the rest is a blur. I went straight back to the apartment and drank a beer, then another. Anything to dull the actual physical pain I was feeling. I'd lost my partner, my child, my whole life had changed in a matter of weeks and—"

"Darling, I'm sorry, I'm so sorry!" She stirred in his arms and raised her eyes to his. "If I'd been thinking normally I wouldn't have been so…so stupid as to break up what we had between us. What happened to you after that? What did you do the next day?"

"I wasn't fit for work. I wouldn't have let myself loose on the patients. I phoned in sick for a couple of days. Then I got a phone call from my old tutor in London—the one I told you about. He asked me if I'd thought about the post in London. I told him my circumstances; told him I was in a terrible emotional state. He advised me to resign and come straight over to London, told me I would feel better once I got away."

"So you went."

"There was nothing to hold me in Australia. I remember going through the interview, answering questions automatically, not even caring whether I got the job or not. I simply wanted the pain of losing you—and our child—to go away. And when I got the job, and started working, the pain started to ease. It wasn't so much physical then as a mental nagging at me that something wasn't right."

"But you had your new…girlfriend to comfort you."

"Yes, I suppose I had. But I couldn't help mentally comparing what I'd had with you, Tanya. I threw myself into my new job and it helped to be doing something I was trained to do, something that would help other people."

"Work always helps. I threw myself into my studies, worked hard at the practical work on the wards, tried not to think about what I'd lost, and little by little I returned to some sort of normality. Yes, the pain eased…" She swallowed hard as her voice began to falter.

"We've both suffered," she said softly as she started again. "Let's just take one day at a time. It's wonderful to be together again and…" Dared she say it? "And have a second chance at…at happiness together."

His lips sought hers. He'd wanted to kiss her as she struggled with her words, her emotions still confused, he could see. This time he wouldn't rush things. Wouldn't ask her to make decisions. His precious darling had to be treated gently, with great tenderness.

His kiss deepened as he felt himself become aroused once more. Tanya was responding, her beautiful body opening up to him. His breathing quickened.

Tanya cried out as they became one. Her body felt as if it

was on fire with the sensual flames flickering through her. She climaxed over and over again until she lay spent with exhaustion, fulfilment and happiness in his arms…

CHAPTER SEVEN

ON THAT wonderful night when Manolis had taken her home after their lengthy session in Theatre, Tanya hadn't dreamed that it would be more than two weeks before the long-awaited day out on Manolis's boat. As she hurriedly packed a small bag with towel and spare bikini—she was already wearing her favourite white one under her jeans—her thoughts drifted back to that exquisite night they'd spent together.

It had certainly been a turning point in their relationship. She remembered how he'd carried her up the narrow stairs to her bedroom. They'd laughed at the romantic gesture that had always made them giggle when they'd been living together in his tiny apartment in Sydney.

The people who owned the apartment had been Greek and had built a small mezzanine floor with a moussandra—a raised platform—for the bed. Manolis had so often insisted on carrying her up the small staircase when it had been obvious to both of them that they were going to fall on to the bed and make love.

He'd carried her upstairs so gently when he'd come to terms with the fact that she was expecting their baby. For a few days after she'd first told him she could tell he was shocked but it hadn't taken long before he'd said he was looking forward to being a father. He'd insisted on cooking supper for them that evening, she remembered, making her sit with her feet up on the sofa.

Afterwards he'd scooped her up in his arms and carried her carefully up the stairs.

"Our first child," he'd said as he'd laid her gently on the bed, treating her as if she were made of Dresden china. "I shall carry you upstairs from now on."

She'd laughed, telling him when she got as big as a house she wouldn't hold him to it. But that hadn't happen anyway because she hadn't got very far on the motherhood road…

She zipped up her bag and told herself she wasn't going to continue that train of thought. Their present relationship was sailing along beautifully now. She wouldn't allow herself to dwell on the past or the future. Only the present was what she cared about when she was with Manolis. They'd both established that fact when they'd made love a couple of weeks ago. It was as if they'd never had that six-year split. Their bodies were so tuned to each other's that…

She drew in her breath and shivered with remembered sensual passion. It had been the most wonderful night of her life—until the next night and the next night…

"Are you up there, Tanya?" came the recognisable voice of Chrysanthe.

Tanya's door was always open and Chrysanthe often wandered in when she knew that Tanya was home.

"Yes, come on up, *agapi mou*. I'm nearly ready."

"Daddy says we've got to go soon. He was using his cross voice so I think he means now."

The little girl arrived panting at the top of the stairs that led straight into Tanya's bedroom. She held out her arms for a hug. Tanya lifted her up and hugged her, revelling in the clean smell of soap and shampoo. She sat her down on the edge of the bed.

"Let me look at you, Chrysanthe. I love the new shorts!"

"Daddy bought them ages ago because I was sad we couldn't go out in the boat. He said it was because you both had to work every day because the tourists kept on breaking their bones or cutting their skin or getting sick."

"That's very true. But we've got a whole day off today."

"Why do the tourists make such a lot of work for you and Daddy? In the winter when it's just the people who live on the island you won't have to work so hard, will you? You and Daddy will be able to look after me properly, won't you?"

"What's that about looking after you properly?" came a whimsical deep voice from down below. "If you girls don't get a move on, I'll have to go without you."

Manolis took the stairs two at a time and stood at the top, half in and half out of her bedroom. It was as if his heart missed a beat when he saw the two people most precious to him. Together, just like mother and daughter. Only they weren't. They should have been if… Don't go there!

"What was that I heard you say, Chrysanthe? You don't think we look after you properly when the tourists are here? Are you trying to say you feel neglected?"

He was using a jocular tone but his daughter's words had reinforced the worry he had about the way his precious child was being brought up.

"What does neglect mean?"

Manolis looked across at Tanya as if he wanted her to help him out.

"Well it's a bit difficult," she began cautiously. "Would you like to spend more time with Daddy?"

"Yes, and you as well, Tanya. You're like my mummy now, aren't you?"

Tanya's eyes locked with Manolis's, both of them now pleading for help in a delicate situation.

It was Tanya who spoke first to ease the tension. "Well, I

help to look after you, Chrysanthe, but you've already got a mummy in England, haven't you?"

"Yes, but you could be my mummy here on the island, couldn't you? I'd like that."

Manolis could feel his heartstrings pulling. He noticed that Tanya's eyes were moist. She was holding back her tears. He wanted to draw her into his arms, tell her he loved her, ask her to become the second mother to his daughter, make some more babies of their own…

Thoughts rushed through his head about all the things he wanted to do but didn't dare suggest. He had to take it more slowly this time round. He'd rushed her the last time when he'd asked her to marry him after only a few weeks together. They needed time to simply enjoy being together again.

"I enjoy looking after you and being with you, Chrysanthe," Tanya said carefully, deliberately avoiding Manolis's eyes.

"I think we should set off now," Manolis said briskly. "The harbour's getting busier by the minute and I've always found it hard to extricate my boat when the place is full of tourists."

Tanya rolled her eyes at Chrysanthe as she scooped her up into her arms. "Now he tells us!"

Chrysanthe dissolved into a fit of giggles. "I'll drive the boat, Daddy! I know how to do it. Uncle Lakis showed me. You just put your hand on the steering-wheel and—"

"OK, child genius," Manolis said, taking her from Tanya's arms and beginning the descent of the stairs. "I'll let you have a go with the boat when we're safely at the tiny island where we're going to have lunch."

"Can we have a barbecue?"

"Of course! But only if you help me catch a nice big fish."

It was, they all agreed, one of the biggest fish that had ever been caught on Ceres. Well, at least on the small rocky island where they'd moored the boat. It had taken Manolis and Chrysanthe only half an hour before it had taken their bait and got hauled in. Chrysanthe and Tanya had then spent a long time swimming and playing in the water while Manolis had gutted the fish and put it on the barbecue he'd rigged up at the edge of the sea.

"When's the food ready, Daddy?" Chrysanthe had called several times, only to be told it wouldn't be long but he needed a swim before he served it. They were finally all able to swim together, amid a lot of laughter and splashing about. As they came out of the water, the three of them holding hands with Chrysanthe in the middle, Manolis glanced across at Tanya, his heart full of love for the family that seemed to have emerged so suddenly.

She swallowed hard as she looked at him. Was this what parenting was about, would be about if only she could commit to Manolis again? But did he still want her? He needed her...yes...but...

"Smell that wonderful fish!" Manolis called, clambering back up the rocks to rescue the precious fish from the grill of the barbecue where an inquisitive goat was wondering if it dared brave the fire.

Manolis told the girls to sit down so that he could serve them and they crouched by the fire, accepting delicious offerings of fish, Greek salad and crusty bread, washed down with wine or fresh lime juice in Chrysanthe's case.

Tanya stretched out on her sandy towel and chewed on the delicious piece of fish that Manolis had just handed to her on the end of his fork. She'd taken it with her fingers and popped it into her mouth.

"Mmm, delicious! What is it?"

"It's some kind of *psari*, rather like tuna—I don't know it's name in English." They were talking in Greek, as they often did.

"It's *psari*, fish," Chrysanthe said.

Manolis smiled. "We know it's fish, darling, but we were wondering exactly what kind."

Chrysanthe shrugged. "I'll look it up in my picture book of fish when we get back. I often have to translate words when we're having our English lesson at school because my teacher says I'm bi-biling…something."

"Bilingual," Tanya supplied.

"What does it mean?"

"It means you can speak two languages."

"Can't everybody?"

"They often can if they've got one English parent and one Greek parent. That's why I'm bilingual."

"Just like me!" Chrysanthe snuggled closer, oblivious to the fact that she was putting her sticky fingers on Tanya's towel.

"Have you had enough fish, you two?"

"Absolutely! That was wonderful!"

"Would madam care for dessert?"

Tanya picked up a flat pebble and pretended to study the menu. "I'll have the crème caramel."

"I'm afraid it's off. Would madam settle for an orange?"

"If it's freshly picked from the tree."

Manolis reached up and pretended to take an orange from the branch overhanging their shady spot.

Chrysanthe had gone past giggling and was laughing loudly now. "Daddy, you and Tanya are so funny," she spluttered. "I like it when you don't have to work. You're much more fun. I'd like to live on this island, wouldn't you?"

"Oh, you'd get bored eventually," Manolis said as he rummaged through the hamper in search of the oranges.

Tanya stretched out on her towel, Chrysanthe having suddenly decided to run down to the edge of the sea in search of some more shells.

She looked up at the blue cloudless sky and then glanced across at the smart new motorboat bobbing on the water nearby. It had been such fun as they'd left the harbour far behind and Manolis had been able to speed along over the waves. Chrysanthe had shouted with delight when they'd reached their little island. It was little more than a few rocks surrounded by sand but Chrysanthe had announced that it was their own special island from now on.

"We're completely alone on this island, aren't we?" she breathed as she took the orange that Manolis was handing to her. "It's like playing at Robinson Crusoe. I agree with Chrysanthe. I'd like to live here and eat nothing but fish and oranges."

He leaned across her and kissed her gently on the mouth. She responded, but not as much as she would have done if they'd been alone. Glancing across at the small figure by the water, she saw that Chrysanthe was fully occupied in gathering shells, which they would soon have to inspect. She allowed herself the luxury of parting her lips and savouring the moment. Her body was stirring with desire. She pulled away as gently as she could so as not to destroy the delicious ambience they'd created.

"Mmm, it's so peaceful."

"Utter bliss," Manolis said, his fingers lightly moving down her arm. "I'm having difficulty controlling myself."

"Me too!"

"Are you free this evening?"

"I'll have to check my diary first."

"Cancel everything," he murmured, drawing her closer.

"I might just do that," she murmured, before dragging herself away and holding out her hand to be pulled up. "It's time we gave some quality time to our little darling."

The word "our" wasn't lost on Manolis as he drew Tanya to her feet. "Is that how you think of her?"

She hesitated. "I'm afraid it is now," she said, slowly.

"Don't be afraid, Tanya. Enjoy this feeling of family that we now have. We're all so close and—"

"Daddy, Tanya, come and see this little fish in the water. It's nibbling my toes, come and see it."

They inspected the fish, before going further out into the bay to swim. Tanya was relieved to find that Chrysanthe swam like a fish. There was no need to worry about her, although she and Manolis swam one on each side of her.

When they came out of the sea Chrysanthe stretched out on the sand under the trees in their picnic spot at the edge of the shore where the sand turned to rocks. "I'm quite sleepy," she murmured as she curled into a ball, closed her eyes and drifted off to sleep like a baby.

Manolis took hold of Tanya's hand. "I'm quite sleepy too," he murmured as he gently took her to one side of the sleeping child and moved across to a shady spot where they could still keep an eye on Chrysanthe.

"You're so wicked," Tanya said as he drew her down on to the sand beside him.

"I know." His fingers toyed with the strap of her bikini top.

"No," she whispered, her hand covering his. "Not in front of your daughter."

He gave her a wry grin. "Prude!"

"I'm not! And you know it. It's just that if she were to wake up she'd be so shocked. Oh, I don't know. It's all part of learning about being a parent."

She stopped, knowing she'd said more than she meant to. "And I'm not even a parent so…I know my place in this family. I'm just a friend."

"My darling, you're more than a friend and you know it. You mean…such a lot to me. Now that you've come back into my life it's so natural that you're part of the family. That's how Chrysanthe thinks of you anyway."

"But I'm not part of the family!"

He drew her closer and kissed her gently as he felt her shoulders shaking. She was crying now. He didn't know how to handle this. He hadn't known how to handle her when she'd lost their baby. She'd cried and he'd felt so useless—just as he felt now. The last time she'd cried in his arms he'd begged her to marry him so he could take care of her. But she'd pushed him away, told him she wanted to be alone.

So this time he remained silent. Held her until the sobs subsided, kissed her gently on the lips and then released her from his embrace.

She was calm now as she turned to him. "I'm sorry. I just felt a bit strange, that's all. It sort of brought back memories I want to forget. I'm happy with the way we are now, aren't you, Manolis?"

"I'm glad you came back into my life," he said carefully.

He was holding himself in check now. One word too many and the whole bubble of his happiness would burst.

"We've been through such a lot together and now...I just don't know how to handle the parent thing." She looked into his eyes so earnestly locked with hers. "How do you think Victoria will feel when she finds out Chrysanthe regards me as a mother figure here?"

"Victoria was never very maternal. She was anxious to get on with her career and insisted on employing a nanny right from day one. I used to bring Chrysanthe out to Ceres as often as I could because she was so happy here. She adores my mother and her cousins. When she was about three she asked if we could come and live here with Grandma. That was when I handed in my notice in London and bought the house on the island. Victoria's reaction was one of relief. Oh, don't get me wrong. She loves Chrysanthe but she doesn't give out that natural warmth that she needs—like you do.

You're doing magnificently, especially as you're not a parent. I mean…"

"I know what you mean. I should have been a parent. We should have been parents together…"

"Darling!" He held her close again as her sobs renewed.

She rubbed her eyes with the back of her hand. "Hey, I'd better snap out of this. I don't know what came over me. Haven't cried so much since…well, a long time ago, you know."

"I know." His tone was very gentle, so scared to break up the newfound bond that was developing between them. "Look, we've both been there, done that and survived." He cleared his throat. "So, how about we have a party tonight to celebrate?"

"A party?"

He reached forward again at the alarmed expression on her face. "Not a party party. Just the two of us at my place. A bottle of champagne—oh, yes, we can now get champagne on Ceres. Thing have changed since you lived here."

"Well, I certainly was never allowed to drink the imported champagne at any of the family weddings."

"You were too young." He ran his fingers through her hair. "But you started to grow up and I remember looking at you when you were sixteen or seventeen and thinking if you were only a few years older, you would be perfect for me."

"Did you really?" She snuggled against him.

"Of course I did! So did all my friends. You were absolutely gorgeous—but completely unaware how attractive you were."

"I wish I'd known I was attractive. I was so caught up in the idea of proving myself clever enough to be a doctor like my dad, my brother and you that I never wore make-up or short skirts or anything like that. Relationships with the opposite sex were all pushed to one side."

A thoughtful expression flitted across his face. "That might account for a lot of things."

"Like what?"

She lay back in his arms, looking up through the leaves above her head. A large heron was flying above her. It skimmed above her head, swooping down towards the sea before expertly lifting a small fish into its jaws and flying away over the calm blue waters.

"Like why it took all my powers of persuasion to get you to move in with me in Sydney. You'd grown up to be a beautiful young woman by then but you still seemed completely unaware of the fact that you were enormously fanciable."

She grinned mischievously. "Oh, I was totally aware. I was just fed up with playing the little-woman bit. I'd realised that at long last friends and family took me seriously. At last I'd got the power to be independent. And I wasn't going to surrender all that so easily."

He swallowed hard. "So when you surrendered to me, as you put it, it was a kind of testing time, was it?"

"It was a wonderful time in my life…while it lasted."

"And now…back to the present. Will you come to my party tonight?" he said. "I promise, we won't talk about the future."

She smiled. "You know me so well."

He gave her a wry grin. "I'm beginning to."

"Then I'd love to come to your party."

She glanced across at Chrysanthe who was sitting up now, looking around her, slightly bewildered.

"Tanya! Daddy! Let's go swimming again, shall we?"

Tanya went in through the open door and sat down in Manolis's small kitchen.

"I'm here!" she called as her eyes became accustomed to the twinkling candles on the kitchen table and took in the champagne holder full of ice, waiting for the bottle, which was obviously chilling in the fridge.

"Come on up! I'm in the bedroom."

"Is that wise?"

"Probaby not, but come up anway."

He was standing at the top of the staircase. He was wearing one of the faded sarongs they'd bought from an Indonesian trader when they'd been in Australia. He looked like an Olympic athlete, every muscle of his well-honed body hard and ready for action. She stood up. In a couple of seconds he reached the ground floor and drew her into his arms.

He nuzzled her hair. "I've been waiting all day for this moment."

"Me too!"

"So you didn't enjoy our day on our island?"

"It was wonderful!" She raised her head for his kiss. "But like a tired non-parent, I'm ready for some adult fun."

"Adult fun! Well you've come to the right place." He bent down and blew out the candles. "Just in case we don't get down here for an hour or so."

He reached into the fridge, took out the bottle of champagne and dumped it into the champagne cooler. Holding this in one hand, he scooped her up into his arms with the other and made for the stairs.

This time when they made love it was exquisitely tender, each body dovetailing into the other as if they'd never been apart. He held her so close, so much part of him, so loved, that she thought she had never known such happiness.

And when she reached the pinnacle of her climax she cried out at the impossible wonder of being once more with the man she'd loved first in her life and maybe would go on to love…for…for a long time.

As she lay back against the pillows and looked into his

eyes she knew she'd really come home this time. She would give up everything for him, she was ready now. She'd gone through the independent bit. It was possible to be a wife, a mother even and still have it all with a man like Manolis. If she could only convey this to him now. He'd asked her before and been turned down. Would he ever ask her again?

He stroked her cheek, his eyes locking with hers. "Why so serious now?"

"Am I serious?"

"If I didn't know you so well I'd say there was something important on your mind. You're going to make an announcement."

She hesitated. He wouldn't like it if she proposed to him. He really wouldn't. He was this macho Greek man, steeped in centuries of male dominance. The last thing she should do was make the first move—even if she wanted to. After the way she'd treated him in Australia she was probably the last woman on earth he'd ever propose to. Anyway, why was she so suddenly getting soft about marriage? She didn't need to be married, did she? Her love for Manolis was strong enough to survive anything now.

"No, I'm not going to make an announcement," she improvised. "Except to say I'm starving and about to call room service."

He kissed the tip of her nose before reaching for the champagne bottle on his bedside table.

"Room service coming right up."

As he was deftly pouring the fizzy liquid into her glass and handing it to her, the thought occurred that it could be a good time to pop the question uppermost in his mind. But even as the thought came into his mind he dismissed it.

This woman would never surrender her independence. He could feel that she loved him again now but anything more was pure fantasy.

He would settle for the present, wonderful as it was, and leave the conventional ideas to other couples. Tanya still needed her freedom and he had to respect that.

CHAPTER EIGHT

"I'M GOING to see Mummy in England next week, Tanya—my English mummy—not you. Daddy told me this morning. But you'll still be here when I get back, won't you? You'll never leave me, will you?"

Tanya lifted the small excited girl into her arms and kissed her soft cheek. The beautiful, sensitive dark brown eyes—just like her father's—were pleading with her to stay for ever. How could she answer such a poignant request? Over the summer weeks she'd grown so close to Chrysanthe, to love this child as if she were her own. But how could she predict what the future held for Manolis and herself at this delicate stage in their relationship? She was going to do all she could to ensure that they continued to trust each other more and more but she still wasn't sure how Manolis felt about a permanent relationship now.

She swallowed hard. "Of course I'll be here when you get back from England." That was definitely true.

Chrysanthe looked around proudly as she saw her other small friends greeting their mothers at the school gate. A couple of her friends had already asked if the pretty doctor lady was her mother. She'd wanted to say yes, but she knew that would have been a naughty lie so she'd had to tell the truth. So she'd told them she had two mummies—one in England and one in Ceres.

Tanya was putting her down on the ground now. That was good. Lots of her friends had seen her being greeted by her wonderful Ceres mummy.

She grabbed hold of Tanya's hand and called goodbye to her nearest friend, who'd kept on all day in school about her new baby brother. She must find out about the possibility of a new baby brother or sister for herself. She wasn't quite sure how it worked. It was something to do with mummies and daddies getting together to plant a seed somewhere but her English mother had told her it probably wouldn't happen till her daddy got married again.

She squeezed Tanya's hand tightly. She'd have to work on that one. Grown-ups could be so difficult about things that seemed so simple. If Katia's mummy could get a baby brother for Katia, why couldn't one of her mummies get one for her?

"I told my friends you were my Ceres mummy." Chrysanthe looked up at Tanya as she skipped along beside her, anxious to see her reaction. You never knew with grown-ups. They had funny ideas about what was proper and what wasn't.

Tanya stopped walking for a moment and looked down at the adorable little girl. She loved her to bits but she could be so precocious at times. They'd reached the section of the *kali strata* where the steps became steeper before the final slog to the top. She looked away for a moment, trying to draw inspiration from the beautiful view of the harbour and the hills beyond, but nothing came into her head to resolve the situation.

"Did you, darling?" She knew this was no resolution but she had to say something when Chrysanthe was looking up at her so anxiously, obviously seeking approval.

"Well, they wanted to know if you were my mummy so I had to tell them you were my second mummy," Chrysanthe said quickly. "That wasn't a lie, was it?"

Tanya wasn't sure what to say now. She'd had a busy day in hospital and questioning from Chrysanthe was hard work right now. Especially when you weren't a parent! If only Manolis were here.

She'd left him in Theatre reconstructing a mangled leg. Their patient had somehow managed to get caught up in a two-car collision and been shunted by a car with dodgy brakes. Manolis had taken her to one side just before he'd started the operation and told her it was time she went off duty. He would get assistance from Yannis, their new doctor who'd trained in Athens but had recently returned to Ceres, where he'd been born. He'd applied for the temporary post during the tourist season that they'd recently advertised.

"I took him on for the season because he has excellent references. He comes from a good family here on Ceres. His wife died a couple of years ago and he's decided to make a break from their life together in Athens. Anyway, I'd like to give him a chance to show what he can do," he whispered. "If he's anything as good as you are…"

"Flattery will get you everywhere, Doctor," she told him. "I must admit that the thought of a long hot bath would—"

"Well, actually, I wondered if you could pick up Chrysanthe from school?"

"I knew there'd be a catch in it! Only joking! I'd love to. Haven't seen her for a couple of days."

"That's what she told me this morning. She asked if you could pick her up like a proper mummy."

Tanya had groaned. "She's obsessed with mummies at the moment."

"I think it's because she's off to London next week. And also she likes her friends to think you're her mummy."

She brought herself back to the current dilemma as Chrysanthe repeated the question that had to be answered now. "It wasn't a lie when I said you were my Ceres mummy, was it?"

"If that's how you think of me…then…"

"Oh, thank you, Tanya! I do love you!"

"And I love you too, Chrysanthe."

Tears were pricking her eyes as she held onto the hot, sticky hand that was tightly clinging to hers. She sniffed and wiped a tissue over her eyes with her other hand before they continued the final section of the steep steps.

"Now, what shall we do when we get back home?"

"Your home? We're going to your home, aren't we? I like your house. Can we do some baking like we did last time I came to see you? We could make some more of those little jam tarts."

"Yes, we could."

Tanya took a deep breath as she realised she must draw on her inner reserves of strength. She had to keep going at the end of this long, tiring day. She couldn't disappoint Chrysanthe.

By the time Chrysanthe had mixed the flour with butter and water, plunging her little fingers into the dough-like substance, they were both laughing. Tanya was reinvigorated and had completely forgotten she was tired as she joined in the excitement of producing the tarts, which they were planning to eat as soon as they were ready.

"Can I invite my cousins round to help us eat them?"

Tanya wiped a damp kitchen towel over Chrysanthe's sticky hands. "Of course. The more the merrier!"

Chrysanthe reached up her hands and put them round Tanya's neck so that she could pull down her face for a kiss on the cheek. "I'll go and see who's with Grandma today. Don't go away, will you, Tanya?"

"No, I won't go away…"

* * *

The following week, when it was time for Chrysanthe to go to London, Tanya felt sad that she wasn't going to see her little surrogate daughter for two whole weeks. She placed the chicken casserole she'd made on the kitchen table and looked across at Manolis, who'd come round for supper.

"I'm really going to miss her, you know."

She picked up the large soup ladle and put a generous helping on Manolis's plate.

"Mmm, this smells delicious. You always could make a good casserole." He put down his spoon and looked directly into her eyes. "Did I tell you I'm going to stay in London for three days when I take Chrysanthe to Victoria's house?"

She sat down and busied herself with the wax dripping onto the table from one of the candles she'd lit to make the little kitchen seem romantic.

"No, I don't believe you did," she said nonchalantly. "I rather thought you were coming straight back."

"Well, Victoria says it's time I got to know Toby, her boy-friend. She's moved into his big house near Hyde Park. Apparently, it was his idea that I should stay until Chrysanthe settles in."

"Sounds a very understanding sort of person."

She tried to swallow a small spoonful of chicken and look as if she was unaffected by the idea of Manolis spending three days in London with his ex-wife.

"He's a retired cardiac surgeon, I believe."

"Retired? So he's older than Victoria?"

"Oh, yes. He's got grown-up children and a couple of small grandchildren. His wife left him for a younger man, I believe. Victoria told me they started off having a platonic friendship and then one thing led to another. I don't think it's a passionate love affair but it seems to suit them both."

Manolis bent his head and applied himself to the casserole, hoping they could now drop the subject. He'd explained what was going to happen but Tanya seemed concerned.

Tanya swallowed her spoonful of chicken and tried to think of a different subject than the one now uppermost in her mind. Was she jealous or was it just that she couldn't bear the thought of being without Manolis for the best part of four days?

She cleared her throat. "How do you know all this…er… stuff about Victoria?"

"Oh, she often phones to ask about Chrysanthe…how she's getting on at school, that kind of thing… May I have some more of this fantastic casserole?"

"Help yourself."

"You've hardly eaten anything. Let me serve you."

"No, thanks. I'm OK. But you go ahead."

There was an awkward silence for a while as Manolis finished his food and Tanya toyed with hers.

After a while she spoke. "What time do you leave tomorrow?"

"The boat leaves at seven."

He reached across the table and took hold of her hand. "What is it, darling? You don't look your usual self tonight."

"I'm tired, that's all." She picked up her plate and took it over to the sink. "I think I'll have an early night—"

He rose slowly, languidly from his seat and came round the table, a seductive smile on his face as he stood looking down at her. "How about I join you?"

She looked up into his dark liquid eyes and thought he'd never looked more desirable.

He drew her into his arms and kissed her tenderly, first on the lips and then on her neck. She felt his hands undoing the top button of her blouse and her body began to quiver with the renewed passion that always rose when they were close together.

"Why not?" she whispered.

* * *

Their love-making was tinged with a certain sadness that night. As Tanya revelled in their intimate embrace afterwards, legs entwined together, she was feeling much more relaxed than she had done at the supper table.

"You said you would miss Chrysanthe," he whispered, his hands gently running through her hair. "Are you going to miss me?"

"You know I am!"

"I don't know unless you tell me. I never know what you're thinking about me. I never did understand what goes on in that pretty little head of yours."

He leaned on his elbow and looked down into her eyes. The moon was so bright that they hadn't put the light on, both having agreed wordlessly that it was more romantic to make love by moonlight.

"I shall miss you a lot," she said quietly. "Just like I did in Australia after you left me."

"I left because you told me to go."

"I know. I was confused. As I told you before, I thought your proposal was simply you being dutiful. I didn't realise you…had strong feelings for me. Yes, we'd always enjoyed making love together but a lifetime commitment was too big for me to contemplate. You know I'd do things differently now, don't you? I hope I've made that clear if you're in any doubt about it."

She looked up at him thinking he'd never looked more handsome, more desirable. His dark rumpled hair was partly obscuring his face but she'd memorised his seductive expression over and over again as they'd made love. She wanted to be able to conjure up his image in her mind during the time when he wasn't with her.

She knew, without a shadow of a doubt, that she wanted to move their relationship on a level. If he were to propose to her now…If only he would! Surely he could read her thoughts. Surely she was making it obvious that she wanted their relationship to be permanent this time round.

He watched the worried expression that was flitting across her face. Something was disturbing her. Was she still scared of commitment? She'd always been a strong, independent person who needed to be as free as a bird. If he were to voice his innermost desire to make her his wife, would she clam up and go all cold on him again? Better to enjoy the relationship they had now than risk losing her again. She'd said she would do things differently this time, but had she really thought about the consequences, the lifetime commitment?

A rasping sigh escaped his lips as he ran a hand through his hair, pulling it back from his eyes so that he could appreciate how beautiful, how infinitely desirable but how totally inaccessible she was.

"Why the big sigh?"

He took a deep breath. "I was thinking it was time...it was time I finished my packing."

"Packing! I'll set my alarm. You can't do it in the middle of the night!"

"Oh, but I can!" He was already out of bed, pulling on his trousers. "No, don't get up. You need your sleep. I'll see myself out. Goodnight, darling. Sleep well. I'll phone while I'm away."

He was leaning down, taking her in his arms for a final kiss. He really was leaving! She felt a moment of panic— not like when he left her before but something akin to that.

And then he was gone.

She buried her face in the pillow but she didn't cry. Her eyes were totally dry as she closed them and forced herself to remember that he was only going away for three nights. Three whole nights when he wouldn't come round from his house next door, take her in his arms, hold her through the night in his embrace...

The tears were beginning to make themselves felt behind

her closed eyelids. She didn't want to cry. It was her own fault that their relationship had reached stalemate. She hadn't cried the first time round when she'd asked him to leave.

Yes, her hormones had been all over the place after her miscarriage. But at that stage in her life she hadn't realised that it would pass and she would arrive at the other side of the tragedy longing for the only man in the world who could help her put her life back together again.

She sat up in bed and reached for the box of tissues on the bedside table, rubbing her damp face vigorously. The moon had gone behind a cloud and her bedroom was dark now. She switched on the bedside lamp and leaned back against the pillows, staring up at the ceiling.

Supposing she were to bring up the subject of marriage with him? Couples sometimes just seemed to agree on marriage nowadays. It didn't seem to matter who brought up the idea. She'd met couples who'd just sort of drifted into marriage by common consent. But not with the background that Manolis had! Born here on Ceres, he was steeped in the importance of family. The man was the head of the family. When he was planning to take a wife and start his own family it was he who did the running, he who proposed to the woman of his choice.

He was macho through and through! As a boy he'd been made to feel how important he was. His mother, grandmother, sisters had all spoiled him, as was right and proper with the male of the species. With a family background like that he wouldn't dream of breaking the rules of life that had been set out long before his birth.

But she loved him more than life itself now. So it was up to her to make it clear—in a subtle way, of course—that she'd changed, that she was waiting for him to propose again and this time her answer would definitely be yes, yes, a thousand times yes!

* * *

When she got into hospital next day she went straight to see Patras, the patient who'd been involved in the car crash the previous day. She'd promised Manolis last night that she'd give him extra attention while he was away in London.

The doctor leaning over the patient's bed, inspecting the leg which Manolis had operated on, turned to look at her as she joined him.

"*Kali mera.* You must be Tanya. Manolis told me you would be here to help me while he's in London. I'm Yannis. I've recently come over from Athens and joined the team as a temporary doctor for the rest of the tourist season."

He smiled and held out his hand. She felt a firm grip as she reciprocated the introduction, thinking all the while what a pleasant addition he was to the medical team. Tall and dark and definitely handsome, he would probably find the single members of the hospital staff fawning all over him! And some of the married ones too!

But not herself. She was so head over heels in love that she couldn't imagine how any woman could contemplate cheating on her man.

He was a consummate professional and a gentleman—she could see that by the deferential way he stepped back to allow her to examine their patient. He waited as she washed her hands at the sink close to the bed. When she turned round she saw something she hadn't noticed before—the aura of sadness that surrounded him in spite of his welcoming smile.

She remembered Manolis saying something about the new doctor having lost his wife a couple of years ago. How long did it take for someone to recover from the death of a loved one? Perhaps you never did.

He handed her the patient's notes. "I assisted Manolis yesterday in Theatre," he said quietly. "It was a difficult operation. These are the X-rays."

Yannis slotted them into the screen on the wall and

switched on the light. She could see the shattered tallus had been pushed upwards and had impinged on the tibia, causing it to shatter into several fragments. She could see where Manolis had inserted screws and pins to hold the tibia in place so that it could, hopefully, knit together and form part of a viable leg when the healing process took over. Manolis had told her that Patras was basically a fit young man whose bones were very strong. It was only the intensity of the impact with part of the engine of the car he had been driving that had caused the bone to shatter.

Yannis removed the top part of the cast covering the leg so that Tanya could see the extent of the injury.

"How are you feeling, Patras?"

The young man grinned. "Better than I was. How long will I have to stay in, Doctor? Only I've got a hot date with a new girlfriend tonight and I'd rather like to get out. Couldn't you just give me some crutches and I'll be on my way?"

Tanya straightened up and looked down at her patient. "I'd love to be able to say it was that easy, Patras, but the fact is we're going to have to keep you in for a few days. At least until Dr Manolis gets back from London. This is a complicated break that's going to take—"

"When will Manolis be back?"

"In three days. He'll probably keep you in for a week at least, I'm afraid. So my advice is to phone your girlfriend and see if she wants to come in and see you. Have you got a mobile with you?"

Patras pulled a wry grin. "It sank in the harbour along with my car. I got dragged out just in time. The driver of the other car—the one that was too far over on my side of the road and made me swerve—escaped without a mark on him."

"I'll bring you a landline and plug it into that socket by your bedside table," Tanya said. "We'll be taking you down to X-Ray soon. Manolis has requested new X-rays for his post operational records."

"Well, that's something to look forward to," the young man quipped. "I'm going to get so restless when I'm in here."

"I'll get you a television," Yannis said. "There's a football match you might you might like to watch this afternoon."

"Great! Thanks very much, Doctor."

CHAPTER NINE

SOMEHOW she got through the three nights and four days knowing that Manolis was living it up in London with his ex-wife. Well, that's what it seemed like to her! He'd phoned every day to give her an account of what was happening there but the phone calls were brief and to the point.

He seemed to be having a great time. Victoria's husband was a good host and entertained them well in the evenings. Mostly, he had "things to do, meetings with friends and colleagues during the day" so it was left to Victoria to take them around London seeing the sights and generally making sure that Chrysanthe was happy.

And it certainly sounded as if Victoria was making sure her ex-husband was happy. He always sounded exhilarated, relaxed. He never told her he was missing her. But why should he miss her? He'd spent six years without her. What was four days and three nights?

On the fourth day, the day he was coming back to Ceres, she lay in bed staring at the ceiling, trying to contain her excitement but failing miserably. She still had to work a whole day before he arrived. She had to be a good doctor to her patients. She mustn't think about Manolis, not at all! Until she went down to the harbour and met him off the boat at 8.30 that evening.

She showered, dressed, somehow got herself to eat a piece of yesterday's bread and drink a cup of coffee before hurrying to the hospital.

Yannis was already there, going round the patients. She'd decided he was an excellent, conscientious doctor, someone who would be a great asset to the permanent medical team. She must remember to recommend him to Manolis—and she must stop thinking about Manolis until this evening!

Patras was much happier today, having been allowed out of bed for a short while and given a pair of crutches. His wound, when she examined it, was beginning to heal and the X-rays were promising. She predicted to Yannis that they would be able to take the stitches out in a few days and put a permanent walking cast on. Well, permanent as in the next six weeks when hopefully the bone fragments would have knitted together.

"But we'll have to see what Manolis thinks," Yannis told their patient. He turned to look at Tanya. "What time does he get back today?"

"He'll be on the evening boat from Rhodes," she said calmly, though her pulses started racing every time someone reminded her of their evening reunion.

They settled their patient, answering his questions, making sure he was comfortable, before leaving his room together.

"So Manolis won't be coming in to the hospital?" Yannis asked as they walked down the corridor.

"I really couldn't say. I'm meeting the boat…well, I'll be down in the harbour anyway at 8.30 so… Was there something you wanted to see him about, Yannis?"

"Actually yes." He paused as if wondering whether to discuss it with his colleague. "I've been wondering if there would be a permanent post going in the near future. I'm enjoying my work here at the hospital and it's great to be back on Ceres again. I went to medical school in Athens and then after my wife and I married—she was a fellow student—we both worked in the hospital where we'd trained. Since she died I've felt there's nothing to keep me away from my family here on Ceres, parents, nephews and nieces, and, well, it's where I was brought up. I feel very much at home here."

She heard the crack in his voice when he spoke of his wife. She didn't want to pry and ask questions which might upset him.

"Leave it with me. I don't know what the staffing situation will be when the tourists stop coming in the winter but I'll speak to Manolis as soon as I can. From working with you while he was away I can tell we would be mad not to keep you on the team here."

She smiled at him. "You're a definite asset so I'll put in a good word for you."

He smiled back, relief showing on his handsome face. "Thanks." He hesitated. "Have you known Manolis long?"

"Since I was born—apparently. Manolis is eight years older than me. He was a friend of my brother so he remembers me from a very early age. I became aware of him much later, of course. But we…well, we didn't get together until we were both attached to the same hospital in Australia. I was still a medical student while he was a doctor, of course."

Her final sentence was delivered very quickly. "Sorry, I don't want to bore you with my life history."

"Not at all. I'm intrigued. I'm only a couple of years younger than Manolis but our paths didn't cross when I was a boy here. We lived on the other side of the island and communications weren't as good as they are today. So, when you met Manolis in Australia I presume… Look, I don't want to be impertinent but it's obvious there's a strong bond between you."

She sighed. "You could say that. We lived together for a while in Australia. We were very happy…and then it all went wrong. We've met up again six years later and…well, who knows what will happen the second time around?"

"Oh, but you've got to make it work! It's obvious the two of you are so much in love. I've never seen you together but I've heard Manolis speaking about you, unable to disguise the fact that he adores you. And every time you mention his name I just know you've got the kind of love that my wife and I shared."

His voice trailed away but then he took a deep breath and resumed in a hoarsely quiet tone of voice, "You've been given a second chance at a special relationship. You're so lucky. I'd give anything to be able to bring my wife back. Life's too short to…"

She swallowed hard as she saw the moistness in Yannis's eyes. Her heart ached to see the sadness he was fighting against.

"I won't let our happiness together disappear a second time," she told him. "I was determined even before we had this conversation but you've made me doubly determined— if that's possible!"

"Go and meet the boat tonight. Don't let Manolis worry about the hospital. I'm on duty and I'll make sure that everything's in order. I had a very responsible post in Athens. Tell Manolis I'll only contact him if it's absolutely necessary. And make sure you have a good reunion."

She reached out and squeezed his hand. "Thank you, Yannis. And I'll make sure Manolis and I do everything we can to keep you on the hospital team."

She stood on the quayside, watching the evening ferry come in. All around the harbour lights twinkled in the waterside tavernas. The hillsides looked like dark velvet studded with diamonds. Above her the moon beamed down, lighting up the mysterious canvas of the night sky. The usually blue sea was black tinged with gold as the boat came ever nearer to her. Manolis's boat!

Would he be standing up on deck or would he be down in the saloon, chatting to friends, perhaps drinking a coffee, unaware that they were drawing into Ceres harbour? He must have done this journey so many times before that it was probably like taking the underground in London. Just another journey to get through, just another...

There he was! Standing on the deck, right at the front, his eyes scanning the quayside.

"Manolis!"

Her voice rang around the harbour, cutting through the noisy chatter, alarming or amusing the people nearest her. But she didn't care about their reaction. She was a young girl again, in love with the most wonderful, handsome, caring...

"Tanya!"

He'd seen her. He was waving madly. For a brief instant it occurred to her that they both had to maintain their decorum in hospital but out here they could behave as they wanted.

The boat was close to the harbourside now. One of the sailors threw a chain. A colleague caught it and began the arduous task of securing the large vessel as the captain cut the engines. The passengers were coming down the steps onto the boat deck. The people meeting the boat were surging forward. Now more people were calling out the names of the people they'd come to meet. She wasn't the only one excited. Manolis had disappeared somewhere in the stairwell.

Her heart turned over as she caught sight of him reaching the bottom of the stairs. She called his name again. He was smiling, waving to her now, hurrying down the landing board, making his way through the crush of people, the confusion of travellers and welcomers and…

She felt his arms wrap around her and she turned her face up to his, her eager lips seeking reassurance that he loved her.

"I've missed you so much," she whispered against his lips as he moved to release her from his embrace.

"I've missed you too."

She felt an enormous surge of happiness running through her. She'd perhaps engineered that he would tell her if he'd missed her but she wasn't going to dwell on that.

"Is everything OK at the hospital?"

"No problems at all," she said hastily, revelling in the feel of his large hand encasing hers. "Yannis, our highly efficient and well-qualified new doctor, is on duty and he's promised to contact you if necessary. But he's given his blessing for us to enjoy our evening together and not to worry."

"Sounds good to me."

An important-looking car was easing its way through the crush of people and vehicles.

"That's our car," she told Manolis as she glimpsed the peaked-capped chauffeur driving it. "I happened to meet Alexander, our ex-mayor…"

"Our ex-patient," Manolis said with a wry grin. "Don't tell me you persuaded him to send the mayoral car he's still allowed to use in his retirement!"

She laughed. "It was actually his suggestion—so how could I refuse?"

"Well, he's been so grateful since we operated on him and then looked after him so that he could resume his enjoyable life. That's what he said the last time he bought me a drink. I can't go into any taverna where he happens to be without him sending over a drink."

The chauffeur was opening the doors at the back of the

limousine. It was so incredibly over the top for a small island like Ceres that the two of them were having difficulty in concealing their laughter as they were ushered inside into the back seat.

"Where to, sir?" the chauffeur asked.

"To Chorio. We'll get out at Giorgio's and walk the rest of the way. I don't think you could get this large car down the street where we live."

As she leaned back against the fabulously comfortable leather seat she felt his arm sliding around her shoulders.

"What a homecoming!" he whispered as his lips sought hers.

"This is why celebrities have tinted windows in the back of their stretch limousines." Tanya giggled as they both came up for air. "So they can get up to whatever they like and nobody can see them."

"I don't think we've time to get up to what I would like because we're nearly there."

"Later," she whispered. "I've prepared a special welcome-home supper in my candlelit kitchen."

"I'm not hungry," he murmured huskily, holding her face in his hands as if he couldn't believe he was actually with her again. "Not yet. But I will be…later…"

They were hardly able to contain their passionate excitement as they removed each other's clothes in the candlelit kitchen. Manolis had remembered to secure the outside door to the street when they'd come in so that they wouldn't be disturbed. He'd turned off his mobile phone. Now reassured by Tanya that the hospital was running smoothly, he could relax. He'd secretly planned to take a couple of off-duty days which were due to him and mentioned the fact that he would confirm this when he returned from London if he was sure that the hospital team could function without him during this period.

He'd actually been in contact with Yannis by phone and email while he'd been away and was impressed with the support this new member of the team was giving him. If by any chance he wanted to stay on at the end of his temporary contract, he would ensure that he was appointed to a permanent post.

All these thoughts had gone through his mind as he'd come over on the boat just now. The world didn't revolve around him. He could now relax with the most wonderful woman in his life. The woman he wanted to make his wife…if only he could be sure she would say yes. If only he dared propose without upsetting the delicate balance of their relationship.

He gathered her up into his arms, taking care not to bang his head on the low beamed ancient ceiling as he carried her up the narrow stairs to the top of the house. The bedside lights were already on. He smiled to himself. So Tanya had thought through the possibility that they might have a romantic interlude before they had supper.

He laid her gently on the bed and gazed down at her beautiful naked body. Oh, how he'd missed her!

She looked up into his eyes as she felt his tantalising fingers delicately tracing the paths she knew they both loved the most. Deep down inside she could feel the familiar awakening of her sensual desires and her body melted into the passionate embrace as they joined together in perfect harmony…

Waking up was like a wonderful dream. He was here in her bed, not miles away in another country. He looked so desirable. Even though she'd felt totally satiated by their love-making a short time ago, when he languidly opened his eyes, his lips moving in a seductive smile, his arms reaching out to draw her closer, her body melted once more with delirious passion.

* * *

The dawn was breaking over the windowsill with a rosy glow when she awoke again to find Manolis leaning over her, resting himself on one elbow.

"I didn't want to wake you," he murmured before kissing her gently, first on the lips, then nuzzling the nape of her neck before leaning back against the pillows, his arms still around her.

She'd always loved the aftermath of their love-making. The feeling that she was utterly adored by her man. This wonderful hunk who she loved to distraction. Six years ago she hadn't looked any further than the next moment of their relationship but now she was aching to look into the future. A future where she would be part of Manolis for ever, where she would bear his children, happy in the knowledge that they belonged to each other for ever and ever.

They would grow old together with the memories of a full and happy life. And, of course, the children and grandchildren.

He traced the side of her cheek with his finger. "What are you thinking about?"

She swallowed hard. "I was thinking…"

Dared she broach the subject of marriage? No, it had to come from him. She mustn't force the issue.

She sat up quickly, extricating herself from his arms. "I was thinking about making something to eat. Shall we have supper or breakfast?"

She was reaching for her robe. He leaned across and drew her back into bed. "Don't worry about food. Come back to bed. Stay here, my princess, and I'll bring you something to drink. What would you like? Champagne? I brought a bottle from the airport and stashed it in your fridge before we came upstairs last night."

She snuggled against him, her resolve to be practical disappearing as her skin touched his.

"That's better." His arms wrapped around her so that she couldn't escape. "We ought to celebrate."

She held her breath for a moment. "What are we celebrating?"

"Our reunion, of course! I know I was only away for four days but it seemed like for ever."

"I thought you were having a great time."

"I was. Great to the extent that I could see Chrysanthe settling into the London life, getting used to sightseeing, shopping, visiting museums, and one time we even took her to the Theatre. So I was completely sure she wouldn't be homesick when I left her with Victoria."

"Well, she is her mother."

"Yes, but it wasn't always this easy when she was very small and we were trying not to row in front of her, so that she wouldn't get upset. Anyway…"

He released her from his embrace, kissing the tip of her nose before springing out of bed and wrapping a towel around his waist.

"Don't go away while I'm downstairs."

She smiled. "I wouldn't dream of it."

She snuggled down into the warm place where his body had been, watching him through veiled lashes before he disappeared down the stairs. His firm, brown, muscular legs showing beneath the towel excited her more than she needed at this moment. She simply wanted to wind down, calm her feelings and enjoy the rest of their time together this morning.

In a few minutes she found herself drifting off to sleep so she just let herself go. It had been a fabulous but exhausting night…

The sound of an explosion awakened her.

"What the…?"

"Sorry, I didn't mean to wake you. I was simply opening the champagne."

She rubbed her eyes and looked at the delightful scene in front of her. Manolis, still wrapped around by a towel, was pouring champagne at her dressing table. She could smell hot croissants.

"It took me ages to put your oven on for the croissants. I remember standing by that same oven when I was a child, waiting for your grandmother to pull out the cake and cut a piece for Costas and me. It must be positively antique by now."

He turned and handed her a glass of champagne. "To the most beautiful girl in the world."

He entwined his arm with hers as they both took their first sip together.

"Another toast!" he said, his eyes firmly on hers. "To us…to…to the future, whatever life may hold."

"To us!"

It was all becoming so impossibly formal she began to fantasise that he was leading up to a proposal. In your dreams, said the still sane voice in her head. You had your chance, girl, and you blew it.

He unwrapped the towel, threw it in the direction of a chair and climbed back into bed, carrying the tray of croissants and apricot jam. The champagne was already firmly placed on the bedside table.

She took another sip of her champagne. "How long was I asleep?"

"Long enough for me to phone the hospital and establish that we're both taking two days off duty."

She stared at him. "But who did you speak to? It's only seven o'clock."

He smiled broadly. "When I switched on my mobile I found a text from Yannis asking me to phone him this morning. He said he was going to be on duty there all night.

He told me that Alexander, our beloved chairman of the hospital board and ex-mayor and very difficult ex-patient, had called in to the hospital yesterday evening to ensure that you and I were going to have two days off duty before we resumed our work."

"Whatever is the man up to?"

Manolis laughed. "I think he's matchmaking, as you would say in English. Perhaps he doesn't approve of our affair and wants us to…to make it…more formal."

She held her breath. He was leading up to it…he was…he really was. He was looking at her with a strange enigmatic expression that could only mean…

As Manolis studied her face he misinterpreted the expression of anxiety. She looked terrified! And that could only mean that she thought he was going to propose again. He hadn't given up hope but in the meantime they could continue as they were. Life was getting better by the minute.

"More champagne?" He picked up the bottle and leaned across the bed to top up her glass. A wicked thought passed through his mind that if he got her a bit tipsy she might be open to saying yes if he proposed. But would she regret it when she was sober and sensible again? Probably.

"So what's the plan if we're not going to work today, Manolis?"

"Would you like to go out to the little island where we took Chrysanthe?"

"I'd love it! We can take everything we need for a barbecue and a picnic."

"If we take some breakfast-type food, we could sleep overnight in the cabin."

He put down his glass and took her in his arms. "Would you like to sleep under the stars with the boat rocking gently on the waves as they lap the shore?"

"Sounds so…so romantic."

He began kissing her face, nuzzling her neck. She could feel his arousal as he drew her even closer.

"The boat will start rocking by itself when we settle ourselves in the cabin," he told her with a wry smile. "But there'll be nobody there to see it but a few sheep and maybe the odd goat…"

By midmorning they were all packed up and ready to set off. Tanya had made sure that Manolis phoned London to speak to Chrysanthe because he'd told her there would be no mobile signal on the island. Chrysanthe as usual was excited to speak to Manolis and also wanted to talk to Tanya.

"We'll call you as soon as we get back home tomorrow, Chrysanthe," Tanya told the little girl.

"Tomorrow! Are you going to sleep with the sheep?"

"Well, the sheep will be on the island but we'll be sleeping in the cabin on the boat."

"Oh, I wish I was with you! Will you take me with you some time when I get back to Ceres?"

"I'll ask Daddy."

"Tanya, will you meet me at the airport in Rhodes when I come back and take me back to Ceres on the ferry?"

"I'll see what Daddy's arranged, darling. He may have planned to meet you himself."

"Oh, I meant both of you to come and meet me. My London mummy is flying with me to Rhodes and then going straight back. You could meet her. I've told her all about you being my Ceres mummy."

"I'll let you know what Daddy's planned as soon as I can. Goodbye."

"Goodbye. I love you, Tanya."

"I love you too."

Manolis was standing by the door. "What was all that about?"

"Oh, I'll explain later. Decisions, decisions…!"

"Come on, let's leave it all behind. For one day only we're going to be completely alone."

"Bliss!"

CHAPTER TEN

THE sound of the sea lapping around the boat and the movement as the gentle waves took them by turn nearer then further away from the shore created an idyllic end to a perfect day. She revelled in the warmth of her suntanned skin contrasting with the coolness of her pillow as she lay relaxed and refreshed by her wonderful day on the island, waiting for Manolis to come back from securing the boat to its mooring.

Everything had gone right today. They'd even seen dolphins dancing in their remote bay as if to welcome them when they'd arrived. Manolis had caught a tuna, and had been well pleased. They'd feasted royally on their barbecued fish, sheltering under the trees to escape the rays of the hot mid-afternoon sun. Then they'd had a decidedly sensual, sexy siesta curled up together, a couple of lovebirds in their shady nest, before rousing each other to go for another cooling swim.

The dolphins had disappeared by this time and the sun had slowly begun to make its descent over their little island. So they'd gathered up their belongings, which had been strewn all over the small pebbly beach and begun to prepare the boat for their evening and night aboard.

Tanya had spread the sheets out in the sun as soon as they'd arrived earlier in the day and the pillows, which had been stored in a locker, had needed a good airing. But by suppertime they both agreed there was nothing more to do except enjoy the feta cheese, salad, taramosolata and spinach pies they'd bought in Ceres town on their way to the boat. Washed down with a special bottle of wine from Crete, which Manolis produced from his small wine rack in the galley, they made themselves comfortable on deck to watch the sun making its descent into the sea.

Tanya gave a sigh of contentment as it seemed to plunge into the depths on the horizon, spreading a gold and red carpet of light over the surface of the sea, which extended as far as their boat.

"Happy?" Manolis asked her.

She smiled. "What do you think?"

"I don't think I needed to ask you. I can tell that…"

He drew her against his side and together they looked out over the darkening sea before he suggested she go inside the cabin and prepare for the night while he finished up the chores on deck and in the galley.

She'd listened to him moving about above her, jumping off the boat at one point, presumably to check the moorings. And now she could hear his footsteps coming down the ladder that led to the cabin.

She smiled as he came in and began stripping off his clothes. "Everything OK? The sea's calm now. The rocking of the boat won't be a problem tonight unless…"

He moved with one virile, seductive movement to climb in beside her on the bunk. She felt his hands beginning their impossibly arousing exploration of her eager body as his lips sought hers.

"Your skin feels so cool," he whispered. "Let's make the boat rock so that you can warm up…"

They lay back against the pillows after they'd made love. She could hear a sheep bleating on the shore, probably calling to its lamb. She'd seen the mother and baby that afternoon and noted the lamb was being particularly frisky. The mother would find it soon. Yes, she heard the lamb now, calling to its mother, and then she was sure she could hear the gentle sound of the baby sucking as it fed. Or maybe she was just imagining it, she thought idly.

It was so utterly peaceful here. Not a sound except the soft murmur of the lapping water. Nothing more except Manolis breathing beside her. If only this could go on for ever, just the two of them, nothing to impede their romance, no customs and conventions to say what they should or shouldn't do.

She turned to look at him, his profile illuminated in the moonlight that was streaming through the cabin window.

"I wish we could stay like this for ever," she told him, leaning over to brush her lips across his face.

"No reason why we shouldn't." He tried to keep his tone light and mischievous, entering into the spirit of make-believe. "We could set up an annexe of the hospital here. Request that the patients be shipped out here."

She laughed. "Will you arrange that?"

"Of course! We could live like Robinson Crusoe—apart from the hospital patients, who would require some attention occasionally."

"And Chrysanthe, of course."

He smiled down at her, propped up on his elbow now. "But she'll grow up and look after us soon."

"And the hospital," Tanya said, wishing life was always as easy as this fantasy game they were playing.

She raised her head and kissed him gently on the lips. "Goodnight, darling. It's been the most perfect day."

"Another one coming up tomorrow. And then back to the real world."

"Yes." She turned on her side. "We've got a good life out here, haven't we?"

"Couldn't be better now that we've found each other again," he murmured.

She lay quite still until she felt his breathing becoming steadily deeper as he fell asleep.

It couldn't be better, she told herself. Very soon he's got to broach the subject of a permanent relationship. It's all so nebulous at the moment. He talks about the future all the time and I'm always part of it.

For the moment she'd have to be satisfied with that. Sometimes she felt she was drowning in happiness. She mustn't spoil what they'd got.

The warm sun streaming through the cabin window woke her. She stretched out her hand to touch Manolis, but he wasn't there. She could hear him moving about on deck. Throwing back the sheet, she wrapped herself in a towel and went up the tiny wooden ladder.

The morning sun had already warmed the surface of the deck. She curled up against the cushions at the front of the boat and watched Manolis pouring out a cup of coffee from the ancient, blackened coffee jug.

"I thought you might surface if I made the coffee," he said, handing her one of the small coffee cups.

He squatted down beside her. "Sleep well?"

"You know I did," she murmured in mid-sip of the strong black coffee.

He put down his cup on the side of the boat. "When I wasn't disturbing you," he whispered, taking her face in his hands, tracing her beautiful skin with his fingers.

The coffee went cold as they made love. It was exquisite, Tanya thought as she lay back afterwards, the hot sun on her bare skin, listening to Manolis making more coffee in the galley. This life has to continue. Oh, not the make-believe

Robinson Crusoe life they were emulating at the moment. A real relationship that would stand the test of time.

Her eyes were moist as she turned to watch the sheep trotting along the shoreline, its errant lamb following behind, looking docile today. Mother sheep was getting the message through that it shouldn't stay out late where there might be danger. When the sun set it should make sure it was safe with its mother.

Mother love was a wonderful thing. She found herself thinking about the baby she'd lost. Their baby. But they could have another baby…babies even! Manolis never talked about the baby they'd lost. Perhaps men didn't feel the pain of losing a baby as much as women did…or maybe they just put on a brave face and got on with life.

"Why are you looking so serious?" He was handing her a cup of fresh coffee.

"Do you ever think about the baby we lost?" she said quietly.

He swallowed hard. "Often. Especially when I'm with Chrysanthe. I think how wonderful it would be if our baby had lived. We wouldn't have split up, we would have been together all through those six years when we were both having a tough time." He looked up at the blue sky. "When Chrysanthe was a baby she helped me to forget some of the pain I'd felt at our loss. But it's always there, isn't it?"

He reached out and took her face in his hands. His voice had been so poignantly tender when he'd spoken. She hadn't realised he'd suffered their loss as much as she had.

"It must have been awful for you, just as it was for me," she whispered.

"It was…but life went on around me and I simply went with the flow for a while until the pain eased."

"I wish I could make it up to you."

"Oh, you can, you are now." He gathered her into his arms, revelling in the scent of her, which was so nostalgic of their previous affair. "Today we're going to live out our dream. No plans, no patients, no children—no worries, as we used to say out in Australia."

She laughed as he drew her to her feet so that they could both dive off the side of the boat together.

"Wow! The water's still cool." The dive had taken her breath away. As she came up for air now she found Manolis nearby, treading water.

"Cool but not cold. It's going to warm up as the day goes on." He hesitated. "I thought it would be a good idea to call in at the hospital on our way home tonight, just check that everything's OK."

"Why not? We've got to return some time."

"Meanwhile, how about scrambled eggs for breakfast?"

"Fantastic! My favourite breakfast."

He swam nearer. They trod water together while discussing the breakfast menu.

She was so glad that the macho image the Greek men liked to keep didn't exclude them from cooking when they were out in the open air. Kitchen utensils on land were regarded as OK for the fairer sex but anything to do with a barbecue or a boat was definitely their territory.

She swam back slowly and stretched out on deck, turning her face up to the sun. It was going to be another deliciously sexy, highly memorable day…

Yannis seemed surprised to see them when they turned up at the hospital that evening.

"I thought you were taking two days off duty, Manolis."

"This is only a social call. You haven't been working all the time, have you?"

"I've only just come back again. I slept all day. The team worked extremely well. I'm going to stay on till midnight and then I'll take the rest of the night off. By tomorrow my body clock will be normal again for day work."

He hesitated. "There's an operation scheduled for tomorrow morning."

"What is it?"

Yannis began to explain. "It's Alexander's wife's hip replacement. He's kind of exerted pressure to jump the queue."

Manolis groaned. "I'll say he has. We prefer to send hip replacements over to Rhodes. In fact, I've put her on the list and she's got a date for next month."

"I know. I explained all that because I checked her notes and phoned him back. But he was adamant that she couldn't wait. And she also wouldn't have any other surgeon but Manolis. She remembers you as a little boy."

"Yes, yes. I'm sure she does but—"

"She's a great fan of yours—and Alexander was singing your praises over the phone to such an extent that—"

"Well, I'll have to do it! Always best to stay on the right side of the chairman of the board."

Tanya smiled indulgently. "Maybe that's why he's been so charming to us. Giving us the VIP treatment for the past two days."

"The wily old fox." Manolis frowned. "Well, I'll admit her to hospital tomorrow but I'm not operating on her till she's been fully prepared. I'll postpone surgery until the day after tomorrow. Any other problems, Yannis?"

"No, everything under control. Patras, the smashed tallus and tibia, keeps asking when he can see you."

"I'll go and see him now. No, it's OK, Tanya. You don't need to come. I'll only be a few minutes. Yannis, would you take Tanya for a decent cup of tea? I forgot the tea bags and I can see the English part of her is getting withdrawal symptoms."

The medics' staffroom was empty. Tanya put the kettle on and sat down in the comfiest chair by the window, waiting for it to boil.

"How was the honeymoon?" Yannis asked, with a wry grin.

"Wonderful!"

"And the proposal?"

She shook her head. "My English mother used to tell me an old English saying that you could lead a horse to water but you couldn't make it drink. I couldn't have made it clearer that I wanted us to stay together for ever."

The kettle was boiling. She half rose but Yannis got there first and was already pouring the boiling water over the tea leaves in the pot.

"Real tea leaves! What a treat!"

"That's how we make it in Athens."

"And here on Ceres—but not usually when we're on a boat." She sighed. "Yes, everything was perfect. So perfect that I wanted to propose to Manolis myself."

"Oh, you couldn't do that!" Yannis looked genuinely shocked. "Manolis would have been scandalised! And all his family too if the news had got out."

"But it's so old-fashioned!" She took a sip of tea to calm her frustration at the impossible situation.

"You must have realised by now that Ceres is old-fashioned. That's what makes it so charming. I always stick to the rules here. They've been bred into me and I certainly wouldn't have wanted my wife to propose to me."

"I know, I know. I was born here too, remember. I remember my English mother crying with frustration at something my stubborn Ceres-born father wouldn't allow her to do."

"Well, are you sure you want to marry a Ceres-born macho, stubborn, bossy, authoritarian—?"

"Wonderful man," she finished off for him. "Yes, I do. I'm utterly convinced about that."

"Well, you'll just have to be patient, I'm afraid. It certainly looks like it. If only I could—"

The door swung open and Manolis walked in. Tanya put down her cup and made to cross the room to pick up the teapot.

"No tea for me, thanks." He looked from one to the other again. "I could swear you two were talking about me when I came in. You both went suddenly quiet."

"I was telling Yannis about the dolphins."

"No, you weren't." He gave her a wry smile.

She took a deep breath. "I was saying how conventional you men are on Ceres. Always sticking to the old-fashioned customs where it's not the done thing for a woman to propose marriage to a man."

"There would be a scandal if that happened in my family," he said lightly, his eyes scrutinising her expression. "How about your family, Yannis?"

"The same as yours. But, then, nobody's ever tried it, as far as I know."

"Of course not." Manolis hesitated, wondering if Tanya had been asking his advice. No, she must know the conventional rules on Ceres. They'd just been having a light chat together—or had they? Could she possibly be thinking about marriage? Never had he ever thought... No, he was jumping to conclusions—wasn't he?

"Come on," he said briskly. "Let's go home and have a long soak in the bath."

"The same bath?" Yannis pretended to look shocked.

"I wouldn't like to say," Manolis replied lightly. "Otherwise I might compromise Tanya's reputation."

Manolis placed his arm around her waist possessively and began to guide her to the door.

"Whatever happens, Yannis, we'll both be on duty tomorrow."

They were both down in the kitchen early the next morning, trying to get themselves into the mood for work.

"Come on, Manolis, it's not as if we don't like our work. You'll soon be back in the saddle again."

She was leaning over him to pour a cup of coffee from the fresh jug she'd just made. He took hold of the jug, placed it on the table and pulled her onto his lap.

"I was getting used to our idyllic life out there on the island," he whispered. "I'm glad I'm a doctor but the last two days have made me wish I'd been born a fisherman like my ancestors."

"That fish you caught wouldn't have fed a large family," she joked. "You'd have had to have a second string to your bow."

He laughed. "Quite right. OK, let's go and do some work, Doctor."

He kissed her on the lips before she could escape from his lap. They separated for their different tasks before meeting by the door to walk down to the hospital.

The pattern of their lives that evolved while Chrysanthe was in London soon became the norm. On the evening before she was due back, as Manolis lit the candles on the table in Tanya's kitchen she knew that they'd both enjoyed probably the most wonderful period of living together that they'd ever experienced.

Manolis blew out the match and looked across at her, his eyes tender and expressive.

"Are you thinking what I'm thinking, Tanya?"

"Probably. I love Chrysanthe to bits but we've had a great couple of weeks just the two of us, haven't we?"

He came round the table and drew her into his arms. "I'm looking forward to seeing my daughter again tomorrow, but this time when we've been completely alone in the evenings and that two days of fantasy on our little island without a care in the world. That was like our…"

He broke off. He'd been going to say "our honeymoon"

but that would have meant he couldn't avoid bringing up the subject of marriage. And that could be enough to burst the bubble of their happiness.

She held her breath. "Like our what?"

"Like our first days together when we first moved into our flat. We were like a couple of kids."

"Well, let's face it. We were a couple of kids. I think we've both matured in the last six years, don't you?"

"Possibly," he said, a whimsical smile on his face.

He reached inside the fridge and took out the bottle of champagne he'd put in there when they'd first arrived back from the hospital.

Tanya placed the glasses on the table in front of him. They clinked their glasses together, linking arms, as had now become something of a ritual.

"I had a phone call from Victoria today."

"Yes?" She was immediately alert, waiting to hear what his ex-wife wanted.

"Apparently, Chrysanthe would like you to meet her at Rhodes airport. She wants you to meet Victoria. Don't ask me why because I haven't a clue."

"It's the afternoon plane, isn't it?"

"Yes, you'll need to be there by about three."

"Oh, so you want me to go?"

"It's by special request. I thought I'd give you the day off and you can be the perfect Ceres mummy doing the transfer from Chrysanthe's English mummy."

"I think she might want you to be there."

"Impossible from a work point of view! It's you that Chrysanthe wants to meet her. You three girls can have a pleasant chat together. Victoria only has a few minutes before she takes the same plane back to London. Don't worry, she won't bite you. She's very civilised. Now, just relax and enjoy the rest of our evening."

He came round the table and drew her into his arms. She felt a frisson of excitement at the evening ahead…

Getting off the Rhodes ferry in the early afternoon, she walked along the harbourside to the taxi rank.

It was just as well that Manolis had given her the day off today because they hadn't had much sleep. It had been as if they'd both been clinging to the fantasy life they'd led and changing to become responsible adults with a child to consider was going to somehow intrude. But they'd both agreed that the totally selfish life they'd enjoyed couldn't continue. They were both longing to have Chrysanthe back.

Tanya felt that their love for each other had grown stronger while the darling little girl had been away, but without children in their lives it would be a false sort of relationship. Sooner or later, Manolis would realise that. He had to! He had to propose sooner or later.

The taxi was drawing into the airport waiting area. She could feel her excitement mounting. It would be so good to have Chrysanthe back with them again.

CHAPTER ELEVEN

THE arrivals hall was in its usual state of turmoil. Tanya made her way through the crowds, her eyes scanning the nearest screen. Chrysanthe's plane had just landed. She moved as near as she could to the glass door where the people meeting those coming off the plane were waiting. She was lucky enough to find a seat in the corner where she could watch the door, which was now being opened.

Good sign. Hopefully she wouldn't have to wait long. She whiled away the time looking out through the glass windows, which gave a good view of the arriving coaches and taxis. A pleasant cooling stream of air was coming down from a vent just above her. Air-conditioning had been unheard of when she'd been small and had sat here with her parents, waiting to meet visiting relatives. The airport had been much smaller, much less organised and hopelessly chaotic in those days. As a child she'd wondered why on earth her parents had dragged her away from her island home to come to this noisy place to politely say hello to some unknown person. She'd had to be on her best behaviour, wear impossibly clean clothes, speak when she was spoken to and…

There she was! Her darling Chrysanthe was coming through the door, clasping the hand of a very elegant, tall slim woman whose eyes were searching around the spot where she was sitting. Her chic blonde hair was cut in a style that suited the high cheekbones and general air of elegance and sophistication.

She leapt to her feet, feeling all of a sudden hot and flustered compared to this vision who looked as if she'd spent the morning in a beauty shop but obviously couldn't have done. She must be one of these women who remained cool, calm and collected under difficult conditions.

"There she is," cried an easily recognisable little voice. "There's Tanya. Tanya, it's me, I'm home, I'm…"

And the tiny bundle of energy unleashed herself against Tanya's legs. Tanya picked her up, feeling tiny hands round her neck.

"Tanya, I've missed you so much! Has Daddy come?"

"No, he had to work at the hospital."

"Hi, I'm Victoria."

A firm, cool hand gripped hers.

"Good flight?"

"Not bad." She pulled a wry face. "I've had worse. Now, I've only got a few minutes before I've got to get along to Departures and go back to London on the same plane when they've managed to clean it out. There were so many kids on the plane it was in an awful state by the time we got here."

Chrysanthe had wriggled free and jumped down from Tanya's arms. "Mummy, Mummy, can I go to the crèche now? I'm going to meet that girl who was on the plane."

"Yes, just a moment, Chrysanthe. I'm talking to Tanya. Now, we must have a chat. I've arranged for Chrysanthe to go into the crèche for a short time. She's been in there before and is desperate to play with her new friend."

"It's over there, Mummy! I know the way. I'll just—"

"No, I'll take you then you must stay with the stewardess till Tanya or I come to pick you up."

"If you've only got a few minutes, Victoria, it's best if I pick up Chrysanthe."

"Good thinking! After all, you're her Ceres mummy, I hear." It was said in such a tone of approval that Tanya felt reassured that Chrysanthe's birth mother obviously didn't mind her stepping into her shoes when they were apart.

"So Chrysanthe explained that was how she describes me to her friends on Ceres."

"Oh, she talked of you all the time. I'll say goodbye now, darling. Tanya will collect you soon."

"OK. Bye, Mummy."

Chrysanthe disappeared into the crèche after a stewardess had taken details from Victoria and Tanya about who was collecting her and when.

"Well, that's a good innovation," Tanya said. "Wish they'd had that when I was a child. Hours I spent in this place, kicking my heels."

"We've just time for a cup of tea—or would you prefer coffee?" Victoria was heading over to the drinks dispenser. "It all comes out of the same container, I think, but… There you go."

They found a corner where there were two seats. "It's great to meet you at last. As I say, Chrysanthe is besotted with you. And also with the idea that you and Manolis are going to get married and give her a baby brother or sister just like the rest of her friends seem to be having."

Tanya tried a sip of her tea and put it straight into the nearest waste bin. "The tea hasn't changed!"

Victoria agreed as she also binned hers.

Tanya didn't mind the tea being awful. The bonding of the two women in Manolis's life was going much better than she'd dared to hope.

"I think it's a kind of one upmanship to have a baby brother or sister," she said carefully. "I'm not taking it too seriously."

"Oh, but you must! It's so obvious that you and Manolis were made for each other—just as it was obvious from the start that Manolis and I would never make a go of it. Talk about on the rebound! The poor man didn't know what to do with himself. He was utterly bereft. I felt so sorry for him. It was obvious he'd left his heart in Australia. He never stopped talking about you. I suppose I just wanted to comfort him at first and, well, you know how things develop when you've had too much to drink. Manolis was hell bent on drowning his sorrows. Somehow the comfort turned into sex...and then in no time at all I found I was pregnant."

Victoria fidgeted on the uncomfortable plastic chair. "Of course, Manolis did what he thought was the honourable thing and asked me to marry him. You know, they're so old-fashioned over there on that quaint little island, aren't they? I would have been content to split up at that point and bring up the child myself—well, with the help of a nanny, of course, so I didn't have to take a career break—but, oh, no. Manolis said his child had to be legitimate. His family on Ceres... Oh, you must have come across the sort of thing I'm talking about."

"Absolutely! That's the problem at the moment with our relationship. Manolis actually proposed marriage when we were in Australia and I turned him down—for various reasons which we don't need to go into. Anyway, we have a marvellous relationship now but...well, I'm waiting and waiting for the third proposal, which just isn't coming. And I daren't propose to him because it would be so frowned on."

"Well, of course it would. Oh, it's so easy to talk to you, Tanya." Victoria broke off as she looked at her diamond-encrusted watch. "Look, we must keep in touch. I'm sure you'll find a way of prompting Manolis. Oh, there's the announcement for my departure. I'd better go. Stick to your guns because, as I say, you two were made for each other.

You could stick your neck out and just tell him it's for Chrysanthe's sake. She's desperate for a baby brother or sister."

They were both laughing together now as the woman who'd been sitting next to Victoria, leaning nearer so that she could take in the bizarre conversation, got up from her seat and walked away looking thoroughly shocked.

They stood up and air-kissed each other on both cheeks. "I feel as if I've known you for ages," Tanya said, feeling relieved that their short introduction to each other had gone so amicably.

"Well, in a way you have—through Chrysanthe. I wish we had more time to chat through this problem. When you've solved it—as I know you will—please invite me to the wedding. I'll just lurk in the shadows at the back of the church and I won't cause any problems. I won't hurl myself at the altar weeping and wailing…"

Tanya was giggling now. "I can't imagine you weeping and wailing about anything, Look, you'd better go or you'll miss your flight. I'll go and collect Chrysanthe."

She watched the slim figure disappearing through the crowds in the direction of the departure lounge. She turned as she went through the doors and waved, still smiling.

Tanya waved back. This certainly wasn't the meeting she'd dreaded. She'd made a true friend in a matter of minutes. That was a part of the relationship that would be easy. Chrysanthe having two mummies. It was the daddy who was the difficult one.

They enjoyed a smooth crossing on the ferry. So smooth that Chrysanthe fell asleep snuggled up to Tanya in the saloon. She had to be woken up a few minutes before they were due to dock.

The little girl smiled sleepily and was soon in conversational flow. A never-ending stream of thoughts and dreams had happened while she'd been asleep and she needed lots of answers from her Ceres mummy.

"Did my London mummy tell you that you and Daddy could easily get a baby brother or sister for me if you really tried?"

"I think she might have mentioned it but she was in such a hurry to catch her plane... Oh, look, we're nearly there. Daddy said he'd try to get out of the hospital in time to meet us. He's got such a busy day today."

"Mummy said all the daddy has to do is to plant a seed in the mummy. He's got this kind of injector thing. Does my daddy know how to do that?"

"I'll have to ask him. But not just now because, as I say, he will have had a busy day and he's probably tired."

Chrysanthe put her head on one side so that she could look up at Tanya and judge her mood. Grown-ups could be so weird. You could never tell what they were thinking. Best to change the subject because Tanya seemed really tense.

"Is Daddy cutting people up today? He really likes cutting up people, I think."

Tanya was relieved they'd been speaking Greek together since Chrysanthe woke up. The English tourist listening next to Chrysanthe didn't flinch at the little girl's words and smiled with complete incomprehension at the continual flow of Greek words from such a small child.

"I think he probably is. Can you pass me your jacket and I'll help you put it on."

"Is it difficult to put people back together again once you've cut them up? I mean, knowing which bit goes where?"

"Daddy's a very good surgeon so he knows exactly what to do. You have to train a long time to be able to work like Daddy does."

"I'm going to be clever like Daddy and train for a long

time. I think I'd like to cut people up. It's probably like doing jigsaw puzzles. Must be fun sorting out which bit goes where. You can do it, can't you, Tanya? Daddy was telling Grandma one day that you were the best doctor he'd had helping him in the operating theatre."

Tanya took hold of Chrysanthe's hand and led her firmly towards the top of the stairs that led to the boat deck.

"Grandma said your daddy used to cut people up and he was ever so good at getting babies for people. Didn't your daddy ever tell you where he got the babies from? Didn't you ever ask him?"

"Careful on the stairs, darling. Watch your step. Hold my hand tightly for this last little bit... There he is! There's Daddy."

Manolis had somehow managed to board the ferry as soon as it arrived. He could usually find the odd grateful patient who would bend the rules and let him aboard.

"Daddy!" Chrysanthe ran forward as Manolis bent down to greet her. He lifted her high in the air and swung her round. "Daddy! You're not tired, are you?"

"Of course not. Why should I be tired?"

"Well, Tanya wants to ask you... Oh, look, there's my new friend from the plane. Let me go and see her before she gets off the boat." Chrysanthe had wriggled her way out of Manolis's arms and was halfway down his legs, scrambling to the floor.

"No, hold onto my hand, Chrysanthe," Manolis said, as he reached for the escaping child.

Tanya screamed out. "Hold onto her, Manolis. They're letting the lorries off the car deck. They're—"

A deafening thud, the screech of brakes and then an awful silence around them. The worst thing had happened. Every parent's nightmare. Their child under the wheels of a vehicle.

"Chrysanthe, darling." Tears were streaming down

Tanya's cheeks as she bent to reach the motionless child beneath the wheels of the large truck.

The driver was crying as he climbed out of his cab. "I slammed on my brakes as soon as I heard you call out. I never saw her. She came from nowhere. Is she OK? She's not…?"

Manolis was on his knees, crouched over his daughter. The wheels of the truck were resting against her head. She'd received a blow to the head but the wheel hadn't passed over her.

The driver was trembling with shock. "Get an ambulance! Quick. I couldn't help it. Nobody said the passengers were on this deck."

"It's OK," Manolis said quietly to his unconscious daughter.

Tanya was at his side.

At that point the captain arrived, saying frantically, "I've called an ambulance. I'm sorry, I'm sorry! There was a new sailor in charge of disembarkation today. He shouldn't have given the signal for the trucks to start their engines and move off early like that."

He was pleading with Manolis now. "Is there anything I can do, Doctor? She's not…?"

"I just need to get my daughter to the hospital…"

"Your daughter? Oh, Manolis I wouldn't have…"

They waited in silence until the ambulance arrived and the paramedics stabilised Chrysanthe's neck and head for the journey. The normally noisy, loquacious, lovable child lay pale and motionless while they tended to her and Manolis and Tanya looked helplessly on.

As Chrysanthe was carried to the ambulance, Manolis strode through the crowd with Tanya beside him in a state of total shock. She just knew she had to get Chrysanthe to the hospital before she allowed herself to cry. She had no idea how badly injured her daughter was. She wasn't her daughter—she knew that. But that was how she now thought of her.

They all went to the hospital in the back of the ambulance, Manolis checking out his little daughter with a paramedic en route. She was very still, eyes closed but she was breathing.

As the driver pulled in to the hospital forecourt and slammed on the brakes, Tanya opened the door and got out.

A porter with a trolley arrived and, with Chrysanthe lifted safely onto it, Manolis led them all hastily straight past Reception and along to the X-ray department.

"X-ray of skull please...now!"

In a very short time Manolis and Tanya were examining the X-ray images on the screen.

"There's no fracture of the skull," he said in a relieved tone. "No discernible subdural haematoma, which sometimes happens in a concussion like this. I'll get a CT scan to make sure. If blood has collected beneath the skull it won't be a problem for me to remove the haematoma provided I can do it quickly so— Ah, Yannis, don't you agree with me that—?"

"Absolutely, Manolis. But I think you should let me take over at this point if you don't mind me saying so. You're bound to be in a state of shock because this is your daughter. I'll take Chrysanthe for a CT scan and report back to you as soon as possible."

Tanya put her hand on his arm. "Manolis, my darling, just let Yannis take over for a little while. Sit here with me for a moment. I need you by my side, my love. You're shaking with the shock of it all."

"OK. Yes, you're probably right. I think I am in shock. But, Yannis, get back to me as soon as you can."

Gently, Yannis took the motionless child from her distraught father. "Chrysanthe will be fine with me. Take it easy, Manolis, and I'll keep you informed."

* * *

The lights in Chrysanthe's hospital room had been dimmed. The child was breathing steadily but was still unconscious. Tanya clung tightly to Manolis's hand as they sat together at the side of her bed. She was exhausted but knew she would never be able to sleep even if she'd taken up the offer of the bed in the corner of the room.

"Why don't you try and get some sleep, Manolis? You've been working all day."

He tried to smile but failed miserably. "I don't expect your day has been all that easy. How did you get on with Victoria?"

"Very well. She's easy to get on with."

"Really? What did you talk about?"

"Oh, this and that. Chrysanthe mainly."

He attempted a wry grin and succeeded. "And me?"

She smiled. "Possibly."

Yannis walked in. "All the tests show there's no haematoma. She has concussion, which we all know can be unpredictable. She could come round any minute or…or we may have to wait a while longer."

"Thank God! How about the swollen arm I pointed out to you? What did the X-rays show?"

"The ulna is cracked. I'm going to take her along to the plaster room and put a cast on now."

Manolis half rose. "Do you want me to do it?"

"No, I'd like to do it," he said, firmly taking the lead.

Tanya put her hand on his arm. "Better you rest while you can. Why don't you stretch out on the bed over there?"

"I might just do that while Yannis is putting the cast on Chrysanthe."

CHAPTER TWELVE

As THE morning sun tipped over the windowsill of the small room in Ceres Hospital, Manolis opened his eyes and took in the all too familiar scene. Tanya was still sitting by Chrysanthe's bed, holding her motionless hand, looking down at her with the gaze of a concerned mother and an experienced doctor.

Twice during the last three hours he'd got up from the bed in the corner of the room reserved for the patient's relatives and tried to persuade Tanya to take some rest. But she'd been adamant that she wanted to be there when Chrysanthe came round.

She'd looked at him with those intense, beautiful eyes where the sad expression told him that she knew as well as he did that it wasn't when she came around, but if. He'd stayed with her for a short time, hoping to give her some support. But she was one tough lady who'd done exactly what she felt was the right thing to do all her life. There was no changing her.

He watched for a few moments wondering what life would be like if she ever left him. They'd split up before and it had been hell. It mustn't happen again!

He threw back the light sheet that was covering him. He was still wearing the clothes he'd worn yesterday morning.

At some point he'd try to have a shower—but not yet. Like Tanya, he didn't want to leave their precious daughter. He'd seen how Tanya had completely bonded with his child. Chrysanthe was only slightly younger than their child would have been.

In fact, looking at the scene of mother and child now, he doubted if Tanya could differentiate her feelings from what she would have felt if she'd actually given birth to Chrysanthe.

Tanya looked across the room at Manolis sitting on the narrow bed in his crumpled clothes, his dark hair flopping over his forehead, and her heart went out to him. Was his anguish worse than hers because he was the biological father of this precious child? She couldn't imagine anything worse than the agony she was going through.

A nurse came in through the half-open door. Tanya looked up expectantly.

"Do you have any more results of the tests?"

The nurse shook her head. "I came to see if you'd like some breakfast, Tanya."

"No, thank you."

The nurse looked across at Manolis. "Doctor?"

"No, thank you," he said in an absent tone of voice. He stood up and walked across to the bedside. "Maybe some coffee, strong please."

He sat down on the other side of Chrysanthe's bed and took hold of her limp, seemingly lifeless hand. His eyes scanned her face for any sign of life. Then he raised her arm, which was encased in a cast. He checked on the fingers.

"They're only slightly swollen," Tanya said. "I've been working on them every few minutes."

"Let me take over now. Why don't you go and have a shower?"

She gave him a faint smile. "Do I look grubby?"

"You look wonderful, darling. But if you feel anything like I do…"

"OK, I'll go off for a short time when I've had some coffee. Find some clean clothes to put on."

The nurse brought in a large coffee pot and two cups. Beside it she'd placed a plate with some small bread rolls.

"You must eat," she told them. "It could be a long time before…before your daughter regains consciousness. These rolls are freshly baked. I've just been out to the bakery in the harbour to get them."

The nurse hesitated by the door on her way out. She was much older than these two doctors. She'd become very fond of both of them since she'd come back to work now that her family were grown up.

"Please eat something to keep up your strength. Life must go on."

She closed the door quietly behind her.

Tanya picked up the plate and held it towards Manolis. "Sound advice. Take one of these."

Manolis dutifully finished his bread roll and took a gulp of the strong coffee.

Tanya forced something down. "This drip needs changing." She stood up. "Have we any more glucose saline in that fridge?"

"Yes, I checked a short time ago." He handed her a pack.

She scrubbed her hands and put on some sterile gloves before changing the nearly empty pack for a full one.

"Got to keep Chrysanthe hydrated."

Manolis nodded. "I'll send another blood sample to the path lab this morning for a full blood count and checks on how her body is coping."

"She'll need to be strong when she comes round and starts…" Tanya hesitated. "Starts talking again."

Her voice cracked as she came to the end of her sentence.

She looked across the bed at Manolis. "It will be so wonderful to hear that little voice chattering again, won't it?"

He swallowed hard. "Yes. It will happen, you know, Tanya."

"I know, I know." She was choking back the tears now.

He stood up and came round the bed, drawing her to her feet so that he could take her in his arms. He pressed his lips against her tousled hair, murmuring gently.

"I'm so glad you're with me, darling. I love you so much."

He lowered his head and kissed her on the lips. It was a gentle kiss, devoid of all passion but infinitely soothing to her. But what was most reassuring to Tanya was his assertion that he loved her. She couldn't remember him saying that since they'd been together in Australia.

"I love you too, darling," she whispered.

He kissed her again, before smoothing away the tears from her face with his hand.

She gave him a long slow smile as she looked up into his swarthy but still handsome face.

"I'll go and take that shower. Won't be long. Don't go away."

"As if!" He was already holding his daughter's hand, checking her pulse. "You know, as long as she's breathing and her heart is beating..."

He broke off as Tanya turned at the door, listening to him clutching at straws.

"Look, we've both been with unconscious patients who've recovered and we've been with some who haven't," she said quietly. "We're doing all we can but medical science can only do so much." She took a deep breath. "I'm hopeful."

"So am I!"

She went down to the female staff shower room. It was empty. She'd checked the contents of her locker and found a brand-new packet of cotton knickers which she'd brought over from Australia. Not at all glamorous but perfectly serviceable. She'd picked up a clean white short-sleeved coat from the doctors' clean laundry pile outside the shower room.

The hot water tumbled down, washing over her sticky skin. Yesterday afternoon, waiting outside the airport, her clothes sticking to her skin, she'd promised herself that the first thing she would do when she reached home would be to have a bath. Hours later, it felt as if she'd died and gone to heaven.

She made a point of trying not to think about Chrysanthe. Manolis was with her. A large number of the hospital medical team were devoting their combined skills and energy to ensuring that this little girl wasn't going to die.

She stepped out of the shower wrapped in a hospital issue towel, ready to face whatever the day threw at her.

Somehow, they both got through the day without losing hope. But it was a tough one. As they resumed their places beside Chrysanthe's bed Manolis reached across the bed and took hold of her hand.

"She's going to make it!" he said firmly.

"Absolutely!"

Whenever her hopes dwindled during the day she'd taken hold of Manolis's hand and they'd both said their mantra together. Heaven knew, they'd done all they could during the day. And the rest of the medical team had been amazing. They'd pooled their ideas and theories, tried every test that could possibly give them a clue as to what was happening inside that little head. There was no evidence of a blood clot.

They sat either side of the bed for a while, both of them in deep contemplation. Manolis was first to break the silence.

"An unconscious state like this could last for weeks, months, years even before…before…"

"Before it's resolved," she put in quickly as she saw him floundering to find the right words without demolishing the hope they were hanging onto.

"Exactly!" He reached across the bed with his spare hand and squeezed Tanya's.

Neither of them must admit that their hope had grown thin during the day. Neither of them must give in to the temptation to face the medical facts of the situation. The longer this unconscious state lasted, the less likely they were to get their daughter back so that she could lead a normal life.

Tanya glanced once more at the clock across the room. Two a.m. This second night was proving harder than the first. She forced her heavy eyelids to stay open. They'd decided to take turns to have a two-hour sleep while the other watched. It was time for her to wake Manolis but he looked so peaceful. She'd give him another five minutes.

Her heart missed a beat as she thought she saw the faint fluttering of Chrysanthe's eyelashes. She leaned closer, not sure if it had really happened. Chrysanthe was completely still again. The small hand remained cold and motionless in her own. She'd imagined it.

Tomorrow she was going to play some of Chrysanthe's favourite CDs to see if there was any response to the music. She remembered a young patient in Australia who'd been roused from a coma after several weeks by the sound of his favourite music. But unfortunately his brain had been damaged by the length of his vegetative state.

That wasn't going to happen to Chrysanthe. Oh, no! She was going to…

That was a definite fluttering of the eyelids! She hadn't imagined it this time.

"Manolis, Manolis!"

He was immediately awake, throwing back the sheet, padding across the floor in his bare feet.

"She's opening her eyes. She's opening…"

A strange gurgling sound came from Chrysanthe's mouth as her lips began to move. They leaned over her, clinging to her hands.

"Chrysanthe," Manolis said gently. "Can you hear me, darling? Can you…?"

The eyelashes fluttered again and she opened her eyes. For a few seconds it appeared as if she couldn't focus her eyes on the faces hovering above her. And then she uttered another sound, a gentle animal sound like a small lamb calling for is mother.

"Mmm…mmm…Mummy. Mummy." Slowly she turned her head towards Tanya, then Manolis. "And Daddy…"

"Oh, thank God! She's OK." Tanya choked on her words as she leaned down to kiss the child's forehead.

"I was dreaming," Chrysanthe said slowly and very faintly. So faintly they both had to bend down as closely as they could to catch what she was saying. "I was dreaming. We were on the boat…. The sun was hot…"

She closed her eyes and became quiet again as if the effort of those first few words had exhausted her.

"We must be patient, not rush her progress," Tanya whispered.

Manolis nodded, his heart too full of emotion for him to speak.

Several hours later, Tanya had made her small patient comfortably propped up against her pillows. The few words she'd spoken had indicated that all her faculties were well and truly in place. Time, the great healer, would do the rest.

For the next seven days they all lived in the small hospital room. The medical team involved with Chrysanthe's care had insisted that they keep their patient in hospital until they all agreed that she was back to normal again.

Manolis and Tanya both agreed. They knew the odds on a case like this and didn't want to take any risks until Chrysanthe was out of danger. But exactly one week and two days since she'd been admitted to hospital the entire team agreed that the patient could go home.

It had helped that both parents were doctors and would pick up on any sign of deterioration in the patient's condition. Even so, Alexander had insisted that they have round-the-clock nursing care on hand at home. He didn't want the parents to tire themselves. And he'd also insisted his chauffeur drive them home. Only the best for the sleeping princess.

It was Alexander who'd first called her that when he'd visited her the first day she'd woken from her sleep as he'd put it.

"You were like Sleeping Beauty," he'd told her.

"Was I really?" Chrysanthe's eyes had become wider than they'd been since she'd fallen into her coma. "Am I a princess?"

"I think you are," Alexander said. "And so do your mummy and daddy."

And Manolis had whispered into Tanya's ear, "There's nothing wrong with our daughter's brain!"

"She'll soon be running rings around us again," Tanya said happily.

It seemed as if the whole of Ceres had heard about the doctor's sick child who'd woken from her coma. People were lining the streets down by the harbour. As the mayoral limousine drove slowly along the water's edge they were actually cheering.

"I'm not really a princess, am I, Daddy?"

"You are to us, my darling. And for the people of Ceres you're a princess for the day."

"Wow!"

Manolis closed the bedroom door behind him and walked quickly across to the bed.

"Don't you think we should leave the door ajar?" Tanya said, as she snuggled back against the pillows to admire Manolis's athletic muscles as he stripped off his robe.

"No reason why we should," he said firmly. "There's a trained night nurse in Chrysanthe's room ready to come and alert us to any change in her condition. But the way our little princess has been behaving today—even with the inconvenience of the cast on her arm—leads me to believe that she's completely OK."

He climbed into bed and drew her towards him.

"Completely OK? Is that your clinical diagnosis now, Doctor?"

"It is indeed. It's you who needs your head examined."

"Me? What clinical signs have drawn you to that ridiculous conclusion?"

"I've done a lot of thinking while we were going through the awful crisis of almost losing our precious child. I can't live without you, Tanya. Everybody who knows us—friends, colleagues, the world at large—acknowledges we are a great couple. Made for each other is the phrase often bandied about."

"Yes," she said, drawing out the word as slowly as she could.

"Chrysanthe regards you as her mummy now and—"

"Manolis, I think I know where this is going—"

"Please, hear me out before you start saying anything. I know what you're going to say but—"

"You do?" She was impatient with hope that he might, he just might be going to…

"Tanya. Six years ago I asked you to marry me and you turned me down—twice! But I'm going to ask you again anyway because it doesn't make sense to go on as we are doing. I agree with the general consensus of opinion that—"

"Ask me, Manolis," she said, breathlessly.

"What?"

"Ask me to marry you."

"Well, against all the odds I am going to ask you to marry me even if—"

"And I'm going to say yes."

"But no matter what you think or… What did you just say?"

"I'm thinking that if you were to get out of bed and go down on your bended knee I could give you my answer— the answer I've longed to give you for ages. So please put me out of my misery. The suspense is killing me."

He looked completely stunned as he climbed out of bed and went down on one knee. He felt as if he'd turned into a robot. He was simply obeying orders. This couldn't be the girl who'd turned him down twice admitting that maybe, just maybe it could be third time lucky.

He swallowed hard. "Tanya, will you marry me?"

"Of course I will. What took you so long?"

Waking up in Manolis's arms, the details of the previous evening when Manolis had proposed to her were sketchy to say the least. But the love-making that had ensued had been out of this world. That bit she did remember! She remembered him climbing back into bed after his proposal, covering her with kisses as she settled into his arms.

And waking up in his arms just now, stretching out as a new day began. A day when she would have to start planning the wedding of the year! Everybody on the island would want to be invited. And her mother and stepfather and all of Manolis's enormous family.

He was opening his eyes, drawing her closer to him.

"Manolis, darling, before we…before we… I need to talk to you about the wedding so… Mmm…well, perhaps later…"

Just over a month from Manolis proposing to her they were standing in the beautiful church on the hill overlooking the entrance to the harbour. Neither of them had seen any point in waiting to tie the long-awaited knot.

Tanya was intrigued by the knots of ribbon that were being made around the two of them by the priest and his assistants in front of the altar. It was at this point that she began to realise that she was actually going to be Manolis's wife after all these years of longing.

She felt little fingers touching the ivory silk of her fabulous long gown and bent to see Chrysanthe admiring the texture and feel of the hastily but beautifully made garment. Two of the best seamstresses on Ceres had worked flat out to have it finished in time for the wedding of the year.

She bent down to whisper to Chrysanthe, who was chief bridesmaid, looking pretty and demure in her ivory silk mid-calf-length dress. She'd wanted a long dress like Mummy Tanya but Manolis was so afraid she'd fall over in her exuberance at some point during the long day that he'd suggested she would look better in a shorter version. He'd X-rayed her arm yesterday and decided that after six weeks in a cast the ulna had healed perfectly. She'd parted happily with the cumbersome plaster regretting only the fact that she could no longer show off all the signatures from friends and family.

"Are you OK, Chrysanthe?" Tanya whispered.

Chrysanthe nodded. "Why are they tying you up with Daddy?"

"To show that I'll always be with him."

"And me?"

"Of course."

Chrysanthe squeezed Tanya's leg encased in the layers of silk. "How much longer do we have to stay here? I need to go to the loo. I ever so need a…"

Tanya could see Victoria watching from the back of the church. She nodded her head down towards their daughter. Victoria hurried forward and put out her hand to take hold of the chief bridesmaid. Tanya smiled and mouthed her thanks as mother and daughter walked off down the aisle.

This was the first contact she'd had with Victoria that day. She'd arrived at the last minute and had been keeping a low profile at the back of the church. Not exactly lurking, as she'd so poignantly put it when they'd talked about the possibility of a wedding, more trying to remain unobtrusive in her chic silver grey designer suit and impossibly high stilettos.

The service continued all around her with the priests chanting loudly and the guests becoming restless in the hot airless church. They'd deliberately chosen the wedding to be at the end of the holiday season so that the island wasn't too crowded and the weather was still good.

The weather today was hot, almost too hot, but she was so happy that she hardly noticed. Only the sight of the ladies in the congregation fanning themselves with their wedding programmes made her hope that the service wouldn't last much longer.

As soon as it ended, she and Manolis were surrounded by their guests before they'd had chance to leave the altar.

"Let's go outside," Manolis suggested to the nearest and dearest of his family, who were clinging to him, congratulating him, kissing him and generally holding him back from his bride, who was signalling to him they should leave.

They finally found a way of getting together before walking down the aisle and escaping into the fresh air, hands firmly clasped together, Chrysanthe holding onto Tanya's skirt so that she didn't fall over in the crush of people all trying to reach her Mummy and Daddy.

"Thanks, Victoria," Tanya said as she passed by the London mummy.

Victoria smiled. "Glad I could help. You look absolutely gorgeous. And so do you, my poppet." She bent to kiss her daughter. "What a good girl you've been."

Chrysanthe beamed and looked up at her Ceres mummy. "Are you and Daddy married yet?"

"We are," Tanya said as they posed for the cameras outside the porch.

"When will you start to make the new baby?"

"Let's talk about it later, Chrysanthe. Smile now for the camera."

She looked around at the enormous crowd. It had been a mammoth task to get all her relatives here. She had a particularly special smile for her brother Costas who'd miraculously phoned a couple of weeks before to say that he was going home to Australia from South Africa to introduce his new fiancée to his mother.

According to their mother—who was now coming forward to join the large family photograph to be taken on the grass to the side of the church under a large tree that would give them some shade—it hadn't occurred to Costas that the family might be worried about his whereabouts. So he'd simply got on with his work out there in the back of beyond.

Tanya's mother came closer to her now, kissing her cheek before moving to the appropriate place for the mother of the bride.

"I think Costas's fiancée is going to be a good influence on him," her mother whispered, before taking up her place.

Tanya smiled. "About time someone took my brother in hand."

"I heard that," Costas said, coming up to stand behind her. "Hey, Manolis. We've got a lot of catching up to do, my friend. How about I meet you tonight for a drink—after this show, of course."

"Sorry, Costas," Manolis said. "I've got an important date with the most wonderful woman in the world."

Costas looked around him. "So when's she arriving?"

"Quiet, Costas!" Tanya's mother said.

"And now just the bride and groom by themselves!" the fraught photographer boomed above the laughter and chattering.

Manolis took hold of her hand as the crowds moved back. "Happy?" he whispered.

"What do you think?"

"A kiss! The wedding kiss," the photographer called.

"This is the best bit," Manolis said as he drew her into his arms and kissed her. His kiss deepened and the crowd cheered.

Tanya pulled herself gently away. "Later," she whispered.

"Promise?"

Her eyes shone with the promise of the night to come, their first as a real married couple. "Can't wait…'

CHRYSANTHE climbed into bed, snuggling down between her mummy and daddy, taking care not to speak until they opened their eyes. Since her baby brother had arrived they'd been keen that she shouldn't talk and wake him up when they'd just got him to sleep. She glanced at the cradle at her mummy's side of the bed. He was a very small baby. She hoped he would start growing soon. He hadn't seemed to get any bigger since he was born three weeks ago.

Tanya lay very still, pretending she was still asleep. Baby Jack had needed two breastfeeds in the night and it seemed only a short time since she'd fed him.

Chrysanthe stared hard at her mummy. She was sure she wasn't really asleep. Perhaps if she just whispered to her, that would be OK.

"Are you awake, Mummy?"

"I am now."

"It's morning time. Look, the sun's shining outside. Daddy, can you see the sun?"

"Mmm?"

"The sun. It's shining. Must be time we all got up, don't you think?"

"Morning, darling." Manolis planted a kiss on his daughter's cheek before reaching across to his wife and kissing her on the lips. "How were the feeds last night? I think I might have slept through them."

"I think you did. But I forgive you because you had a long busy day at the hospital yesterday whereas—"

"Mummy and I did nothing all day yesterday but look after Jack. I loved it! Do I have to go to school today? I know it's Monday but—"

"Don't you want to go to school and tell all your friends how brilliant it is now that you've got a baby brother?" Tanya said.

"Yes, OK. But will you come and meet me and bring Jack in the pram?"

"Of course I will. Now, don't make a noise as you climb out of bed. Just go back to your own room for a couple of minutes and start putting on your clothes."

"OK. You'll come and help me, Mummy, won't you?"

"Yes, I'll be with you in two minutes. I just want to discuss something with Daddy."

Chrysanthe paused at her mummy's side of the bed and looked gravely at the eyes that were firmly closed again.

"You know, I told you it was easy making a baby, Mummy. You did really well. It seems to be the looking after the baby that tires you. But you've got me to help you, haven't you?"

Tanya opened her eyes and smiled at the child who now seemed as if she was her true firstborn. "Of course I've got you to help me. I don't know what I'd do without you, darling."

She held out her arms and closed them around Chrysanthe. "Now, off you go and start getting ready for school, my love."

"What was it you wanted to discuss?" came a sleepy voice as the door closed behind their daughter.

Manolis drew her into his arms and she snuggled as close as she could get.

"I've forgotten. It will have to wait until this evening."

"Like everything else," he told her in his most seductive, provocative tone. "Unless…"

"Not now, Manolis!" She moved out of range and put her feet on the floor. "You won't be late tonight, will you? Because… I've forgotten what I was going to say again! It must be all these broken nights."

"They won't go on for ever. Can't wait to have you all to myself again." Manolis looked down at his sleeping son. "But I wouldn't be without this wonderful gift you gave me, darling. As Chrysanthe just said, you did well making our baby."

She laughed. "It was an absolute pleasure, I assure you."

"We could maybe make another one in the not too distant future," Manolis said gently.

She blew him a kiss. "It would be fun trying…"

MILLS & BOON®

The Rising Stars Collection!

1 BOOK FREE!

This fabulous four-book collection features 3-in-1 stories from some of our talented writers who are the stars of the future! Feel the temperature rise this summer with our ultra-sexy and powerful heroes. Don't miss this great offer—buy the collection today to get one book free!

Order yours at www.millsandboon.co.uk/risingstars

MILLS & BOON®

It's Got to be Perfect

* cover in development

When Ellie Rigby throws her three-carat engagement ring into the gutter, she is certain of only one thing. She has yet to know true love!

Fed up with disastrous internet dates and conflicting advice from her friends, Ellie decides to take matters into her own hands. Starting a dating agency, Ellie becomes an expert in love. Well, that is until a match with one of her clients, charming, infuriating Nick, has her questioning everything she's ever thought about love…

Order yours today at
www.millsandboon.co.uk

MILLS & BOON®
By Request

RELIVE THE ROMANCE WITH THE BEST OF THE BEST

A sneak peek at next month's titles...

In stores from 21st August 2015:

- **His Virgin Bride** – Melanie Milburne, Maggie Cox & Margaret Mayo

- **In Bed With the Enemy** – Natalie Anderson, Aimee Carson & Tawny Weber

In stores from 4th September 2015:

- **The Jarrods: Inheritance** – Maxine Sullivan, Emilie Rose & Heidi Betts

- **Undressed by the Rebel**
  – Alison Roberts